Eclipse

I felt the increasing energy in the air around me; goose bumps broke out on my arms, and my hair felt full of static. I could feel that every animal and bird had left the area. I didn't blame them.

When I looked down, I saw that the star, the pentagram, had begun to glow with a whiter light—their energy. I knew what was coming next, and my stomach clenched. I drew my knees up again and held them tightly against myself and felt that I would bear the scars of this night forever.

. . .

SWEEP

Book of Shadows (Book One)

The Coven (Book Two)

Blood Witch (Book Three)

Dark Magick (Book Four)

Awakening (Book Five)

Spellbound (Book Six)

The Calling (Book Seven)

Changeling (Book Eight)

Strife (Book Nine)

Seeker (Book Ten)

Origins (Book Eleven)

Eclipse (Book Twelve)

Reckoning (Book Thirteen)

Full Circle (Book Fourteen)

Night's Child (Super Edition)

SWEEP

Cate Tiernan

VOLUME IV

SEEKER

ORIGINS

ECLIPSE

speak

An Imprint of Penguin Group (USA) Inc.

To my three nephews:
Paul, Daniel, and Coltrane

SPEAK
Published by the Penguin Group
Penguin Group (USA) Inc., 345 Hudson Street, New York, New York 10014, U.S.A.
Penguin Group (Canada), 90 Eglinton Avenue East, Suite 700, Toronto, Ontario, Canada M4P 2Y3
(a division of Pearson Penguin Canada Inc.)
Penguin Books Ltd, 80 Strand, London WC2R 0RL, England
Penguin Ireland, 25 St Stephen's Green, Dublin 2, Ireland (a division of Penguin Books Ltd)
Penguin Group (Australia), 250 Camberwell Road, Camberwell, Victoria 3124, Australia
(a division of Pearson Australia Group Pty Ltd)
Penguin Books India Pvt Ltd, 11 Community Centre, Panchsheel Park, New Delhi - 110 017, India
Penguin Group (NZ), 67 Apollo Drive, Rosedale, Auckland 0632, New Zealand
(a division of Pearson New Zealand Ltd)
Penguin Books (South Africa) (Pty) Ltd, 24 Sturdee Avenue, Rosebank, Johannesburg 2196, South Africa

Registered Offices: Penguin Books Ltd, 80 Strand, London WC2R 0RL, England

Published by Puffin Books, a division of Penguin Young Readers Group, 2002
Published by Speak, an imprint of Penguin Group (USA) Inc., 2008
This omnibus edition published by Speak, an imprint of Penguin Group (USA) Inc., 2011

3 5 7 9 10 8 6 4 2

Produced by 17th Street Productions,
an Alloy company
151 West 26th Street
New York, NY 10001

17th Street Productions and associated logos
are trademarks and/or registered trademarks of Alloy, Inc.

Speak ISBN 978-0-14-241025-7
This omnibus ISBN 978-0-14-242010-2

Printed in the United States of America

BOOK TEN

SWEEP
SEEKER

1

Invitation

Poor Dagda is still clomping around the house in his kitty cast. He has another week before it can come off. In the meantime he keeps giving me baleful stares, as if it were my fault that he ran in front of that car.

Since Hunter dropped the bomb about Sky's lead on his parents, I've been waiting for him to say, "Today's the day—I'm off." But he hasn't yet. Hunter. He makes me crazy; he keeps me sane. He seems so . . . English sometimes, kind of distant or reserved, but then he'll look at me, and his eyes see right through to my soul, and I go all shivery and want to kiss him. He makes me feel safe, and at the same time he makes me feel like I'm standing on the edge of a cliff. Does love always feel like this?

—Morgan

Since Sky's been gone, I'm amazed by what her presence meant in this house. There's less laundry. There's more food, but of *a less interesting kind. The post is piling up—why does she get so many bloody catalogs? I always get the good parking spot right in front of the walkway. And the house is quiet: there are no vibrations that tell me I'm not alone, that my cousin is with me.*

Now I'm here, and there's no getting around it—male laundry is boring. I wear jeans and shirts and socks and underwear. Those four things, day and night, summer and winter. Sky's clothes are so much more complicated—all sorts of weird girl-type articles of clothing, things I couldn't even name. Morgan doesn't seem to have as many varieties of clothes as Sky. She mostly wears corduroys or jeans, shirts or sweatshirts. Plain underwear, no bra, ever. (Excellent.) It's funny—she doesn't ever deliberately try to be sexy. She doesn't have to. Just looking at her, in her regular clothes, and knowing what she feels like wrapped around me, pressed hard against me, knowing what her skin feels like, knowing the scent of her, the vibration of her, her aura . . . my brain cells start fusing, and I cease being able to form coherent sentences. Like right now.

I still can't get over Sky finding a lead on my parents. Seeing them again is something I've dreamed of for more than half my life. And now that my employer, the International Council of Witches, has given me permission and helped narrow down their whereabouts, I'm ready to go. I just need to make plans.

Alwyn, who was only four when they left, can barely remember them. Linden died trying to see them again. He failed. In some ways, it seems too huge. In the years they've been gone, my parents have taken on almost mythical proportions—witches say their names with reverence or curiosity or even disdain; they look at me as though their legacy was stamped on my forehead.

This is simultaneously the most exciting and most terrifying thing that has ever happened to me. More, even, than our run-in with Ciaran in New York. Or when Morgan shape-shifted into a wolf, tracked me, and almost ripped me apart. Goddess, what we've been through together... I just wish Morgan could go with me now.

If Sky were here, she would offer to go. I wouldn't let her, though. She is still fairly battered emotionally from her breakup with Raven. Spending time in France will be good for her.

But to have Morgan by my side as I see my parents for the first time in over a decade would make this so much easier. She is practical, powerful, able to face almost anything. I need her so much.

Morgan met me at Practical Magick, one of the area's only occult bookstores. It was a popular Wiccan hangout, and I was good friends with the owner, Alyce Fernbrake. The bells over the door jangled, and I looked up to see Morgan coming toward me, a little smile on her face.

I'm over six feet, so I'm used to looking down at people, but Morgan always seems to be eye to eye with me. Objectively speaking, though, she's about seven inches shorter than me, which still makes her taller than a lot of women. At seventeen, Morgan's face shows no lines of age or wisdom, pain or laughter. Only striking bones, features that seem strong and womanly and intensely attractive. Her eyes are almost frighteningly knowledgeable, her expression solemn, her mouth generous yet not prone to vacuous smiles or asinine giggles. She is one of the most stubborn, strong-willed, prickly, reserved, and irritating people I have ever met. I love her so much, my knees buckle every time she's near.

"Hi," she said.

"Hi. Let's go in the back."

Morgan and I passed through the tattered orange curtain that separates the back room from the rest of the shop. It fell closed behind us, and then we were standing, looking at each other in the poorly lit room.

Her hair was loose and needed brushing. It fell in unsmooth waves past her elbows, almost to her waist. Her black peacoat was unbuttoned; her jeans flared slightly, with thready bottoms, to the tops of her scuffed leather clogs. Her large, brownish-green eyes watched me, and her strong, classic nose was faintly pink from cold. This was Morgan Rowlands. The daughter of Maeve Riordan, the last, powerful witch of Belwicket, and of Ciaran MacEwan, who was one of the darkest Woodbanes that Wicca had ever known. Adopted daughter of Sean and Mary Grace Rowlands. My love.

My desire for her came with no warning, like a snake striking, and suddenly I pulled her to me by her jacket, pushing my hands beneath the heavy coat and around her back, feeling the sweater she wore. I had a brief glimpse of her startled, uptilted eyes before I closed my own and slanted my mouth across hers, kissing her with an urgency that both scared and embarrassed me.

But Morgan met fire with fire; she has never backed down from anything in the months I have known her, and she didn't push me away with false modesty now. Instead, she clung to me, her arms moving around my waist, and kissed me back, hard, stepping closer to me and putting her feet between mine.

Finally, who knew how long later, we eased apart. I was

breathing hard, every muscle in my body tense and wired and urging me forward. Morgan's lips were red and soft; her eyes were searching mine.

"I missed you," I said, surprised to hear my voice sounding hoarse and breathless. She nodded, her own breath coming quick and shallow. "Come on, sit." I led her toward the battered wooden table, and we both sank onto chairs as if we had just finished a marathon. Every bit of idle chitchat I could have summoned fled my brain, and, instead, I just held her hand tightly and blurted out my news.

"I'm leaving Saturday for Canada, to see my parents."

Morgan's dark brown eyes widened, and for a moment she looked afraid. But that impression faded instantly, and I wasn't sure if I had really seen it.

She nodded. "I've been expecting this."

I gave a short laugh. "Yeah. The council contacted me again this morning. They actually gave me directions to my parents' *house*. Can you believe that? They think Mum and Da moved about three months ago."

She nodded thoughtfully, not meeting my eyes.

"I'm driving," I told her. "I think it'll take about eleven hours. They live in a little town north of Quebec City. Morgan—will you go with me?"

Surprise lit her eyes, almost immediately replaced by clear longing.

"I don't know how long I'll be gone," I said quickly. "But if you need to get back before I do, I can put you on a plane or train or rent you a car."

As we held hands across the little table, we both pictured what it would mean. Long, intimate conversations in the car.

Hours and hours of time alone together. Being together day and night. Meeting my parents, her being with me during this incredibly meaningful experience. It would take our relationship to a whole new level. I wanted her to say yes so badly.

"I want to go," she said slowly. "I really want to go." She fell silent again. In her mind, she was probably having an imaginary conversation with her parents. I groaned to myself. What had I been thinking? Her parents don't even allow boys in the house. There was no way they'd let their daughter take off to Canada without at least one chaperone, like we'd had in New York. And this would be a much bigger trip.

Her face fell, and I could feel her disappointment because it was mirrored by mine.

"I can't," she said. "Why am I even thinking about it? I'm still trying to get my grades out of the toilet, my parents are still twitchy around the edges, there's no school vacation anytime soon—it's impossible." Her voice held frustration and impatience.

"It's all right," I said, covering her hand with both of mine. "It's all right. I just thought I'd throw the idea out there. Don't worry about it. There will be plenty of time for us to take trips in the future."

She nodded, unconvinced, and I felt sorry for bringing the subject up, sorry for making her feel guilty that she couldn't accompany me on this important journey. Looking into her face, I brought her palm to my mouth and kissed it. She sighed, and I watched the heat flare in her eyes.

2

Preparation

Goddess, I feel stupid. Stupid and childish and mad and guilty about not being able to go to Canada with Hunter. Why am I only seventeen? After what I've been through in the last five months, you'd think I would be at least twenty-three by now. I can't stand being my age. I want to live in my own place, make all my own decisions, study the craft as much and as openly as I'd like. I want to be an adult. I should be an adult. Until I discovered Wicca, I'd always assumed I'd finish high school, go to college, and get a job that was incredibly satisfying, fun, creative, and that paid a ton of money.

Now the whole rest of my life seems up in the air. Eoife wants me to go to Scotland to study with some important teachers. I want to be with Hunter. My parents expect me to go to college. What for? I have to *take the SATs this spring, have to start collecting college brochures. Suddenly everything seems so pointless.*

Oh, Hunter, how long will you be gone?

—Morgan

Alyce Fernbrake recommended a friend of hers, Bethany Malone, as someone to lead my coven, Kithic, while I was gone. When I rang her doorbell on Thursday night, I had no idea what to expect and wondered if my being a Seeker would have a negative effect on our meeting.

She opened the door almost immediately. As soon as I saw her, I realized that I had seen her at least a couple of times at various witch gatherings here and there. Bethany was almost as tall as I am, big boned, with large, strong hands and a sturdy-looking body. Her short black hair was fine and straight; her eyes were huge and so dark, they seemed to have no pupils. I guessed her age to be about forty-five.

"Hunter Niall," she said, looking at me consideringly. "Come in."

"Bethany," I greeted her. "Thanks for agreeing to see me."

She led me through the short foyer into her lounge. Despite the building's boxy, modern appearance, Bethany had created her own haven here, and this room was warm and felt familiar.

"I'm having some wine," she said, getting down a glass. "Will you have some?"

"Yes, thank you," I said, watching her pour the dark, rich fluid. I took the glass and looked into it, inhaling the scents of fruit, tannins, earth, and sun. I drank.

"This is terrific," I said, and she smiled and nodded. We sat across from each other, me on the sofa and Bethany in a large, overstuffed chair that was draped with a mohair throw. The room was lit by shaded lamps and several candles; there were herbs hanging in neat rows along one wall. I sipped my wine and felt a bit of the day's tension start to melt away.

"Alyce told me you're looking for someone to lead your circles for a while," she said.

"Yes. I'm going out of town. Kithic is a fairly new coven, and I'd hate for them to get out of rhythm while I'm gone."

"Tell me about them," she said, folding her long legs beneath her. "Are you all one clan? I'm Brightendale—did Alyce mention it?"

"Yes, she did, and no, we aren't," I said. "In fact, out of the twelve, only three are blood witches—me, my cousin Sky, and a girl named Morgan Rowlands. And Sky's on holiday right now, so there would be only eleven, including you."

"Morgan Rowlands," said Bethany. "Goodness. She's in your coven? What's that like?"

I grimaced. "Unpredictable. Exciting. Frightening."

Nodding, Bethany swirled the wine in her glass. "What about the rest of them?"

"They're all in high school," I explained. "They've all known each other, more or less, for most of their lives. Widow's Vale is a pretty insular town, and there aren't many different schools. One girl, Alisa Soto, left the coven recently, but I have a feeling she'll be coming back. She was the youngest, at fifteen. The others are Bree Warren, Robbie Gurevitch, Sharon Goodfine, and Ethan Sharp. They're all juniors. Simon Bakehouse, Matt Adler, Thalia Cutter, Raven Meltzer, and Jenna Ruiz are all seniors."

"So many young people, coming to Wicca," said Bethany. "That's really nice. How sincere do they seem? Are they just flirting with it, or do you think they take it seriously?"

"Both," I said. "Some are more sincere than others. Some are more sincere than they realize. Some are less sincere than they realize. I'll leave it up to you to figure it out—I don't want to prejudice you."

Bethany nodded and sipped her wine. "Tell me about Morgan."

I paused for a few moments. How to put this? "Well, she's powerful," I said lamely. "She grew up in a Catholic family. She only started studying Wicca five months ago—and only found out about being a blood witch maybe four months ago. And she was, you know, involved with Selene Belltower and her son."

I tried to keep my face neutral as I said this. Cal hadn't been dead long enough. Anytime I thought of Cal and Morgan together, of his convincing her he loved her, of the black plans he and Selene had for her, an overwhelming rage came over me and shattered my usual self-control.

"Yes," said Bethany, her dark eyes on me. As with Alyce, I got the impression that she wasn't missing much. "I'd be interested in meeting her."

"In my opinion," I went on, "Morgan desperately needs to learn as much as she can as fast as she can. It's nerve-racking being around her, feeling like she could blink and make a building collapse."

"She's as powerful as that?" Bethany looked very interested.

"I think so. This is someone who has had barely any instruction, who's uninitiated and who has never even thought about going through the Great Trial. Someone who grew up having no idea of her powers, her heritage."

"Yet she shows such great promise?"

"She lights fires with her mind," I said, shrugging helplessly. "No one taught her how to do that. She has an inherent knowledge of power chants and other quite complicated spells that would be very difficult for a well-educated witch to do. She scries with fire. And a few weeks ago, she shape-shifted."

"Holy Mother," Bethany breathed. "What did she shift into?"

"A wolf."

For a few minutes Bethany Malone and I sat looking at each other, drinking our wine. "Goddess," Bethany said finally.

"Yeah," I said wryly. "It gets rather tense sometimes."

"I see," she said. "Tell me a bit about how you conduct your circles."

I went over our usual rites, our check-ins and meditation and energy-raising. Bethany listened attentively as I briefed her on the lessons I had led so far, about basic correspondences, purifying the circle, focusing skills. "Kithic has had some ups and downs," I concluded. "But in general the members are coming together in an interesting way, and I'm committed to helping them as long as they want to continue and as long as I'm in the States. It would be easy for them to get off track if they missed several circles."

"Yes," Bethany agreed. She set down her empty glass. "I'm intrigued, Hunter. I want to meet Morgan. I'm curious to meet these kids. I'd be happy to take over your circles while you're gone."

Relief flooded my body. Instinctively I felt that Bethany would bring good energy to the group, and the fact that she was recommended by Alyce set my mind at ease. "Brilliant," I said. "Thanks very much. The circles meet every Saturday night at seven, but the location changes. This Saturday it'll be at Jenna Ruiz's house—I'll give you directions."

I left half an hour later, a huge weight off my shoulders. Bethany was both strong and sensible; Kithic, and especially Morgan, would be safe in her hands.

"What time is it there?" I asked. I had called Sky when I got home but guessed I hadn't calculated the time difference correctly. Sky sounded sleepy and uncharitable.

"It's . . ." I pictured her craning around for a clock. "It's oh-dark-thirty," she finally said irritably. "What's up?"

Sky and I had grown up together; though I had two siblings and she had four, we were the same age and had compatible temperaments. Though neither of us was much given to sappy emotional outbursts, we were as close as brother and sister, and we both knew it. Now I told her my news as briefly as possible, picturing her almond-shaped black eyes widening under her golden eyebrows.

"Oh, Giomanach," she breathed, lapsing into my coven name, the name she had called me through childhood. "Oh, Goddess, I don't believe it—after all this time."

"Yeah. I leave on Saturday. It's about an eleven-hour drive, I think."

"I just can't believe it," Sky repeated. She paused. "How about I catch a flight back and go with you?"

I smiled with gratitude. "Thanks, Sky, but I'm all right going solo. Besides, you've done enough—I'd have never found them without you. You're on holiday."

I paused, and changed the subject. "How's the mighty Cara?" Sky's sister Cara was living in Paris.

Sky gave an uncharacteristic giggle. "She's pretty much the same: beautiful, successful, extremely popular, blokes panting at the door, constant promotions at work, the usual."

"Gross," I said. "And of course she's still sweet and kind and impossible to hate?"

Sky sighed. "Yes, damn her. She's been great. I'm glad I'm here. I still feel so—drained. Tired. Achy. I keep expecting to get the flu, but it hasn't come yet."

I waited, wondering if she would ask for news of Raven, but she didn't. "Listen," I said, "I'll call you from there and let you know what's happening. Who knows what I'll find? Anyway—I'll keep in touch."

"Do," she said. "I might be back in England, or maybe even America, by the time you get home. I don't know how much more fabulousness I can stand."

"Paris or Cara?"

"Both."

We rang off, and I sat for a moment, hoping that being away was doing her good. I frowned, thinking about how she was still feeling run-down. Was it just a simple mental thing, caused by stress or unhappiness, or was she really sick?

I knew Morgan's number by heart and braced myself to talk to one of her parents if they answered the phone. But it was Morgan who said, "Hello, Hunter."

Morgan's slightly husky voice sent shivers down my spine, and I realized I was gripping the phone a little tighter. You are pathetic, Niall, I told myself. "Hi," I said. "How are you?"

"Okay. Have you been getting ready for your trip?"

"Yes. I've lined up a replacement circle leader. Her name is Bethany Malone. Alyce recommended her, and I went to see her tonight. She seems terrific—I hope you'll like her. I think she'll be really good."

"Hmmm. I guess I just like it best when you lead the circles."

Morgan wasn't being coy or trying to inflate my ego. She was naturally shy, and it took her a while to be comfortable with new people. Making magick with people is an intimate thing: it's very hard to hold on to your barriers and defenses when you're connected by the energy. And Morgan wrote the book on defenses and barriers.

"I know," I said. "But Bethany is very learned, and it's a good opportunity for you to work with someone new. You know I'm not the best teacher for you." Because I want to ravish you.

She remained quiet, and I sensed that she was feeling conflicted about things.

"Hunter—I know you have to go," she said finally. "It's incredible that your folks are alive. You have to go see them. I know that. It's just—I'll miss you while you're gone."

"Love," I said. "I'm going to miss you, too. I wish I knew when I'll be back. I mean, I might be back in three days, or it might take a week . . . or longer."

"Uh-huh," she said, sounding down.

"I'll be thinking of you the whole time," I said. "I'll try to call as often as I can. And I'll be so glad when I'm back." Part of me felt almost guilty saying that. The truth was, I really had no idea what would happen. What if my parents no longer had to live in hiding? What if they could live openly and we could be a real family? Maybe they were planning to move back to England, to be near Beck and Shelagh. We would have actual family holiday celebrations, like for Ostara, coming up. Maybe next year's Yule would be truly joyous, with all of us together at last.

And if they did return to England, where would that leave me? I can easily work in England—plenty of witches are there. And I knew the council would be eager to send me out on another job soon. Nothing was holding me in Widow's Vale except Morgan. What if I had to choose between being with my parents or being with Morgan? If I could be near my parents, see them, make magick with them, learn from them . . . that would carry a lot of weight. And Morgan wouldn't be able to join me in England, not for at least a year and a half.

A lot can happen in a year and a half. A lot can happen in three months.

"I'll be glad when you get back, too," Morgan said. I sensed her taking charge of herself, deliberately deciding to be stronger. "But I know it'll be wonderful for you to go." Her voice sounded much more brisk and matter-of-fact.

"Thanks," I said softly, feeling the warmth of my love for her.

"I can't believe I can't go with you," she said. "But anyway—I was thinking, if you're leaving early Saturday, maybe we could have dinner together tomorrow night, just the two of us. Unless you think you're going to be really busy getting ready."

Terrific idea. "No, I'll make sure to get everything done before then. Dinner alone tomorrow sounds wonderful. Let's do it at my house—I'll try to put something special together."

"Great," she said, and I picked up on her waves of relief and anticipation.

"I'll look forward to seeing you, love," I said.

"Me too," she said, and we rang off.

3

Good-bye

I can't believe Hunter is leaving tomorrow. I feel a sense of dread when I think about his being gone. I tried to scry last night but really didn't pick up on anything except images of woods. Frustrating.

Now, on to the main thing. I've read in Maeve's Book of Shadows that blood witches can do spells to either get pregnant or not get pregnant. I went yesterday to Practical Magick and tried to find a spell, but I couldn't and was too embarrassed to ask Alyce. So this afternoon after school, I drove over to Norton, to the Planned Parenthood office there, and got a three-month supply of the Pill and a prescription to fill if I need to.

I parked down the street (so original) and crept up the block to the building, which of course had humongous letters on the side screaming Planned Parenthood! Catholic teenagers having premarital sex against their parents' wishes, step right up! Goddess, by the time I got inside the building, I was shaking with mortification. If only I were Bree! Bree has her own gynecologist and suavely went on the Pill when she was fifteen. The whole thing only underlines how immature I am. Yet I do absolutely feel ready to go to bed with Hunter. I mean, I'm dying to. I've been wanting to, but things just haven't worked out. But tonight is going to be the night—I feel it. I came home and took the first pill as instructed. We'll need to use a condom, too, because the Pill doesn't kick in for a month and even though I trust Hunter, I'd rather be safe than sorry.

I can't believe I thought about doing this with Cal. I still feel incredibly sad when I think about him—sad that he's dead, that Selene destroyed his life, that I had anything to do with it. But I'm so glad I'm not with him and didn't go to bed with him. What I feel for Hunter is so different than what I felt for Cal. I love Hunter truly and deeply; I trust and admire and respect him. I feel sure that he loves me, that he will take care of me and not hurt me, and that he respects me as a person and doesn't just want to remake me into what he thinks would be a perfect girlfriend. I feel comfortable with him; I feel safe. I trust him.

And physically, oh, Goddess, he makes me crazy. So tonight's the night. Tonight I'm going to quit being a kid, a little girl. By tomorrow morning, I'll be a woman.

—Morgan

By Friday evening I was tightly wound. Everything was weighing on my mind: Should I stop the mail or ask a neighbor to gather it? Would my car make it to Canada? Did I have enough money? Thoughts consumed me as I surveyed the table I had set. I looked at it suspiciously, certain I'd forgotten something. Something for the trip, something for dinner? I couldn't think. Shaking my head, I tugged at the tablecloth and leaned over to light the candles. Dinner was basically done and waiting in the kitchen. I like to cook. I frowned: had I ever seen Morgan be picky about food? I couldn't remember—my brain was fried. In general, she has an appalling diet. For example, she considers Diet Coke to be an appropriate breakfast food. And she eats these thin, horrible pastries with a teaspoon of jam in the middle and frosting on top. Pop-Tarts. Goddess, it makes me ill just to think about it.

The doorbell rang, and I jumped about a foot in the air—I hadn't felt her coming up the walk. Automatically I pushed my hand through my hair, then remembered too late that always makes it stand up in a stupid way. Goddess, help me.

I opened the door, my heart already thudding. It was dark out, of course, and Morgan stood framed in our weak porch light, her brown eyes huge.

"Hi," I said, feeling awash in love for her. "Come on in."

She came in wordlessly and took off her coat. Hmmm—she was wearing some long skirtlike thing that swept the top of her clogs. Usually she wears jeans, so she had made a special effort for tonight, and I felt oddly pleased in an old-fashioned, male-chauvinist-pig kind of way. Her clingy brown sweater showed off her broad shoulders and her arms, which I knew were strong and toned. Once again the knowledge that she never wears a bra popped into my fevered brain, and I felt my knees start to go wonky. Her skin, and the curve of her waist, and the way she responded when I—"Hunter?" she said, watching my face.

"Ah, yes," I said, snapping my mind out of the gutter. "Right. Hi, love." I put my hand on her back and leaned down to kiss her. She kissed me back, her lips gentle on mine, and I was struck by how alive she felt, how vibrant.

"Are you hungry?" I asked when we pulled apart.

She smiled, her eyes lighting up, and I laughed. "What am I saying? You're always hungry."

Half an hour later I was pleased by the fact that Morgan wasn't picky about food. While I wasn't sure if she knew the difference between bad food (instant tarts and diet soda) and good food (the linguine I had made for dinner), still, the fact that she ate everything and seemed to enjoy it was heartening.

"How did you learn to cook?" she asked, taking another thin slice of bruschetta.

"Self-defense. My aunt Shelagh was pretty uninspired. I couldn't blame her—she had years of cooking for twelve people at every meal before she caught on and started making the oldest kids help out."

Morgan laughed, and I felt the same kind of inner glow that came over me when I had worked a particularly nice bit of magick. I loved her. I didn't want to leave her. I wanted her to be packed, to be ready to get in my car tomorrow morning and drive off with me. Like her, I was frustrated by the fact that she was only seventeen.

"I brought dessert," she said, going into the parlor. She

returned with a white pastry box and opened it at the table.

"Voilà. Two éclairs."

"Brilliant," I said, reaching for one. Witches and sweets seem to go together. I know that after spell-working, I tend to fall upon whatever sweet carbohydrate there is. Even Aunt Shelagh, during her macrobiotic period, had been observed wolfing down a brownie after a Lammastide rite.

As I fixed a pot of tea, I began to realize that Morgan was coiled almost as tightly as I was. I knew she was upset about my leaving tomorrow. I was both upset and incredibly excited. Part of me was aching to go jump in the car right now and set off, every minute bringing me closer to my long-lost parents. I tried as unobtrusively as possible to feel her aura. Regular people can't feel someone do this; even a lot of witches would be pretty unaware of it. I'd had a lot of training in feeling auras as a Seeker. It was literally my job to know people, to be able to detect nuances about their behavior, their energy.

"What are you doing?" Morgan asked.

I sighed. Served me right for trying to scan someone as strong as she was.

"Feeling your aura," I said, turning on the hot water in the sink. "You seem kind of . . . tense. Are you okay?"

She nodded, not looking at me, and drank the last of her tea. "Um, could you leave that till later?" she asked, gesturing toward the kitchen mess. "I just—want to be with you now. It's our last night, and I want us to spend time together, just us."

"Sure, of course," I said, turning off the water. I put my arm around her shoulders and led her from the kitchen.

She leaned against me. "Let's go up to your room."

All my senses jumped to full alert. "All right," I said, feeling my throat contract. Our chances to be alone and physical were few and far between, and I had been hoping we could take advantage of the opportunity tonight.

We walked upstairs, where Sky had one bedroom and I have the other. As we walked in, I could see all at once how impersonal the room seemed. Even after being in Widow's Vale for months, I hadn't spent much time settling in. The room contained my bed, my almost bare desk, and three boxes of books, which remained unpacked. There were no curtains, no rugs, no photographs or knickknacks. It was almost like walking into an abandoned dormitory. I felt a sudden embarrassment at the complete lack of mood.

Morgan left me and walked to the bed, which was still, after months of my living here, just a box spring and a mattress on the floor. She kicked off her clogs, sat down, and leaned back against the pillows. Then she looked at me and smiled. I smiled back.

My nerves jolted awake as desire flared to life. For once we didn't have to worry about Sky coming home; it was a weekend night, so Morgan wouldn't have to leave by nine; we had the rest of the evening together and an empty house with no disruptions. Then we were lying next to each other, and I was kicking off my boots and my hands were reaching around her sides, feeling her curves. The idea that Morgan was lying on my bed went right to my head, and then all thoughts fled as we kissed deeply, our mouths joined, our bodies pressed together. Goddess, she felt good. I have always found her intensely attractive, everything about her: her body, her face, her scent, how she moved against me, the sounds she made as we kissed, tiny whimpers of pleasure. I leaned into her, deepening our kiss.

"Hunter, Hunter," she said, pulling her mouth away from mine.

"Mmm." I followed her mouth, but her hands pressed against my chest and pushed. I swam toward coherence and looked into her eyes to see her gazing at me seriously. "What, love, too much?" Please don't say it was too much. "What?" I asked again.

"Hunter, I want us to make love," she whispered, her eyes glancing at my mouth. "I love you. I'm ready."

My brain struggled to process the words. Had I really heard that, or was this some cruel fantasy? I looked down at her face, her incredible, sculptured face. Was she serious?

I swallowed hard. "You want to—"

"I'm ready, Hunter," she said, her voice soft but sounding confident. "I want to make love with you."

It was as if the entire universe had just dropped literally into my lap. We had come close several times, and I had been keen to since practically the first moment I saw her, but it had never quite worked out.

"Are you sure?" I felt compelled to ask. *Please, please, please.*

She nodded, and my heart began to pound. "I started taking the Pill."

My eyebrows rose. She was serious; she had thought it out; she was ready. I sent out a huge, silent thank-you to the universe and pressed against her, holding her close.

"I really want that, too," I murmured against her hair. "I've been wanting to." I tried to quell the urgent impulse to simply leap on her—don't scare her off—and instead kissed her gently down the side of her face and neck. She wriggled to give me better access and made little sounds in her throat.

"Do you know about conception spells?" I asked, stroking her hair away from her face.

"Yes—but I couldn't find any, and I couldn't ask Alyce."

"When did you start taking the Pill?"

"This afternoon. I brought condoms, too."

I grinned at her, and after a moment she grinned back. "Right. We better do a barrier spell just to be safe," I said, and she nodded, her cheeks flushing a beautiful rose color. Pathetically, it had been a long time since I had needed one, and I had to look it up. In the interests of continuing her education, I explained the basics to Morgan and saw her eyes widen as she grasped the basic image. "Let me go do this, and I'll be right back," I said, running the tip of my tongue along the curve of her ear.

"Hurry," she said, looking extremely witchy, and I almost raced out of the room and stumbled down the hall to Sky's.

When I came back a few minutes later, Morgan was under the covers up to her shoulders. I took in the sight of her skirt, jumper, camisole, and her socks on the floor. *Oh, yeah,* I thought, yanking my shirt over my head and unsnapping my jeans.

"Come here, come here," she said, smiling and holding out her hands, and I almost tripped getting out of my pants. Then I was sliding under the covers, feeling her skin against mine, her knickers against me, and I practically lost my mind. At last, at last, at last. I held her head in my hands and kissed her deeply, again and again until we were both breathing fast and Morgan's eyes were glittering, her pupils wide and dark.

This was something I had been dreaming about for months. Her arms were clasped around my back, holding me close, pressing her small, beautifully shaped breasts to my chest. Our legs were tangled together, hers long and smooth.

"I love you so much," I whispered, stroking her, caressing her, watching her eyes unfocus as she moved under my hands. I knew she hadn't done this before, and I wanted to make sure this was fabulous for her, that she was comfortable and happy.

"I love you, too," she said, her voice sounding tight. She moved against me restlessly, twining closer to me as if she had been doing this all her life. Her hands moved over my skin, over my chest, around my back, stroking my face. . . . I held my breath as her hand tentatively touched me, and I leaned closer to touch her in the same way. Morgan gave a little gasp and stilled, her eyes locked on mine. I could hardly breathe—it was incredibly exciting, incredibly sexy, like falling off a cliff, falling down endlessly and being able to see only Morgan's eyes, her soft mouth.

"Oh my God," she breathed, moving so I could touch her more.

"Yes," I said, lost, leaning in to kiss her neck.

"Hunter," she whispered back. "Yes."

"This is so right," I muttered, kissing her. "You're everything to me."

She made an indistinguishable reply and hooked one leg over my side, curling around me. I never dreamed my last night here would end so perfectly, I thought dimly. Morgan's eyes were closed; the only sounds she was making were anxious little "mm, mm, mms." Tonight we were going to make love.

I couldn't believe this was actually happening, that Morgan had decided she was ready. What timing—this would be the perfect memory to have when I was far away in . . . uh, far away in . . . Canada.

Morgan clutched my arm hard and pushed herself against me, and I thought, Yes, this is going to work, this is fantastic. . . . I will miss this so much when I am . . . in Canada. Far away in Canada. Tomorrow. Uh . . . I quickly tried to push away those bothersome thoughts. Focus, I ordered myself. Concentrate. You have Morgan close to naked in your bed. Get it together. You're almost home.

"I'll think about this the whole time you're gone," said my love's voice, and I felt her breath against my cheek.

The whole time you're *gone*. "Mmm," I breathed as I felt her tongue tickling my ear. Goddess, this was fun, this was perfect; I was here with Morgan, *Morgan,* whom I loved and wanted so much. So much for having an early night—I wanted to do this all night long until the sun came up and—

Oh, bloody hell. When the sun came up, I would be taking off. I didn't know how long I would be gone. I didn't know what I was going to find. I could find something that would change my life forever. My parents had been on the run from Amyranth for eleven years. I could be heading into serious danger. Or I could be heading into having a family for the first time in eleven years. A family I wouldn't want to leave.

And then where would I be? Away from Morgan. And who would I be? Someone who slept with his girlfriend right before leaving her.

Damnation.

"Hunter?" She sounded worried, and I looked down and touched her face.

"It's nothing," I told myself as much as her. I closed my eyes and kissed her again, feeling how right it was, how incredible. What was I doing? Should I be doing this? Was this a good idea?

It was a fantastic idea, and I pulled her against me more tightly, feeling sweat break out on my forehead. Morgan had thought about this, had decided she was ready, and Goddess knew I was. We were going to do this tonight. How could I possibly stop now?

I couldn't; there was just no way. Tonight was all about Morgan and me. Morgan, who trusted me. Trusted me not to hurt her. Oh, no. No. I pulled my weight back onto my arm. Morgan's eyes were wide. "Did I—is something wrong?"

The insecurity in her voice made me jerk my head down to look at her. "No!" I said strongly, holding her closer. "No, of course not."

"Then what's going on?" She snuggled closer to me, and once again I had to fight a vicious battle between the top half of my body and the lower half. The top half, which included my barely functioning brain, won, but only by a minuscule margin.

I sighed. "Morgan—I'm wondering . . . is this the best idea?" The words caught in my throat, but I forced them out, feeling like I should be awarded a *big* medal for valor and chivalry.

"Whaaat?" she said, drawing back from me. I felt her aura, her vibrations instantly change. They had been incredibly strong, vibrant, involved, excited. Now they were cooling, stilling rapidly as she retreated. No, no, no, I wanted to howl.

Talk fast, Niall. "Morgan," I said, still trying to hold her close. "Listen—I want to make love with you practically more than I want to breathe at this very moment. But is this really the best thing? I mean, I'm leaving tomorrow; I don't know when I'll be back; I don't know what I'll find or what will happen to me while I'm there. I'm saying my future is somewhat up in the air at the moment. It seems—irresponsible for me to make love with you now."

"Irresponsible?"

I winced at the cool tone in her voice, and she pulled away from me physically and emotionally while I swore to myself in four different languages, including Middle Gaelic, which isn't easy.

"Love, this is killing me," I said with complete sincerity. "I want this very much. And here you are, giving yourself to me, and it's our first time, and it's incredible. I absolutely don't want to hurt you. But—what if something happens that keeps us apart? I don't want to do this just once and then forget about it. I want our first time to be only the first in a long, long series of us being together."

"I don't understand."

"Wait—stop." She had scooted to the side of the bed, and the sight of her bare, beautiful back, stiff with anger and hurt, pained me almost as much as the athame she had once sent into my neck a long time ago. "Please, Morgan, wait. Hear me out." I lunged and grabbed her around the hips, my cheek pressed against her back as she tried unsuccessfully to get up. "I'm dying to sleep with you!" I said. "I'm mad with wanting you! There's nothing more that I want than to be in bed, making love, all night long!"

"Except to be responsible."

"Morgan! Just think for a minute. Do you really think that the night before I leave for Goddess knows how long is the best time for us to sleep together for the first time? I mean, if we *had* been sleeping together for a while, this would be fine. But this is our first time together. It should be perfect. It shouldn't be part of a good-bye."

Her jaw barely moved. "In your opinion." Icicles dripping. She took advantage of my momentary appalled shock to leap out of bed. I scrambled after her, wondering where the hell I had thrown my underwear. In seconds she had pulled on her camisole with the lace and was reaching for her sweater and socks.

"Morgan, Morgan," I said, looking desperately around the floor. "This isn't my decision alone. We need to agree on this. I mean, I *hate* this. All I want to do is make love with you. But can you try to see where I'm coming from, a little bit?"

The look she gave me was distant, and my heart dropped down to my bare knees. She shrugged and sat on the bed to pull on her socks. "I don't get it. You want to, but you won't. You love me, but you won't sleep with me. I feel like a leper."

I ditched all thoughts of underwear and pulled on my jeans, being careful with the zipper. "Morgan, I want you more than I've ever wanted anyone in my whole life. And I'm ecstatic that you feel ready for us to go to bed. That's what I've wanted ever since I met you." I knelt down in front of her and looked up into her eyes, her shuttered face. "I love you. I'm so attracted to you. Please believe me. I mean, you *felt* it. This has nothing, *nothing* to do with how much I want you or how sexy you are. It's just about timing."

"Timing." She sighed and lifted her long hair away from her neck, then let it fall. I thought of it spread over my sheets, over my pillows, and began to think I was completely mad.

"Morgan, I don't want to hurt you. But either option is bad: if I ask you to wait for the next time we can be together, it hurts your feelings and makes you think I don't want you. Which isn't true. But if we go to bed tonight and then something happens and we're apart for a long time, would that be better?"

She glanced away, seeming for the first time to examine the state of my room. Great. I saw her gaze trace the bare floor, the gutted candles on my desk, the boxes still unpacked. With no warning, an image of Cal Blaire's bedroom came to mind. I had seen it when I'd been in Selene's house, undoing spells, setting other spells. Cal's bedroom had been huge, quirky, and romantic. His bed had been an antique, hung with mosquito netting. Everything in that room had been beautiful, luxurious, interesting, seductive. Feeling bleak, I rested my face on my outstretched arm, wondering if I had just buggered things up in a really huge way.

"Morgan, please," I said. When I raised my head, she was examining me calmly, and I damned her ability to rein in her strongest emotions. I covered her hand with one of mine, and she didn't flinch. "Please don't be angry with me or hurt. Please don't leave like this. Please let's have tonight be a good thing for both of us. I don't want this to be the moment we both look back on while I'm gone."

My words seemed to reach her, and I felt the sharp edges of her anger soften. A tiny bit. Then her face crumpled, and she said, "Hunter, you're leaving tomorrow. I want us to be joined together in a real way before you go. Here I am, I'm seventeen"—she threw out her arm in a disgusted, disbelieving gesture—"and you're *nine*teen and can be with anyone you want, and I want you to feel con*nect*ed to me!" Her voice broke and she clenched her fists, looking embarrassed and angry with herself for seeming weak.

Her words completely threw me, and I gaped at her. One of my favorite Tynan Flannery quotes came back to me: "Women are impossible, witches are worse, and women who are powerful witches are going to be the death of me."

I reached up and enfolded her in my arms, resting my head against her chest just under her chin. "Love, we *are* joined together in a real way because I love you, and you love me. We're *mùirn beatha dàns*," I said quietly. "You say I can be with anyone I want—well, you can be with anyone you want, too. I choose to be with you. Who do you choose?" I tilted my head back and looked up at her.

"I choose you," she muttered ungraciously, and I wanted to laugh but had enough sense left not to.

"I feel connected to you," I went on. "And it doesn't have anything to do with us having sex. Not that I don't want to have sex!" I added hastily. "I definitely want to have sex! Make no mistake! The second I come back, I'm going to jump you, wherever you are, and initiate you into the sublime joys of womanhood."

She burst into laughter, and I grinned. "My mother will be thrilled," she said dryly.

"Me too," I promised with intense sincerity, and she laughed again.

We sat there, hugging, for a long time. I hoped that we

had somewhat mended our earlier rift, and I again started to question whether or not I should just go for it. Hell, Morgan wanted to, I wanted to, it would make us happy . . . for the next couple of hours. What about after that? I was conducting a debate within myself when Morgan gently disengaged from me.

"It's late. I better go."

"Uh . . ."

She kissed me, holding my face in her strong hands. "Drive carefully tomorrow. Call me when you can. I'll be thinking about you."

Then she stood up and left, her clogs loud on the stairs. I trotted after her, still trying to figure out what I wanted. She turned and gave me a last, wistful smile, and then she was gone. I sat down on the steps, unsure of what had happened between us, unsure if I had done the right thing, unsure about everything.

4

The Journey

February 1992

Today the world seems like a different place than it did yesterday. I've always loved the winters here, but now the sky seems cold and pitiless. The beauty of our world seems to have dimmed a little. Yesterday Mama and I were calm and safe, secure in our lives and most especially in our magick. But last night Mama got a witch message from Aunt Celine. A Seeker had come to "investigate" her library, and he found some dark spells she had written—a weather spell and a spell for bending another's will, spells Mama says she never even used. But according to the council—the idiot council, Mama calls them— just writing these spells shows a leaning toward dark magick that can't be tolerated. And Aunt

Celine committed what Mama calls the cardinal sin: she argued with the Seeker, tried to make it seem like the spells aren't all that dangerous. Mama says the Seeker couldn't accept another point of view; he thought it was dangerous. And Aunt Celine was stripped of her powers today.

Oh, Goddess, it is such a horrible ceremony, but Mama insisted that we scry to watch it all. She says that I am old enough to see such things, that I have a duty to make myself aware of the abuses of power that are committed in our world. Aunt Celine cried and shook, and when she was finally stripped, she looked like a broken bird: no longer able to fly, only half the person that she was before. Mama says that the council is corrupt and stupid, that they don't understand the value of knowledge. I don't know what to believe. I only know that what happened to Celine was terrifying. I can't imagine anything she could have done to deserve such a terrible fate.

—J. C.

After Morgan left, I felt sad and wished I could have the whole evening to live over again. When would I ever learn?

I awoke at six in the morning, in the dark and inhospitable dawn. The house seemed empty and too quiet, and once again I missed Sky's presence. I hoped she was feeling better in France.

A hot shower revived me, and I finished loading the car, seeing my breath come out in dragon puffs. I decided to have breakfast on the road and set off for the highway. Just before leaving Widow's Vale, I pulled over and performed one last spell, sending it out into the world, knowing it would come to fruition about twenty-four hours from now.

Then I headed north, toward Canada and my parents.

"A room!" I bellowed into the barely functional intercom. "Do you have a room!"

I rubbed my bleary eyes and waited for the crackly response, hoping they spoke English. For the last sixty miles every sign had been in French. I don't speak French—not well, anyway. I was forty minutes away from Quebec City, had been driving for hours, and was starting to nod with tiredness, though it wasn't much past seven. I needed food, another hot shower, and a bed.

My parents' town, Saint Jérôme du Lac, was only about four hours away, and the temptation to press on was strong. But that would involve crafting wake-up spells for myself or drinking a hell of a lot of coffee, and it meant I would get to my parents' house after ten o'clock at night. A worrying thing—I had been unable to reach them by phone or scrying or witch message. I doubted they knew I was coming. If I was going to show up unannounced after eleven years, it should probably be in the daytime.

The intercom crackled back at me, and I took the garbled response to be an affirmative. Twenty minutes later I was tucking into some *jambon* and *oeufs,* washing them down with *bière,* in the tiny restaurant next door. Half an hour after that, I was facedown on the bedspread in my small, cinder-block room, dead out. I didn't wake up till nine the next morning.

On Sunday the first thought I had, after "Where the hell am I?," was about Morgan. I pictured her slowly coming to recognize the spell I'd crafted before I left. I pictured her eyes widening, a smile softening her mouth. It had been hardly more than a day, but I missed her, ached for her, and felt lonely without her.

But today was the day. I was within four hours of seeing my parents, and the thought shook me to my very bones. This was the day I had been waiting for for more than eleven years. My heart sped up in anticipation.

I leaped up, showered, and hit the road by ten. I'd bought a road map of Quebec Province back in New York. Now it led me up Highway 40, around Quebec City, then off to a smaller, two-lane highway, number 175, that would take me north to Lac Saint Jean, a big lake. Saint Jérôme du Lac was about forty minutes from there, from what I could tell.

This far north, any signs of approaching spring were wiped out. Trees were still bare and skeletal, patches of crusted snow lay everywhere in shade; no crocuses or snowdrops bloomed anywhere. Spring's warm tendrils had not yet touched this country and wouldn't for some weeks, it appeared.

Following my map carefully, I turned off onto Highway 169, still heading north. I knew I had to go about 120 kilometers to reach Saint Jérôme du Lac and, with any luck, could do it in about an hour. Now that I was so close to my parents' home, a strange, quivery feeling was beginning in my stomach. My hands felt sweaty on the steering wheel; my pulse quickened; my gaze darted around the scenery surrounding me, attuned to any movement. I was nervous. I hadn't seen my parents in eleven years. What would they be like?

Eleven years ago, I had barely come up to my da's breastbone. Now I was probably as tall as he. The last image I had of my father was that he was big, stern, and invincible. He hadn't been scared of anything. Sometimes I had seen a deep sadness in his eyes, and when I had asked about it, he'd replied that he'd been thinking about the past. I didn't understand it then but now knew that he'd probably been thinking about his life before he married Fiona, my mum. He'd been married before, to Selene Belltower, a fact that still stunned me. He'd had another son, a few months older than I, whom he'd abandoned. That had been Cal Blaire. Now both Cal and Selene were dead, and people were glad of it. I wondered if Da knew. Probably not.

My mum was Da's perfect counterpart: soft, smiling, feminine, with a ready laugh, a sense of mischief that delighted us kids, and an easy, immediate ability to show emotion. It was Mum who explained Da's moods, Mum who comforted us, cheered us on, encouraged us, loved us openly. I had been desperate to please both of them, for different reasons. Childishly, as I drove closer to them with every mile, I felt a barrage of different emotions—loss, anger that they had been gone, a quickening sense of anticipation. Would I, when I saw them, be once again able to lean on my da, to rely on his strength? Would I feel that he would protect me still, though I was now grown and come into my full powers? Hell, I was a Seeker for the council—the youngest ever. Yet I was still a nineteen-year-old kid, and the thought that I could abandon the weight of being a Seeker, even if just for a short while, was very seductive.

They would have changed in the past eleven years, I knew. Of course I knew it. I had changed, too. But we were still family, blood family, still father and mother and son. Somehow we would make those relationships fit us once more. And soon I would contact Alwyn, too, and the four of us could be a true family again.

The small turnoff road to Saint Jérôme du Lac was clearly marked. Suddenly I was bumping down a road that hadn't been retarmacked in what looked like twenty years. Huge potholes caught me off guard, and I bottomed out twice before I wised up, dropped down to about twenty miles an hour, and drove like an old lady.

The farther off the main road I got, the less prosperous the land felt. I went through several tiny, poor-looking towns, each with a petrol station that might or might not function. I also saw a lot of Canadian Indians, who called themselves First Nations people, and signs for First Nations crafts and displays.

I had no idea how far down this road I was supposed to go; after that first sign, I hadn't seen any more indications that I was heading in the right direction. Finally, when it seemed that I had gone impossibly far, I gave up and pulled over to get petrol. After I had filled the tank, I went into the small store attached to the station to pay. The storekeeper had his back to me; he was on a small wooden ladder, stocking packages of sandpaper. I hoped he spoke English.

"Excuse me," I said, and, when he turned around, I saw that he must be part Indian.

"Yes?"

"I put in ten dollars of regular petrol," I said, laying the Canadian money on the counter.

"Okay." The cash register was beautiful: an old, manually operated one.

A sudden thought struck me, and in desperation I said, "Do you by any chance know of any English or Irish people who live around here?"

He thought for a moment. "You mean the witch?" he said, and I gaped at him.

"Uh . . ."

"The only English I know around here is the witch," he said helpfully. "He moved here two, three months ago."

"Um, all right." My mind was spinning. It was unheard of to be known so casually in a community. Even witches who weren't hiding from Amyranth were always very circumspect, very private. We never would have identified ourselves as witches to anyone. Why did this man know? What did that mean? And why did he only mention a "he"?

"Could you tell me where they live?" I asked, with a sense of dread. Surely if this man knew about them, knew where they lived, then Amyranth did, too. What would I find when I got there?

"Sure. Let me draw you a map."

I watched in a daze as the man quickly sketched a rough map. I thanked him and headed back to my car. I didn't know what to think, so I started the engine and set off. The crude but accurate map led me down back roads that were even more bumpy and ill kept than the access road had been. I wished I had rented an SUV and hated the thought of what my car's undercarriage must look like.

I was hungry, thirsty, and exhausted. I began to wonder if this whole trip had been an unworkable spell. Then I came upon a little wooden shack, the first building I'd seen in ten minutes, set back from the road. A battered Ford Escort minus its wheels stood on cinder blocks in the yard. Dead ivy vines clung to it. The yard was a wintry mess—untidy, overgrown, littered with trash. It didn't look like anyone lived here. Obviously this wasn't my parents' house, though it seemed to be in the correct place on the map. I must have gotten it wrong. No witch would live in a house in this condition, with this kind of general air of neglect and poverty. A glance around the back confirmed my suspicions: Even in Canada, in winter, I should have been able to detect a cleared plot for an herb garden. But there was nothing, no sign of one. I sighed and rubbed my cold hands together.

Finally I decided to at least knock and try to get directions. I climbed up onto the porch, pulling my coat around me. This close, I felt I could detect the presence of a person, though it wasn't strong or clear, which was unusual. I knocked on the rough, unpainted door, wincing as my cold bare knuckles rasped the wood.

Inside, there was a slight shuffling, then silence, and I knocked again. Come on, I thought. I just want directions. With no warning I felt something touch my presence, as if someone had cast their senses to identify me. My eyes widened in surprise, and then the door slowly creaked open, admitting dim light into the dark interior. My eyes instantly adjusted, and I saw that I was standing before Daniel Niall, my father, for the first time in eleven years.

5

Grief

This morning I woke up, and yes, Hunter was still gone. My heart went thunk, and I thought of the days stretching before me without him, no Hunter to talk to or see or hold. Dagda and I were pondering this bleak reality when Mom tapped on my door and asked if I was going to church with them. Spontaneously I said yes, knowing that services would take up two hours of Hunterless time and maybe distract me for a while. So I showered and dressed and went downstairs and got sent back upstairs by my parents because I looked like a schlub. I borrowed a dress from Mary K. that fortunately is too long for her.

It started when we stepped outside. At first I thought I was imagining things—it didn't make sense. But then I thought, Oh, Goddess, and realized that Hunter must have crafted a spell before he left town yesterday.

It was beautiful magick. I had no idea how he had done it, but I knew that he had, and I almost started crying. It *was almost everywhere I looked, all morning: in the shapes of tree branches, in the plume of smoke from Dad's car's exhaust, in the curve of Mom's scarf as it lay over her shoulder. Somehow Hunter had woven letters and symbols and runes into almost everything I saw: crossed branches made an H, for Hunter. A crooked line of leaves in the street made an M, for Morgan. I saw the rune Ken, for fire and passion, and blushed, remembering Friday night. My heart lightened when I saw Geofu: One of its uses is for strengthening relationships. And in the line of pale gray clouds floating above us I saw Peorth: hidden things revealed and also female sexuality. Oh, Goddess, I love him so much.*

—Morgan

I've read books where people are "struck speechless," and to me it always sounded like they just couldn't think on their feet. The ability to think on my feet has always been one of my strengths, but it deserted me now as I gazed at the man before me.

I knew what my father looked like: Though I had brought no photographs with me to America, I had my memories, and they had always seemed accurate and consistent and full. But they didn't match this person in the doorway. This couldn't be Da. It was an incredibly bad Da imitation, a hollowed-out husk of what once had been my father. My gaze darted restlessly over him, taking in the sparse gray hair, the hollow cheeks with their deep lines, the thin, almost emaciated body. His clothes were shabby, his face unshaven, and there was a dank smell of stale air emanating from the dark house. My father is only forty-six. This person looked about sixty.

He frowned at me consideringly but without wonder: He didn't recognize me. I had a sudden, irrational urge to turn and run—something in me didn't want to know how he had come to be in this state. I was afraid. Then, slowly, as I stood there, a dim light entered his eyes; he looked at me more closely; he measured me up and down, trying to calculate how much his son would have grown in eleven years.

A vague disbelief replaced the suspicion in his eyes, and then we were hugging wordlessly, enfolded in each other's lanky arms like tall spiders. In my memories, my father was tall, huge. In real life I had an inch or two on him and outweighed him by maybe two stone. And I'm not hefty.

My father pulled back and held me at arm's length, his hands on my shoulders. His eyes seemed to memorize me, to memorize my pattern, my imprint. Then he said, "Oh, Gìomanach. My son." His voice sounded like a thin, sharp piece of slate.

"Yes," I said, looking behind him for Mum. Goddess, if Da looked like this, what would *she* look like? Again I was afraid. In all my thoughts and wishes and dreams and hopes and expectations about this meeting, it had never occurred to me that I would be hurt emotionally. Physically, yes, depending on what happened with Amyranth. But not emotionally. Not feeling pain because of who my parents had become.

"You're here alone?" Da rasped, and looked around me to examine the yard.

"Yes," I said, feeling incapable of intelligent speech.

"Come in, then."

I stepped through the doorway into the darkness. It was daylight outside, but every window was shuttered or curtained. The air was stale and unpleasant. I saw dusty herbs hanging from nails on the wall, a cloth that looked like an altar cloth, and candles everywhere, their wax spilling over, their wicks guttered and untrimmed. Those were the only signs I could see that a witch lived in this house.

It was filthy. Old newspapers littered the floor, which was black with dirt. Dust was thick on everything. The furniture was old, shabby, all castoffs, put out on the junk heap and rescued—but not fixed up. The one table I saw was covered with piles of paper, dried and crumbling plants, some Canadian coins, and unsteady stacks of plates with bits of crusts and dried food.

This house was shocking. It would have been shocking to find anyone living in it, but to find a witch living in it was almost unfathomable. Though witches are notorious pack rats—mostly related to their ongoing studies of the craft— just about all of us instinctively create order and cleanliness around us. It's easier to make magick in an ordered, purified environment. I looked around to find Da shuffling his feet awkwardly, glancing down as if embarrassed for me to be seeing this.

"Da, where's Mum?" I asked outright, as tendrils of fear began to coil around my heart. My father staggered as if hit and bumped against the doorway leading into what I guessed was the kitchen. I reached out to steady him, but he pulled away and ran his bony hand through his unkempt hair. He looked at me thoughtfully.

"Sit down, son," came his thin, stony voice. "I've imagined this conversation a thousand times. More. Fancy a cuppa?"

Through the doorway I saw that the kitchen was, if anything, even more filthy than the lounge. Unwashed pots and crockery covered every surface; the tiny cooker was black with burned grease; packages of opened food bore unmistakable signs of having been shared by mice. I felt ill.

"I'll make it," I said, and started rolling up my sleeves.

Twenty minutes later Da and I were seated in the room's two armchairs; mine wobbled, and the vinyl seat was held together with silver duct tape. The tea was hot, and that was all I could say for it. I'd run the water in the sink till the rusty hue had gone and scrubbed the kettle and two mugs. That was the best I could do.

I wanted to cry, "What the hell is going on? What's happened?" but instead sipped my tea and tried not to grimace. I hadn't known what to expect—I'd had images, thoughts, but no solid way of knowing what my reunion with my parents would be like. However, this scene, this reality, hadn't come close to being on the board.

"Where's Mum, Da?" I repeated, since no answer seemed forthcoming. Something deep inside me was afraid I already knew the answer, but there was no way I couldn't ask it.

Da visibly flinched again, as if I had struck him. The hand holding his tea mug trembled almost uncontrollably, and tea splashed over the rim onto the chair's arm and onto his raggedy brown corduroys.

"Your mum's dead, son," he said, not looking at me.

I gazed at him unwaveringly as my brain painfully

processed the words one by one. They made no sense to me, yet they also made a horrible kind of sense. My mother, Fiona, was dead. In our coven some people had called her Fiona the Bright because being around her, with her flaming red hair, was like raising your face to a ray of sun. Da had called her Fiona the Beautiful. Us kids, when we were little and childishly angry, sometimes called her Fiona the Mean. And giving no respectful weight to our words, our anger, she would laugh at us: Fiona the Bright. Da was telling me she was dead, that her body was dead and gone. I had no mother and so no future chance of experiencing a mother's love, ever again in my life.

I couldn't cry in that house, that horrible, dark, lifeless house, in front of this person who was not the father I had known. Instead, I rose, put down my tea, and staggered out the door to my car. I climbed in, coatless, and stayed out there until I was half frozen and my tears were under control. It was a long time, and Da didn't come after me.

When I went back in, Da was in exactly the same place I had left him, his cold, undrunk tea by his hand. I sat down again and shoved my hair off my forehead and said, "How? Why?"

He looked at me with sympathy, knowing all too well what I was feeling. "Fiona had battled ill health for years—since right after we left. Year after year we went from place to place, searching for safety. Sometimes she would do a little better, mostly she did worse. In Mexico, seven years ago, we had another close call with the dark wave—you know what that is?"

I nodded. As a Seeker, I had all too much experience with the dark wave.

"And after that it was pretty much downhill." He paused, and I stayed silent. "Your mother was so beautiful, Gìomanach," he said softly. "She was beautiful, but more than that, she was good, truly good, in a way few witches are. She was light itself, goodness itself. Do you remember what she looked like?" His eyes on me, suddenly sharp.

I nodded again, not trusting myself to speak.

"She didn't look like that anymore," he said abruptly. "It was impossible for her not to be beautiful, but every year that passed took its toll on her. Her hair was white, white as a cloud, when she died. She was thin, too thin, and her skin was like . . . like paper, like fine paper: just as thin, just as white, as brittle." He shrugged, his shoulders pointed beneath his threadbare flannel shirt. "I thought she would die when we found out about Linden."

My head jerked up. "You know?"

Da nodded slowly, as if acknowledging it created fresh waves of pain that he could hardly bear. "We knew. I thought that would kill her. But it didn't—not quite. Anyway. This past winter was hard. I knew the end was coming, and so did she. She was tired, so tired, Gìomanach. She didn't want to try anymore." His voice broke, and I winced. "Right before Yule she gave up. Gave me one last beautiful smile and slipped away, away from the pain, the fear." His head dropped nearly to his chest; he was trying to not cry in front of me.

I was upset, angry, devastated—not just at the news of my mother's death, but at the haggard condition of this man who appeared to be my father. Tense with inaction, I jumped up and began throwing open curtains, opening shutters.

Pale, watery wintry sunlight seemed to consider streaming in, then decide against it as too much trouble. What light did enter only illuminated the pitiable condition of the house. I could see now why Da kept it dark.

This wreck of a man, this shell with his caved-in chest, his head bowed in pain and defeat, this was my da! This was the man whose anger I had feared! Whose love I had craved, whose approval I had worked for. He seemed pathetic, heartbreaking. I could only imagine what he had been going through, and going through alone, all this time. Had my mother's death done this to him? Had Amyranth? Had years of running done it? I sank back into my chair in frustration. Two months my mother had been dead. Two months. She had died just before Yule, a Yule I had celebrated back in Widow's Vale, with Kithic. If I had come here before Yule, I would have seen my mother alive.

"What about since then?" I asked. "What have you been doing since then?"

He looked up, seeming bewildered at my words. "Since then?" He looked around the room as if the answer was contained there. "Since then?"

Oh, this was bad. Why had he agreed to talk to the council? What was the point in all this? Maybe Da knew what bad shape he was in. Maybe he was hoping for help. He was my father. And he had the answers to a thousand questions I'd had since I was eight years old.

I tried again. "Da, what made you and Mum leave in the first place? How could you—how could you leave us behind?" My voice cracked and splintered—this was the question that had tormented me for more than half my life.

How many times had I cried it aloud? How many times had I shouted it, screamed it, whispered it? Now here was the one person who could answer it, or so I hoped. Mum no longer could. Da's eyes, once deep brown, now looked like dim pools of brackish water. They focused on me with surprising sharpness, as if he had just realized I was there.

When he didn't answer, I went on, the questions spilling out like an unchecked river—once started, impossible to stop. "Why didn't you contact me before Mum died? How did you know Linden died? How could you not have contacted us when each of us was initiated?"

With each question my father's head sank lower and lower. He made no reply, and I realized with frustration that I would get no answers, at least not today. My stomach rumbled with alarming fierceness, and I remembered I had eaten nothing since that morning. It was now five o'clock, and dark.

"Come on, Da, let's get something to eat. We could both use it." Without waiting for a reply, I went into the kitchen and began opening cupboards. I found a tin of tomatoes, a tin of sardines, and some half-eaten, stale crackers. The refrigerator offered no joy, either: nothing but a lone turnip, whose shriveled, lonely form increased my confusion, my concern. Why was there no food in the house? What had he been eating? Who the hell eats *turnips*? I went back out to the living room, seeing again how thin Da was, how fragile he seemed. Well, I was here, and I was the only son he had left, and I would take care of him.

"On second thought, let's go out. I saw a diner in town. Come on, my treat."

6

Turloch-eigh

June 1997

Today my cottage seems filled by a cloud of sadness. I know that this isn't a day for sorrow; it should be a day for happy memories, for quiet contemplation and reminiscing. Yet the sorrow comes along unbidden. Today is the fifth anniversary of Mama's death.

It seems so long ago that we lived in this house together, yet I remember so much about her—her intensity, her passion for learning, the way she strove to kindle in me an appreciation for the complexity of the world. And her morality. If they knew the truth of her beliefs, many witches who revere her today would not consider my mother a moral person. Yet her heart was large, her empathy complete. She taught me healing spells and did her utmost to help animals, children, anyone who was vulnerable. She had a strong sense of right and wrong, and she felt that our family had been wronged too many times. I miss her so terribly, even five years after her death. I would like to believe that somewhere, wherever her soul is on its journey, she is aware of the work I am doing, and she is proud.

Today I stayed away from the library. I did not want to be tempted; it would be so easy to hurt my mother in my nostalgia and my sadness. But tomorrow I will return to my work. I will continue compiling . . . continue learning.

I cannot think of a better gift that I could give to Mama.

—J. C.

"Sorcier."

My head jerked at the French word, so casually spoken, as a man walked past Da and me. We were in the town proper of Saint Jérôme du Lac, which was basically one street, no stoplight. One petrol station. But at least there were sidewalks and some small shops that had a quaint, frontiersy charm. I had parked my car not far from the town's only diner, which was right next to the town's only grocer. It was dark and colder than an ice cave. I pulled my coat tighter around my neck and wondered that my father didn't get knocked over by the stiff breeze. And then I'd heard it: "*Sorcier.*" Witch. I know the word *witch* in at least seventeen different languages: useful for a Seeker. *Bruja* in Spanish. *Hexe* in German. Italians call us *strega*. Polish people say *wiedźma*. In Dutch, I listen for *toverheks*. Once in Russia I had old potatoes thrown at me while kids yelled, "*Koldunya!*" Long story. In Hungary one says *boszorkány*. And in French Canada one says, "*Sorcier.*"

But why anyone from the town would identify my father as a witch was still a mystery. I resolved to ask him about it later, after we ate. Two more people greeted Da as we went into the diner. He acknowledged them with a bob of his head, an embarrassed nod. I scanned them with my senses: they were just townspeople.

I, for one, felt better after a dinner of sausage, potatoes, canned green beans, and four thick slices of a rough brown bread that was incredible. I felt self-conscious, sitting with Da; I felt eyes on me, speculation. Da introduced me to no one, never said my name aloud, and I wondered if he was being careful or if he had forgotten who I was.

"Eat that," I encouraged him, gesturing at his plate with my fork. "I paid good money for it."

He gave me a slight, wan smile, and I found myself hungrily looking for a trace of his old, broad grin. I didn't see it.

"Your mother would be amazed to see my appetite so small," he said, forcing a laugh that sounded more like a cough. "She used to tease me about being able to eat for three."

"I remember," I said.

Da picked his way through his meal and left so much on his plate that I was forced to finish it for him. He did seem a little less shaky afterward, though. I bet he would be a hundred percent better after I got a couple more good meals into him. Luckily the grocer's was still open after dinner. I bought a cabbage, some potatoes, some apples. Da, not even pretending to take an interest, sank down into a rocking chair near the door, his head on his chest, while I shopped. I bought meat—missing the somewhat intimidating sterile American packaging—chicken, fresh fish, and staples: flour, rice, sugar, coffee, tea. Inspired, I bought laundry detergent, other cleaning supplies. I paid for everything, collected my dim ghost of a father, and loaded groceries and Da into the car.

By the time we got back down the road to the cabin, Da was a waxy shade of gray. Worriedly I helped him into the dark house, felt unsuccessfully for a light switch, gave up, and used witch sight to lead him to a tiny, bleak, horrid bedroom—the only one in the house. It was about the size of a walk-in freezer and had about as much charm. The walls were unpainted pine planks spotted with black, age-old sap. The rusty iron bed, like the furniture in the living room, looked like it had been saved from a garbage heap. Unwashed clothes were piled in small heaps on the floor. Next to the bed was a small, rickety table, covered with candles, dust, and old cups of tea. Da sank down onto dingy sheets and rested his arm across his eyes.

"Da—are you ill?" I asked, suddenly wondering if he had cancer or a death spell on him or something else. "Can I get you something? Tea?"

"No, lad," came his reedy voice. "Just tired. Leave me be; I'll be fine in the morning."

I doubted that but awkwardly pulled a thin coverlet over him and went out into the lounge. I still couldn't find a light switch but brought in the groceries, lit some candles, and looked around. The cabin was freezing. As cold as outside. Shivering, I searched for a thermostat. Ten minutes later I came to the sinking realization that there was no thermostat because the cabin had no electricity.

Smothering a curse, I lit more candles. How had Da managed to live like this for any length of time? No wonder he looked so bad. I'd thought all the candles and lanterns had been witch gear—but they were his only light sources as well.

There was a fireplace with some handfuls of pale ashes scattered on its hearth. Of course there was no firewood inside—that would be too easy! I pulled on my coat and tramped around in the snow outside. I found some firewood, wet with snow. Inside I kindled a fire, and the flames leaped upward, the damp wood sizzling. Instantly the room seemed cheerier, more inviting. The fireplace was small but threw back an impressive heat into the frigid room.

Da was sleeping, and I was bone tired but filled with a frenetic energy that wouldn't admit to fear. I had been on the road since morning; it had been a long, strange, awful, sad day. I was in a cabin in the backwoods of Canada with my unrecognizable, broken father. I heard wolves in the distance, thought of Morgan, and missed her with such a powerful ache that I felt my throat close. I wanted to sit down in one of the vinyl recliners and weep again but knew that if I started, I wouldn't stop. So instead I rolled up my sleeves and went into the kitchen.

At midnight I sank down onto a couch I hadn't even realized was there because it had been covered with litter. I pulled an ancient, ugly crocheted afghan over me and closed my eyes, trying to ignore the hot tears that burned my cheeks.

In the morning I was awakened by the sounds of my father shuffling out of his room. He walked through the lounge without noticing me on the couch, then stopped in the kitchen doorway. I waited for his response. Last night, after thanking the Goddess for the propane-run refrigerator, stove, and hot water heater, I had done a major clean of the kitchen. Da stood there, and then he seemed to remember that if the kitchen looked like this, someone else must be in the cabin, and he looked for me. I sat up, swinging my long legs over the side of the couch.

"Morning, Da," I said, standing and stretching.

He managed a smile. "I'd almost forgotten you were here. It's been too long since someone said good morning to me," he said wistfully. He gestured at the kitchen. "You do all this?"

"Aye."

"Ta. I just haven't been up to much lately—I know I let the place get into a mess." Then he went into the kitchen and sat down at the table, and suddenly I remembered how he used to do that in the morning, just come in and sit down, and Mum would make him a cup of tea. Grateful for any reminder of the old days, I filled the kettle with water and set it on the stove. I fixed him tea and toast with butter, which he managed to eat a little bit of. For myself I fried eggs and some rashers of bacon: fuel for the day's labor ahead. I sat down across from Da and tucked in. I still had a thousand questions; he was still the only man who could answer them. I would have to choose my time.

After breakfast I set him to work, helping me clean the rest of the house. While I was piling papers and things neatly on the desk so I could wipe the surface, I couldn't help noticing letters from people, crude notes written in broken languages, handwritten thank-you notes in English and French, praising my da, praising his skill as a *sorcier*. With shock I realized that Daniel Niall, Woodbane, formerly of Turloch-eigh, son of Brónagh Niall, high priestess of Turloch-eigh, was basically the local medicine man, the village witch. I couldn't believe it. Surely this was incredibly dangerous. As far as I knew, Da hadn't worked real magick for years because it would be one way for Amyranth to trace him. Was it now safe? Why, and how?

Burning with questions, I went to find Da and sighed when I found him asleep again, on the bare mattress in his room. It had only been about an hour since I'd started him on the candles and lanterns. Well, sleep was probably good for him. Sleep and food and someone looking out for him.

In the meantime, I couldn't just sit around this place. I felt a need to get out, breathe fresh air. In the end I made Da a sandwich and left it covered on the kitchen table. Then I bundled up every piece of cloth in the place, threw it into the boot of my car, and headed for the laundromat in town.

"What do you do with your trash?" I asked Da at dinner. There was quite a mound of black plastic trash bags in the front yard. Sadly, they actually didn't make the yard look that much worse.

He looked up from his boiled potato. "Take it to the dump, outside town."

I groaned silently. Great. Now I'd have to haul it all in my car. After we ate for a few more minutes, I said, "Da, all I know is what Uncle Beck told me, what I've heard whispers of from other people through the years. But now I'm here, across from you, and you've got the answers. I need to know: Why did you and Mum leave us? Why did you disappear? And why is it now all right for me to know where you are?"

He didn't look at me. His bony fingers plucked restlessly at the cuff of the clean flannel shirt I had given him to put on. "It's ancient history, lad," he said in a voice like a dry leaf. "It was probably all a mistake. Won't bring your mother back, anyway." A spasm of pain crossed his face.

"I know it won't bring Mum back," I said. I took a swig of beer, watching him across the table as though he might disappear in a puff of smoke to avoid my questions. "That doesn't mean I shouldn't know the answers. Look, Da, I've waited eleven years. You took my life apart when you left, and Linden's, and Alwyn's. Now I need to know. Why did you and Mum leave?"

Though I'm only nineteen, I'm a Seeker. Which means I make my living by asking people questions. I've grown used to waiting for answers, asking over and over until I find out what I want to know. I'm very good at my job, so I said again, very gently, "Why did you and Mum leave? It's almost unheard of for a coven to split up if trouble's coming."

Da shifted in his seat. He held his fork and patted a piece of cabbage on his plate, pushing it this way and that. I waited. I can be very patient.

"I don't want to talk about it," he said at last. His eyes flicked up at mine, and I noticed again how their color had faded, had clouded. But there was a hint of sharpness in his gaze, and in an instant I knew that my father still had some kind of power and that I needed to remember that. "But you always were like a bulldog—once you got your teeth in something, you didn't let it go. You were like that as a lad."

I met his eyes squarely. "I'm like that still, Da," I said. "Actually, I've made a career of it. I'm a Seeker for the council. I investigate people for a living."

I watched Da's eyes, waiting for his reaction. Would he be proud of me? I had always imagined he would be, but then, so many of my imaginings had been proven hopelessly wrong in the last twenty-four hours. My father looked at me considering, and then his face broke into a sudden smile.

"So you are," he said softly. "Well, that's quite an accomplishment, son. Right, then, bulldog, if you'll have it out of me—Selene sent the dark wave after us, at Turloch-eigh."

I frowned, my brain kicking into gear.

"Us who?" I asked.

He cleared his throat. "Your mother and me. Both of us. Your mother felt it that night, felt it coming, knew who it was aimed at. Knew who it was from."

"Was Selene finally getting you back for leaving her? The dark wave that killed the entire village was about Selene's jealousy?"

He gave a short bark of a laugh. "Yes. She'd always said that I would need to look over my shoulder the rest of my life. And she was right. Well, until now." He paused. "At least *they* were able to come together again safely."

"How's that?" I wasn't sure if I had heard him correctly. "Who came together again?"

Da was looking at me, frowning. "Gìomanach, what have you been thinking all these years? That we were gone, along with everyone else, and we never came back for you and you didn't know why?" He shook his head. "Oh, Goddess, forgive me. And I ask your forgiveness, too, son." He swallowed, then went on. "No. That night Fiona felt the dark wave coming. We knew it was for us, and us alone, but that Selene and Amyranth would be happy to destroy the whole village if it included us. So, taking a chance, the only chance we could, we fled, leaving you three there, spelled with protection circles. We thought if we left, we would draw the dark wave away from the village. That it would follow us, instead of concerning itself with Turloch-eigh. Later, when I scried and saw the village gone, I was devastated—our flight hadn't saved anything. But years later Brian Entwhistle found me. You remember Brian, right?"

I searched my memory and came up with a big, ruddy bear of a man. I nodded.

"It wasn't safe to contact you kids or Beck. Too risky. But once or twice we were contacted by older witches, powerful ones who could protect themselves. Brian was one. I was astonished when he found us—thought he'd been dead all those years."

I was sitting on the edge of my seat, my hands gripping the arms. Here it was, the whole story, after so long. It wasn't what I'd thought it would be.

"Brian told us that you kids were safe, that Beck had gotten you. He told me the village had actually been spared."

"But wait a minute," I said, remembering something. "I went back there, not three years ago. The place is deserted and has been for years. No one lives there. I saw it."

"Yes, they all returned a short time after the dark wave left—trickled back in one family at a time. They tried to make another go at it there, but apparently the dark wave came too close. It left a destructive spell in its wake. After everyone had come home and settled down, things started happening. Accidents, unexplained illnesses. Crops failed, gardens died, spells went wrong. It took a year of that before the whole village up and moved closer to the coast. They made a new town there, thirty miles away, and Brian told me they had prospered."

I was dumbfounded. "So everyone left and no one bothered to look for us? They left me and Linden and Alwyn to die?"

"They didn't know you were there, lad. Susan Forest knocked on our door that night. Mum and I had already fled. You kids slept like the dead and were spelled besides. Fiona and I wanted you to sleep soundly, not to wake up in the middle of the night and find us missing and be afraid." Da's voice caught there, and he shook his head as if to clear it. "Anyway, when she got no answer, she figured we'd all taken off."

I shook my head, frowning in disbelief. "All this time I've been mourning not only my parents, but everyone I knew, everyone in our village. And now you're telling me they're hale and hearty, living thirty miles from home. I don't believe this!" I said. "Why didn't anyone contact us at Beck's? Why hasn't anyone told me this before?"

Da shrugged. "I don't know. I guess Beck probably knows. Maybe he thought that if you knew, you'd leave him and go back to the village."

"Why didn't Brian Entwhistle bother to tell us that our parents were alive?" I was feeling a growing sense of indignation. All those years of tears, of pain . . . so much of it could have been avoided. It made me ill to think about it.

Da met my eyes. "What would you have done if you'd known?"

"Come to find you!" I said.

"Right."

Oh.

"Your mum and I thought that if we sacrificed ourselves, we could save our children, save our coven. When I scried and saw the village gone, it was a hard blow. I thought it had been for nothing. I was relieved when I found out my vision had been wrong."

"But after you learned that the coven was safe, why didn't you come back?"

"The dark wave was still after us. I'm not sure if it was always Selene, but at the time we reckoned it was. No one's ever hated me like that. Goddess willing, no one ever will. At the time, it seemed that if we kept Selene occupied with finding us, she'd have less time to go after other covens, other witches. It seemed worth it." He shrugged, as if that were no longer so clear.

"Why aren't you in hiding now?" I asked. "Are you not in danger anymore?"

My father let out a deep breath, and again I was struck by how old he seemed, how frail. He looked like my grandfather. "You know why. Selene's dead. So's Cal."

I nodded. So he *did* know. I figured the council must have told him when they'd found him with Sky's lead. I drank my tea, trying to digest this story. It was light-years away from anything I had imagined.

"So now you work magick, now that you're not hiding from Amyranth?"

Da shrugged, his thin shoulders rising like a coat hanger in his shirt. "Like I said, Fiona's dead," he said. "No point in hiding, in keeping safe. The one thing I wanted to protect is gone. What's the point in fighting anymore? It was for her I kept moving, kept finding new sanctuaries. She wanted us to stick to this plan; I wanted to do what she wanted. But she's gone now. There's nothing left to protect." He spoke like an automaton, his words expressionless, his eyes focused on the table in front of him.

By the time he finished talking, my face was burning. On the one hand, I was glad that he and Mum had had some noble cause behind their disappearance, glad they had acted unselfishly, glad they had been trying to protect others. But it was also incredibly hurtful to listen to my own father basically negate my existence, my dead brother's, my sister's. Obviously staying alive now for our sakes hadn't occurred to him. I was glad he had been loyal to my mother; I was angry that he had not been loyal to his children.

Abruptly I got up and went into the living room. I undid the huge bundle of washing in the lounge, then made up Da's bed with clean sheets and blankets. He was in the same position when I got back to the kitchen.

"I'm so sorry, son," he said in a thin voice. "We thought we were acting for the best. Maybe we helped some—I hope we did. It's hard to see clearly now what would have been best."

"Yes. I see that. Well, it's late," I said, not looking at him. It was only eight-thirty. "Maybe we should turn in."

"Aye. I'm knackered," Da said. He got up and shuffled with his old man's walk toward the one bedroom. I sat down at the kitchen table, had another cup of tea, and listened to the deep silence of the house. Again I missed Morgan fiercely. If she were here, I would feel so much better, so much stronger. I imagined her arms coming around me, her long hair falling over my shoulder like a heavy, maple-colored curtain. I imagined us locked together, kissing, rolling around on my bed. I remembered her wanting to make love with me and my saying no. What an idiot I'd been. I resolved to call her the next day as soon as I could get into town.

I washed up the few dishes and cleaned the kitchen. By ten o'clock I felt physically exhausted enough to try to sleep. I wrapped myself up in a scratchy wool blanket and the ugly afghan. After being washed, the afghan was only about half as big as it had been. Oops.

From the couch I extinguished the lanterns and candles with my mind, and after they were snuffed, I lay in the darkness that is never really darkness, not for a witch. I thought about my unrecognizable da. When I was younger, he'd seemed like a bear of a man, huge, powerful, an inevitable force to be reckoned with. Once when I was about six, I had been playing near an icy river that ran by our house. Of course I fell in, got carried downstream, and only barely managed to grab a low-hanging branch. I clung to it with all my strength while I frantically sent Da a witch message. It was long minutes before he came leaping down the bank toward me and splashed into the strong current. With one hand he grabbed my arm and hauled me out, flinging me toward the bank like a dead cat. I was shaking with cold, blue and numb, and mainly he felt I'd gotten what I'd deserved for being so stupid as to play near the river.

"Thanks, Da," I gasped, my teeth chattering so hard, I almost bit my lip. He nodded at me abruptly, then gestured to my wet clothes. "Don't let your mum see you like that." I watched him stride up the bank and out of sight, like a giant, then I crawled to my knees and made my way home.

But he could be so patient, teaching us spells. He'd begun on me when I was four, simple little spells to keep me from burning my mouth on my tea, to help me relax and concentrate, to track our dogs, Judy and Floss. It's true I caught on quickly; I was a good student. But it's also true that Da was an incredibly good teacher, organized in his thoughts, able to impart information, able to give pertinent examples. He was kind when I messed up, and while he made it clear he expected a lot from me, still, he also made me feel that I was special, smart, quick, and satisfying to teach. I used to swell like a sponge when he praised me, almost bursting in the glow of his approval.

I turned on my side, trying to find a position that coordinated the old couch's lumps with my rib cage. I heard Da sleeping restlessly in the other room, as if he didn't even know how to do a soothing spell. Like yourself, idiot, said my critical inner voice. I rubbed the bridge of my nose with two fingers, trying to dispel a tension headache, then quickly sketched a few runes and sigils in the air, muttering words I'd know since childhood. *Where I am is safe and calm, I am hidden from the storm, I can close my eyes and breathe, now my worries will all leave*. What second-year student doesn't know that? I said it, and instantly my eyes felt heavier, my breathing slowed, and I felt less stressed.

Just before I fell asleep, I remembered one last scene with my father. I had been seven and full of myself, leagues ahead of the other third-year students in our coven. To show off, I had crafted a spell to put on our cat, Mrs. Wilkie. It was to make her think a canary was dipping about her head so she would rear up on her hind paws and swat at it over and over again. Of course, nothing was there, and we kids were hysterical with laughter, watching her pointlessly swipe at the air.

Da hadn't found it so funny. He came down on us like the wrath of heaven, and of course my companions instantly gave me up, their fingers pointing at me silently. He hauled me up by my collar, undid the spell on poor Mrs. Wilkie, and then marched me to the woodshed (a real woodshed) and tanned my bum. I ate standing up for three days. Americans seem to be much more skittish about spanking, but I know that after that, I never again put a spell on an animal for fun. His approval was like the sun, his disapproval like a storm. I got love and affection from Mum, but it was being in Da's good stead that mattered.

Today his approval or disapproval would mean little to me. With that last sad thought, I fell asleep.

7

Le Sorcier

December 2001

Today I found a bit of rock that had a thread of gold running through it. I held it in my hand and closed my eyes and felt its ancient fire warming my hand. I came home, crunching through the snow, and set the rock on my kitchen table. I stoked the fire and made myself some mulled cider. Then we sat together, the rock and I, and it told me its secrets. I knew its true name, the name of the rock and the name of the gold within it. Using the form as described by Davina Heartson, I gently, slowly, patiently coaxed the gold out of the rock. It came to me, running like water on fire, and now it sits in a tiny lump in my hand, the rock being empty where it was. It was such a beautiful thing, such a pure power, such a perfect knowledge, that I sat there and wept with it.

This is the value of my research. This is why I've gone to such lengths to collect true names. Knowing true names elevates my magick into something different from what most witches have. I was born strong—I'm a Courceau. But the collection of true names I have gives me almost unlimited power over the known ones. Think of what I could do with some particular names. Think of what power I would wield. I could be virtually unstoppable. Then I could avenge my family, all those who have had their power stripped, who have been persecuted, misunderstood, judged by small-minded bureaucrats. They didn't understand who they were dealing with. I will make it my life's work to teach them.

—J. C.

When I got up the next morning, Da was gone, just like he had been the day before. I wondered if the extra food he'd been getting had given him more energy, because he'd said he was going to "work." Work? What work? I tried to engage him in a conversation about it but got nowhere. I could only assume that this had something to do with the notes thanking him for his skill as a *sorcier;* perhaps he was out on medicine-man business. I wished he would tell me more about it, because he scarcely seemed strong enough to go to the grocery store, never mind tending to the magickal needs of villagers. The previous afternoon when he had come home, his face had been the color of a cloudy sky. I wondered if his heart was okay. When was the last time he had seen a healer? I wished I could get him to one. As far as I knew, though, he was the only witch around.

But he was gone again, already gone when I woke up.

I meditated, fixed myself breakfast, then drove to town to call Morgan. Naturally, I discovered that if you phone your seventeen-year-old girlfriend at ten o'clock on a Tuesday, she'll be in school. After that disappointing episode, I hung around the house. I was starting to feel like a professional maid. I scrubbed the lounge floor (it was wood—who'd've known?), whapped all the dust out of the furniture, and did a complete overhaul of the kitchen cabinets. I didn't know how long I'd be there or what Da would do after I was gone, but I'd laid in a good store of supplies.

Back in New York, I had pictured quite a different family reunion. I'd pictured my parents—changed, to be sure, but still themselves—overjoyed to see me, my mum crying tears of joy, Da clapping me on the back (I've grown so tall!). I'd pictured us sitting round a table, the three of us, sharing good stories and bad, sharing meals, catching each other up on our lives of the last eleven years.

I hadn't pictured a gray ghost of a father, my mother being dead, and me being Suzy Homekeeper while my da went off to his secretive work that the whole bloody village knew about but I didn't. I'd wondered if my folks would be impressed or unhappy about my Seeker assignment from the council. I'd wondered if they'd test my magickal strength, if they would be happy with my progress, my power. I'd wanted to tell them about Morgan and even talk to them about what had happened with Linden, and with Selene and

Cal. But Da had showed no interest in my life, asked no questions. Two of his four children were dead, and he hadn't asked any more about it. He hadn't asked about Beck or Shelagh or Sky or anyone else.

Goddess, why had I even come? And why was I staying? I sighed and looked around the cabin. It gave me a sad satisfaction: everything was tidy and scrubbed, clean and purified, the way a witch's house should be. I had sprinkled salt, burned sage, and performed purifying rites. The cabin no longer jangled my nerves when I walked into it. I had dragged it into the light. It was too bad the ground outside was still frozen—I was itching to start digging up earth for a summer garden plot, every witch's mainstay. Sky and I had planned ours back in January. I hoped she would come back soon to help me with it.

Then my senses picked up on someone approaching the cabin—Da returning? No. I turned off the gas burner on the stove and cast my senses more strongly.

When I answered the knock, I found a short First Nation woman standing on the porch. I didn't think I'd seen her in town.

Her dark eyes squinted at me, and she didn't smile. *"Où est le sorcier?"*

I still found it hard to believe that my father was identified as such so openly. In danger or not, it's never considered a good thing to be so obvious, so well known. Witches had been persecuted for hundreds of years, and it always made sense to be prudent.

I searched my mind for the little French I'd learned to impress an ex-girlfriend. *"Il n'est pas ici,"* I said haltingly.

The woman looked at me, then reached out her hand and

touched my arm. I felt her warmth through my sweater. She gave a brisk nod, as if a suspicion had been confirmed. *"Vous être aussi un sorcier,"* she said matter-of-factly. *"Suivez-moi."*

My jaw dropped open. Where was I? What was this crazy place where witches lived openly and villagers could tell them from nonwitches?

At my hesitation she said again, more firmly, *"Suivez-moi,"* and gestured toward a dark blue pickup truck that looked as though it had fallen down a rocky ravine, only to be hauled out and pressed into service again.

"Oh, no, ah . . . " I began. I had no intention of getting into a truck with a strange woman, not in the backwoods of Canada, not when my da wasn't around.

"Oui, oui," she said with quiet insistence. *"Vous suivez-moi. Maintenant."*

"Uh, *pourquoi?"* I asked awkwardly, and her jaw set.

"Nous besoin de vous," she said shortly. We need you. *"Maintenant."* Now.

Oh, blimey, I muttered to myself. *"D'accord, d'accord,"* I said, turning inside. I banked the fire in the hearth, grabbed my coat, and, wondering what the hell I was getting myself into, followed the woman out into the rapidly falling darkness.

The inside of the truck felt as rough as the outside looked. Nor did this driver believe in seat belts. I clutched the door handle, feeling my kidneys being pummeled by every stone and hole in the road, and there were too many to count. After what felt like a whole evening but was really only about twenty minutes, we slowed and the truck's head-lights illuminated a cabin much like my father's, and in the same state of decrepitude.

As soon as I unfolded myself painfully from the truck, I picked up on waves of searing pain and distress. My eyes widened, and I looked at the woman. What the hell was this about? Did she need a witch or a doctor? My driver came and took my arm in a deceptively strong grip and almost hauled me up the steps. I braced myself and started summoning strength, spells of power and protection, ward-evil spells.

Inside the cabin my ears were immediately assaulted by a long, howling wail of pain, as if an animal were trapped somehow. There were three other First Nation people in the lounge, and I saw another, older woman bent over the stove in the kitchen, which looked marginally better equipped than Da's. Four sets of black eyes fastened on me as I stood there, dumbfounded, and then I cringed as the unearthly wail came again.

The woman tugged off my coat and pulled me toward a bedroom. Inside the bedroom I was confronted by something I never could have predicted: a woman in childbirth, writhing on a bed, while an elderly woman tended to her. In a flash I realized I had been brought here as a healer, to help this woman give birth.

"Oh, no," I began lamely, as the woman screamed again. It made all the hairs on the back of my neck stand up, and I was uncomfortably reminded of the time when Morgan had shape-shifted into a wolf.

"Vous elle aidez," said my driver in a no-nonsense tone.

"Oh, no," I said, trying to find my voice. "She should be in hospital." Did anyone here understand some English? I was rapidly running out of French. I glanced at the bed again and saw with dismay that, in fact, it wasn't a woman in childbirth—it was a teenager who couldn't have been more than sixteen or seventeen. Morgan's age. And she was having a hard time of it.

"Non. Vous elle aidez," my companion said, a shade more loudly and with more tension.

"A hospital?" I said hopefully, and couldn't help shuddering when the girl screamed again. She didn't seem to know I was there. Her shoulder-length black hair was soaked with sweat, and she clutched her huge belly and curled up as if to get away from the pain. Tears had wet her face, so there was no dry skin left. The older woman was trying to soothe her, calm her, but the girl was hysterical and kept batting her away. The tension in the room was climbing rapidly, and I could feel coils of pressure surrounding the whole cabin. Oh, Goddess.

The older woman looked at me. "The 'opital is five *heures* far. Far." She gestured with her hand to mean "extremely far away." "Is big money, big money."

Bloody hell. The girl wailed again, and I felt like I was in a nightmare. A huge swooping attack from Amyranth right now, with Ciaran trying to rip my soul away, would almost have been more welcome. The older woman, who I guessed was a midwife, came toward me. The girl sobbed brokenly on the bed, and I felt her energy draining away.

"I get *bébé* out," the older woman said, using descriptive hand motions that made my face heat. "You *calmez* 'er. *Oui? Calmez.*" Again she gestured, with soothing, stroking motions, then pointed toward the girl.

There was nothing for it: I had to step into the fray. The girl's eyes were wild, rolling like those of a frightened horse;

she was fighting everyone who was trying to help her. My nerves were shot, but I reached deep inside my mind and quickly blocked things out, sinking into a midlevel meditative state. After a few seconds I began to send waves of calmness, comfort, reassurance to the girl. I didn't even try to interact with her present self but sent these thoughts deep within her, into her mind, where she would simply receive them without examining or questioning them.

The girl's wild, terrified eyes slowly turned and focused on me. Then another contraction racked her, and she coiled and screamed again. I had never done anything like this before and had to make up a plan as I went along. I kept sending waves of calm, comfort, reassurance toward her while I desperately searched my spell repertoire for anything that might help. *Right, come on, Niall, pull it out of your hat.* I stepped closer to the bed and saw where it was soaked from her water breaking. Agh. I wanted to run from the room. Instead, I looked away and began to sketch sigils over the bed, muttering spells to take away pain, spells to calm fears, spells to make her relax, to let go, to release.

The girl made harsh panting sounds, *hah, hah, hah,* but kept her eyes on my face. As if in a dream, I slowly reached out and touched her wet hair, like black silken rope beneath my fingers. As soon as I touched her, I got a horrible wave of pain, as if someone had run a machete through my gut, and I gasped and swallowed hard. The girl wailed again, but already her cry was less intense, less frightened. She tried to slap my hand away, but I dodged her and stayed connected, pushing some of my own strength and energy into her, transferring some of my power. Within half a minute she had quit struggling, quit writhing as much. Her next contraction broke our connection, but I came back, touching her temple, closing my eyes to focus. The poor teenage girl couldn't begin to understand, but the deep-seated, primal woman within her could respond. Concentrating, I tuned that woman into the cycles of nature, of renewal, of birth. I sent knowledge that the contractions weren't the pain of injury or damage, but instead signs of her body's awesome power, the strength that was able to bring a child into the world. I felt the consciousness of the child within her, felt that it was strong and healthy, a girl. I smiled and looked up. My driver and the midwife were nearby. The midwife was sponging the girl's forehead and patting her hand. *"Une fille,"* I said, smiling. *"Le bébé est une fille. Elle est jolie."*

At this the girl met my eyes again, and I saw that she understood, that she was calm enough to hear and understand words. *"Une fille,"* I told her softly again. *"Elle est jolie."* I tried to think of the word for healthy but couldn't. *"Elle est bonne"* was the best I could come up with. The midwife smiled, and so did the woman who had fetched me, and then I sensed another contraction coming.

This time I reached down and held the girl's hand, and as her muscles began their tremendous push down, their intense concentric pressure, I tried to project the feeling that these contractions were just her body working hard to accomplish something. This was what she needed to do to get her baby out; she had to release her fear and let her body take over. Her body, like the bodies of women since time began, knew what to do and could do it well. Together we rode the wave of her contraction, squeezing our hands together as it crested, and then I think we both panted as the force ebbed and her muscles relaxed again.

"*Oui, oui,*" murmured the midwife. She was down at the end of the bed, pushing the girl's knees up, and besides that I didn't want to know. I stayed near the head of the bed, looking into the girl's bottomless black eyes, holding her hand, sending calming waves. Her eyes were much calmer and more present; she looked more like a person.

"*Elle arrivé,*" the midwife murmured, and the girl's face contorted, and fast, fast, I sent images of things opening up, flowers blooming, seeds splitting, anything I could think of in my panicked state. I thought relaxation, concentration, releasing of fear, surrendering to her own body. As I looked at her, her eyes went very wide, her mouth opened, she said, "Ah, ah, ah, ah," in a high-pitched voice, and then suddenly it seemed like she kind of deflated. I made the mistake of glancing over to see the midwife pulling up a dark red, rubbery-looking baby, still connected to her mother by a pulsing blue cord. Sweat broke out on my forehead, and my skin grew cold, as if I were about to faint. The baby squinched up its quarter-size mouth, took a breath, and wailed, sounding like a tiny, infuriated puppy.

My patient's face softened, and she instinctively reached out her arms. The midwife, beaming now, wrapped the kicking, squalling baby in a clean towel and handed her to the mother, the cord stretching back behind her. As if the entire episode of terror and gut-splitting pain had never happened, the girl looked down at her baby and marveled at it. Feeling somewhat queasy, I looked at the infant, this end product of two people making love nine months earlier. Her face was red and raw looking. She had a cap of long, straight black hair that was glued to her little skull with what looked like petroleum jelly. Her skin was streaked with blood and white goop, and suddenly I felt like if I didn't have fresh air, I would die.

I staggered to my feet and lurched from the room, through the lounge and out the front door. Outside, I took in great, gulping breaths of icy air and instantly felt better. Somewhat embarrassed, I went back in to find that some of the other women had come into the bedroom. They were smiling, and I felt their waves of relief and happiness. They praised the girl, who was now beaming tiredly, holding her new daughter close. The midwife was still busy, and when I glanced over, she was picking up the cord, so I looked away fast.

I had never seen a human birth before and wished I hadn't seen this one. Yes, it was a miracle, yes, it was the Goddess incarnate, but still. I would have given a lot just then to be sitting in a pub, knocking back a pint and watching a football game on the telly.

The girl looked up and saw me, and she smiled widely, almost shyly at me. I was struck by how regular she looked, how girlish, how smooth her soft tan skin was, how white her teeth were. The contrast with how she'd been, while racked with pain and fear, was amazing. I smiled back, and she gestured to the baby in her arms.

"*Regardez elle,*" she murmured, smoothing the baby's cheek. The baby turned her head toward her and opened her rosebud mouth, searching.

Quickly I said, "*Elle est très jolie, très belle. Vous avez bonne chance.*" Then I cornered the woman who had brought me and took her arm. "I have to go home now."

We were interrupted by other women thanking me gravely, treating me with distant gratitude, then turning, all warmth and smiles, to the girl. They knew I had helped the girl but also knew I was a witch and probably couldn't be trusted. I had mixed feelings. Surely a girl this young ought not to be having a baby. From looking around, I could see these people had no money; who knew how many of them lived in this four-room cabin? Yet seeing how the women clustered around the girl, praising her, admiring the baby, tending to them both, it was clear that the girl was safe here, that she would be treated well and her baby looked after. There was love here, and acceptance. And often, that was most of what one needed.

I tapped my driver's arm again—she was cooing over the baby, who was now attempting to nurse. I kept my eyes firmly away from what I considered a private thing (I was the only one who thought so—there were at least five other people in the room). "I have to go home now," I said again, and she looked up at me with impatience, and then understanding.

"Oui, oui. Vous avez fatigué."

Right. Whatever. I looked for my coat and shrugged it on. My right hand was sore from being squeezed so tightly. I suddenly felt bone weary, mentally and physically exhausted, and I was ashamedly aware that out of all of us, I had done the least work. Men might have bigger muscles, bigger hearts and lungs, but women have greater stamina, usually greater determination, and a certain patient, inexorable will of iron that gets hard things done. Which is why most covens are matriarchal, why lines in my religion usually went from mother to daughter. Women usually led the hardest, most complicated rites, the ones that took days, the ones that took a certain ruthlessness.

I sighed and realized I was punchy, my shoulder brushing against the door frame as I went through. The night air woke me up, making me blink and take in deep breaths. I groaned audibly as I saw my nemesis, the blue pickup truck from hell. The woman, whose name I had never learned, walked briskly to it and pulled herself into the driver's seat. I climbed into the passenger's seat, pulled the door closed, and reflexively clutched the door handle.

Then the door of the cabin opened, and a sharp rectangle of light slanted across the dark yard. *"Attendez!"* cried a woman, and she came toward us. She gestured to me to roll down my window, but it didn't unroll, so I opened my door. *"Merci, merci beaucoup, m'sieu sorcier,"* the woman said shyly. I saw that it was the older woman who had been in the kitchen.

I smiled and nodded, uncomfortable about being openly identified as such. *"De rien."*

"Non, non. Vous aidez ma petite-fille," she said, and pushed a package toward me.

Curious, I opened the brown paper and found a warm loaf of homemade bread and, beneath it, a somewhat new man's flannel shirt. I was incredibly touched. Right then I broke off a piece of the bread and bit it. It was incredible, and I closed my eyes, leaned back against the truck seat, and moaned. The women laughed. *"C'est très, très bon,"* I said with feeling. Then I unfolded the shirt and looked at it, as if to assess its quality. Finally I nodded and smiled: it was more than acceptable. The woman seemed relieved and even proud that I thought her gift was fine. *"Je vous remercier,"* I said formally, and she nodded, then clutched her shawl around her shoulders and ran back into the house.

Without another word, my chauffeur started the engine and hurtled us down an unpaved road that I couldn't even see, but she obviously knew by heart. By holding on to the door handle with one hand, I was still able to break off chunks of warm bread with the other and eat them. I was happy—I had done a good day's work—and then I remembered that I had been there only because Da hadn't.

"Daniel—*souvent il vous aidez?*" I said, butchering French grammar.

The woman's dark eyes seemed to become more guarded.

I motioned back to the cabin. *"Comme ça?"* Like that?

"Comme ça, et ne comme ça," she said unhelpfully.

"Do you speak any English at all?" I asked, frustrated.

She slanted a glance at me, and I thought I saw a glimmer of humor cross her face as I flinched, going over a pothole.

"Un peu."

"So Daniel helps you sometimes?" I asked in my neutral Seeker voice. As if the answer didn't matter. I looked out my window at the dark trees that flashed past, lit momentarily by the truck's unaligned headlights.

A slight frown wrinkled the skin between her brows. *"Quelquefois."* She hesitated, then seemed to make up her mind. "Not so much *maintenant*. Not so much. Good people, only when so desperate. Like today."

Every Seeker instinct in me came to life. "Good people?"

She looked away, then said in a voice I could barely hear

over the engine, "People who don't walk in the light—they go to *le sorcier* more often."

Oh, Goddess, I muttered to myself. That didn't sound good. We were both silent the rest of the ride. She pulled up in front of Da's cabin but didn't shut off the engine.

"*Merci*," she said quietly, not smiling. "*Elle est ma fille, vous aidez.*"

"*Soyez le bienvenue.*" Then I got out of the truck, knowing that I would probably never see her, her daughter, or her new granddaughter again. Her tires spun on the snowy dirt behind me as I went up the steps to the porch. Inside, my father was there, in the kitchen, eating some meat I had browned hours ago. He looked up as if surprised to see me still around.

"We have to talk," I said.

8

Answers

In the time I've been here, I've come to fully appreciate the pristine and harsh beauty of winter. Five years ago it was spring that made me feel alive, the unstoppable power and bursting rawness of life renewed. Now that seems so naive. For me, winter is the culmination of nature's beauty, winter that shows the perfection, the bare bones of the world I live in.

Today I walked for miles, up to Grandfather's Knee. The air was sharp and cold, like a knife, and by the time I reached the top, every breath seared my lungs. I felt alive, completely connected to everything around me. The sound of ice cracking in the sun, the rare, startled flight of a bird, the occasional wet drop of snow from a tree limb —all these things filled me, awoke my senses, until I felt almost painfully joyful, painfully ecstatic. I fell to my knees in the sun-softened snow and blessed the Goddess and the God. My entire life felt like a song, a song that was reaching a crescendo, right then.

Ahead of me lay a meadow, its snowy surface marked by animals who had come to break through the crust to forage. As I knelt there, I was startled by a flash of dusty white—a winter hare, zigzagging crazily across the meadow, running so incredibly fast that I could hardly follow it with my eyes. It was beautiful, a slightly darker white than the snow, designed to run, its feet sure and strong. A second later I saw the reason for its flight: a red-tailed hawk, its wingspan more than four feet, was swooping toward it. In the time it took me to blink, the hawk had swung its feet down and up and was already beating the air with its wings, heading skyward with its prize.

I didn't think. There was no time. Instinctively I traced a sigil and cried, "Israthtac! Israthtac!"

As if shot, the hawk faltered in midair, one shoulder dipping, its wings beating arrhythmically. I sent the message, "Drop it. Release." And in the next moment the hare was falling like a soft-bodied stone toward the earth. I was already on my feet and running.

The hare lay stunned, near death, its eyes wide and yet unseeing. Its dusky fur was streaked with blood from the hawk's talons; I felt its labored breathing, its pain, the panic that went beyond fear. It blinked once, twice, and then its life began to ease away. "Sassen," I murmured, not touching it. Its little sides had quit heaving for breath. "Sassen," I said softly, tracing several sigils in the air above it, calling it back. "Sassen." I sang it coaxingly, and then the hare blinked, its eyes taking on a new awareness. It breathed deep, its velvet nose twitching. I watched as it rolled to its feet in a smooth movement and bounded off to the brush.

I know that some would say that what I did today is wrong, that it is interfering with nature's will, which should be held sacred. But I believe that as witches we should have the ability to use our own judgment. Nothing I have done today will throw off the balance of the universe: The hawk will catch more prey, the hare will die sooner or later. Both will go on with their lives, unaware of what I've done.

Animals are innocent. People never are.

—J. C.

I told Da about helping the First Nation girl give birth. He seemed interested, his eyes on me, as he finished eating.

I gave him the tiny piece of bread I had left, and he ate that, too, though it seemed to take effort.

"It sounds like you handled it well, son," he said in his odd, raspy voice. "Good for you."

My heart flared, and I became humiliatingly aware that part of me still longed to impress him. Impress *him,* this pale imitation of my father.

"Da," I began, leaning forward. "I need to talk to you about how you've been helping people around here. I'm a Seeker, and you must know that some of the things I've seen and heard concern me. I need to understand what you do, what role you play, how you've made it safe to be known openly as a witch."

For a moment I thought he might actually try to answer, but then he raised one hand in a defeated gesture and let it fall again. He glanced at me, gave a faintly embarrassed half smile, then stood and headed to his room, just like that.

I sat back in my chair, unreasonably stunned—why had I expected anything different? Maybe because when I was a child, my da had never turned away from answering a question, no matter how hard, how painful. He had given it to me straight, whether I really wanted the answer or not. I had to let go of that da—he was gone forever. In his place was this new man. He was what I had to work with.

That night I lay on the lumpy couch, unable to sleep and unwilling to do a calming spell until I had thought things through. I was a Seeker. Every instinct I had was on alert. I needed to find out what my father was up to. I needed some answers. If Da couldn't give them to me, I would find their answers myself. Then I would have a decision to make: whether to notify the International Council of Witches or not.

On Wednesday, I awoke early with renewed determination. I was going to follow Da today. All I had to do was wait for him to get up, then track him, something I was particularly good at.

Within moments of waking up, however, my senses told me the cabin was empty except for me. I frowned and swung my legs off the couch. A stronger scan revealed no other human around. How could that be? It would have been impossible for Da to wake and leave without my knowing. I was a light sleeper to begin with, and the couch of torture had only increased that. Then it occurred to me: it *was* impossible for Da to have left without my knowing. Which meant that my father had spelled me to keep me asleep. I sprang up, my hands clenching with anger. How dare he? He'd spelled me without my knowledge. There was no excuse for that, and it only emphasized how shady his business must be.

Swearing to myself, I shoved my feet into my boots and tied them with jerky movements. I pulled on the flannel shirt I'd earned, grabbed my coat, and stomped outside.

Outside, I saw that it was still early, and the air smelled like coming snow. The big pile of black garbage bags filled a corner of the front yard, and the thin, half-melted snow was tracked with my footprints. There were no tracks leading away from the house; none headed into the woods. Obviously Da had covered his trail.

I stomped a small circle into the snow and stepped into

it. It took several minutes for me to release my anger, to summon patience, to center myself and open myself to the universe. At last I was in a decent state, and I began to craft revealing spells.

I had to say this for him, Da still knew his spells. His concealing spells were in several layers and included some variations that took work and thought on my part to break through. Either he was a naturally gifted and innovative spellcrafter, or he had considered me a real threat. Or both.

When I was done, I felt cold and drained and wanted nothing more than a cup of tea and a warm fire. Instead I got up and retraced my steps around the cabin. I saw the repeated tracks of my feet leading to the woodpile, but this time I also saw a set of new footprints, one that definitely hadn't been there earlier: tracks leading from a corner of the porch into the woods. My mouth set in a firm line, I followed them.

How had my emaciated, malnourished father been able to hike this far the last couple of days, I wondered some forty minutes later. Granted, it was taking me longer because the tracks doubled back on themselves, I had to clear away other concealing and illusion spells, and I had to watch out for traps—but still, it had to be something desperately important to compel Da to trek this far every day in his weakened state.

A few minutes more and I became aware of a growing uneasiness, a bad taste in my mouth. I felt nervous; the back of my neck was tingling; all my senses were on alert. It was unnatural for the forest to be this quiet, this still. There were no animals, no birds, no movement or life of any kind.

Instead, a feeling of dread and disturbing silence pervaded the area. If I hadn't been on a mission, if I hadn't known I was tracking a witch—my father—I would have fled. Again and again, every minute, my senses told me to bolt, to get the hell out of there, to run as fast as I could through the thick forest, to not stop until I was home. It took all my self-control to ignore them, to push those feelings ruthlessly down. Goddess, what had he done?

I pressed forward and came at last to a smallish clearing. To one side of the clearing stood an old, round-roofed hut, made of sticks and covered with big strips of birch bark, like an Indian house. A fire burned unenthusiastically outside the hut. It was surrounded by huge logs, easily two feet in diameter, that looked like benches.

I felt ill. Nausea rose in my throat; my skin felt clammy, cold, and damp with sweat. From the strong pulls on my senses I could tell I was at a huge power sink, much like the one in the cemetery in Widow's Vale. But this one was made up of crossed lines, light and dark—it would be easy to work dark magick here, I realized, and my heart clenched.

I approached the hut. Every sense in me was screaming for me to get away from this place, to leave, that I was about to die, that I was suffocating. Dimly I was able to understand that these feelings were the effects of spells designed to ward off anyone who stumbled upon this place by accident, and I forced myself to ignore them. Taking a deep breath, I ducked down and pushed myself into the hut through its low doorway.

Immediately I was assaulted with feelings of out-and-out terror. My mouth went dry; my eyes were wild; my breath caught in my throat. Fighting for control, I looked around the hut with magesight. There was Da, crouched on the floor in a deep trance, his face alight with an unearthly eagerness. He was leaning over a dark . . . hole? Then it came to me, and my throat closed as if a fist were squeezing my windpipe shut. Dear Goddess. I had never seen one of these before, though of course I had read about them. My father was in front of a *bith dearc*, a literal opening into the netherworld, the world of the dead. My brain scrambled to understand, but nothing came to me except a horrified recognition. A *bith dearc* . . . if the council knew about this . . .

Da was oblivious to my presence, deeply entrenched in the shadow world. The atmosphere inside the hut was wretched, oppressive. I was reeling from shock and horror, wondering with panic how the hell this had become part of my life. Then, vaguely, my tortured senses picked up on the presence of a person outside. I stumbled back out through the opening, toward the clearing, to see a woman sitting on one of the log benches. She was poking listlessly at the fire with a stick, apparently used to having to wait and not seeming to feel the same terror and dread that was shredding my self-control.

I must have looked crazy, with my face white, my eyes wild, but she didn't seem to think anything of it, nor was she surprised to find someone here besides herself.

"*Bonjour*," she said, after a quick glance at me.

I sat down on a log across from her, my head between my knees so I wouldn't throw up. "*Bonjour*," I muttered. I sucked in cold air, trying to clear my head, but the air here felt poisoned. How could my da be doing this? What to do, what to do?

"C'est ma troisième visite à le sorcier," the woman confided.

It took me a moment to translate. Her third visit to the witch. I wished I had thought to brush up on my French before I had come to this hateful place.

"Il m'aide de parler avec mon cher Jules," she went on, a stranger chatting in a doctor's waiting room. *"Jules mourut l'année dernière."*

My stomach roiled as I took in this information. My father helped this woman talk to her dear Jules, who died last year. Bloody hell. My father was helping people talk to their dearly departed. He had opened a *bith dearc* into the netherworld and was selling this service to his neighbors. It was appalling on so many levels, I didn't know what to react to first.

Apparently not bothered by my lack of response, the woman mused, *"Le sorcier, il est très compatissant. Le dernier fois, moi, je ne peut pas payer. Mais aujourd'hui, pour lui j'ai deux poules grosses."*

Great. My father was a prince. She couldn't pay last time, but today she had two nice chickens for him. My father was breaking some of the most seminal laws of the craft and being paid in chickens for it. I felt like I was losing my mind.

There had been times in history where it had been necessary, even imperative, to contact souls on the other side, times when it was sanctioned. But to commune with the dead on a regular basis, for payment—it was an affront to nature. It would never be allowed. This was exactly the kind of thing a Seeker would be sent to investigate, to shut down. This realization caused a sickening drop of my stomach.

Eventually, I wasn't sure how much later, Daniel came out, ashen-faced. When he saw me sitting there, white with illness and misery, he staggered. His dull eyes went from me to the woman, who was still waiting patiently. Ignoring me, he went over to her and spoke gently to her in French, telling her today wasn't a good day, that she must return at another time. The look of utter disappointment on her face was heartbreaking. But she dutifully stood, offered my father her chickens, which he refused, smiling, and left. Leaving us alone, father and son, witch and Seeker.

9

Fiona the Bright

I haven't heard a thing from Hunter, besides his phone message on Tuesday. (Why did he call while I was at school? Was he trying not to talk to me?) I'm starting to get worried. Either he's run into trouble and hasn't been able to contact anyone, or he's having a great time, doesn't want to come home, and hasn't been able to contact anyone. Either way, I'm scared.

I finally sent him a witch message last night, but I have no idea whether it reached him since I haven't heard anything back. It's getting harder and harder for me to concentrate on the rest of my life. I think about Hunter all the time. I think about last Friday night, how close we came, and wonder if we'll ever finally go all the way.

I went to Bethany's apartment yesterday after school. I'm comfortable with her. We talked some about healing herbs. I told her about the research I had done online, and she lent me one of her own books: <u>A Healer's Herb Companion</u>. I can't wait to get into it.

Bethany asked me about my plans for this year's garden, and I admitted I hadn't gotten far with them. She told me that she has a plot in the Ninth Street Community Garden, two blocks from her apartment. Without being pushy or making me feel guilty, she helped me think about mine a little more, and now I'm excited all over again about my first one.

Right now, though, I would give anything to hear the phone ring. Hunter, where are you? What are you doing? Are you coming back to me?

—Morgan

"You've got to talk to me!" I shouted. My father turned away and paced into the kitchen, his shoulders stiff, his gaunt face set with anger.

I followed him, crossing the tiny lounge in four big paces. A bleak sunshine was trying to stream through the newly washed windows, but it was weak and seemed incapable of entering this house of darkness, death, and despair.

"How could you possibly think it's all right?" I demanded, pursuing him. Ever since we had gotten home, I had been trying to get answers from him. He had retreated into cold silence, regarding me as from a distance, as if I were nothing more than an annoying insect. I had spent most of the night awake, pacing in front of the fireplace, sitting on the couch, rubbing the back of my neck. Da had been in his room—if he slept, I didn't know it. I would bet he did. Nothing much seemed to get to him. Certainly not my revolted reaction to his *bith dearc*.

The next morning I jolted awake, slumped against the back of the couch, unaware of when I had fallen asleep. Our ugly fight started again. He looked, several times, as though he wanted to say something, to explain himself, but couldn't. I was alternately cajoling, supportive, angry, insistent. I never let down my guard, never left him alone.

Seeing him in the kitchen, hunting through the cabinets for something to eat, through food I had supplied, filled me with fresh anger. I had been here five days, five awful, disappointing, shocking days. I'd had enough.

"When I got here, you could hardly walk," I pointed out, coming closer. My anger was starting to spiral out of control, but for once I didn't rigidly clamp it down. "Now you're stronger because *I've* been taking care of you. And you're going out into the woods, to your *bith dearc*. Are you *mad*?"

Daniel turned and looked at me, his eyes narrowed. I almost wanted him to explode, to show me a side of my old father, any side, even anger. He paused, his hand on a cupboard shelf, then looked away.

"What would Alwyn say if she saw you, if she knew about this?" I demanded. "This is what killed her brother."

He looked at me, something flickering behind his dull brown eyes. Answer me, just answer me, I thought. "Please, stop," he said, sounding helpless. "You just don't understand."

"Explain it to me," I said, trying to calm down. "Explain why you've done this terrible thing."

"It *is* terrible," he agreed sadly. "I know that."

"Then why do you do it?" I asked. "How could you take payment for contacting the dead?"

We were face-to-face in that cramped kitchen. I was taller than he and outweighed him; I was a young, strong, healthy man, and he was a broken wreck far older than his years. But there was something latent in him, a reserve of ancient power lying coiled within him, awaiting his need for it. I sensed this; I'm not sure if he did.

His face twisted. "I have to," he said.

"It's making you ill. And you know it's wrong," I said, as if talking to a child. "Da, you've got to stop this."

His shoulders hunched, he looked away. Then, stiffly, as if holding back a cry, he nodded. "I know, lad. I know."

"Let me help you," I said, calming down more. "Just stay here today—don't go. I'll make you some lunch."

He gave another short nod and sat abruptly in his armchair, staring at the fire. His fingers twitched, a muscle in his jaw jumped—he looked like an addict facing withdrawal.

"Tell me about your town," Da said at lunch. It was the first question he had asked of me, the first interest he had shown in my life. I answered him, though I suspected he was only trying to change the subject.

"I've only been there about four months," I said, not mentioning the reason I had first gone there: to investigate his first wife, his first son. "But I've stayed and kept it my base in America. It's a little town, and it reminds me of England more than a lot of other American towns I've seen. It's kind of old-fashioned and quaint."

He bit into his BLT and almost looked like he enjoyed it for a second. Every once in a while he glanced at a window or the door, as if he would somehow escape if I let him. He was trying not to go to the *bith dearc*. He was trying to let me help him.

"Do you have a girl there?"

"Aye," I admitted, taking a huge bite of my own sandwich. The thought of Morgan sent a tremor through my body. Goddess, I missed her.

"Who is she?"

"Her name is Morgan Rowlands," I said, wondering how to broach the topic of her parentage. "She's a blood witch, a Woodbane."

"Oh? Good or bad?" At his little joke he gave a small cough and took a sip of his juice.

"Good," I said wryly. How could I tell him what Morgan meant to me, who she was? That I believed she was my *mùirn beatha dàn?*

"What's her background? Tell me about her."

My pulse quickened. He sounded almost like a real father, the father I had always wanted. "She's amazing. She's only just found out about being a blood witch. But she's the strongest uninitiated witch I've ever seen or heard of. She's really special. I'd like you to meet her."

Da nodded with a vague smile. "Perhaps. How did she just find out about her powers? Who are her parents?"

My jaw tensed. I had no idea how my father would react to this. "Actually . . ."

Da looked up, sensing my hesitation. "What is it, lad?"

I sighed. "The truth is, she's the biological child of Maeve Riordan of Belwicket . . . and Ciaran MacEwan. Of Amyranth."

All expression seemed to drain from Da's face. "Really."

"Yes. But she was put up for adoption. . . . It's a long story, but Ciaran killed her mother, and Morgan just learned the truth about her heritage recently. She was adopted by a Catholic family in Widow's Vale."

My da's eyes flicked up at me. They were full of suspicion.

My father had been fleeing Amyranth and their destruction for eleven years, and now his son was involved with the leader's daughter. It had to be hard to take. "Does she . . . has she met Ciaran?"

"Yes," I admitted, remembering Ciaran's odd recent reunion with his daughter. "But she's very different from him. She wants to work for good, like her mother worked for good. She helped the council find him. You know that he's in custody now."

Da nodded and went on eating. I had no idea what he was thinking.

"Did you know Cal?" he asked.

My jaw almost dropped. When I was young, Selene and Cal were never, ever mentioned in our house. In fact, I hadn't found out about them until right before I had come to Widow's Vale. I still remember how stunned I had been by the news.

"Only a bit," I said.

Da put down his sandwich, took a sip of beer. "What was he like?"

He was a bloody criminal, I wanted to say, letting out my still white-hot anger at the person who almost destroyed Morgan. He was evil personified. But this was Da's son—my half brother. And I suppose, deep down, I knew that Cal hadn't really had a chance, not with Selene Belltower for a mother.

"Um. He was very good-looking," I said objectively. "He was very charismatic."

"You hated him." It was a statement.

"Yes."

"I don't know what I was thinking, leaving him with her," Da said, his voice dry and aged. "All I knew was I was in love with your mother; she'd already had you. I wanted to be with her. I didn't want Selene and her evil tendrils wrapping around my life. At the time, I told myself that a child that young should stay with his mother. And Selene always said there was no way I could take him from her. Ever. But now I wonder if I could have—if I'd tried hard enough. And I wonder if I didn't try because I hated Selene so much, I didn't want any part of her near me—not even our son."

Crikey. I'd never heard Da talk like this. It made him seem so much more human somehow.

"Well, anyway. Old days," he said blithely, seeming embarrassed to reveal so much. Yet it was just this that allowed me to get past my new vision of him—the disappointing father—and see him as the man I remembered. A good man, who had loved, made mistakes, had regrets. It was a side of him I liked.

"I'm knackered," he said, sounding shaky. He stood up and walked past me with hesitant steps. I followed him to his bedroom, where he lay down on clean sheets. I guessed that the pull of the *bith dearc* was still working on him.

"Da, let me help," I said, coming to stand by the side of the bed. He looked up at me with uncomprehending weariness, and gently I laid my fingers on his temple, the way I had with the First Nation girl. I sent waves of soothing calmness, feelings of safety, of relaxation. In moments his eyes had fluttered closed, and his breathing changed to that of a man asleep. I stayed for a moment, making another spell of deep rest. If I could just keep him away from the *bith dearc*, if he would rest, I knew that I could help him get stronger. And perhaps then . . . when he was back to his old self . . . perhaps then I could get him away from this place, back home with me in Widow's Vale.

He would be out for hours, I figured, watching his sunken chest rise and fall. I went into the lounge, got my coat, and headed to town.

In town I was startled by how normal things seemed. I checked my watch—it was after three. Please be there, I thought, punching in my phone card number, then Morgan's number. Mary K.'s bright voice answered the phone.

"Hunter!" she said happily. "Where are you? Morgan's been so awful lately because she hasn't talked to you."

"I'm sorry," I said. "My mobile can't get a signal here, my father doesn't have a phone, and it's hard for me to get to town sometimes. Is she there? Can I speak to her?"

"No, she hasn't gotten home yet. Jaycee's mom gave me a ride from school. I don't know if Morgan's with Bree or what. You want Bree's cell phone number?"

"Yes, thanks. It's been too long since I talked to her."

"I know *she* thinks so," said Mary K. primly, and I smiled to myself, wondering how grumpy Morgan had been all week.

Mary K. gave me Bree's number, and I called it as soon as we hung up. But a recorded voice told me that the mobile customer I was calling was not available. I wanted to smash the phone receiver against the booth wall. Dammit. I needed to talk to Morgan, needed to hear her voice, her comforting, encouraging reactions to my horrible situation. I called Bree's cell phone again and left a message, asking her to tell Morgan that I had tried to call her and really missed her and hoped we could talk soon.

Next I tried calling Sky. I didn't even bother to calculate what time it would be in France—I needed to hear a semi-friendly voice. No one was home. I was starting to feel desperate. Talking to my father was full of emotional highs and lows. I needed some medium.

In the end I talked to Kennet. Kennet had been my mentor, had taught me much about being a Seeker. But I didn't mention any of my fears about Da, didn't talk about the *bith dearc* or Da's transgressions. Kennet, however, had news for me.

"It's convenient you're up there, actually," he said.

I leaned into the phone booth, watching my breath come out in little puffs. "Yeah? Why's that?"

"The council has a job for you to do," he said.

"All right," I said with unusual eagerness. Anything to take my mind off the situation with my father. "Tell me what's going on."

"About three hours west from where you are, a Rowanwand witch named Justine Courceau is collecting the true names of things."

"Yes?" I said, meaning, so what? Most witches make a point of learning as many true names of things as they can.

"Not just things. Living creatures. People. She's writing them down," said Kennet.

I frowned. "Writing them down? You have knowledge of this?" The idea of a witch compiling a list of the true names of living creatures, especially people, was almost unthinkable. Knowing something's true name gives one ultimate power over it. In some cases this is useful, even necessary—for example, in healing. But it is all too easy to misuse someone's true name, to use it for power's sake. Writing this information down would give that power to anyone who read the list. And knowing the true name of a human or witch would give someone ultimate power over them. It was very, very difficult to come by someone's true name. How had she been gathering them?

"Yes, she doesn't deny it," Kennet said. "We've sent her a letter, demanding she stop, going over some of the basic protocols of craft knowledge, but she hasn't responded. We'd like you to go see her, investigate the matter, and determine a course of action."

"No problem," I said, thinking about how relieved I would be to get away from here, if only for a short while.

"If it's true that she's keeping a list, then she must be stopped and the list destroyed," Kennet went on. "For such a list to fall into the wrong hands would be disastrous, and this Justine Courceau must be made to realize that."

"I understand. Can you tell me where she lives?"

Kennet gave me directions, and I fetched the map from the car and traced the route, making sure I understood. She lived in Ontario Province, near a town called Foxton. It appeared to be about three hours' drive from Saint Jérôme du Lac.

When I rang off with Kennet, it was almost dark. I stopped in at the grocer's to get more milk and more apples, feeling the irony of wanting to feed Da and yet resenting the fact that it gave him the strength he needed to get to the *bith dearc*. But I felt we had made real progress today. He had stayed away from the *bith dearc*. We had talked, really talked, for the first time. I hoped it was just the first step.

However, when I got back, the cabin was empty, the fire burning unbanked in the fireplace. I knew immediately where he had gone. As fast as that, my anger erupted afresh, and in the next second I had thrown the groceries across the kitchen, seeing the container of milk burst against the wall, the white milk running down in streams. This wasn't me—I had always been self-control personified. What was happening to me in this place?

This time it took only twenty-five minutes to get to the hut, despite the fact that the path was still spelled and it was dark outside. My anger propelled me forward, my long legs striding through the woods as if it were daylight. The closer I got to the hut, the more I was assaulted by waves of panic and nausea. When I could hardly bear the feelings of dread, I knew I was close. And then I was in the clearing, the moonlight shining down on me, witnessing my shame, my anger.

Without hesitation I stormed into the hut, ducking through the low doorway, to find Daniel crouched over the eerily black *bith dearc*. He looked up when I came in, but this time his face was excited, glad. He flung out his hand to me.

"Hunter!" he said, and it struck me that this was perhaps the first time he had used my given name. "Hunter, I'm close, so close! This time I'll get through, I know it."

"Leave off this!" I cried. "You know this is wrong; you know this is sapping your strength. It's not good, it's not right; you know Mum would have hated this!"

"No, no, son," Da said eagerly. "No, your mum loved me; she wants to speak to me; she pines for me as I pine for her. Hunter, I'm close, so close this time, but I'm weak.

With your help I know I could get through, speak to your mother. Please, son, just this once. Lend me your strength."

I stared at him, appalled. So this was what the *bith dearc* had *really* been about. Not helping others—that was incidental. His true goal had always been to contact Mum. But what he was suggesting was unthinkable, going not only against the written and unwritten laws of the craft, but also against my vows to the council as a Seeker.

"Son," Da said, his voice raspy and seductive. "This is your mother, your *mother,* Hunter. You know you were her favorite, her firstborn. She died without seeing you again, and it broke her heart. Give her the chance to see you now, see you one last time."

My breath left my lungs in a whoosh; Da's low blow had caught me unaware, and I almost doubled over with the pain of it. He was wily, Daniel Niall, he was ruthless. He had seen the chink in my armor and had rammed his knife home. It was a mistake for anyone to discount him as weak, as helpless.

"It's a powerful magick, Hunter," he wheedled. "Good magick to know, to be master of."

I snorted, knowing that anyone who thought he was master of a *bith dearc* was telling himself dangerous lies. It was like an alcoholic insisting he could stop anytime he wanted.

"It's your mother, son," said Daniel again.

Oh, Goddess. The reality of this opportunity suddenly sank in with a power that was all too seductive. Fiona . . . I had missed seeing my mother by two short months. To see her now—one last time—to feel her presence . . . Fiona the Bright, dancing around a maypole, laughing.

I sank to my knees across from my father, on the opposite side of the *bith dearc*. I felt sick and weakened; I was angry and embarrassed at my own weakness, angry at Da for being able to seduce me to his dark purpose. Yet if I could see my mother, just once . . . I knew how he felt.

Da reached out and put his bony hands on my shoulders. I did the same, clasping his shoulders in my hands. The *bith dearc* roiled between us, a frightening rip in the world, an oddly glowing black hole. Then together, with Daniel leading, we began the series of chants that would take us through to the other side.

The chants were long and complicated; I had learned them, of course: they were part of the basic knowledge I had to prove before I could be initiated. But naturally, I had never used them and had forgotten them in places. Then Daniel sang, his voice cracked and ruined, and I followed as best I could, feeling ashamed for my weakness and his.

I don't know how long we knelt there on the frozen ground, but gradually, gradually I began to become aware of something else, another presence.

It was my mother.

Though I hadn't seen or spoken to her in eleven years, there was no mistaking the way her soul felt, touching mine. I glanced up in awe to look at Daniel and saw that tears of joy were streaming down his hollowed cheeks. Then I realized that my mother's spirit had joined us in the hut. I could sense her shimmering presence, floating before us.

"At last, at last," came Da's whisper, like sandpaper.

I was scared, my mouth dry. I was not master of this magick, and neither was Daniel. This was wrong, it was trouble, and I should have had no part of it. This was how my brother had died, calling on dark magick to find a *taibhs* that had turned on him and taken his life.

"Hunter, darling." I felt rather than heard her voice.

"Mum," I whispered back. I couldn't believe that after eleven years, I was near her again, feeling her spirit.

"Darling, is it you?" Unlike Da, Mum seemed genuinely happy to see me, genuinely full of love for me. From her spirit I received waves of love and comfort, welcome and regret—more emotion than my father had spared for me so far. "Oh, Giomanach—you're a man, a man before my eyes," my mother said, her pride and wonder palpable. I started crying.

"My sweet, no," came her voice inside my head. "Don't spoil this with sadness. Let's take joy from this one chance to express our love. For I do love you, my son, I love you more than I can say. In life I was far from you; you were beyond my reach. Now nothing is. Now I can be with you, always, wherever you are. You need never miss me again."

I've never been comfortable with crying, but this was all too much for me—the pain of my last five days, my fear and worry for my father, my anger, and now this, seeing and hearing my long-lost mother, having her confirm what I thought I would wonder about my whole life: that she loved me, that she'd missed me, that she was proud of me, of who I had become.

"Fiona, my love, you've come back to me," said Da, weeping openly.

"No, my darling," said Mum gently. "You've called me here, but you know it can't be. I am where I am now and must stay. And you must stay in your world, until we can be together again."

"We can be together now!" my father said. "I can keep the *bith dearc* open; we can be together."

"No," I said, pulling myself back to reality. "The *bith dearc* is wrong. You have to shut it down. If you don't, I will."

His eyes blazed at me. "How can you say that? It's given you your mother back!"

"She's not back, Da," I said. "It's her spirit; it isn't her. And she can't stay. And you can't make her. This isn't good for her, and it's going to kill you."

Angrily my father started to say something, but my mother intervened. "Hunter's right, Maghach," she said, a slight edge to her voice. "This isn't right for either of us."

"It is. It could be," Da insisted.

"Hunter is thinking more clearly than you, my love," Mum said. "I am here this once. I can't come here again."

"You must come back," my father said, a note of desperation entering his voice. "I must be with you. Nothing is worthwhile without you."

"Be ashamed, Maghach," my mother said in her no-nonsense tone. It gave me joy to hear it, bringing back memories of my childhood, when I'd had parents. "To say that nothing is worthwhile dishonors the beauty of the world, the joy of the Goddess."

"If you can't stay, then I'll kill myself!" Daniel said wildly, his hands reaching for her spirit. "I'll kill myself to be with you!"

My mother's face softened, even as I despised the weakness my father was showing. "My darling," she said gently. "I love you with all my heart. I always did, from the first moment I saw you. I look forward to loving you again, in our next lives together, and again, in our lives after that. You will always be the one for me. But now I am dead, and you are not, and you mustn't desecrate the Goddess by wishing to be dead yourself. To deny life is wrong. To mourn in a negative, self-centered way is wrong. You must live for yourself, and for your children. Hunter and Alwyn need your help and your love."

I was glad to hear my mother confirm the feelings I'd had about this. I felt a mixture of pathos and disgust, pity and shame, watching the despair on Da's face.

"I don't care!" he cried, and I wanted to hate him. "All I want is to be with you! You are my life! My breath, my soul, my happiness, my sanity! Without you there is nothing. Don't you understand?" My father fell forward onto his arms, sobs shaking his thin frame. Once again I felt this couldn't be the father I had known. I was horrified at how weak he had become.

"Don't judge him too harshly, Hunter," came Mum's voice, and I sensed she was speaking to me alone. "When you were a child, he was a god to you, but now you see that he's just a man, and he's mourning. Don't judge him until you too have lost something precious."

"I did lose something precious," I said, looking in her direction. "I lost my brother. I lost my parents."

Her voice was sad and regretful. "I'm so sorry, my love. We did what we thought was best. Perhaps we were wrong. I know you've suffered. And Linden suffered, too, perhaps most of all. But that wasn't your fault; you know that. And please believe me when I say that I loved you, Linden, and Alwyn with every breath, every second of every day. I made you, I bore you, and I will be with you forever."

I hung my head, unwilling to start crying again.

"My son," she said, "please take your father away from here. Destroy this *bith dearc*. Don't let Daniel return. My shadow world will eventually sap his strength and take his life if he doesn't stay away. And if he keeps calling me back, my spirit will be unable to progress on its journey. As much as I love your father, you, and Alwyn, I know that it's right for my spirit to move on, to see what more lies ahead of me."

"I understand," I choked out. My father was still bent double, weeping. I felt something brush me, as if Mum had touched me with her hand, and as she faded away, I saw a flash of her beautiful face.

"Fiona! No!" Da cried, reaching futilely for her, then collapsing again. When she was gone, I swallowed hard and rubbed the sleeve of my shirt against my face. Then, getting to my feet, I grabbed hold of my father's arm and dragged him outside, into the cold air. As awful as it was outside, it was still better than the wretched sickness of the hut.

Daniel crumpled to the ground, and I stumbled, trying to catch him. I felt weak, light-headed, and sick, as if someone had dosed me with poison. At first I didn't understand why I felt so terrible, but then I realized that Mum had meant her words literally: contacting the shadow world saps one's life force. I looked at my father, facedown on the ground, clawing at the snow-encrusted dirt, and realized exactly why Daniel looked so awful—who knew how long he'd been doing this? Two months? It was a wonder he was alive at all, if I felt like this after only one time, and I was a young, strong, healthy man.

It came to me that I might have to turn Daniel in to the council to save his life. I wondered whether I would have the strength. I staggered to my feet and pulled my father up by one arm. Then, with him leaning heavily on me, we headed back to the cabin.

10

Shadows

There is somebody coming.

I first became aware of it this morning as I tried to concentrate on my work down in the library. I had laid out the salt, I had lit the candles, and I felt like I had been chanting for hours but to no avail. I wasn't breaking through. My shadow friends seemed hesitant to meet me. It was almost as if they were afraid—of something or somebody. I went upstairs to scry, and there I had my vision. A Seeker, coming here. I had a vague sense of youth, of emotional turmoil. Whoever this Seeker is, I do not fear him. He has his own troubles. He will not sway me from my life's work.

On Wednesday, I made an amazing breakthrough. I have developed a host of friends in the shadow world—many of them fellow Rowanwands who see the value of my research and are eager to help. One of these friends, an older man who will only give the name Bearnard, brought to me a new and eager associate, a woman who calls herself Naible and who brought with her a wealth of knowledge. Never before have I come across anyone—in the living world or the shadow world—who has such an extensive knowledge of true names as this woman. From her I obtained nearly twenty true names that day, and she has promised to return with more knowledge, more names. Oh, Goddess, I have only gratitude for this generous woman and her love of knowledge. I wish that I had known her while she was among the living; what a remarkable team we would have made.

The Seeker is coming, and once he arrives, I will not be able to continue my research until he is gone. Goddess, give me the courage to remember my objectives and the intelligence to prevent this Seeker from truly learning what I seek. If only Naible could give me the true name of this Seeker . . . then he would stand no chance against me.

—J. C.

On Sunday, I woke up to find my father's bed empty. Hell! I had been right: it was like living with a junkie, and I always had to be on alert in case he tried to score. I immediately threw on some clothes, feeling a mixture of anger, a reluctant empathy, and a tight impatience.

It was amazing what desperation could lead a man to do, I thought twenty minutes later. My father was so weak that a trip to the grocery store could exhaust him for hours, but here, in his overwhelming desire to reach his *bith dearc*, he was able to trudge for miles through a Canadian forest in winter.

As I neared the place of darkness, feeling the familiar senses of nausea and fear, I wondered bleakly what I was going to do with my father—let him kill himself? Try to save him? Steeling myself, drawing on any strength I had, I ducked into the low opening of the hut and found my father, his face lighting with ecstasy. As my eyes focused, I felt my mother's spirit take shape above the glowing opening into the shadow world. Daniel looked up, joy making him seem twenty years younger. He reached out his hands to her ethereal form.

I crept close, awed by my mother's presence as I had been the first time. Kneeling by Daniel, I couldn't help allowing myself to enjoy the feel of her presence, which would be all I could have until I joined her one day in the shadow world.

"Daniel," Mum said, "I'm telling you that you must stop this. You must remain among the living. It is not your time." Her voice sounded more firm, and I was glad. If she had been truly needy or welcoming, Da would have been dead a month ago.

"I don't know how, Fi," Da answered, shaking his head. "I only know how to be with you."

"That isn't true," my mother said. "You had a lifetime of other people before me." I felt a warmth from her directed at me, almost like a smile, and I smiled back, though I was feeling queasy and weakened by the *bith dearc*.

"I don't want other people," Da said stubbornly.

"You will learn to want other people," Mum said firmly, taking on a tone that was so familiar to me—the one she took when one of us kids had persisted too long in lame excuses for a wrongdoing. "Now I'm telling you, Daniel, you must not call me back again. You are hurting me. My spirit must move on. You're not letting that happen. Do you want to hurt me?"

"Goddess, Fiona, no!" said my father, looking appalled.

My mother's voice softened. "Daniel, you were the strong one in our marriage. You kept us going when I would have given up. It was your strength I relied on. I need to rely on that strength now. You must be strong enough not to call me back, to stay with the living. Do you understand?"

Da looked at the ground, seeming lost, bereft. Finally he gave a broken nod and covered his face with his hands.

Once again I felt the warmth from my mother, but tinged with sadness—a sadness borne of understanding and empathy. She knew how much my father was suffering; she knew how much I had suffered. She loved us both with all her heart, and in return I felt an intense love for her, the mother I had lost.

Silently Fiona's spirit brushed a shadowy kiss across us both, and floated through the *bith dearc*. As soon as she was gone, my father collapsed on his side on the ground. I sagged myself, hating the feeling of weakness and sickness that pulled me down. But I struggled to sit up and quickly performed the rite that would shut the *bith dearc* down. When the last of it had faded and I could see solid, frozen ground again, I sat back, trying not to throw up.

As soon as I could, I got Da out of there, and again we sank down outside in the snow, too weak to move. Ten minutes later I felt together enough to call to my da, who was lying, gray-faced, on the ground a few feet away from me.

"I can't believe you!" I said, letting fly with my frustration. "Could you possibly be more stupid, more self-destructive? Could you be a little more selfish?"

Da's eyes fluttered open, and he sat up slowly, with difficulty. If he had been the old da, he would have come over and backhanded me. But this da was weak, in mind, body, and spirit.

"Why are you choosing death over being with your live children?" I went on, feeling my anger ignite. "I'm the only son you have left! Alwyn's the only daughter you'll ever have! You don't think you should stick around for our sakes? Not only that, but you're deliberately hurting Mum. Every time you contact her, every time you draw her to the *bith dearc*, you're slowing down her spirit's progress. She needs to move on. She must go on to the next phase of her existence. But you don't give a bloody flip! Because you can only think about *yourself*!"

Da's eyes were focused intently on me now, and his ashen cheeks were splotched pale red with anger. "I've tried to resist—" he began, but I cut him off.

"You haven't tried bloody hard enough!" I shouted, getting to my feet. My stomach roiled, but I stood, looming over him like a bully. "You just keep giving in! Is that what you want to teach me, your son? You want to teach me how to give in, give up, think only about myself? That's what you're showing me. You never would have been this way eleven years ago. Back then you were a real father. Back then you were a real witch. Now look at you," I concluded bitterly. I could count on one hand the number of times I had been this hateful, this mean to someone I cared about. I hated the words coming out of my mouth but couldn't stop them once I started.

"You have no idea how hard it is," my father said, his voice scraped raw.

I snorted and paced around the spent fire in the middle of the log benches. I felt ill, exhausted; I needed to get out of there. I knew I had to bring Da back to the cabin, but I had to talk myself out of leaving him there to freeze. Minutes passed, and I wondered what the hell I was going to do with myself. Everything in my life right now was miserable. The only person who could make me feel at all better wasn't here, and I couldn't seem to reach her. Bloody hell, why did I ever come here?

At last, after a long time, Da said, "You're right." He sounded impossibly old and broken down.

I looked over at him, and he went on, struggling to find the words.

"You're right. I'm being selfish, thinking only of myself. Your mother would have been stronger. She should have been the one to live."

My eyes narrowed as I readied to nip his self-pity in the bud.

"But it was me who lived, and I'm making a hash of it, aren't I, lad?" He gave a crooked, fleeting smile, then looked away. "It's just—I can't let her go, son. She was my life. I gave up my firstborn son for her."

I gave a short nod. Cal.

"And then," he went on, "for the past eleven years it's been only me and Fiona, Fiona and me, everywhere we went, every day. We were alone; we didn't dare make friends; we went for months without seeing another human, much less another witch. I don't even know how to be with other people anymore."

I looked away and let out a long breath. When Da sounded like this, somewhat rational, somewhat familiar, it was impossible to hold on to my anger. Mum had reminded me that he was just a man, in mourning for his wife, and I needed to cut him a huge swath of slack.

I raised my hands and let them fall. "Da, you could learn how—"

"Maybe I could," he said. "I guess I'll have to. But right now there's no way I can give up the *bith dearc*, no way I can give up Fiona. The only thing that will stop me is to be stripped of my powers. If I have no power, I can't make a *bith dearc*; I won't be able to. So that's what I need from you. You're a Seeker; you know how. Take my powers from me, and save me from myself."

My eyebrows rose, and I searched his eyes, hoping to find any trace of sanity left. Was he joking about such a terrible thing? "Have you ever seen anyone stripped of their powers?" I asked. "Do you have any idea how incredibly horrible it is, how painful, how you feel as though your very soul has been ripped from you?"

"It would be better than this!" Da said, his voice stronger.

"Better than this half existence. It's the only way. As long as I have power, I'll be drawn to the *bith dearc*."

"That's not true!" I said, pacing again. "It's been only two months. You need more time to heal—anyone would. We just need to come up with a plan, that's all. We need to think."

He made no answer but allowed me to pull him to his feet. It took almost forty minutes for us to get back to the cabin, with our slow, awkward pace. Inside, I stoked up a fire. A dense chill permeated my bones, and I felt like I would never get rid of it. Keeping my coat on, I lowered myself to the couch. Da was sitting, small and gray and crumpled, in his chair. I felt exhausted, ill, near tears. Frustrated, pained, joyful at seeing my mother. Horrified and shocked at my father's demand that I strip him of his powers. I had too many emotions inside me. Too many to name, too many to express. I was so overwhelmed that I felt numb. Where to start? All at once I felt like a nineteen-year-old kid—not like a mighty Seeker, not like the older, more experienced witch that Morgan saw me as. Not like an equal, like Alyce felt. Just a kid, without any answers.

Finally I just started talking, my head resting against the back of the couch, my eyes closed. "Mum was right, you know," I said without accusation. His request that I strip him of his powers had blown my anger apart. "I understand how you felt about her, I really do. She was your *mùirn beatha dàn*, your other half. You only get the one, and now she's gone. But you were a whole person before you met Mum, and you can be a whole person now that she's gone."

My father kept silent.

"I don't know how I would feel if I lost my *mùirn beatha dàn*," I said, thinking of Morgan, the unbelievable horror of Morgan being dead. "I can't really say if I would have the strength to behave any differently. I just don't know. But surely you can see how this is going down the dark path. Ignoring life in favor of death isn't something you would have taught us kids. This is the path that killed Linden. But two of your children are still alive, and we need you." Looking at him, I saw his shoulders shake, perhaps with just exhaustion.

I made up my mind. The council wanted me to head west, to go interview Justine Courceau. I decided to take Da with me, whether he wanted to go or not. Mum was right— if Da stayed here, he would keep using the *bith dearc* and eventually kill himself. It wasn't a great plan, a long-term fix, but it was all I had.

Standing up, I went and threw clothes for both of us into a duffel. Da didn't look up, showed no interest. I made tea, packed some food and drinks for the three-hour drive, and loaded the car. Then I knelt by his chair, looking up at him.

"Da. I need to go west for a few days on council business. You're going with me," I said.

"No," he weakly, not looking up. "That's impossible. I need to rest. I'm staying here."

"Sorry—can't let you do that. You'll end up killing yourself. You're coming with me."

In the old days, Da could have lifted me up and thrown me like a sack of potatoes. These days, I was the strong one. In the end, pathetically, he didn't have much choice.

Half an hour later he was buckled into the front seat next to me, his mouth set in a defeated line, his hands twitching at the knees of his corduroys, as if waiting for the day when he would be strong enough to fasten them around my neck. I had no idea whether that day would ever come, whether my da would ever resemble the father I had known before. All I knew was that we were headed for Foxton, a small town in Ontario, and after my job there was done—I didn't know what I was going to do.

Justine Courceau lived at the very edge of the Quebec-Ontario province border. I endured three and a half hours of stony silence on the way. Fortunately the scenery was incredible: rocky, hilly, full of small rivers and lakes. In springtime it would be stunning, but here, at the tail end of winter, it still had a striking and imposing beauty.

The small town Kennet had directed me to, Foxton, had one bed-and-breakfast. First I got Da and me settled there and brought up our lone duffel. Da seemed completely spent, his face cloud-colored, his hands shaky, and he seemed relieved enough to curl up on one of the twin beds in our room. I felt both guilty and angry about his misery. Since he seemed dead asleep, I performed a few quick healing spells, not knowing whether they were strong enough to have any effect on a man in my da's condition. Then I put a watch sigil on one of his shoes, figuring he couldn't go anywhere without it and that he would be less likely to feel it than if it was on his body. This way I could stay in contact with him, be more or less aware of what he was doing, be aware if he tried to do something stupid, like harm himself. Then I grabbed my coat and car keys and locked the door behind me. Regretting it, I spelled the door so it would be hard for him to get out. In any other circumstance, such a thing would be unthinkable, but I didn't trust Da to be making the best decisions right now.

This was never how I'd thought I'd be using my magick. It left a bad taste in my mouth.

Kennet had told me Justine Courceau was a Rowanwand, and I had to deliberately put aside my personal feelings about the clan before I got to her house. Frankly, I've often found Rowanwands to be rather full of themselves. They make such a production of their dedication to good, of their fight against dark, evil Woodbanes. It just seems a bit much.

Kennet had been able to give me very accurate directions, and, barely twenty minutes after I had left Da, I was bumping down a long driveway bordered on both sides with hardwoods: oaks, maples, hickories. It was a pretty spot, and again I imagined how it would look in springtime. I hoped I wouldn't be here to see it.

After about a quarter mile, the driveway stopped in front of a cottage that to my eyes screamed "witch." It was small, picturesque, and made of local stone. Surrounding it was the winter version of a garden that must, in summer, be astounding. Even now, dormant and dusted with snow, it was well tended, tidy, pleasing.

Before I left my car, I went through my usual preparations. When a Seeker approaches someone she or he is investigating, anything can happen. An unprepared Seeker can soon be a dead Seeker. I took a moment to focus my thoughts, sharpen different defenses, physical and magickal, that were in place, and did the usual ward-evil, protection, and clarity spells. At last I felt sufficiently Seekerish, and I got out of my car and locked it.

I walked up a meandering stone path toward the bright red front door, wondering what Ms. Courceau would be like. Judging by the cottage, I was already picturing her as something like Alyce, perhaps. Gentle, kindly, with three or four cats. I hoped it would be as easy as it seemed. Unfortunately, I've learned that isn't always the case.

While I had been sitting in my car, no face had peered out through the thick-paned, old-fashioned windows, bordered with dark green shutters, and I hoped Ms. Courceau was home. I didn't see a car. Glancing toward the back, I saw a small greenhouse attached to the cottage, plus quite a few well-ordered squares of garden behind. Maybe there was a garage back there as well.

At the front door I put all my senses on alert and rapped the shining brass door knocker. I felt someone casting their senses toward me and instinctively blocked them. The door opened hesitantly, and a woman stepped forward. I was momentarily taken aback.

"Justine Courceau?" I asked.

She nodded. "Yes. Can I help you?"

My first, instantaneous impression was that she was much younger than I had assumed. I realized Kennet hadn't mentioned her age, but this woman couldn't have been more than twenty-two or twenty-three. She was strikingly pretty, with shoulder-length dark red hair. Her skin was clear and ivory-toned, and her eyes were wide and brown, kind of like Mary K.'s.

"I'm Hunter Niall," I said. "The council sent me here to

talk to you." This sentence can create any number of different reactions, from defiance, to fear, to curiosity or confusion. This was the first time someone had laughed at me outright.

"I'm sorry," Justine said, stifling her laughter but still smiling widely. "Goodness. A Seeker? I had no idea I was so scary. Come in and have some tea. You must be frozen."

Inside, her cottage was charming. I cast my senses and picked up on nothing but the usual frissons of lingering magick, regular magick—nothing odd or out of place. I detected faint traces of mild spellcraft, the pleasing scents of herbs and oil, and a quiet sense of joy and accomplishment. I could feel nothing dark, nothing that set off my radar. Instead I felt more comfortable in this room than I had in most of the places I had been in the last six months.

"Please, sit down," said Justine, and I processed the musical notes of her voice, wondering if she sang. "The kettle's already on—I won't be half a minute." She spoke perfect English but with a soft French accent. I was just glad she spoke English. It would have been hard going, doing all this in French.

The sofa in the lounge was oversize, chintz-covered, and comfortably worn. On the table before it rested a circular arrangement of pinecones, dried winter berries, some pressed oak leaves. It was unpretentious and artistic, and the whole cottage struck me that way. I wondered if this was all her taste or whether she had lived here with her parents and then inherited all their decor.

As soon as I sank onto the couch, two cats of undistinguished breed approached me and determinedly climbed into my lap, curling up, kneading my legs with their paws, trying to both fit into a limited space. I stroked their soft, winter-thick fur and again picked up nothing except well-fed contentment, health, safety.

"Here we go," said Justine, coming in with a laden tea tray. There was a pot of steaming Darjeeling tea, some sliced cake, some fruit, and a small plate of cut sandwiches. After the past week of my doing all the cooking, it was nice to have someone feed me for a change.

Holding my tea over the cats on my lap, I said, "Obviously you know why I'm here. The council sent you a letter that you didn't respond to. Do you want to tell me what's going on, in your own words?"

Her brown eyes regarded me frankly over her Belleek teacup. "Now that I look at you, you seem quite young for a Seeker. Is this your first job?"

"No," I said, unable to keep the weariness out of my voice. "Do you want to tell me what's going on, in your own words?" Witches tended to prevaricate and avoid a Seeker's questions. I had seen it before.

"Well," she said thoughtfully, "I assume you're here because I collect the true names of things." She took a sip of tea, then curled one leg underneath her on her chair.

"Yes. Every witch uses them to some degree, but I hear you're collecting the names of living beings and writing them down. Is that true?"

"You know it's true," she said with easy humor, "or you wouldn't be here."

I took a bite of sandwich: cucumber and country butter on white bread. My mouth was very happy. I swallowed and looked up at her. "Talk to me, Ms. Courceau. Tell me what you're doing."

"Justine, please." She shrugged. "I collect the true names of things. I write them down because to learn and remember all of them would take me a lifetime. I don't do anything with them; I don't misuse them. It's knowledge. I'm Rowanwand. We gather knowledge. Of any kind. Of every kind. This is what I'm focusing on right now, but it's only one of many areas that interest me. Frankly, it doesn't seem like the council's business." She leaned back in her chair, and another cat leaped up on the back of it and rubbed its head against her red hair.

I was aware that there was, if not exactly a lie, then a half-truth in what she had just told me. I continued to question her, to explore her motives.

"Many clans gather knowledge," I said mildly, breaking off a piece of cake with my fingers. "It's the very nature of a witch to gather knowledge. As Feargus the Bright said, 'To know something is to shed light on darkness.' But it makes a difference what kind of knowledge you collect."

"But it doesn't, don't you see?" Justine asked earnestly, leaning forward. "Knowledge in and of itself cannot be inherently evil. It's only what a person chooses to do with that knowledge that makes it part of good or evil. Do we want to take the chance that something precious and beautiful will be lost forever? I don't have children. What if I never have children? How will I impart what I've learned? Who knows what later generations might be able to do with it? Knowledge is just knowledge: it's pure; it's neutral. I know that I won't misuse it; I know that what I'm doing is going to be hugely beneficial one day."

Again I had just the slightest twinge of something on the

edge of my consciousness about what she had said, but I would look at it later. Anyway, I could see her point of view so far. Many witches would agree with her. It wasn't my job to agree or disagree with her.

We talked for another hour. Sometimes Justine pressed her beliefs, sometimes we just chatted, learning about each other, sizing each other up. At the end of my visit I knew that Justine was very bright, extremely well educated (which she would be: I had recognized her mother's name as one of the foremost modern scholars of the craft), funny, self-deprecating, and strong. She was wary; she didn't trust me any more than I trusted her. But she wanted to trust me; she wanted me to understand. I felt all that.

Finally, almost reluctantly, I needed to go. It had been a nice afternoon and such a great change from the hellish disappointment the last week had been. It was nice to talk to an ordinary witch instead of someone hell-bent on his own destruction, someone mired in grief and pain.

"I'd like to meet with you again before I make my report to the council," I said. I carefully dislodged the cats in my lap and stood, brushing fur off my jeans. Justine watched me with amusement, making no apologies.

"You're welcome here anytime," she said. "There aren't any other witches around here for me to talk to. It's nice to have company I can really be myself with." She had a nice smile, with full lips and straight white teeth. I put on my coat.

"Right, then, I'll be in touch," I said, opening the front door. As I started down the stone path, I became suddenly aware of Justine's strong interest in me. I was surprised; she hadn't given a sign of it inside. But now I felt it: her physical attraction to me, the fact that she liked me and felt comfortable with me. I didn't acknowledge it but got into my car, started the engine, and waved a casual good-bye.

11

The Rowanwand

The Seeker arrived yesterday. I don't know how to describe my reaction—he's an invader, and I should resent his being here, yet he is so . . . interesting. He is an Englishman, young, scarcely even twenty. Yet he carries himself with a confidence, a maturity that makes me think he has great potential. I do sense turmoil in him—whether it is a result of this assignment or a personal problem, I can't say. Still, he is so attractive to me, so stimulating to talk to, I find myself wondering if I could win his heart.

Of course, I haven't been able to do any research since I sensed him coming. I've stripped the library of any traces of magick and have *performed endless purification rituals to keep him from sensing the taint of the other side. I miss my work and my friends in the shadow world more than I can express, but I can be patient. The Courceaus know much about patience, biding our time, waiting until the right moment to make our intentions known.*

Goddess, help me to keep my focus and remember that it is my work that is most important—more important than any temporary attraction I might have. If only there were some way to make him understand. If only I could get his true name . . .

—J. C.

This morning I spent time in Foxton proper, hanging out at the local bookstore, the coffee shop, the library. It's a bigger town than Saint Jérôme du Lac and has more resources. Basically I was casting my senses, trying to listen for gossip about Justine. Unlike my father, no one here seems to have identified her as a witch, though quite a few people knew who she was. I mentioned her name in a few places, and people had only good things to say about her. The previous autumn she'd led a fund drive for the library, and it had been their most successful ever. One woman told me how Justine had helped when her dog was ill—she'd been a godsend. The general impression was that she was something of a loner but friendly and helpful when needed. They thought of her as a good neighbor.

The way Kennet had talked about her, I had been prepared for another Selene Belltower—an amoral, ruthless user who felt she was above the council laws. Justine didn't seem that way at all. Though, of course, appearances can be deceiving.

Back at the bed-and-breakfast, Da was doing a lot of lying around, staring at the walls. I had brought several books to read, and I offered them to him. If he knew about the watch sigil or the spelled door, he didn't mention them. Mostly he seemed incredibly depressed, hopeless, uninterested in anything. I wanted to jolt him out of his stupor but wasn't sure how. I wished there was a healer around.

That afternoon Daniel lay down with a book, and I headed back to Justine's. She greeted me cheerfully, and soon I was again sitting in her comfortable lounge, with cats appearing out of nowhere to take naps on me.

"I've been thinking about what you said yesterday," she began. "About the council laws and why we have them. And I'm just not convinced. I mean, I obey all Canadian laws, and I recognize their right to have and enforce them. After all, I'm choosing to live here. If I don't like their laws, I can decide to move somewhere else. But I have no choice about being a witch. I *am* one, by blood. It would be impossible for me not to be one. So why should I accept the council's laws as valid over me? They set themselves up almost two hundred years ago. Nowadays they're elected, but the entire council, in and of itself, wasn't created by the Wiccan community or even by the Seven Clans. To me they seem arbitrary. Why should I subject myself to their laws?"

I leaned forward. "It's true that the council created itself long ago. But the original members were witches, just as all members are today. The council wasn't created by humans, who have nothing to do with witch affairs. The creation of the council signifies the intent of the witch community at large to be self-governing. And yes, we're all subject to whatever human laws govern the places in which we live, but those laws don't address the sum of our existence. Everyone who practices the craft, everyone who works with magick is a part of a different world. That world intersects with the human world but doesn't overlap." I adjusted one of the cats on my lap, whose claws were digging into my thigh. "We're not talking about golf here, Justine. We're talking about magick. You know as well as I do that magick can be incredibly powerful, life-altering, dangerous, misused, destructive. You don't think it's a good idea to have some sort of mutually agreed-upon guidelines for it? Do you really think it would be preferable to have no laws in place? So that every witch could make any kind of magick she or he wants, with no fear of reprisal?"

Her brows came down in a thoughtful V, and she pulled a corner of one lip into her mouth: she was thinking. "It's just that the laws seem arbitrary," she argued, crossing her legs under her. Today she wore faded jeans and a fuzzy pink sweater that showed the neck of a white T-shirt underneath. She looked very fresh and pretty. "I mean, look at the rules about uninitiated witches making certain kinds of magick. Why does someone need some stranger's stamp of approval just to do what comes naturally? I hate that."

"But *what* comes naturally, Justine?" I asked. I was enjoying this back-and-forth discussion. I hardly ever got to have this kind of interesting, stimulating conversation. Among the witches I knew, we all just accepted the council's laws. And other people, like Morgan, don't really know enough about

Wiccan history or the witch community to be able to fully form an opinion. "What kind of magick did you make as a child? That was natural, wasn't it? But was it always good?" I thought about my own spell on poor Mrs. Wilkie. "I don't believe either people or witches are always born naturally good," I went on. "I think that as people get older and more educated, they learn to channel their goodness, to identify it, and to express it. But I think witches, and people, too, are born with a capacity for light or dark. It's up to their parents, their community, their teachers to educate them to see the consistent benefit of good and the consistent detriment of darkness. The council and its laws only serve to reinforce that, to provide guidelines, to help people learn where the boundaries are."

"But is that all they do?" asked Justine, and we were off again. For the next hour we went back and forth, discussing the various merits of laws versus no laws, outer-determined behavior versus inner-determined behavior. It was really fun, though at times I was uncomfortably reminded of the scientists who had figured out how to make an atom bomb. They had seemed to divorce the idea of how to create it from the idea of what its natural consequences would be. They hadn't wanted to see it. In a way, I felt that Justine was doing the same thing: closing her eyes to the potentially destructive effects of her actions.

But we talked on. Justine was sure of herself, sure of her own intelligence and attractiveness, and didn't let insecurity get in the way of her speaking her mind. For a moment I wondered if I should be concerned that I was enjoying her company so much, but then thought, Nah. I knew I loved Morgan more than anything. I was doing my job, being a Seeker, finding out what made Justine tick. It was all for the report.

I had talked to Morgan the night before, but it had been kind of stilted. Hearing her voice had brought back my unhappiness about my parents, about how much I missed Morgan herself, about how much I didn't want to be here. Widow's Vale seemed so far away from here, both physically and emotionally.

"I was wondering—are you interested in seeing my library?" Justine asked.

"Yes," I said immediately, aware that this was a show of trust on her part. For my part, a Seeker never turns down an invitation into someone's private world. It's often where I find the answers to my questions.

She led me through a tidy, well-stocked kitchen to a small door in a hallway. She passed her hands over the door frame: dispelling protection spells. Once opened, the door led to steps going downward. I immediately became alert and quickly cast my senses to see if anything unpleasant was waiting for me at the bottom of the stairs.

"It's underground," Justine explained, turning on the electric lights. She didn't seem to pick up on my momentary suspicion, or maybe she was just being polite. "That helps keep it safe from fire. I think the people who owned this house before me used the cellar as storage, as a wine cellar. I enlarged it and waterproofed it."

At the bottom of the stairs she flicked another light switch, and I blinked, looking around. Justine's library was enormous. We were in one good-sized room, but doorways led to at least two other rooms I could see. The floor was made of rough wooden planks, and the walls were a crude stucco. But most bare surfaces had been painted with stylized designs of runes, hexes, words, and even some sigils I didn't know the names of. I picked up on a general air of light, of comfort and pleasure and curiosity. If dark magick had been worked here, I couldn't feel it.

"This is incredible," I said, walking slowly into the room. Despite the lack of windows, the room looked open and inviting. A fireplace took up one wall, and by gauging the rooms above, I figured its chimney must run through the kitchen fireplace's. Big, cozy armchairs were strewn here and there. There were closed glass cases, regular bookshelves, wooden tables piled with stacked books. Unlike Selene's personal library, this one wasn't cold or intimidating. It was all laid out neatly and beautifully organized.

"This is quite an accomplishment for someone so young," I said, wandering into the next room. I saw that it led to another room, and that there was a lavatory off to one side.

"I'm twenty-four," Justine said without artifice. "I inherited a lot of this from my mother when she moved into a smaller house. Most of what I've contributed myself are the books on the use of the stars' positions to aid or hinder magick. It's another interest of mine."

I ran my fingers lightly over books' spines, skimming titles. There were one or two books on the dark uses of magick, but that was to be expected of almost any witch's library. The vast majority of the books were legitimate and nonthreatening. Or as nonthreatening as a manual of how to make magick can be. Just about anything can be misused.

"My father would have loved seeing this," I murmured,

remembering the Da of my childhood, surrounded by books in his library at home. Candles burned down around him and still he read, late into the night. He'd often impressed on us kids how precious books were, learning was.

"Is he no longer living?" Justine asked sympathetically.

I bit back a snide retort about the definition of living and answered instead, "No, he's alive. He's at the B and B in Foxton."

"Why don't you bring him next time, then?" Justine said. "I'd be happy for him to see my library. Is he a Seeker, too?"

"No," I said, unable to suppress a quick dry laugh. "No, but he's in bad shape. My mum died at Yule, and he's taken it hard." I was surprised to hear myself confiding in her. I tend to be very closemouthed and don't often share my personal life with anyone, besides Sky and Morgan.

"Oh, how awful," Justine said. "Maybe the library will be a good distraction for him."

"Yes, maybe you're right," I said, meeting her brown eyes.

"This place is nice," I said, looking around the small restaurant. It was Monday night, and Justine had recommended the Turtledove as a likely place for Da and me to have a decent meal. Across from me, the etched lines of his face thrown into relief by the flickering firelight, Da nodded without enthusiasm. Since I had gotten back to the B and B this afternoon, he had been alternately withdrawn, confrontational, and wheedling. I figured a nice meal out would help stave off my overwhelming desire to shake him.

Not that I felt that way every second. Every once in a while, I would get a glimpse of the old da, the one I knew and recognized. It was there when he almost smiled at a joke I made, when his eyes lit with momentary interest or intelligence. It was those moments, few and far between, that had kept me going, kept me reaching out to him. Somewhere inside this bitter husk was a man I'd known as my father. I needed to reach him somehow.

"More bread?" I asked, holding out the basket. Da shook his head. He'd barely picked at his beef stew. I was going to give him another five minutes and then finish it off for him.

"Son," he said, startling me, "I appreciate what you're doing. I do. I even think you're right, most of the time. But you just can't understand what I'm going through. I've been trying and trying, but I need to talk to Fiona. I need to see her. Even if the *bith dearc* saps my strength or my life force. I just can't see any kind of existence where I wouldn't need your mother."

His hand shook as he reached for his wineglass, and he downed the rest of his drink. This was the most direct he'd been with me since we'd left the cabin, and it took me a moment to find my footing.

"You're right—I don't understand what it's like to lose your *mùirn beatha dàn*, not after you've been married and had children, made a life together," I said. "But I know that even with that tragedy, it doesn't make sense for you to kill yourself by continuing to contact the shadow world. Mum wouldn't have wanted it that way."

Da was silent, his clothes hanging on his thin frame.

"Da, do you believe that Mum loved you?"

His head jerked up, and he met my eyes.

"Of course. I know she did."

"I know she did, too," I agreed. "She loved you more than anything on this earth. But do you think that she would be doing this if *you* had died? Or would she be doing something different?"

Da looked taken aback by my question and sat in silence for a moment.

Changing the subject, giving him time to think, I repeated Justine Courceau's offer of letting Da see her library. "It's quite amazing," I said. "I think you'd be very interested in it. Come with me tomorrow and see it."

"Maybe I will," Da muttered, tapping his fork against the tablecloth.

It wasn't a total victory, but maybe it was a step forward. I sighed and decided to let it go for the present.

On Tuesday, I called Kennet and gave him a preliminary report. I had more background checks to do on Justine and more interviewing, but so far I hadn't turned up anything of great alarm.

"No, Hunter, you misunderstand," Kennet said patiently. "Everything she's doing is of great alarm. Under no circumstances should any witch have written lists of living things' true names. Surely you see that?"

"Yes," I said, starting to feel testy. "I understand that. I agree. It's just that you made Justine sound like a power-hungry rebel, and I don't see that in her. I feel it's more a matter of education. Justine's quite intelligent and not unreasonable. I feel that she needs reeducation; she needs to be made to understand why what she's doing is wrong. Once she understands, I think she'll see the wisdom in destroying her lists."

"Hunter, she needs to be shut down," Kennet said strongly. "Her reeducation can come later. Your job is to stop her, now, by any means necessary."

I tried to keep my voice level. "I thought my job was to investigate, make a report, and then have the council make a judgment. Have you already decided this matter?"

"No, no, of course not," Kennet said, backpedaling at the implication of my words. "I just don't want you to be swayed by this witch, that's all."

"Have you known me to be easily swayed in the past, by man or woman?" I asked with deceptive mildness. Deceptive to most people, but not to Kennet. He knew me very well and could probably tell I was working hard to keep anger out of my voice.

"No, Hunter," he said, sounding calmer. "No. I'm sure we can trust your judgment in this matter. Just keep reporting back, all right?"

"Of course," I said. "That's my job." After I hung up, I sat on my twin bed for a long time, just thinking.

That afternoon I brought Daniel to Justine's cottage. As before, she was welcoming, and though I detected her shock at my father's haggard appearance, she made no mention of it.

"Come in, come in," she said. "It's gotten a little warmer, hasn't it? I think maybe spring is on its way."

Inside, Da instinctively headed for the fireplace and stood before the cheerful flames, holding out his hands. Back at the cabin, it had been as though the fire hadn't existed, so I was interested to see his reaction to this one.

"Are you warm enough, Mr. Niall?" Justine asked. "I know it can be chilly in these stone cottages."

"I'm fine, thanks," said Da, turning his back to the fire but keeping his hands behind him, toward the heat.

Justine and I talked for a while, and she told us stories about growing up with Avalen Courceau, who sounded like an intimidating figure. But Justine spoke of her with love and acceptance, and again I was impressed by her maturity and kindness. She got even Da to smile at the story of when she had built a house of cards out of some important indexed notes her mother had made. Apparently sparks had flown for days. Literally.

"Mr. Niall," said Justine, "I wonder if you could do me a favor?" She gave him a charming smile, sincere and without guile. "I don't get many opportunities to try new magick— no one around here knows I'm a witch, and I want to keep it that way. I was wondering if you would consent to be a guinea pig for a spell I've just learned."

Da looked concerned but couldn't think of any reason not to and didn't want to refuse in the face of her hospitality. "What for?"

She smiled again. "It's a healing spell."

Da shrugged. "As you wish."

"It's all right with me," I said, and she turned to give me a teasing look.

"It's not your decision," she pointed out. Feeling like an overbearing clod, I sat down on the sofa, relaxing against the plump pillows, waiting for some cat to realize I was there.

She had Da sit down in a comfortable chair, then cast a circle around it, using twelve large amethysts. She invoked the Goddess and the God and dedicated her circle to them. Then she stood behind my father and gently laid her fingertips against his temples on either side. As soon as she started on the forms and opening chants, I realized I wasn't familiar with it.

It went on for more than an hour. At different times Justine touched my father's neck, the back of his head, his forehead, the base of his throat, his temples. Da seemed patient, tired, disinterested. I myself felt almost hypnotized by the warm crackling of the fire, the deeply felt purring of the apricot-colored cat who had finally settled on me, the soothing tones of Justine's low-voiced singing and chanting.

At last I recognized the closing notes, the forms of completion, and I sat up straighter. Slowly Justine took her hands away from Da and stood back, seeming drained and peaceful. I looked at Da. He met my eyes. Was it my imagination, or was there more life in them?

He turned to find Justine. "I feel better," he said, sounding reluctant to admit it. "Thanks."

She smiled. "I hope it helped. I found it in a book I was cataloging last month, and I've been anxious to try it. Thank you for allowing me." She took a deep breath. "Now, how about some tea? I'm hungry."

Ten minutes later, watching Da tuck into his cake with the faint signs of an actual appetite, I smiled my gratitude to Justine. She smiled back. To me, this healing was one more indication that Justine was just misguided, overenthusiastic in her quest for knowledge, but basically good-hearted. There was no way someone like Selene could have performed that healing rite, not without my picking up on her dark underlying motives. I'd felt none of that with Justine. She seemed genuinely what she was.

"My son told me how impressed he was with your library," Da said.

"Would you like to see it?" Justine asked naturally, and my father nodded.

I felt something like gladness inside—this was the first time he had called me his son, in front of another person, since we'd been reunited. It felt good.

12

Trust

Today is Saturday, but I feel so incredibly bizarre that I need to come up with a whole new name for this day. "Saturday" doesn't cover it.

Last night, to take my mind off things, I agreed to go ice-skating with Mary K., Aunt Eileen, and Paula at the big outdoor rink outside of Taunton. I hadn't seen Eileen and Paula in ages—I've been busy saving my grades, and they've been fixing up their new house.

It was one of the last times we could go skating—spring is coming, and soon they won't be able to maintain the outdoor ice. I felt like a little kid, lacing my skates. Mary K. bought a caramel apple. Eileen and Paula were happy and light-hearted, and all four of us were being incredibly silly and goofy. I felt happy, and I didn't think about Hunter more than about a thousand times, so that was good.

Then Paula was zipping along backward when she lost

her balance and went down hard. The back of her head slammed against the ice with a crack so loud, it sounded like a branch breaking. Immediately Eileen and I were there, and Mary K. rushed up a few seconds later.

I watched in horror as a spreading, lacy design of blood seeped across the ice.

A little crowd had gathered around, peering over our shoulders, trying to see what was happening, and Aunt Eileen rose on her knees and shooed them back. I could tell she was starting to freak out, so I took hold of one of her shoulders and told her to go call 911.

Her eyes took a second to focus on mine, then she nodded, got shakily to her feet, and skated carefully to the side of the rink.

Mary K. was trying not to cry and failing. She asked me if Paula was going to be okay.

I told her I didn't know and gritted my teeth at the amount of blood I was seeing. Paula's eyes fluttered open once, and I took her hand, patting it and calling her name. She didn't respond and closed her eyes again. I had seen that one of her pupils was tiny, like a pencil point, and one was wide open, making her iris look black. I didn't know what that meant, but I had watched TV often enough to know it was bad. Crap, I thought. Double crap.

I stroked Paula's cheek, cool beneath my hand. My hands

felt so warm, even without gloves. My hands . . . a couple of weeks ago, Alisa Soto had been very ill. I had touched her, and all hell had broken loose. Did I dare try to touch Paula now? The situation with Alisa had been really weird, way different from this one. But what if I made Paula worse?

Cautiously I traced my fingers over Paula's hair, now cold and wet. I hoped no one was paying attention to what I was doing. Beneath my fingers, I felt Paula's life force pulsing unsteadily, becoming overwhelmed by a cascading flood of injuries it couldn't recover from.

I closed my eyes and concentrated. It took me a moment to orient myself, to feel my consciousness blend with Paula's. But then I was at home in her body, and I could tell what was wrong. There was bleeding inside Paula's skull. The blood on the ice was from her skin being split, but there was also bleeding inside her skull, and it was pooling at the back of her head. It was compressing her brain, which had nowhere to go. Her brain was swelling dangerously, pressing against her unmovable skull, and it was starting to shut down. Paula was going to die before the ambulance got there.

My eyes flew open at this knowledge. Eileen was white-faced, crying, trying to be brave. I saw Mary K., stroking Eileen's arm and weeping.

Very slowly and quietly, hoping no one would stop me, I closed my eyes again and rested my fingers lightly beneath

Paula's head. In moments I had sunk into a deep meditation, had sent my senses into Paula again. Now I could see all the damage. Without having to search for them, ancient words came into my mind. It was a spell from Alyce, I realized. Silently I repeated them as they floated toward me, hearing their powerful, singsong melody. I pictured the pooled blood dissipating, seeping away; I thought about gently opening the collapsed veins, branching off smaller and smaller, infinitely delicate and perfect and beautiful.

As Paula's systems steadied—her breathing more even, her heart pumping more strongly, her brain returning to its pre-accident state—I felt a wave of exhilaration that almost took my breath away. This was beautiful magick, perfect in its intent, powerful in its form, and gracefully expressed by the ancient voices through me. There was nothing more wonderful, more satisfying, more joyful, and I felt my heart lighten and a smile come to my face.

Then Paula's eyes fluttered open, and my happiness increased.

I sat back on my heels, exhausted, and glanced at my watch. My hand was covered with blood; I wiped it hastily on my jeans. I had done everything in three minutes. Three crucial minutes that meant the difference between life and death for someone I cared about. It was the most amazing thing that had ever happened to me, and I couldn't even take it in.

The ambulance came almost ten minutes later. Paramedics raced out onto the ice, stabilized Paula's neck and head, then moved her carefully to a stretcher. Aunt Eileen went with the stretcher, promising to call us later with news. I said I'd take her car back to my mom's house, and she could come get it later. She tossed me the keys and then ran to catch up.

After the flashing red lights had disappeared and the crowd of anxious bystanders had drifted away, Mary K. and I got stiffly to our feet. We were chilled through and bought some hot chocolate from the stand, then walked back to Aunt Eileen's car.

As I unlocked the door, I told Mary K. I thought Paula was going to be all right. She had stopped crying but still looked very upset. She got into the passenger seat without saying anything, and I looked over at her before I started the engine.

Mary K.'s large brown eyes met mine and she asked me what I had done.

I looked out the windshield into the salt-stained street—winter was ending, and it seemed like I was seeing the bare ground, bare trees, bare sidewalks for the first time. I thought of Alisa and her brief illness, how Mary K. still seemed to think I'd healed her.

I didn't know what to say.

"Nothing," I whispered.

—Morgan

On Saturday morning I finished writing my Justine Courceau report for the council. I'd spent quite a bit of time with her, discussed all the different facets of true names, had further interviews with the people in Foxton, and gone through her library. The summary of my report was that she needed reeducation but wasn't dangerous and that no serious action need be taken, once I witnessed her destroying her written list of true names.

I signed it, addressed an envelope, put the report inside, and sealed it. Da was sitting in the room's one chair. I told him what the report said, and to my surprise, he looked like he was actually listening. He rubbed his hand across his chin, and I recognized the gesture as one I make myself when I'm thinking.

"Reeducation, eh?" he said. "You think so? I mean, you think that will be enough?"

"That and destroying her list," I said. "Why wouldn't it be?"

He shrugged. "I think there's more to Justine than meets the eye."

I gave him my full attention. "Please explain."

He shrugged again. "You don't really know her. You might not want to accept her at face value."

"Do you have anything concrete or specific that should change what I said in my report?"

"No," he admitted. "Nothing more than I feel suspicious. I feel she's hiding something."

"Hmmm," I said. On the one hand, the report was written, and I didn't want to redo it, though of course I would if I turned up new information. On the other hand, Da, despite his many *enormous* faults, was still nobody's fool, and it would be stupid of me not to pay attention to what he said. On the third hand, Da had just spent eleven years on the run and was probably pretty likely to be suspicious of everyone.

"Right, well, thanks for telling me that," I said. "I'll keep that in mind this afternoon."

"Yup," Da said. "Anyway, she's got a nice library."

"Hunter! Welcome back. Come in," Justine said.

"Hello. I've wrapped up my report, and I wanted to give you the gist of it before my father and I take off." I got out of my coat and draped it over the back of the sofa, then sat down across from her.

"Oh, great. Where *is* your father?"

"Back at the B and B. He gets tired very easily, though he definitely seems better since you did the healing rite."

"I'm glad. Okay, now tell me about your frightening report on the evil and dangerous Justine Courceau."

She was openly laughing at me, and I grinned back. Not many people feel safe teasing me—Morgan and Sky are the only ones who came to mind. And now Justine.

Briefly I filled her in on what I had reported to Kennet, expecting her to be relieved and pleased. But to my surprise, her face began to look more and more concerned, then upset, then angry.

"Reeducated!" she finally burst out, her eyes glittering. "Haven't you heard a thing I've said? Have our talks meant nothing?"

"Of course I've heard what you said," I responded.

"Haven't you heard what *I've* said? I thought you'd come to agree with the council's position on true names of living beings."

"I said I *understood* it," Justine cried, getting to her feet. "Not that I *agree* with it! I thought I'd made that perfectly clear."

I stood up also. "How can you not agree? How can you possibly defend keeping a written list of the true names of living beings? Don't you remember that story I told you, about the boy in my village and the fox?"

She threw her arms out to the sides. "What has that got to do with anything? That's like saying don't go to Africa because I knew someone who tripped and broke their leg there. I'm not an uneducated child!"

Before I realized it, we were shouting our views and shooting the other's down. It turned out that all week we had been dancing around each other, skirting the issues, avoiding openly confronting each other and, in so doing, had made incorrect assumptions about what we agreed on, how we felt, what we were willing to do. I had thought I was being a subtle but influential Seeker, but Justine had chosen not to be influenced.

Ten minutes into it, our faces were flushed with heat and anger, and Justine actually put out her hands and shoved against my chest, saying, "You are being so pigheaded!"

I grabbed her arms below her shoulders and resisted the temptation to shake her. "Me pigheaded? You have pigheaded written all over you! Not to mention self-centeredness!"

At that very instant, as Justine was drawing in a breath to let me have it again, I became aware that someone was watching me, scrying for me. I blinked and concentrated and knew that Justine had just picked up on it, too. It was Morgan, trying to find me. She must not have cast concealing spells. As soon as I made that connection, she winked out, as if she were only trying to locate me to see where I was. I looked down at Justine, saw what we looked like, with her hands pressed against my stomach and me holding her arms, both of us arguing passionately, and realized what it might have looked like to Morgan. "Oh, bloody hell," I muttered, dropping my hands.

"Who was that?" Justine asked, her anger, like mine, deflated.

"Bloody hell," I repeated, and without warning, my whole life came crashing down on me. I loved Morgan, but she'd been spying on me! I was a Seeker but growing increasingly uncomfortable with the council's secrecy and some of its methods. And my da! I didn't even want to go there. My father who wasn't a father; my mother who was dead. It was all too much, and I wanted to disappear up a mountainside, never to be seen again. I rubbed my hand against my face, across my jaw, feeling about forty years old and very, very tired.

"Hunter, what is it?" Justine asked in a normal voice.

I raised my head to look at her, her concerned eyes the color of oak leaves in fall, and the next thing I knew, she had pressed herself against me and was pulling my head down to kiss me. I was startled but could have pulled back. But didn't. Instead my head dipped, my arms went around her, and our mouths met with an urgency as hot as our argument had been. Details registered in my mind: that Justine was shorter and curvier than Morgan, that she was strong but less aggressive than Morgan, that she tasted like oranges and cinnamon. I drew her closer, wanting her to turn into Morgan, then realized what I was doing and pulled back.

Breathing hard, I looked down at Justine, horrified by what I had just done, even as I acknowledged that I had liked it, that it had felt good. She smiled up at me, her lips full, her eyes shining.

"I've been wanting to do that since the first moment I saw you," she said, her voice soft. "I haven't been this attracted to anyone in I don't know how long." She reached for me again and spread her hands across my chest, splaying her fingers and pressing against the muscle there. Gently I covered her hands with mine and pulled them away from me.

"Justine," I said, "I'm sorry. I don't know what to say. I shouldn't have kissed you, for several different reasons. I don't know what came over me. But I apologize."

She laughed—a light, musical sound—and tried to pull me close again. "Don't apologize," she said, her voice drawing me in without a spell. "I told you, I've been wanting to kiss you. I want you." Her eyes took on more intent, and she stepped closer to me so we were touching from chest to knees. I felt her full breasts pillow against me and the width of her hips against mine. It felt terrific, and I felt awful, guilty.

"I'm sorry, Justine," I said again, stepping back. I crossed the room with big strides and grabbed my coat. "I'm sorry. I didn't mean to hurt you." Then I was out the door like a dog turned loose and rushing toward my car.

I was back at the bed-and-breakfast hours before I had expected to be. All I wanted was to lie on my bed and figure out what the hell had just happened. I knew I loved Morgan sincerely and truly, and I knew I was intensely attracted to her. The fact that we hadn't slept together didn't seem to have any bearing on this—I was sure we would, when it was right. No, this was a freak occurrence, and I needed to figure it out so I could make sure it never happened again. I also just needed to get my head clear about the council and my father. A daunting task.

Groaning to myself, I turned my key in the lock and tried to open the door. It wouldn't budge. I tried the key a couple of times, then realized that the damned door was *spelled* from the inside! Working as quickly as I could, I dismantled all the blocking spells, then crashed into the room. Da was on the floor, hastily brushing a white substance under his bed. I lunged for it, dabbed my fingers in it, and tasted it. Salt.

"What have you been doing?" I demanded while he got up and sat on his bed, brushing off his hands. He was silent, and I looked around the room. Now I saw a small section of the concentric circles of power he had drawn on the floor with salt, and I also found a book, written in Gaelic. Written Gaelic is a struggle for me, but I could read enough to decipher that there was a chapter on creating a sort of artificial *bith dearc*, far from a power sink. I wanted to throw the book across the room.

"Did Justine give you this, or did you take it?" I demanded, holding the book out to him.

He looked at me. "I took it," he said without remorse.

I shook my head. "Why am I even surprised?" I asked no one. Suddenly feeling angry seemed pointless. Instead a deep sadness came over me as I accepted the fact that I wasn't enough of a reason for Da to want to live. I flopped down on my bed and looked at the ceiling. "Why am I disappointed? You don't want to stop contacting Mum. You don't care that it hurts her, that it hurts you, that it hurts me. You don't care that you're going to take away the only parent Alwyn and I have left. I just—I don't know what to do. *You* need a father, a father of your own. I'm not up to it."

"Son, you don't understand," Da began.

"So you say," I interrupted him, turning on my side, my back to him. "No one understands how you feel. No one has ever lost anyone they cared about, except you. No one has felt your kind of pain, except you. You're so bloody *special.*" I didn't try to hide my bitterness. I hated the fact that I cared enough to be disappointed. I hated Da for being who he was, and who he wasn't.

"No, I mean you don't understand what I was doing," Da said, a stronger tone in his voice. "I was trying to help you."

"Help me?" I laughed dryly. "When have I ever mattered enough for you to want to help? I know I'm nothing to you. The only good thing about me is that I'm half Mum."

Silence dropped over the room like a curtain. My father was so still and quiet that I turned over to see if he was still there. He was. He was sitting on the edge of his bed, staring at me, a stunned, confused expression on his face. "You are," he whispered. "You are half Fiona. You, and Alwyn both. Fiona lives on in you."

I sighed. "Forget it, Da. I'm not going to hassle you anymore. I'm giving up."

"Wait, Hunter," he said, using my common name. "I know you won't believe this, but you, Linden, and Alwyn were the most precious things in my life, after your mother. You three were our love personified. In you I saw my strength, my stubbornness, my wall of reserve. But I also saw your mother's capacity for joy, her ability to love deeply and give freely. I had forgotten all that. Until just now."

I rolled over to face him. He looked old, beaten, but there was something about him, as if he'd been infused with new blood. I felt a more alive sense coming from him.

"I liked being a father, Giomanach," he said, looking at his hands resting on his knees. "I know it may not have seemed like it. I didn't want to spoil you, make you soft. My job was to teach you. Your mother's job was to nurture you. But I was happy being a father. I failed Cal and left him to be poisoned by Selene. You and your brother and sister were my chance to make that up. But then I left you, too. Not a day has gone by since then that I haven't regretted not being there to watch my children grow up, see your initiations. I missed you." He gave a short laugh. "You were a bright lad, a bulldog, like I said. You were fast to catch on, but you had a spark of fire in you. Remember that poor cat you spelled to make the other kids laugh? I was angry, you misusing magick like that. But that night, telling Fiona about it, I could hardly stop laughing. That poor cat, batting the air." Another tiny chuckle escaped, and I stared at him. Was this my father?

"Anyway," Da said. "I'm sorry, son. I'm a disappointment to you. I know that. That's bitter to me. But this seems to be where my life has brought me. This is the spell I've written."

"Maybe so, up till now," I said, sitting up and swinging my feet to the floor. "But you can change. You have that power. The spell isn't finished yet."

He shook his head once, then shrugged. "I'm sorry. I've

always been sorry. But—you make me want to try." These last words were said so softly, I could hardly hear them.

"I want you to try, too, Da," I said. "That's why I'm so disappointed today." I gestured at the circles, smudged on the floor, the salt crunching underfoot.

"I really was trying to help you," he said. "I didn't trust Justine. How is she acquiring the true names of living beings? Of people?"

I frowned. "She told me she inherited some of them from her mother. Others she found by accident. Two names have been contributed by their owners, in the interest of her research."

"Maybe so," said Da, not sounding convinced. "But she also gets a lot from the shadow world."

"What?"

"I wasn't contacting Fiona this time," Da explained. "I have no wish to harm her further. But the shadow world does have its uses. One of them is that people on the other side have access to knowledge that not many can get otherwise."

"What are you talking about?" I asked, afraid of where this was going.

"Justine acquires many of the true names of living beings, including people, from sources in the shadow world," Da explained.

I blinked. "How do you know this?"

"Sources in the shadow world. Reliable sources."

I was quiet for several minutes, thinking it all through. Obviously if Da's sources were correct, I had to come up with a whole new game plan. The situation had developed a new weight, a new seriousness that would require all my skill as a Seeker. Da had gotten this information for me. He had risked his own health—not to mention the irresistible temptation of calling my mother—in order to help me in this case.

Finally I looked up. "Hmmm."

Da examined my face. "I have—a gift for you. To help you."

"Oh?"

He went to the room's small desk and took out a sheet of paper. With slow, deliberate gestures he wrote a rune in the center of the paper. Then, concentrating, he surrounded the rune with seven different symbols—an ancient form of musical notes, sigils denoting color and tone, and the odd, primitive punctuation that was used in one circumstance only. Da was writing a true name. At the end he put the symbol that identified the name as belonging to a human.

I read it, mentally transcribing it as I had been taught, hearing the tones in my mind, seeing the colors. It was a beautiful name, strong. Glancing up, I met Da's eyes.

"She is more dangerous than she seems. You may need this."

The paper in my hand felt on fire. In my life, I had known only five true names of people. One was mine, three belonged to witches whose powers I had stripped, doing my duty as a Seeker, and now this one. It was a huge, huge thing, a powerful thing. My father had done this for me.

"I have an idea," I said, feeling like I was about to throw myself into a river's racing current. "I think you need to get away from Saint Jérôme du Lac—far away. It has bad memories for you. Not only that, but Canada is too bloody cold.

You need to start fresh. I think you should come back to Widow's Vale with me. Sky and I have room, and I know she'd be glad to have you. Or we could get you your own place. You could be around other witches, be back in society. You need to rejoin the living, no matter how much you don't think you want to."

For a long time Da sat looking at a blank spot on the wall. I prayed that he had heard me because I didn't think I'd be able to repeat the offer.

But at last my father's dry croak of a voice said, "Maybe you're right. I don't know how long I can resist the pull of the *bith dearc*. I don't want to hurt your mother anymore. I can't. But I need help."

I was amazed and wondered what I had just gotten myself into. I would have to deal with it as it came. "Right, then," I said. "We'll leave tomorrow, after I clear up a few matters with Justine Courceau." I looked again at the true name and memorized it. "We'll stop in Saint Jérôme du Lac, get what you need from the cabin, and be in Quebec City by nightfall."

My father nodded and lay down on his bed with the stiff, jerky movements of an old man.

13

Confrontation

It isn't often that someone truly surprises me, but Hunter did this morning. First he surprised me with that ridiculous report to the council and then by running off like a scared rabbit after I kissed him. I don't understand him at all. I know he wants me, too—all week he's been looking at me like a lovesick puppy, whether he realized it or not. Did he run just because he's a Seeker and I'm the one being investigated? Granted, I'm sure there are protocols in place; I'm sure it would be frowned upon. But according to whom? The stupid council! I don't acknowledge their dominion over me, so why should they stop me from having Hunter? And I absolutely want to have him. He's so compelling, such a portrait of contrasts. He looks young but acts much older. There's a world-weary air about him, as if he's seen it all and hasn't been able to forget enough of it. And there's that intriguing scar on his neck, almost like a burn. I want to know the story behind it.

He seems reserved, but he's funny, passionate about what he believes in, a worthy adversary, and an equal. He has a deep, smoldering sensuality behind his eyes. I want to see those embers ignite. The one problem is his devotion to the council—was I just imagining it, or is that devotion wavering? Given his age, he can't have been a Seeker long. I'm sure it's not too late to show him what the council really is, how insidious they are, how poisonous. In my family alone they've stripped three women of their powers—and that's just within the last fifty years. They're threatened by anyone and anything, and they retaliate far out of proportion. If Hunter understood that, he wouldn't want any part of it.

Hunter. He'll be back. He's not the type to leave unfinished business. I want him in a way I haven't wanted a man before. I want him in my bed, in my life, in my magick. Think of it— two strong blood witches, accumulating so much pure, beautiful knowledge. And using it, only occasionally, to strike down those who have wronged us.

—J. C.

The next morning, after our last breakfast at the B and B, Da and I pulled up to Justine's stone cottage. Our bags were packed and in the boot of the car; by this afternoon Da and I would be back at his cabin, getting ready to leave for the States. I felt a strong sense of reluctance, and the true name I'd memorized seemed to burn in my mind.

This would probably be the last time I would ever see Justine Courceau. Which was fine. But I had to clear up the matter of the kiss, and more importantly, I had to witness her destroying the list of true names. Which meant first I had to convince her to do it. I had never met a witch who so openly defied the council—even Ciaran MacEwan, evil though he was, acknowledged that the council had legitimate power.

"Right, then, show time," I said, starting to open my door.

"Hunter," said my father, and I turned to look at him. "Good luck."

Encouragement from a father. I smiled. "Ta." We got out of the car.

Justine greeted my knock and gave us an easy smile. If she was upset about our kiss yesterday, she didn't show it. Today she wore a deep red sweater that made her look vital and curvaceous. I tried not to think about it.

"*Bonjour,*" she said, letting us in. "I just poured myself some coffee. Would you care for some?"

We both agreed, and she left us in the lounge. On the floor in front of the fireplace was a large wooden crate that had been crowbarred open. I looked inside shamelessly: it was full of leather-bound books, beat-up journals, even some preserved periodicals. All about Wicca, the craft, the Seven Clans. Additions to her library.

"I see you're examining my latest shipment," Justine said cheerfully, handing us each our coffee. It was scented with cinnamon, but other than that I detected no magickal addition, no spell laid on it. I took a sip.

"Yes," I said, tasting the coffee's warm richness. "Are these about anything in particular or just general witchiana?"

She laughed her musical laugh. "Most of these are about stone magick, crystals, gems, that kind of thing. For the gem section downstairs."

"I was hoping to go downstairs again," my father said.

"Certainly," Justine said graciously. She walked Da down the hall, opened the door leading down to the library, and turned on the light. "Call if you need anything."

She came back into the lounge with an almost predatory expression on her face. "At last we're alone," she said, smiling at the cliché.

"I wanted to talk to you about yesterday," I said. I hadn't sat down and now stood before her. I put down my coffee.

"Why did you run?" she asked softly, looking up at me. She stretched out one hand and rested it against my chest. "You must know I want you. And I know that you want me."

"I'm sorry," I said. "Yesterday shouldn't have happened. It isn't just that I'm a Seeker and I'm investigating you. It's just—I find you very attractive, and I've enjoyed our times together."

"Me too," she said, moving closer. I could detect her scent, light and spicy.

"But I'm involved with someone," I pressed on.

She didn't move for a moment, then she laughed. "What does *that* mean?"

"I have a lover." All right, it was stretching the truth a bit. I *almost* had a lover. I would have, if I hadn't been such a git.

Justine's beautiful brown eyes narrowed as she weighed my words. "Where?"

"Home."

She turned away from me and walked across the room to stroke one of the cats that lay sleeping on the back of the couch. Then she dismissed my unseen lover with a shrug. "People get together," she said. "People break up. They move on. Now you've met me, and I've met you. I want you." She gazed at me clearly, and if I hadn't had the tough hide of a Seeker, I would have squirmed. "You and I would be a formidable team. We would be good together—in bed and out of it."

I shook my head, wanting to run again. I'm terrible at dealing with things like this. "Not a good idea."

"Tell me why."

"Because I have a lover. Because I'm still a Seeker and you're still someone who has an illegal list of true names. I'm here to watch you destroy them before I leave town."

She stared at me as if I had suddenly grown antlers.

I had decided not to use my secret weapon unless I needed to. Better to have her achieve true understanding. "Justine, I understand your motives for wanting to collect true names. But there's no reason for any one person to amass that kind of power, that kind of knowledge. Even though I know you're a good person and a good witch, still, power corrupts. Absolute power corrupts absolutely."

Her lip curled the slightest bit. "I've heard that before, of course," she said softly. "I didn't believe it then, either. You know, Hunter, I thought you really understood. I thought you were on my side. But you're still determined to be a council pawn."

Ignoring her dart, I held out my hands. "I'm on the side of balance. It's never a good idea to let things get out of balance, and amassing lists of true names will absolutely tip the balance."

Her face lightened, and she shrugged and looked away. "We'll simply have to agree to disagree," she said easily. "It was nice meeting you, though. How far of a drive do you have today?"

I felt that peculiar sensation of tension entering my body, my mind, my voice. It was like a gear shifting. "No, I'm afraid it isn't that simple," I said mildly. "I'm afraid I have to insist. It isn't that I don't trust you. But what would a malicious witch do with that list? What if it fell into the wrong hands? It would be much better for that knowledge to be disseminated among witches equally, or at least witches who have dedicated themselves honestly to the side of light."

I could feel her interest cool as if I were watching a fire die down. "I'm sorry," she said, her voice sounding harder, less seductive. "I just don't see it that way. So if you'll just be going, I'll continue on my life's work."

"I need to see you destroy your list," I said in a steely voice.

Justine looked at me in amazement, then threw back her head and laughed. Not a typical reaction to a Seeker's demand. Then she caught herself and looked back at me, thoughtful. "I'll tell you what," she said. "I'll destroy my list if you'll stay here and be my lover."

Well, that was an offer I didn't get every day. "I'm sorry," I said. "But that just isn't an option."

She gave me a cool smile. "Then you need to leave now, and neither of us will have gotten what we wanted."

"The list," I said.

Her anger flared, as I knew it would eventually. "Look, get the hell out of my house," she said. "You're a Seeker for the council, but you're nothing to me and have no power over me. Get out."

"Why don't you see how dangerous it is?" I snapped back in frustration. "Don't you see how impossibly tempting it is to control something just because you can?"

Something in her eyes flickered, and I thought, Struck a nerve there, didn't I?

"I'm above that kind of temptation," she spat.

"No one's above that kind of temptation," I almost shouted. "How do you get these true names, Justine? Can you look me in the eye and honestly tell me there's no dark magick involved?"

A spark ran through Justine's eyes; she hadn't known that I knew. Her mouth opened, and she seemed momentarily stunned. Just as quickly as it came, though, she recovered. "I don't know what you're talking about," she said in a low voice. "Whoever told you that, it is a lie."

"Don't waste my time, Justine." I moved closer, raising my voice. "Now destroy the list, or I'll destroy it for you!"

She flung out her hand unexpectedly, hissing a spell. Instinctively I blocked it. It wasn't major; the Wiccan equivalent of slamming a door or hanging up on me. But it was enough to make me see that I needed to up the pressure. I cringed; I had been hoping to avoid this. But it was becoming clear that Justine needed a concrete example, right before her eyes, to see a different point of view.

"Nisailtirtha," I sang softly, looking at her as I traced a sigil in the air. "Nisailtirtha." I sang her name, feeling it achieve its shape in the air between us. It was a very serious thing, what I was doing. I felt extremely uncomfortable.

Across the room Justine's eyes opened in horrified shock, and she quickly began to throw up blocking spells. All of which were useless, of course. Because I knew her true name. That was the seductive power of it.

"Nisailtirtha," I said with gentle regret. "I have you in my power, my absolute power."

She practically writhed with anger and embarrassment before me, but there was nothing she could do. I came closer to her, close enough to feel her furious, panicked vibrations, close enough to smell oranges and cinnamon and fear. "You see," I said softly, leaning close to her ear, knowing that I was eight inches taller, sixty pounds heavier: a man. "Now I can make you do anything, anything at all."

A strangled sound came from her throat, and I knew if she were free, she'd be trying to strangle me. But I held her in place with a single thought. "Do you think that's a good thing, that I have this power over you because I know your true name? Nisailtirtha? I could make you set fire to your library."

She sucked in a breath, staring at me as if a devil she didn't believe in had just materialized in front of her. A thin, stretched moaning sound came from her throat. I hated this kind of threat—of course I would never make her do anything against her will, not even destroy her list. If I did, I would have let power corrupt me. But I was willing to scare her, scare her badly. In my career as a Seeker, I had done much worse.

I said, "Now that I know your name, I could sell it. To the highest bidder. To your enemies. Everyone has enemies, Justine. Even you."

She looked like she was about to jump out of her skin. "Nisailtirtha, I could make you tell me any secret you've ever had." Tears began to roll down her face, and I knew she was about to implode from frustration and fear. She didn't know me, not really. I hated this, hated that she was being so stubborn. I went on. "Do you have any secrets, Justine? Anything you don't want me to know?"

A whimper broke free, and one hand barely clenched. "Now," I whispered, walking in back of her so she couldn't see me, "I can make you destroy your list of true names. Or I can release you, and you can choose to destroy it yourself. Which do you think would be better?"

I released the hold on her enough to allow her to speak, and she broke out in sobs. "I'll destroy it," she cried. I tried not to think about what it had been like to kiss her.

"I won't make you promise," I said, and released her. She collapsed on the couch, as if I had cut her strings. She grabbed one startled cat and held it against her chest as if to make sure I hadn't made her kill it.

"I won't make you promise because I know your true name," I said solemnly. "I have control over you—absolute, unshakable control—for the rest of your life."

Racking sobs shook her, and if I hadn't been a Seeker, I would have folded her into my arms.

"That's the danger of true names," I said. "That's the kind

of control you have over everything and everyone on your list. Is that good? Are you glad I know your true name? Does it seem neutral, like pure knowledge? Or does it seem a little . . . dark?"

"*You* seem like a complete bastard," she said, still crying. Her cat was squirming to get away, but Justine held it closely, her tears wetting its fur.

"You know what? I seem like a complete bastard because I know your true name."

She had nothing to say to that.

14

The Way Home

I hate him. He's gone now, and I'm still shaking with fury. I can't believe Hunter Niall just took my life apart. First I fell for him, hard, but couldn't get him, even with a spelled kiss. Then his insulting, asinine, pointless report to the idiot council. Reeducated! I'm more educated than any member of the council! I can't believe Hunter, who had such promise, would be so pedestrian, so shortsighted. What a disappointment—though I still held out hope that he would see my point of view. But today, oh, today I put Hunter on my list—not the list of true names, but the list of people who have wronged me and my family. He is now at the top.

How did he learn my true name? I have never written it down. How could he possibly have that knowledge? If someone told it to him, then that person knows it, too. I feel completely exposed. I don't want to move from here; this cottage is perfect. But now I know that at least two people—maybe more—know my true name. How will I ever sleep peacefully again?

My house still smells like smoke. Hunter and I performed the spell that would allow the list to be destroyed. Then I burned the list in the fireplace, crying as I watched the flames lick along its edges, making the parchment curl. It was beautiful, and I had worked so hard on it, with the gold leaf and the calligraphy. Hunter stood by, his arms across his chest, that hard chest I had felt. His face was lit by the fire, and the awful thing was that I could tell that part of him regretted destroying something so beautiful. Seeing that on his face was incredibly irritating because it only showed me again how much possibility exists within him, how close he was to being exactly what I needed him to be.

I do know this. I haven't seen the last of Hunter Niall, nor he of me. Now I have work to do.

—J. C.

I felt better once we were fifty miles away from Justine. That last scene had left me with bitter feelings, all sorts of conflicting emotions. But I was glad the list had been destroyed and glad I'd had the presence of mind to also check her computer. There wasn't much there—just a few files she had to purge. I'd have to make an addendum to my report.

Da had little to say about the whole thing—if he had an opinion, he was keeping it to himself. On the drive back to his town he seemed thoughtful, preoccupied.

In Saint Jérôme du Lac, I stopped at the liquor store and picked up several cardboard boxes. Then, back at the cabin, I helped Da pack his few belongings worth saving—some books, a wool shawl of Mum's, her notebooks and papers. He had almost no clothes; none of the furniture was fit for anything but the bin; he had no art or knickknacks. It took us barely half an hour, but even that half hour made me nervous. The longer we were there, the twitchier Da seemed to become. He kept glancing at the front door as if he would bolt. I threw his stuff into the boot of my car and hustled him out to it, leaped into my seat, and motored out of there as fast as I could without causing my entire exhaust system to fall off.

After we had been on the road for six hours, I felt calmer. Da had curled miserably in his seat, as though the act of leaving that area was physically and emotionally painful.

"We'll be stopping soon," I told him, the first words either of us had spoken in hours. "We can get a room for tonight, then tomorrow be back in Widow's Vale by late afternoon. I think you'll like it there. It's an old town, so it has some character. I'll have to call Sky and get her back from France. You'll be so surprised when you see her. Remember how she was kind of a pudge? She's quite thin and tall now."

I was chattering, completely unlike myself, trying to fill the silence. Something occurred to me, something I needed to say. "Da. I wanted to tell you. I was having a hard time with Justine back there, but knowing her true name tipped the balance. I don't know what she would have done if I hadn't been able to use it. So thanks."

Da nodded. "Once upon a time, I was a strong witch," he muttered, almost to himself. He reached down on the floor by his seat and picked up a somewhat battered, black-cloth-bound book. Its spine was unraveling, and black threads hung off it like whiskers.

"What's that?" I asked.

"I took this from Justine's library," he said.

"You *what?*" I said. "You snatched another book from her?"

"I . . . confiscated it," he said. "This is a memoir of the witch who first created the dark wave, back in 1682."

"You're kidding."

"It talks about the Burning Times and the War Between the Clans. . . ."

"What was his name?" I broke in, glancing away from the road to look at the book's cover again.

"Whose name?"

"The name of the witch who created the dark wave." I sighed. It was a terrible, terrible legacy—the creation of a weapon of mass destruction. Ever since that time blood witches had been living in fear. Get on the wrong side of a powerful witch who practices dark magick, and you might be the next victim of the dark wave.

Daniel opened the book and frowned. "Not a he, a she. Let me see here. Her name was—" He frowned. "Rose MacEwan."

"MacEwan," I whispered.

Like Ciaran MacEwan. Morgan's father.

"She lived in a small town in Scotland," Daniel told me. "I didn't have time to read much of it, but as the book begins, she's just a teenager."

Part of Morgan's family was from Scotland. "Do you think— is it possible that she's an ancestor of Ciaran MacEwan?"

Daniel's face clouded over. He looked over at me. "It's possible. Even likely, I suppose. Same name, same country, even." He frowned. "That would make her an ancestor also to your—Mary?"

"Morgan." Dammit, he'd barely even been listening to me.

Daniel nodded. "Not surprising." I turned to him, startled— what was he trying to say?—and he continued gravely. "To be Ciaran MacEwan's daughter—it's a dark inheritance. I wouldn't trust her so easily."

Anger flared in me. Who was he to talk about trust? I had to struggle to keep myself under control. Remember what he's been through, I kept telling myself. He's been on the run from Amyranth for eleven years. Of course he would be skittish about Ciaran . . . and anyone related to Ciaran. Once Da meets Morgan, he'll be fine, I told myself. And until then, hopefully I could keep from throttling him whenever her name was mentioned.

"But I *do* trust her, Da. I have every reason to. She's proved herself to me again and again." I glanced over at him, but I found it hard to gauge his reaction. His expression hadn't changed.

"Well, that's your decision, lad." Da's gaze turned back to the book. "In any case, Justine never should have kept such an important piece of history from the council. Who knows how useful it could be in possibly defeating the dark wave? The council should see this right away."

"Indeed they should."

On the whole, I was feeling unrealistically happy and optimistic about bringing Da home to live with me and Sky, at least until he got his own place. I pictured him six months from now, healthier, heavier, able to function around other people. If I could somehow manage to make that happen, I would feel like I had finally repaid him for the fathering he had done for the first eight years of my life. Even though I'd been without him longer than with him, still, the lessons he'd instilled in me in those years had been the basis of everything I had done since then. I was glad to have a chance to help him now.

Of course, I knew he was occasionally going to drive me stark raving mad—but I would deal with that in time.

This time tomorrow I would be seeing Morgan—I hoped. I would try to call her tonight to tell her I was on my way home. I felt bad about what she had seen when she'd scried, but I also hadn't liked her scrying for me unless she'd really needed me. On the other hand, I hadn't been able to call her much at all. So I could understand how she might have been worried about me.

And I knew I had to tell her about Justine and the kiss. I still couldn't figure out why I'd done it, and I wasn't ready to think about how Morgan would react.

I sighed. I just wanted to see her tomorrow, talk, get everything straightened out, get caught up. My chest actually ached with wanting to hold her, see her eyes, taste her lips. If she had been with me, this trip would have been so different, so much more positive. I wouldn't have felt so crazed and out of control most of the time. And nothing would have happened with Justine. . . .

Which reminded me. I had to make a decision with

regard to the council. I knew that when I got home, I'd have to have a long talk with Kennet. I was becoming increasingly uncomfortable with the council's power—and their methods—and despite whatever Justine was guilty of, I felt she'd been tried and convicted in advance of the facts.

"I'll have to call Kennet when we get home," I said to Da. I wanted to include him in my life, even confide in him. Get him used to being a father again.

"Aye? Is that who you usually deal with?"

"Yes. He was my mentor when I first decided to become a Seeker."

"He's a good man," said Da. "He tried to help with Fiona before she died."

I frowned. "What?"

"Back before Yule," Da said, looking pained again. "I knew Fiona was on the brink. I tried to tell you that time I saw you scrying for us—but we got cut off. I was devastated. In desperation, I contacted the council. Kennet sent a healer to help. We tried everything we could, but in the end, she was ready to leave."

I went very still, a deep, interior stillness. My brain started firing, and I pulled the car over to the side of the highway. It was dark, almost seven, and I left my lights on.

"What's wrong?" Da asked, peering out at the car's bonnet.

"You're saying that Kennet knew where you were, back before Yule?" I asked quietly.

"Aye."

I rubbed my chin hard, thinking. My chest felt tight, and my jaw was clenched as the truth came filtering down to me. The council had learned where my parents were three months ago. Kennet had known their whereabouts for three months!

If he'd told me, I could have come up and seen my mother while she was still alive! This knowledge stunned me. I could have seen my mother alive. I could have seen her, held her.

Kennet had known, and he hadn't told me. Why?

I thought back. Yule. Morgan and I had had the final showdown with Selene Belltower and Cal Blaire. And then we had gone to New York City, had found Killian and Ciaran MacEwan.

Could that have been it? Had the council wanted to keep me in Widow's Vale to help protect Morgan? Had they decided not to tell me, rather than give me the choice of possibly seeing my mother? Had they taken that last chance away from me?

It seemed so, I thought, swallowing hard.

If I was right, the council had treated me like a child, or a pawn. I had been manipulated, betrayed. How could they have decided my fate like that? Who were they to make that kind of decision?

Shaking, I pulled the car back onto the narrow highway. Inside, I felt as if my heart had shriveled up into a charred piece of coal. Why was I working for the council? Once I had absolutely believed in them. Did I now? I didn't know anymore. I didn't know anything. All I knew how to be was a Seeker. If I wasn't a Seeker, what would I do?

"Everything all right, son?" asked Da.

"Yes," I murmured softly.

But I was lying. Nothing was all right, nothing at all. I wondered whether anything would ever be all right again.

Book Eleven

SWEEP
Origins

Origins

SPEAK

Published by the Penguin Group
Penguin Group (USA) Inc., 345 Hudson Street, New York, New York 10014, U.S.A.
Penguin Group (Canada), 90 Eglinton Avenue East, Suite 700, Toronto, Ontario, Canada M4P 2Y3
(a division of Pearson Penguin Canada Inc.)
Penguin Books Ltd, 80 Strand, London WC2R 0RL, England
Penguin Ireland, 25 St Stephen's Green, Dublin 2, Ireland (a division of Penguin Books Ltd)
Penguin Group (Australia), 250 Camberwell Road, Camberwell, Victoria 3124, Australia
(a division of Pearson Australia Group Pty Ltd)
Penguin Books India Pvt Ltd, 11 Community Centre, Panchsheel Park, New Delhi - 110 017, India
Penguin Group (NZ), 67 Apollo Drive, Rosedale, Auckland 0632, New Zealand
(a division of Pearson New Zealand Ltd)
Penguin Books (South Africa) (Pty) Ltd, 24 Sturdee Avenue, Rosebank, Johannesburg 2196, South Africa

Registered Offices: Penguin Books Ltd, 80 Strand, London WC2R 0RL, England

Published by Puffin Books, a division of Penguin Young Readers Group, 2002
Published by Speak, an imprint of Penguin Group (USA) Inc., 2008
This omnibus edition published by Speak, an imprint of Penguin Group (USA) Inc., 2011

1 3 5 7 9 10 8 6 4 2

Copyright © 2002 17th Street Productions, an Alloy company
All rights reserved

Produced by 17th Street Productions,
an Alloy company
151 West 26th Street
New York, NY 10001

17th Street Productions and associated logos
are trademarks and/or registered trademarks of Alloy, Inc.

Speak ISBN 978-0-14-241026-4
This omnibus ISBN 978-0-14-242010-2

Printed in the United States of America

Prologue

"Hey, Morgan!"

Afternoon sunlight bounced off the cars in the high school parking lot as I turned to face my best friend, Bree Warren. I knew that she was eager to catch up with me—I'd been kind of cranky and out of sorts all week—but at the moment I was in a huge hurry. I leaned against the driver's side of my huge '71 Plymouth Valiant, which I'd nicknamed "Das Boot."

"What's up, Bree?"

Bree ran up and stopped a few feet away from me, gasping for breath. "I just wanted to sort of check in, see how you were doing today."

I nodded. "Well, I heard from Hunter last night. I'm supposed to go to his house now."

Her eyes widened in comprehension. "*Oh.* So Hunter's back."

"Apparently so." Hunter Niall, my boyfriend of two months—was it possible it had been only that long? I couldn't imagine life without him. I loved him with all my heart and soul and was fairly certain that he was my *mùirn* beatha dàn, my soul mate. He had left a little over two weeks ago to find his parents.

"Are you nervous?" Bree looked at me sympathetically.

"A little." I sighed. All the time Hunter had been gone, we'd had only one conversation. Worried, I had scried for him and found him with another woman. Not kissing or anything romantic—thank the Goddess for that—but locked in a passionate conversation. I wasn't sure what to make of the whole thing. I was afraid to think too hard about it.

"I'm sure it'll be okay," she said confidently. "Hunter loves you, Morgan. You can see it in his eyes when he looks at you. You have nothing to worry about."

I looked up at Bree, feeling a little comforted. "Thanks. I just love him so much. . . . Well, you know how I feel."

She nodded. "I don't want to keep you, then." She smoothed down a lock of shiny dark hair and gave me a concerned frown. "Listen, I hope everything's okay. I know you've been worried. Let me know if you need to talk, all right?"

"All right." I smiled. It seemed like Bree had gotten even more beautiful, more caring, more empathetic since she had fallen in love with my other best friend, Robbie Gurevitch. Not that she'd been totally selfish before—she just seemed warmer now, more open.

"See you tomorrow."

"'Bye."

Bree headed back toward the school and Robbie, and I climbed into Das Boot and swung out of the parking lot. It was mid-March, and the sidewalks were still covered with glistening, melting snow. I tried to calm my nerves as I drove toward Hunter's rented house on the other side of town. But the truth was, I was very afraid. Afraid of what Hunter would tell me. Afraid that I wouldn't want to hear it.

After I arrived, I sat in Hunter's driveway for a few minutes with the car running, trying to collect my thoughts. On the one hand, this was Hunter. Hunter, whom I loved and had missed terribly—I couldn't wait to see him. But on the other hand, what if he had found something new and wonderful in Canada? What if that was why he hadn't called me? What if he had been afraid to tell me something hurtful over the phone?

Sighing, I pulled the key from the ignition and smoothed my worn cords. I ran a quick hand through my long brown hair and decided that taming it was a lost cause. Taking a deep breath, I climbed out of Das Boot and headed for the door. I reached out my hand to ring the doorbell, but before I could get there, the door opened.

"Morgan."

"Hunter." As soon as I saw Hunter's face—serious, loving—my fears and anger faded away. I wrapped my arms around him, buried my face in the crook of his neck, and breathed in his warm, familiar scent.

"I missed you," I murmured into his collar. "I was so worried."

"I know, love." I could feel Hunter's hand rubbing my back, his other hand reaching up to stroke my hair. "I missed you, too. I wanted you there with me every moment."

"*Every* moment?" I asked, unable to prevent myself from picturing him arguing with the woman from my vision.

"Every moment." Hunter leaned back and looked at me, then turned and gestured to his living room. "Sit down for a moment and let me get you some tea. There's lots to talk about."

I nodded, pulling off my coat and looking around. "Where's your father?" Our phone conversation the night before had been very brief, largely due to the fact that it was after midnight and my mother was standing beside me in the hallway with steam coming out of her ears because he'd called so late. All I had learned from Hunter was that he had found his dad, who was in poor health, and that he had convinced him to come back with him to Widow's Vale. His mother, unfortunately, had died three months earlier, around Yule. Hunter hadn't said as much, but I could sense his frustration at not finding her in time and his grief over losing the mother he'd had so little time with.

"He's asleep," Hunter called, heading for the kitchen. "He's been sleeping almost nonstop since we left his cottage. I'm hoping that all the rest will be good for him. He certainly needs it."

I settled on the sofa, and after a few minutes Hunter joined me, holding two cups of chamomile tea. "For you," he said, handing a cup to me and sitting down. "I think we could both use some soothing after the past couple of weeks."

I sipped my tea, closed my eyes, and tried to let all of my fears, all of my insecurities and anger run out of me. "Hunter," I said finally, feeling more calm, "tell me what happened in Canada."

Hunter's jaw tightened almost imperceptibly, and I saw a darkness pass over his eyes. "It was . . . difficult." He paused and sipped his tea. "I feel like I've been tested in ways I never could have predicted or imagined. My mum is dead." He looked at me briefly, and I nodded slowly. "She and my da had been on the run from the dark wave for all those years—eleven years." He sighed. "It was Selene, you know. Selene Belltower sent the dark wave after them because she couldn't forgive my da for leaving her and Cal."

I gasped. Selene Belltower and her son, Cal, had first introduced me to the world of Wicca. It was Cal who told me I was a blood witch. I'd then realized that I was adopted, that I was the biological daughter of Maeve Riordan and Ciaran MacEwan—two very powerful, and very different, witches. I had thought that Cal was my true love, my *mùirn beatha dàn*, but it turned out that he was a pawn of his mother, who wanted to harness my power for her own dark uses. And I'd learned that before Hunter was born, his father had loved and married Selene, making Cal Hunter's half brother. Both Cal and Selene were dead now—Selene had died trying to steal my power, and in the end Cal had died trying to save me.

"It was Selene?" I asked finally, and Hunter nodded.

"My mum scried for the dark wave in Mexico, and she got too close. She was never the same after that, and she died last December. After that my da moved to a tiny village in French Canada. He was living in filth, like a madman. I found out he was acting as a sort of medicine man to the local population, selling his services as a witch, which was bad enough. But I soon realized that he was also doing something much worse—he was contacting the villagers' dead loved ones through a *bith dearc* and receiving payment for it."

I looked at Hunter in disbelief. "Contacting the dead? I didn't think that was possible."

Hunter nodded again. "It is. A *bith dearc* is an opening into the shadow world where spirits reside after they die. It doesn't naturally occur very often, and it's very rarely used by 'good' witches—only when it's imperative to get information. My father began using the *bith dearc* to try to contact my mother. He's utterly lost without her." Hunter's mouth twisted into a strange expression—he looked angry, sad, and understanding of his father's devotion all at the same time.

"Wow," I said softly. "How horrible for your dad. How horrible for *you.*" I touched his arm, and he looked up at me gratefully.

"Anyway," he continued, "while I was there, he succeeded in contacting my mum. So I got to say good-bye to her, which was—priceless. But a *bith dearc* saps a living witch's strength, and my da was fading every day. I had to get him away from that village before he killed himself. The council gave me an assignment in a town three hours away, and I took him with me. While we were there, he agreed to come here to live with me for a while." Hunter turned to me and smiled and shrugged, as if to say, "The end."

"That's not everything, though," I challenged. "There was a woman. I saw you with her. I know you felt me scrying for you."

Hunter's smile faded, and he nodded. "Justine," he said quietly. "Justine Courceau. She was my assignment from the council."

Hunter was a Seeker for the International Council of Witches, which meant that he investigated witches suspected of using dark magick. "What was she doing?" I asked.

Hunter sighed. "She's a kind of . . . rogue. She's the only witch in her small town, and she believes that knowledge is pure—any knowledge. She was collecting true names . . . of people." My eyes went wide. That was a major Wiccan no-no. "I was sent there to stop her and destroy her list."

"Did you?" I asked, remembering the emotion on Hunter's face when I had scried for him.

"Yes." Hunter frowned, and his voice grew softer. "Justine was very passionate about what she believed in. When you saw us, we were arguing about whether the list was inherently bad. I was under a lot of stress, and she was very . . . persistent."

I stared at him, dreading his next words.

"I kissed her," Hunter continued, and my heart plunged. "I knew as soon as I did it that it was a mistake. I was lonely and . . . sad. I missed you. I wanted you." Hunter groaned softly. I turned away. I felt like I had been kicked in the stomach. I couldn't look at him right now.

"How does kissing another woman . . . mean that you want to spend time with *me?*" I stared at the wall. I couldn't imagine wanting to kiss anyone else, anyone but Hunter, for any reason. I struggled to get it all to make sense, but I just couldn't.

I could hear Hunter's sigh. "I don't know, Morgan, and I'm sorry. So sorry. If there was some way that I could undo it, I would."

I shook my head. "But you can't."

"I know." I felt Hunter's fingers touch my back, but I scooted away. "Morgan, I don't know what to say, how to explain it all to you. I love you very much. You're my *mùirn beatha dàn*, and I know that."

I let out a ragged breath, like I was about to cry. Dammit—no! I took a deep lungful of air, not wanting to fall apart in front of Hunter. I wanted to hear what he had to say about this. I wanted to act like an adult.

Hunter went on. "The whole drive home, you were all I could think about. If you want to know why in that moment I kissed Justine, I can scarcely figure it out myself. It happened quickly. I felt like everything in my life was going the wrong way. My job with the council, my father—"

"—and me," I finished for him. "Because I scried for you. Without asking. And before you left—" My voice caught again. Before Hunter left, we had been planning to make love. But at the last minute Hunter had backed out. He'd said he didn't want to love me and leave me—he wanted to be there for me, my first time, on the morning after. I had felt ridiculous then, and I felt even more so now.

Hunter put his hand on my shoulder, and this time I was too busy trying not to cry to pull away. "Morgan, this has nothing to do with what happened before I left. I love you, and of course I want to make love with you—it just wasn't the right time. You know that. I was startled when you scried for me, and everything else was going wrong. I suppose I was angry. I was wrong, and I'm sorry. Justine means nothing to me. It's you I love."

Sniffling, I tried to calm myself down. I reached for my tea and took a sip, then sighed and slowly turned my body to face Hunter. "I know you do," I whispered. "It just . . . hurts. And I still don't understand."

Hunter frowned, leaning forward to brush my hair out of my eyes. "Maybe I can't make you understand," he said softly. "I can only say again that I love you, and I'm so sorry for hurting you."

I looked up into Hunter's eyes—they were warm, filled with concern and love. But I still hurt. "Maybe," I said softly. "I can't say I forgive you yet. You'll have to give me some time."

Hunter nodded, and I could see sadness welling up in his eyes. "Morgan, I can't say I'm sorry enough."

I looked down at my tea, cradling the cup in my hands. I didn't say anything. I didn't know what to say anymore.

Hunter sat back in the sofa. "Morgan, there's more news—if you want to hear it."

I turned the teacup in my hand, feeling utterly overwhelmed. "What next?" I asked sarcastically. I was dreading his next revelation. Everything up to this point had been awful.

"First," he said after a moment, "the council. Morgan, the council had been in contact with my parents months ago—back when my mother was sick, before she died. They knew where my parents were and didn't tell me."

I turned to look at him. "What? How do you know? Are you sure?"

Hunter nodded. "My da told me. He thought I already knew. My mentor, Kennet—he sent a healer for my mum back in December."

I frowned. "So—"

"So they betrayed me. They probably wanted me here, to protect you. And I don't regret that—truly, I don't regret that at all. But they didn't give me the choice. They let me believe that my parents were still missing."

I stared at him, at the hurt in his face. I could see how this would affect him. He had missed seeing his mother alive because he'd had to stay here and protect *me.* Hunter had placed all of his trust in the council since he had become their youngest Seeker a year ago, and this was how they treated him. "What are you going to do?"

Hunter shook his head. "I don't know."

I slowly put my cup down. "Was there something else?" I asked shortly, dreading the answer.

Hunter nodded, looking stung. I knew he wanted forgiveness, but I wasn't ready to give him that. "Stay here for a moment," he said as he slid off the couch and went upstairs to his bedroom. In a few seconds he thumped back down the stairs, holding an ancient-looking book under his arm.

"What's that?"

Hunter came closer and held it out to me. "This is very interesting. It's a record of sorts. My father found it in Justine's library."

I shuddered at hearing her name again, but I composed myself and took the book from him carefully, so that I didn't have to touch his hands. I ran my hands over the cover, which was made of torn and faded leather. Opening it, I could see that the pages were handwritten. "A Book of Shadows?"

"Not a Book of Shadows, exactly." Hunter flipped the pages back to the beginning, where a handwritten title page read, *A Book of Spelles and Memories, by Rose MacEwan.* "It's more like a memoir."

"Rose MacEwan," I whispered. "Do you think . . . ?"

Hunter nodded gravely. "She lived in Scotland during the Burning Times. It's very likely that she was an ancestor of yours. This book could be invaluable for what it can tell us about the dark wave spell and how it came into being. My da's read most of it, but I haven't looked at it at all." He closed the cover of the book and looked up at me hopefully. "Would you like to read it with me, Morgan?"

I looked into Hunter's clear green eyes. I could see his love for me, pure and unbending, along with the pain he'd suffered and his hope for the future. My heart still ached with the knowledge of what he'd done, but I hoped that we'd be okay . . . eventually. I turned my attention to the book. When I ran my hand again over the worn embossed cover, I felt a rush of energy. My ancestor. I knew it.

"Yes," I said finally. "Let's read it."

1

Scotland, April 1682

The rose stone.

It glimmered brightly in my palm, catching the few rays of light allowed in by the drab portals of the church. The reverend mumbled on, glorifying the Christian God. My thoughts were far from the church altar as I considered the spell I would cast over this precious gem.

Beside me, my mother lifted her head from pretending to pray. I closed my fist suddenly, not wanting her to see the stone that I'd borrowed from her cupboard of magickal things. The crystal, with its soft, pink hue, was known to evoke peaceful, loving feelings. It was a wonder to me that I shared the same name as the stone—Rose—yet I had never come close to falling in love. Ma raised her brows, chastising me without words, and I dropped the stone back into my pocket and clasped my hands the way the Presbyterians did.

Would Ma mind that I had borrowed the stone for Kyra? I wondered. Ever since my initiation my mother had encouraged me to work on my own magick, practice my own spells and rituals. But somehow I didn't think she would appreciate that one of my first attempts would be to cast a love spell for my best friend. My mother had warned me against using spells that tamper with a person's free will, but a love spell was for the good, I thought. Besides, Falkner had been oblivious to Kyra for so long, and I knew she was getting desperate.

A few rows ahead Kyra turned to me, her mouth twitching slightly before she turned back to the front of the church. I knew what she was thinking. That church was tedious. Nothing like our beautiful circles in the woods, gatherings lit by candles, sometimes festooned by ribbons, blessed with the magickal presence of the Goddess. Not that I had any quarrel with the Christian God. Time and again Ma had reminded me that they were all the same—God or Goddess, it was one force we worshipped, albeit different forms. The problem was the ministers, who could not open their minds to accept our homage and devotion to the Goddess. Consequently the king's men and the Christians were ever crossing over the countryside in a mad witch-hunt that brought about dire results.

Makeshift trials. Hangings. Witches burned at the stake.

And so every week my mother and I knelt in this church, our heads bowed, our hands folded. We pretended to practice Presbyterianism so that we might avoid the fate suffered by other members of the Seven Clans who had been persecuted for practicing magick, for worshiping the Goddess. The puritanical wave that had been moving through Scotland

had claimed many a life. The toll across the land was frightening, with tales of so many witches persecuted, most of
them women.

Just last year a woman from our own coven, a gentle wisp
of a lass named Fionnula, had been found killing a peahen
with a bolline marked with runes. Those of us who knew her
understood that the hen was not intended as an offering to
the Goddess but as a very necessary meal. Still, the townspeople could not see beyond the fact of the strange markings
on the small knife she used to kill the bird. Fionnula had been
charged with sacrifice and worshipping the devil.

I lifted my eyes to the altar, staring at the robed back of
the murmuring reverend who had been so instrumental in
Fionnula's fate. At her trial Reverend Winthrop had testified
that the young woman missed his sermon every week, defying the Christian God. He had called her a vassal of Satan.

I clenched my hands, recalling the horrified look in
Fionnula's eyes as she was sentenced to death. Christians
had come from nearby villages to witness the trial—a
ghastly spectacle in these parts—and although every
Wodebayne had wanted to save her, no one spoke in her
defense. 'Twas far too dangerous.

The following day she was hanged as a witch.

Sometimes when I catch suspicious gestures of the
townspeople—a curious stare or a whispered comment—I
can't help but recall the fear in Fionnula's dark eyes. Her
execution brought a new veil of secrecy to our circles. More
rules passed down by my mother, who was sometimes a bit
overbearing in her role as high priestess. Ma wanted me to
see less of my friend Meara, a kind girl who loved to laugh

but was born into a staid Presbyterian family. Everyone in the coven had been warned to take great care in all their associations, whether it be trading baked goods for mutton or simply washing garments in the brook. No one outside our all-Wodebayne coven was to be trusted.

Tools were to be well hidden and guarded by spells that made them unnoticeable. Skyclad circles were no longer safe, and when we gathered for an Esbat or a sabbat circle, coveners went into the woods in small groups of two. We were so afraid of being caught that we tried not to be seen gathering together at market or in the village—nothing beyond a cordial greeting. And now every member of the coven attended church every Sunday.

We were prisoners in our own village. By night we practiced our craft in secret. By day we played at being just like the rest of the townspeople.

The injustice of it fired up a fury within me. That my mother—Síle, high priestess of our coven—should have to kneel amid their wooden pews . . . It was a travesty, to be sure. Just one of the heavy burdens upon my shoulders, making me feel like a trapped animal in a dark sack that was closing in around me. There were so many rules governing my world. I had to hide the fact that I was a blood witch from the townsfolk. I had to avoid contact with other clans, whose members considered themselves our rivals although we were all witches and worshipped the same Goddess. (This was a tedious war, I felt, but I had been told the rivalry among the Seven Clans had worn on through many generations.) I had to make entries into my Book of Shadows, gather and dry herbs, learn to make healing tonics and candles, bless and inscribe my own tools. . . .

Aye, the life of Rose MacEwan was filled with constraints. Was it any wonder that I felt suffocated by them?

When I thought of what would make me happy, the answer was not forthcoming. I wasn't quite sure of my own heart's desire; however, I knew that my destiny was not to spend the rest of my life concocting spells and practicing witchcraft secretly in this remote, provincial village.

At last the prayers ended and townsfolk began to file out of the church. I waded into the aisle, hoping to catch Kyra before her parents whisked her back to their cottage. Kyra was my lifelong friend, a member of my clan and coven, though she was not as adept at casting spells as I was said to be.

Wouldn't she be surprised to see what I'd brought for her? I reached into the pocket of my skirts and closed my hand around the small gem. My fingertips felt warmed by the stone. I planned to give it to Kyra to help her attract Falkner Radburn, a boy from our own Wodebayne coven. Falkner was all Kyra had spoken of since the children jumped the broomstick at Samhain. All winter long I had heard of Falkner's strength and Falkner's eyes. Falkner this and Falkner that. Bad enough that poor Kyra was captivated by him, but to make matters worse, Falkner was unaware of her love.

I had agreed to help my friend, though I didn't really understand why she favored him. Then again, I had never known any attraction like that. In my eyes boys were silly galloping creatures, and men had nothing to do with me. They seemed to me like the wolves who roamed at night, pouncing on their prey without warning. I was a Wodebayne of seventeen years, initiated into the ways of the Goddess at fourteen, and as most girls my age were already betrothed or wed, I had come to the conclusion that I would never meet a man who caught my fancy. Since it hadn't happened as yet, I felt that the Goddess didn't intend it to be.

Outside the church, Ma greeted the Presbyterian villagers cordially. I kept my head bowed, not wanting to meet their eyes or see the cruel faces that had so quickly sentenced Fionnula to death. Some time had passed since her trial, yet I could not forgive these people for their crime. I would never forgive them.

"Good day to you, Rose," said a familiar voice.

I turned to see Meara, her freckled face wrought with shadows. "Meara, I didn't see you inside."

"Da and I were late getting in. Ma was up all night with the pains, but she's back resting again. Da said we should come to church and pray to Christ Jesus for her recovery."

Meara's mother had not truly recovered from the birth of her sixth child a few months earlier, and as the oldest daughter, the burden of taking over her ma's responsibilities fell on Meara's shoulders. I felt sorry for her, having to tidy up the cottage, mind the young bairns, and cook enough porridge for the whole brood of them.

"Who's caring for the children, then?" I asked her.

"Ma's sister, Linette, has come from the south to help for a while." Her eyes were hollow, and I wasn't sure if it was simply tiredness or fear over what might happen to her mother. Ma had visited Meara's mother once, hoping to help. She told me they'd talked awhile and she had tried to raise the woman's spirits, but 'twas all Ma could do. She didn't dare pass on healing herbs or place her hands on the ailing woman's worn belly to perform a spell. And that was the shame of it; Ma had the power to perhaps cure Meara's mother, but since that very act could get Ma hanged as a witch, it would not be done.

"I haven't seen you down by the brook lately," Meara told me. "Do you not draw water for washing?"

"Ma sends me later now," I said awkwardly. "She says the morning chill is too much." It was a lie, and I hated telling it to Meara, who had always been a good friend. But the truth was, Ma had told me to find a different place to draw water so that I wouldn't meet Meara every morning. "It's too dangerous, the two of you talking with such ease," Ma had told me. "One of these days you're liable to slip and speak the Goddess's name or mention the coming Esbat, and that sort of breach I cannot allow."

Meara's father summoned her from the edge of the crowd.

"I'd better go," Meara said reluctantly. "Godspeed."

I nodded, wondering what would happen to my friend if her ma passed. Already Meara was acting as mother to the large family. My own father had died when I was but five years of age, and though I often wished for the protection a father could offer, I remembered so little of him. Losing a mother had to be worse.

"Tell your ma . . ." I wanted to espouse an herbal tea that would help her mother feel better, but I knew it was too dangerous. I sighed. "Tell your ma I will pray for her."

Meara nodded, then went off with her da.

Ma was speaking with Mrs. MacTavish, an elderly woman from our coven who'd been suffering from a hacking cough. As she spoke, I slipped away from Ma's side to find Kyra.

Gently I took my friend's arm and led her away from her ma and da. Feeling whimsical, I touched the stone in my pocket. "I have something for you," I said quietly. "Something to attract your certain someone."

She stared at me, uncomprehending.

I glanced around to make sure that none of the villagers were paying us any mind. Folks were engaged in the usual chatter, complaints of the long winter and worries over the spring planting. I turned back to Kyra. "Can you guess what's in my pocket?" When she shook her head, I whispered in her ear, "I've brought an amulet for you to attract Falkner."

Her cheeks grew pink at my words, and I wanted to laugh aloud. Kyra was so easy to embarrass. She took my hand and pulled me off the stone path, away from the churchgoers. "Would you have everyone in the Highlands hear of my secret love?"

"Harmless words," I said, adding in a whisper, "though I dare not show you the magickal gem before everyone in the village." The sun was still rising in the sky, promising a warm spring morning. Only days before, the last of the snow had melted from the ground. "Come with me to the woods," I said. "I need to collect herbs. We'll do the gathering ritual together, and afterward we'll charge the rose stone."

"Oh, I wish I could, but I promised Ma I would help with the baking." Kyra pressed a hand over her heart. "Are you sure the stone holds power?"

"Ma used to let me hold it whenever we quarreled. It's powerful enough."

Turning slightly, Kyra glanced toward the crowd still spilling out of the church. I knew she was looking for Falkner, a beanpole of a boy who had yet to show any signs of intelligence in my presence. "Nothing seems to work on him," she said wistfully. "He can't even spare me a glance. It's as if I'm just a passing dragonfly, hardly worthy of notice."

I pressed my lips together, wishing that Kyra wouldn't go into it again. It was precisely the reason I had borrowed the rose stone from Ma's cupboard: to put an end to my friend's pining and suffering. "Come to the woods with me, then," I said.

"Kyra!" her mother called. Her parents were ready to leave.

She nodded at her ma respectfully, then tilted her head. "I cannot go," she told me regretfully. One chestnut braid slipped over her sapphire cloak. "But I do want the stone. Can you leave it on my doorstep? In a basket by the woodpile?"

"I dare not. It's too precious a thing to leave out."

"Rose . . ."

"Maybe tomorrow. Stop by our cottage on your way to market," I told her, wishing that Kyra could just once summon the courage to sneak away from her parents. She was my friend, but in every situation I was the bolder. While I dreamed of travel to distant places, of exploring and celebrating all corners of the Goddess's earth, Kyra was content to remain in her small world.

I went off to join my mother, who was getting an earful of unhappiness from Ian MacGreavy and his wife. Once we were out of earshot of the village, I told Ma of the failing health of Meara's mother.

"I fear she is not long with us." Ma shook her head. "'Tis a pity the Christians don't accept the Goddess's healing. I would like to help her."

A feeling of melancholy washed over me. "Poor Meara.

She's already feeling the burden of so many chores to keep the children fed and clean."

"She shall forge ahead," Ma said stoutly.

I wondered if that had been Ma's attitude when my own father, Gowan MacEwan, had died. It made me sad that I barely remembered him, and whenever I asked about him, Ma went cold as the brook in winter. "Do you still miss Da?" I asked suddenly.

Ma sucked in a deep breath of crisp spring morning. "I will always love him. But 'tis not a fit subject to discourse upon, especially when we have pressing matters at hand. The MacGreavys are in a tumult."

"Has the miller asked about dark magick again?" I asked, recalling how he had recently suggested calling on a *taibhs*, a dark spirit, to wreak vengeance against a Burnhyde man who had crossed him.

"As if we don't have enough trouble with the townspeople always on the lookout for witches," Ma said as we tramped down the rutted road to our cottage. "The tension among the Seven Clans is heating up again. Ian MacGreavy is outraged over a snub by a few men of the Burnhyde clan. Seems they won't use his mill, and they're telling all the others in their clan to avoid it, that it's cursed and the evil is spilling into the grain."

The unfairness of it irked me. "If the mill is cursed, it's because of a spell from one of them."

"Indeed. Mrs. MacGreavy found a sprinkling of soil and ashes on the threshold of the mill one morning, swirled in a circle."

"A spell wrought of minerals and soil . . ." Everyone knew that the Burnhyde witches were masters of spells involving crystals and minerals. "A sure sign that the Burnhydes are behind all their trouble."

"Aye, and trouble is rising for the MacGreavys. They fear the mill has been infested by rats." She pressed her lips together, and I could see from the bluish vein in her forehead that Ma was angry. "It's dark magick the Burnhydes are playing with."

"I can't believe it," I said, kicking at a dirt clod in the road. "This isn't about Ian MacGreavy's mill at all. It's about the other clans turning against the Wodebaynes again."

For as long as the Seven Great Clans had existed, there had been strong rivalry among them. Everyone knew of the clans and their distinctions: the healing Braytindales, the master spellcrafters of the Wyndonkylles, the Burnhydes with their expertise in the use of crystals and metals. I had heard of the astute Ruanwandes, who were well schooled in all of the ways of the Goddess, though I had never met anyone from that clan. We knew of trickster Leapvaughns in neighboring villages, and everyone dreaded the war-loving Vykrothes, who were rumored to kick dirt in your face while passing you on the road. Aye, the clans had their reputations, the most slanderous being that of our own clan. For decades the other six clans had looked down upon our Wodebayne clan, their prejudice and hatred stinging like a wound that refused to heal.

Their hatred was prompted by a notion that Wodebaynes practiced dark magick. When a witch tried to harness the Goddess's power for evil purposes—to harm a living thing or to tamper with a person's free will—it was called dark magick. Other clans seemed to think that we Wodebaynes were expert at this black evil. They liked to blame their hardships on our "dark spells," and consequently they had grown to hate all Wodebaynes.

And now, as a result of that hatred, our own village mill was to be overrun by rats. "Can we help the MacGreavys to thwart the spell?"

Ma nodded. "The Burnhyde spell doesn't scare me, but their hatred of the Wodebaynes frightens me deep down in my bones."

Her worry spurred my anger. "Yet again we're back to the same hatred of the Wodebaynes. What did we do to bring on such animosity? Can you tell me that?"

"Easy, Rose."

"They act as if we were marauders and murderers! It's unfair!"

"Aye, it is," Ma said quietly. "But I have always said that the other clans will come to know us through our acts of goodness. The Goddess will reveal the true nature of the Wodebaynes in time."

"That doesn't help Ian MacGreavy, does it?" I asked.

"We will place a spell of protection around the mill," Ma said. "We'll do it tomorrow, on the full moon, the perfect time to cast a spell of protection. You'll need to collect sharp objects—old spearheads, broken darning needles—whatever you can find. They are to be stored in a jar, which we'll take to the mill."

As Ma went over the details of the spell of protection, I felt myself drifting off into an ocean of sorrow. My pitifully small world was growing smaller. With conflict among the clans heating up, we would be forced to become even more closed and guarded than we already were. Members of our coven would stick close to our hopelessly small country village, a tight knot of cottages that was already like a noose around my neck. Beyond my sweet but unadventurous friend Kyra, I was without a friend or possible mate within my own clan. No one outside the Wodebayne clan could be trusted, and any notions I'd ever had of exploration were squashed by the sure and steady evil lurking in new places.

Seventeen years of age, and already my life seemed to be over.

By now we had passed out of the village, which consisted mostly of the church, the mill, the inn, and a tangle of cottages that were built far too close to keep your business private. We came upon a flat, grassy field that was used by one of our own Wodebayne clansmen for herding his sheep, and indeed, two men were there at the edge of the field, talking to a sheep as if it had the sense in its head to understand and heed them.

The scene made me smile. The two men looked like bumblers, but Ma sucked in her breath, as if she'd just come upon a tragedy.

"What is it, Ma?" I asked.

She stopped walking, her hands crossed over her chest as she stared at the men, still not speaking.

"Aye, they could be punished," I observed. "Out on a Sunday, when work is to be set aside to praise the Christian Lord."

"If only they *would* meet with punishment," Ma said. "For thievery."

"What?" I ran ahead, then turned back to her to ask, "Who are they, Ma?"

"Vykrothe men," she said, reaching for my arm and holding it tightly.

Now that she said it, I could feel it. A blood witch can always sense other blood witches, and their presence was now palpable as a bracing cold wind. "Wait . . ." I said. "And now the Vykrothe men are stealing our Wodebayne sheep?" A sheep that would provide wool for spinning blankets and cloaks. A sheep whose slaughter would provide mutton to an entire family through many seasons. I tried to pull away from her. "We must stop them!"

She pulled me off the side of the road, behind the cover of a haystack. "Hush, child. Speak not your mind on this—the danger is too grave. We know not how strong their magick is, and they look much stronger than us physically."

"But—"

"I'll try to stop them." She lifted one hand, drawing a long circle around her body and then around mine. I couldn't hear the words she murmured, but I realized she was putting a cloaking spell upon us so that the Vykrothe men would not know we were blood witches.

Then Ma clasped her fingers through mine, locking me into place by her side as we stepped out of the shadow of the haystack and pressed ahead. I felt her fear, though I wasn't sure if she was frightened of the men or of my own desire to blast them. I pressed my lips together, determined to defer to my strong, noble mother on this.

"Good day to you, sirs," my mother called out to them.

They lifted their heads, mired in suspicion. "Good day," the taller man answered. His hooded eyes seemed sleepy, and he wore his flaxen hair pressed to his skull like a helmet.

"Did the sheep break loose?" Ma asked lightly. "They so often do, and I recognize that one as belonging to Thomas Draloose, who lives in the cottage just beyond the spring. I'll tell him of your act of kindness, returning his lost sheep to its pasture on this fine Sunday."

Act of kindness? I pressed Ma's arm, irked by the way she was coddling these tubs of lard.

But Ma went on. "It's noble of you, gentle sirs, taking the time, and—"

"This sheep is not returning to pasture, but departing," the tall Vykrothe said. "'Tis an evil beast, a harbinger of dark spirits. I know for true that this sheepherder you speak of is not a Christian man but a practitioner of witchcraft."

"You must be mistaken, sir!" Ma cried out.

"'Tis not a mistake at all," the shorter man insisted. He was a bull of a man, with so much flesh on his large bones, he could easily ram through a castle door. "This man is evil, a ghastly witch." He fixed his eyes on us menacingly. "Do you know him well?"

"Aye, I do," Ma answered boldly, "and I must proclaim his innocence of such ungodly pursuits."

The taller Vykrothe yanked on the rope. "Proclaim what you will. We must remove this sheep before it turns into a demon."

Ma shook her head and gave a fake laugh. "A mere sheep, sir? It is but an animal. One of the Lord's creatures, is it not?"

I gave Ma's hand a squeeze. The man could hardly argue with Christian philosophy.

The tall Vykrothe leaned closer, and his unpleasant smell of sweat, dung, and sour cheese rankled the air. "This sheep is possessed. I have seen it bleat at the moon, its eyes red with Satan's fires."

"Aye," Ma countered, "and what reason have you to be lurking in a stranger's fields at night?"

The tall man leaned back, but the bull answered, "And I've heard rumor that the herder is planning to spill its blood in a dreadful spell of harm and destruction." He turned to his friend, dropped his voice to a whisper, and added, "Just like those Wodebaynes."

I felt my fists clenching at the muttered slander. He had thought we would not hear or understand his strike against our clan and likely didn't care that we did since he thought us to be Christian women. But I had heard, and my blood boiled at the insult. These men weren't even common sheep thieves—they were bigots, striking out against one of our own.

"This, sir, I must dispute," my mother said. She sounded so sincere, so earnest. How could these men refuse to believe her? "Do you imply that all Wodebaynes are evil?"

When Ma spoke the word, the bullish man took two steps back. "What Christian woman knows so much of evil?" the man accused.

"How dare you speak to her that way!" I shouted. My fingers twitched with the urge to shoot *dealan-dé* at him and burn him with its flinty blue sparks. But Ma was already pulling me down the road, her other arm having slid protectively around my waist.

"Make haste," she whispered in my ear, "lest they raise their ire toward us. The Vykrothes are known to love war, and raise arms they will."

"But the sheep . . ." I gasped. "They're stealing it . . . and even talking of witchcraft could get Thomas Draloose and his family hanged."

"Hush, child." Ma hurried me along, pressing her head down against mine. "We must choose our battles. I did my best to defend Thomas and save the sheep, but we cannot always win against such cruelty."

"It's unfair," I said, feeling tears sting my eyes. "Why do they hate the Wodebaynes so?"

"I cannot say, child," Ma whispered. "I cannot say."

2

Gathering and Sanctifying Spring Herbs

That afternoon I collected my gathering basket, retrieved my bolline from its hiding place in the seat of one of our wooden chairs, and set off to collect the newest herbs of spring. I knew many small trails through the woods, tiny lanes and hidden paths that led to my favorite gathering places.

A few years ago, when I was around the age of ten, Ma had agreed to let me gather the first herbs on my own. Since then it had been a ritual I performed gladly, grateful for the peace of mind it offered and for the thread of power that laced itself up from the plants through my fingertips. Aye, the feeling of power was sweet when it came my way, though it didn't happen to me often enough in the coven circle.

Sometimes I worried that I had fallen in the shadow of my mother, that somehow Ma was interceding and collecting my blessings until she thought I was ready to deal directly with the Goddess. An odd belief, I know, but I had my reasons. For one, Ma had never given me a significant role at sabbats. And she constantly questioned me when I returned from the woods, having performed a spell or consecration in a solitary circle. She said it was her duty to educate me in the ways of the Goddess, but I sensed that she didn't trust me. And why was that? When I was on my own, I felt a strong connection to the Goddess, and I had always quested to grow in my craft. Why, then, did my own mother question my devotion?

"She's just your ma, doing what mothers do," Kyra always told me. Perhaps she was right. Perhaps Ma didn't realize how difficult it was to be the daughter of a high priestess.

Birds chirped in the woods as I swung my basket gently. I'd spent many a winter's eve sewing pouches of sapphire blue, ruby red, and saffron cloth in preparation for this day. A different pouch for each herb, enough to replenish our supplies. Of course, back at the cottage the herbs would need to be dried in the rafters and eventually ground, but this was my favorite part of the ritual—gathering under the crown of trees and the canopy of blue sky.

I followed the path until I came to my solitary circle, a small natural clearing with a large gray stone that I'd cleansed for use as an altar. Beside a tall oak was my broom, modestly constructed of twigs and a long stick I'd rubbed smooth with the help of a rough stone. I placed my gathering basket on the altar, then began to sweep the circle, swinging my broom as I walked slowly. The spell I chanted was my own, one that I'd created years ago.

Ma had once called it primitive and childish, which wounded me deeply, yet I clung to the spell. It had come from my heart, and I always felt that the Goddess heard it and answered favorably.

> *"Sweep, sweep this circle for me,*
> *By powers of wind, so mote it be."*

My circle complete, I placed the broom at the gateway and closed my eyes. A gentle current of air stirred around me—the breath of the Goddess. I lingered long enough to breathe it in, my breast swelling with the wind. Then I lifted my hands and face to the sun.

> *"Light, light this circle for me,*
> *By powers of fire, so mote it be."*

Warmth shot through my body, from the crown of my head down through my heart. The Goddess was with me today, her power so strong. Reeling with a vivid feeling of life, I lifted the tiny flask of consecrated water from my basket and sprinkled it around my circle.

> *"Water, cleanse this circle for me,*
> *By the powers of water, so mote it be."*

As I stood in the center of the circle, I imagined water flowing around me. My skirts swirled at the center of the tidepool, and the tang of fresh spring water cleansed my throat.

Oh, Goddess, you are with me today. I feel your presence. I treasure it.

I sank to my knees, scraping both hands at the ground beside me. Lifting my hands, I let the soil whisper to the ground as I chanted:

> *"Dirt, bless this circle for me,*
> *By the powers of earth, so mote it be."*

The sun seemed to shine brighter, a lemony halo of light favoring my circle. I thanked the Goddess for lending me Her power, then went to the altar to cleanse and consecrate my basket, my pouches, my knife. I realized I felt lighter, buoyed by Her power. Whatever had been bogging me down earlier had dissipated, turned to dust and carried off in the wind at the Goddess's touch.

Now to set about collecting herbs.

I left the circle and ventured off to a thicket I'd known to produce a variety of plants. My first harvest was a bay plant, a hearty green stem with fat, dark leaves. Gathering my skirts and tucking them between my legs, I crouched beside the plant and pressed the blade of my bolline into the soil.

"Thank you, Goddess, for this beautiful herb," I said, drawing a circle around the plant to protect its energy. Then, cutting off the heartiest sprigs, I thanked the plant for its usefulness as a poultice for ailments of the chest. Ma also used bay leaves in spells of protection, though I'd yet to try this. When I was finished, the plant bounced back jovially, and I felt confident it would thrive and go on to produce many more harvests.

I moved on to other plants—anise for treatment of colic, thyme to rid internal disorders, clover to conjure money, love, and luck. Each time I did a cutting, I repeated the ritual, drawing a circle with my bolline, thanking the Goddess, soothing the plant. My basket was filling. I leaned close to a fennel plant, my bolline held in midair as I wondered whether the plant would be best harvested later.

The forest was silent.

The birds had stopped chirping.

And I sensed that I was not alone.

I froze in place. My heartbeat thundered in my ears as I realized I was holding the bolline—the very same object that had incriminated poor Fionnula. I could be tried as a witch for this gathering ritual, tried and jailed and sentenced to death. Quickly I shoved the bolline into the basket, burying it under the fresh-cut herbs.

Fear-stricken, I clenched the basket and tried to calm myself. Perhaps the intruder had not noticed me yet. With luck, he or she was too far away to spy the runes carved into the handle of my bolline. I wondered if I should cast a blocking spell over myself . . . or a spell of protection. But there was no time.

Say that you're gathering herbs, I thought. The task of gathering herbs is totally innocent.

Unless the intruder finds your tool of witchcraft.

I turned to confront the enemy.

And the enemy smiled at me. 'Twas a tall, solid boy, not much older than myself, and for a moment I wondered if the Goddess had sent him on a jagged bolt of lightning. Even from across the clearing his blue eyes flashed with that intensity, like the night sky lit during a storm.

Clasping the basket to my breast, I closed my eyes, then opened them, sure he would vanish just as readily as he had appeared. He did not. Instead, he came toward me, reaching up to grab an overhanging branch, then swinging closer. He landed a short space away from me, his ginger brown hair falling over one eye.

"Did I startle you?" he asked.

"No . . . aye, that is . . ." I fumbled for words, sensing that he was not a threat, at least not in the way I had feared. For my immediate sense was that he held power . . . not the power to persecute, but the grand, sweeping power possessed only by a blood witch. A blood witch, but from what clan? Certainly not a Wodebayne, as Síle's coven included every living Wodebayne within miles.

"What's that, then?" he teased. "Do you think it wise for a lass like yourself to wander these woods alone?"

"I wander these woods often, gathering herbs," I said, trying to draw out our encounter with conversation. "Though I've not seen you leaping from trees."

"I trust you've not seen many lads leaping from trees," he said, hooking a thumb over his leather belt.

"You're my first, I must admit."

"Well, that's certainly an honor. I'd imagine men would go to battle to be your first." That he would imply something so intimate nearly stole my breath away. He spoke the words of a man, but the humor in his eyes was boyish and full of youth. The drawstrings of his white shirt were open at the throat, revealing a fair amount of skin turned tawny from the sun. More skin than most men laid bare, except in circles. I wondered what he would look like in a circle, his robe slipping away from those broad, tanned shoulders.

I have met my match, I thought, letting the basket drop to one arm.

Aye, he was handsome from head to toe, and his conversation had a certain cleverness that amused. But those qualities merely added to my enchantment. I was drawn to him—inexorably, irrevocably drawn to the power that swirled around him like a visiting wind.

At that moment, I didn't know where he had come from or where he was headed, but with grave certainty I knew that I wanted to be the one to accompany him in his travels. I longed to move close to him and slide the tunic off his shoulders, touch the wall of his chest. And how would it feel to be touched by such a god . . . the sweet press of his lips upon mine, the shimmer of his hands over my body? I slid one hand into the pocket of my skirt and clenched the rose stone. If ever a spell were necessary, this was the time. But what were the words?

He turned and reached up to swing from the tree limb again, giving me a chance to conjure a quick spell.

I set my mind on the power I had felt swirling in my circle. *Oh, Goddess.* I felt the stone's power swelling in my palm, like a quickly blossoming flower. *Thank You for bringing him to me. Let him ever be drawn to me, as a man to a woman, ever in love. Ever after.*

The warmth of the stone rippled up my arm and passed on through my body. I let out a gasp of shock and joy, though I think he was too caught up in showing off his climbing skills to notice. Then he turned toward me and stared.

He stared at me as if he'd only just discovered the answer to his lifelong quest.

My heart clamored with joy that the Goddess had heard me. The magickal stone was now charmed, and we were under its spell.

He slid down from the tree and rubbed his hands on his breeches. "I fear I am more lost than I realized. I thought I had strayed from the path and discovered a maiden, but I was mistaken. I seem to have wandered into an enchanted faerie world, into the realm of a dark, tiny wood nymph. A beauty with glistening black hair and eyes that hold the secrets of the night."

I smiled, feeling myself blossom at his words. I had always viewed myself as small and plain, unworthy of much notice for my appearance. It delighted me to hear myself described so. "You are too kind. I am but a village girl, gathering herbs to make a pottage."

He lifted the basket from my hand. "Bay leaves . . . anise for colic. Thyme to aid in digestion. And clover . . ." He pulled the basket away, teasing me. "These are enchanted herbs, my lady. Tell me, where does your circle gather?"

"I know not of a circle, but for the shape of the full moon," I lied, reaching for my basket. But he stopped my hand with his own, and suddenly we were touching, the sensitive palms of our hands aligned like the stars of a splendid constellation.

His lips moved, forming no words, but his glittering blue eyes told a tale of surprise and desire.

And love? Had my spell worked? I looked into his eyes, begging the question.

His answer was the brush of his lips against mine, a gentle surprise followed by a rich, ripe kiss. I kissed him back, reveling in the feel of his lips on mine, rejoicing in the power that hummed when we touched. This was a passion matched only by the incredible spark I had felt in my solitary circle, and I knew at once that the Goddess was here with us. The Goddess had brought us together. It was meant to be.

And from the way his fingers gently cupped my cheek and followed the line of my jaw to my hair, from the way he held my arm securely as if he would never let go, it was clear that he knew it, too.

He squeezed my arm, letting out a small laugh. "The sun is falling. I'll be on the road after nightfall, but I can't bring myself to care . . . or to leave."

Nightfall. Danger. Looking to the west, I saw only the orange-and-purple glow above the tree line. "I must go, too. But I cannot say good-bye. I can't bear it." My eyes were level with the open ties of his shirt, where a gold pentagram dangled on a leather cord. I reached out and touched it brazenly. In turn, he pressed a finger below the crook of my neck, just above my breasts.

"It will be yours," he whispered. "For I am yours already."

It was a startling admission, coming from a boy I'd only just met. I thought of the boys I had known in my life. None had ever sparked a flame of interest within me, despite a few awkward kisses and groping hands. More than once Meara and I had encountered village boys down by the brook. They were gawky, rough-hewn creatures who teased and chased us, always wanting to steal off into the woods with one of us. More than once I'd had to kick one of them away. Neither boy nor man had held any appeal for me.

Until now.

"Come to me tomorrow," he said, holding my hands to his chest. "Meet me here, at the same time. Please say you will."

"I will," I promised, loving the way my slender fingers disappeared in his large, warm hands. He kissed my fingertips, then backed away, walking awkwardly into the woods.

"You're going to hit your head," I called, gesturing for him to turn around.

"But I can't take my eyes from you," he said.

"Then I must vanish." I hitched up my skirts and raced out of the clearing, resolved not to turn back lest I linger in his arms forevermore. I was breathless from running and from his kisses, but I kept it up, slipping over a patch of dried mud and ignoring the brambles that caught at my stockings. I would run through the heather without shoes, roll down the rocky hills headfirst if it would get me closer to him.

In my deepest heart, I knew that I had met my *mùirn beatha dàn*—my only soul mate. I did not yet know his name. I knew only that he was mine.

I pressed my hand to the side of my skirt, feeling the weight and warmth of the rose stone through my pocket.

Astounding, I realized, the power of a charmed gem.

Even more surprising was the power of my own spell. I hadn't been quite sure of the magnitude of the power—of my power—when I had planned to spell the stone for Kyra. But by the grace of the Goddess, the amulet had brought me love.

3

Charging an Amulet, Esbat, Seed Moon

The next morning I went about the cottage, performing my usual chores with a lightness in my heart, as if a heavy burden had been lifted. Suddenly it did not seem at all tedious to clean the cabin and air the linens and stoke the fire in preparation for breaking fast.

And the last eve I hadn't minded when Ma had questioned me about the herbs I had gathered, nor when I was chastised about the dangers of returning home after sunset. I did not think she had believed my story about the herbs being sparse and difficult to find, and I could feel her eyes upon me, watching curiously. No doubt she was surprised by my suddenly blithe spirit.

As was I. The meeting in the woods had changed everything about my dull, suffocating life. Suddenly the Goddess had filled the very air around me with beauty, and the sure knowledge that I would see him again doubled the pleasure in each moment till then.

When Kyra arrived, I was eager to go off with her and tell her everything. And from the way she switched from one foot to the other, I could see she was equally anxious. Likely eager for her love amulet, which she didn't know the half about.

"I must take some biscuits over to the market at Kirkloch," Kyra said, resting a heavy basket on the table inside the cottage. Kirkloch was a nearby Christian village with a small market-place and a blacksmith. "Ma and Da were hoping you would go along. Otherwise Ma will put off her spinning and go with me."

"May I go?" I asked my mother. I was already untying my apron and brushing soot from my skirt. "I've finished my chores."

But Ma was not so agreeable. "After our encounter with those thieves yesterday, I am not sure it's safe. And what of the preparations for tonight's Esbat?" Her arms crossed, Ma watched me with suspicion. Since tonight was the full moon, our coven would gather in the woods for an Esbat—a meeting of witches. We would worship the Goddess and take care of coven matters such as spells and charms. "Have you gathered what we need for the spell over the mill?"

"No, not yet." I wiped my moist palms on my skirt.

"Then you cannot go. Not when you can't be trusted to complete your chores and be home before sunset." I couldn't believe she was issuing such an edict, but she simply turned back to her spinning, as if I were being punished. Aye, perhaps she was punishing me for glowing with the Goddess's joy. Some-times it was impossible to understand my mother.

"But Ma . . ."

"Please, ma'am," Kyra beseeched her.

"I've made my decision, and that is that!" Ma snapped. Although she didn't bother to look at me, her anger was palpable.

The breath rushed out of Kyra as she gave me a desperate look.

I knew I had to get out of the cottage before my news burst forth like a cinder popping out of the fire. "The sharp objects I need for the spell," I said, thinking aloud. "I've a good chance of finding things like that along the roadside. Broken spearheads and pointed stones and such."

My mother stopped spinning, considering.

"And there's the blacksmith's shop," I said. "He is sure to have some discarded metals and arrowheads."

"Please?" Kyra added.

Ma touched her forehead. "At least you're thinking like a witch now."

"And we'll be back in plenty of time for Esbat," I said. After dark our coven would gather to celebrate April's seed moon. It was a time to banish unwanted influences and cast spells of protection—a perfect time to help the MacGreavys out of their dilemma.

"All right, then, you may go," my mother relented. "But do not forget your chores. I'll not have the MacGreavys without a spell of protection because a daughter of mine neglected her duties."

"Aye, Ma," I said, feeling once again like the put-upon daughter of the high priestess. I hated it, but often I felt as if I did the work while she got the glory.

I grabbed my veil and cloak, not daring to stay to question my mother's change of heart. The rose stone was in my pocket, a glimmering reminder of the fantastical spell I had conjured, and though I had promised it to Kyra, I was now afraid to part with it. Hence I had sneaked into Ma's cabinet that morning and found a stone that might do just as well for Kyra—a pale green moonstone, which was known to promote love and compassion.

Before we reached the end of the path, I told Kyra of my meeting in the woods and of the splendid spell the Goddess had given me. As I spoke, her mouth opened, her jaw dropping in amazement.

"A kiss!" Her hand flew to her face. "You let a stranger kiss you?"

"Not a stranger," I said confidently. "He's a blood witch. My *mùirn beatha dàn*—I'm sure of it."

"Who could he be?" Kyra wondered. "And from what clan?"

"I'll learn his name and clan today. We're meeting this afternoon," I said, smiling at the promise of seeing the sparkle of his eyes again. Reaching into my pocket, I took out the rose stone and held it up to the sky. It glimmered and winked in the sunlight.

"That's the rose stone?" Kyra asked, staring at it. "Oh, by the Goddess, it does exude power."

While I dreamed of meeting him again, Kyra went on and on with dire warnings. How I should not trust a stranger. How I must beware anyone from another coven. How it was wrong to lie to my ma. How I shouldn't have charmed the stone in the first place.

"Aye, but you had no objection when it was to be spelled for you," I pointed out.

"You're right." She flipped a braid over her shoulder and

sighed. "I'm a fool in love, and now I've even lost my chance at having an amulet."

"Don't despair." I took the moonstone from my pocket and presented it to her with a flourish. "This stone promotes love and sympathy. And I heard one of the coven witches go on about its magickal ability to melt a lovers' quarrel. It helps to open up emotions between two lovers."

Kyra's face turned pink. "But Falkner and I are not lovers!"

"Ah, but you shall be," I teased in a singsongy voice. "Come, we'll stop at my circle and charge the moonstone for you."

My circle in the woods was on the way to Kirkloch, and Kyra had been there before for gathering and practicing spells of our own. Kyra always deferred to me, as we both knew my powers with the Goddess were strong. Of late, some of Síle's coveners had seemed to notice my powers. Once while Síle was drawing down the moon, coveners saw a halo of light surround me. *Me*—not the high priestess. My body had trembled with life force that night, but Ma had barely said a word beyond reminding me to ground myself when the rites ended. Sometimes I truly believed she was envious of my powers.

I swept the circle with my broom, cleansing it for the spell. Then I placed the moonstone upon the altar and joined hands with Kyra.

"Do you want to put the spell on your charm?" I asked her.

"Would you do it for me?" She turned to me, her dark eyes beseeching. "You have so strong a bond with the Goddess, I think it's best coming from you. Everyone knows you're to be the next high priestess when Síle steps down."

I squeezed her hand, feeling flattered. "I don't know that everyone has accepted that just yet. My own ma questions my spells and whereabouts every minute of every day."

"She's trying to teach you."

"Well, if chastisement and disapproval are teaching, I'll not be her student." I went to the altar, where the moonstone sat in the dappled sunlight. Ma always said spells were best cast at night, and it was certainly safer, but it was nearly impossible to steal off and make magick under the moonlight with her watching me as she did. After making certain we were alone, I bowed to the Goddess, asking for Her blessing over this stone. As always, I summoned the power of earth, wind, water, and fire. Then I turned and handed the moonstone to Kyra.

"Hold it next to the pounding in your breast," I told her.

She pressed the stone to the bodice of her gown.

I felt the power above me. Lifting my chin, I saw the moon in the sky through a clearing in the circle. It was full and visible today, thrumming with life force and power. So much power for tonight's Esbat. I went to my stash of tools and took out my athame, a long wand I'd made from a tree branch and a lovely pointed stone I'd spied in the river. Standing in the center of the circle, the athame in my right hand, I felt the moon trembling in the crown over the trees. I raised my arms directly above me and clasped them both at the base of the athame.

"I now draw the power of the moon into myself," I said, "merging with her power, the pure essence of the Goddess." My breath came sharp and fast as the moon flashed onto the tip of my athame. I could feel it there, coursing down onto the sharp stone. I let the moon fill the athame, then brought the tool down and pressed its sharp tip to my chest.

At once the power danced through me. Molten silver filled my breast, my body, my whole being. Beside me I heard Kyra gasp, but I could not turn my head to look over, so engrossed was I in drawing down the moon.

When I was fully saturated, I swung around and pointed my athame at Kyra, touching her chest to let the power soar into her. Her dark eyes reflected the silver light as she watched it stream through my athame.

"In this day and in the hour I call upon thee, ancient power." I spoke slowly, steadily. "Kyra has a need that must be met, a true love to draw to her, Falkner to call for her. Charm this stone, O Goddess of Light. Bring her love to cherish and delight."

The spell complete, I pulled the athame away and dropped to the ground, pulling Kyra along beside me. I had learned from coven circles that so much power could sap a witch, making the head light and the body weak. Grounding was essential.

After a few moments Kyra sat up, blowing dirt from her hands. "The Goddess has truly blessed you, Rose," she said. "The way you summon Her power, 'tis like a circle with the elders, who have so much more experience."

"The power runs in my blood," I said, neither bragging nor awed by it. I had come to accept that my destiny was intertwined with the Goddess, even if my own ma wasn't nearly so sure.

It seemed like hours had passed drawing down the moon, but the sun was still high in the clear sky. Carefully I hid away my tools, and we returned to the road to Kirkloch.

When we reached the gathering of cottages at the edge of Kirkloch, Kyra resolved to go directly to the market, but I would not have it.

"We must stop at the blacksmith first," I insisted. "I have grave need of sharp objects for tonight's spell of protection."

Her cheeks turned pink. "Aye, and whose father happens to be the blacksmith of Kirkloch?"

It was none other than Falkner, I knew. "I'm here to help you get beyond your fears," I teased her. "Where would you be without me, Kyra? Hiding in your cottage, under your ma's skirts?"

"I would not," she insisted, but she came close and kissed my cheek lightly. "But you're a good friend, Rose MacEwan. A good friend indeed."

I smiled, sure that our destinies were to be filled with love and happiness. It was such a good feeling after the heaviness that had fallen upon me of late, the pressing danger of persecution from the Christians, the unfair hatred from every rival clan. I took Kyra's hand and skipped ahead merrily.

"I'll drop my basket!" she protested, laughing.

"Well, then, hold on tight," I said as I pulled her along. Outside the blacksmith's shop, I let her compose herself before we ducked around the post and faced the blaring heat of the fires under the overhang. There was the usual wild flurry of activity as the blacksmiths clanged and banged horseshoes and the like, sparks flying and fires hissing. It brought to mind the many times I had accompanied Kyra here and, indeed, to other places in pursuit of her beloved Falkner, who now stood off to the side, prodding the fire with a long poker. How many times had I encouraged her to speak to him, to smile at him, to call his name? All to no avail. He usually gave her a frightened look, then skulked away.

But today would be different.

By the power of the Goddess, my Kyra would have her boy's love.

"Touch the moonstone," I whispered to Kyra.

Reflexively she pressed a finger to her neck, where she'd

strung the stone onto a piece of twine. Her eyes flashed to Falkner, who looked up from the fire . . .

And dropped his poker.

It was as if he'd never seen Kyra before. His heat-ruddy face went pale as he ignored the poker and crossed over to the railing where we stood. Kyra lowered her eyes, but her huge smile revealed her interest as she greeted him and offered a biscuit. Falkner accepted gratefully but didn't take his eyes off her as he lifted the morsel to his mouth and took a bite.

I clapped a hand to my cheek, thrilled that the charm was working.

Blessed be. All thanks to your power, sweet Goddess.

Falkner and Kyra were still gazing at each other when Falkner's father, a witch in our coven, finished with a customer and bade us good day. "And who's been baking here?" he asked. I knew John Radburn from many a circle. He was a jovial man, far more spirited than his son.

"I baked with my ma," Kyra said, lifting the cloth to offer him a biscuit.

He took one and set it aside on a tin plate. "That'll go nicely with my beer at midday, thank you. And what can I help you with, lassies?"

"We came to trade the biscuits at the market," I said. "But while I'm here, do you mind me poking about to find leftover sharp objects? Ma needs them to . . . to scare off the crows from her garden," I lied. Blacksmith Radburn probably knew of the spell of protection to be cast at the mill, but it wouldn't do to have strangers overhear talk of our magick.

"Help yourself." The blacksmith moved the toe of his boot through the dirt to reveal a few jagged pieces of metal. He picked them up and set them on the rail before me. "But mind you don't touch anything that's still heated."

"I'll take care, sir," I said, slipping the sharp items into a thick pouch.

The blacksmith turned back to his work, and I set to searching the ground for sharps. Falkner helped me a bit as he chatted with Kyra; then he, too, returned to tend the fires. When I had a pouch full of splintered nails and shards and arrowheads, Kyra and I thanked the blacksmith and headed away.

Falkner gave an excited nod of farewell, as if Kyra had just brought him a priceless gift.

She squeezed my arm as we made our way toward the market. "Did you see? Your spell worked. The charm is drawing his love!"

"Of course it worked," I said. "You cannot doubt the Goddess."

"No, but I have doubted how strongly one could be connected to Her. Until now. You have summoned Her power to bring me love! Oh, Rose, 'tis the most wondrous thing!"

"Aye." I thought of my mystery boy. I still didn't even know his name.

"And I'll see Falkner tonight at Esbat circle. And at every circle. And from now on, when he looks at me, he'll truly *see* me instead of staring right through me. What could be better?"

"Which reminds me of my appointed meeting this afternoon. Let's make haste at the market so we can return quickly."

Kyra nodded. "I'll sell the biscuits to a vendor, and we'll head home." As she negotiated with merchants at the market, I wandered past carts of brightly colored ribbons, mutton pies, fresh fruits and vegetables. A small black pig squealed as children chased it through the maze of carts. It squeezed past a stout woman's skirts and darted toward the churchyard.

I turned back to the vegetable cart, my fingers pinching a potato. Was it worth the price to thicken our Esbat stew? I could sense that the vendor was a blood witch. Glancing up, I saw that he was eyeing me suspiciously.

"An odd thing, the potato," came a familiar voice. "When digging in the dirt, one has to wonder, is it something to eat or a stone to be cast away?"

My heart sang as I swung around to sparkling blue eyes. It was my boy!

"Aye, sir, I would not eat a stone, but these would do well in a stew," I said, holding two potatoes out to him.

"Hmmm. Or for a jester's tricks." He took the two potatoes and began to toss them, juggling them aptly.

"What's that, now!" the vendor growled. "I'll not have you ruining my wares, boy!" The man, sporting a dense brown beard and red nose, came around his cart, stamping a foot at my love.

"Easy, kind sir." My boy stopped his juggling and held out the potatoes. "I've not damaged them in the least."

The vendor looked angrily from him to me, his eyes narrowing as he took in my petite stature and dark coloring. "And you were touching them." He leaned close to growl softly at me, "You're a Wodebayne, are you not?"

"I am," I answered truthfully, astonished as I was that he would dare speak openly of clans and covens in public. I turned to my boy, wondering if he had heard. Did he know that I was a Wodebayne, one of the so-called evil ones? If he had heard, he did not seem daunted by the fact. He studied the vendor with a mixture of distaste and curiosity.

"Then *you*," groused the vendor, nearly breathing down my neck, "are not permitted to touch my merchandise. How do I know you haven't cast a dark spell upon my wares so that the person who eats them will come down with a racking cough? Or a hideous boil. Or mayhap a burning fever!"

My senses stirred with alarm at his attack. The only consolation was that this man, whatever his clan, would not want to raise the hackles of the people in this Christian village. "Sir, I do not cast harmful spells," I said softly.

"That's what all your kind say," the vendor growled again, suddenly aware that the villagers were taking notice.

All around us it seemed as though people had stopped their business and conversation to watch. I could feel the crowd closing in, watching, waiting. The witches among them were probably hoping the Wodebayne girl would get her comeuppance, as usual. I felt a tightness in my throat, not so much at the disapproval of the crowd as that my boy should be dragged through such turmoil. And surely the hatred of Wodebaynes would frighten him away.

"Just a moment!" the boy interrupted, holding the potatoes high in his hands. He lifted them, weighing and measuring with some degree of drama. "They do not speak, and I see no cryptic message carved among their bruises. There is truly no charm here," he told the vendor. "But the potatoes must certainly be far more delicious for having been touched by a lovely maiden's hands."

A few people laughed, and he nodded at them, his cheekbones high and taut above his broad grin. The crowd began to turn away. Somehow my boy had diffused the swell of hatred against me.

The vendor folded his arms across his chest, still not satisfied.

"I must insist, sir, that you let me purchase these potatoes— these two, no others shall do—for I find that I cannot leave this market without them."

The vendor took a coin from the boy and crept back behind his cart.

"Thank you, sir. A pleasure doing business with you," the boy called. He turned away and handed me the potatoes. "My gift to you. Though it can hardly make up for the way that ogre tried to defame you."

"His hatred does not surprise me," I said. "I've come to expect it, though I don't know that I'll ever become accustomed to it." I dropped the two potatoes into my skirt pockets, where they bounced against my hips.

He watched with awe and reverence. "Would that I could venture where they go," he said huskily.

I laughed at the temerity of his words, here in the wide-open marketplace. "Aren't you the daring one?" I said. "When you're not swinging from trees in the forest, you rescue Wodebayne maidens from mad crowds, then dream of their skirts."

He shrugged and eyed me merrily. "And you despise me for that?"

I looked up at his handsome face and felt the rhythm of my life force increasing. "No, no, on the contrary."

"Rose!" Kyra called, summoning me. "We must go!"

"Rose?" he repeated. "Like the rose on the bush, gentle and sweet, yet ready to prick a finger when approached the wrong way?"

" 'Tis I."

He lowered his head, his hair falling over his eyes in a shroud of secrecy. "We will talk later, Rose."

I nodded, trying to remember every detail of his sultry looks, his feathery light brown hair, his sky blue eyes, his broad shoulders and long legs, coltish yet strong.

With a deep breath I turned away and joined Kyra, who had apparently witnessed the scene with the irate vendor.

"I was so frightened for you!" she said. "What do you think the man wanted? Would he have you locked in jail because you touched his wares? Everyone examines merchandise before trading."

I shook my head, feeling a sense of warm, tender love. It wrapped around me like a cloak of security, just knowing that my boy cared for me, was willing to fight for me. "The man was full of Wodebayne hatred. I don't know what clan he was from, but did you see what happened? The way my boy rescued me? He is the boy I've spoken of. He is a hero. My hero."

"I'm not sure of that," Kyra said regretfully. "Falkner knows him, Rose. His name is Diarmuid, and he's a Leapvaughn. Not one of us."

"Diarmuid," I said, treasuring the sound of his name. I repeated it over and over in my mind.

"He cannot be your true love, Rose. Falkner and I both fear for your heart. He'll hate you as much as his clan hates Wodebaynes."

"Aye, but he doesn't. That's the blessing of the Goddess. It doesn't matter if he's Leapvaughn or Braytindale or Wyndonkylle. He has a good heart. Diarmuid doesn't hate without reason. Didn't you see? He defended me from that peddler. I ought to toss that old ogre's potatoes into the brook!"

"He was a terrible man!" Kyra pressed her hand to her throat, touching her charmed moonstone. "I'll agree Diarmuid did save you. I'll grant you that, and he is a handsome lad. Falkner says he's not of Kirkloch. Where does he live, Rose?"

"That I don't know, but I shall find out. I must cherish this gift from the Goddess."

Kyra shook her head. "But he cannot be a gift from the Goddess, Rose. Not a Leapvaughn boy."

"Would you stop saying that? I'll not allow you to be so small-minded!"

"But to get involved with someone from another clan . . ."

"I know." The reality of it stabbed at me. Diarmuid and I would have to face more than our share of foes. But as I walked along, my mother's words came back to me. She always said that the other clans would one day see the good in the Wodebaynes.

Perhaps I had been chosen to help the world see our goodness.

It lifted my spirits to know that Diarmuid already saw the goodness within me. I couldn't wait to see him again.

Kyra walked alongside me, observing. "You look more in love now than before you knew he was not one of us. But then, you've always been stubborn, Rose MacEwan."

"Aye," I said, thinking of Diarmuid's eyes, his suggestive words, his strong jaw. "I think the Goddess has a plan," I told Kyra. "And I won't let anyone meddle with Her gift to me. I will not be daunted."

4

Drawing Down the Moon

"It worries me, Rose. I know you think you can fight your own battles, but sometimes I fear for you, my child." My mother scrubbed the potatoes furiously, upset by what had happened in the market at Kirkloch.

Of course, I hadn't given her all the details of the story. I'd said that Diarmuid was a traveling peddler, probably a Wodebayne from the north. And although I hadn't mentioned that some in the crowd seemed eager to join in on the Wodebayne bashing, I think she got the complete picture. Whether through her inner sight or simply her experience, Ma had spent her lifetime enduring prejudice from others.

"But it's over, Ma," I reassured her. "'Twas over soon after it began, and we got two fine potatoes out of it."

She turned away, her face in shadow so that I could not

see more than the hollows of her eyes. "I'll thank the Goddess for my supper, not some brash vendor with hatred in his heart." Her voice was strained, and I thought I saw a spot on her cheek—a dark tear. Was she crying?

"What is it, Ma?"

She shook her head. Her chopping was done. "This hatred of the Wodebaynes has to end, Rose. I had hoped it would subside during your youth, but instead it seems to be rising like a river during the spring rains."

I wanted to tell her that the prejudice against us didn't bear down on me so heavily now, not since I'd met Diarmuid. He was a window of light, my escape from the dark hatred that seemed to be closing in around the Wodebaynes. I wanted to go to her and touch her shoulder and ease her pain. . . .

But I couldn't. I knew that talk of a boy, especially a boy from another clan, would rattle Ma all the more. And I feared that if I touched her, if I rested my head on her shoulder or squeezed her arm, she would know the truth.

That the Goddess had interceded, bringing her daughter true love.

I went to her and scooped the potatoes onto my apron, then dropped them into the cauldron over the fire. Already the savory smells of tomato and herbs and beans rose from the kettle.

"The moon is full already," I said, eager to change the subject. "You can see it in the day sky, hanging large as you please." I stirred the stew, talking over my shoulder. "I'd like to go off and draw it down, Ma." Again, a lie, but what could I do?

" 'Tis the seed moon," she said. "We'll have a fine Esbat tonight."

I stepped away from the fire and took off my apron. "I've gathered what we need for tonight's spell. John Radburn was helpful."

She nodded. "You can go. But don't be long. We've a few chores to do before the circle."

I moved slowly, trying to ignore the coursing sound in my ears that urged me to make haste and run off to meet Diarmuid. I hung my apron on the rail outside, measuring my steps while I was in view of our cottage.

One, two, three . . . four steps closer to him.

The waiting was excruciating.

At last I reached the brush at the end of the path. Without looking back, I scooped up my skirts and leaped ahead, startling a small rabbit from the heather at the side of the trail. It darted off into the brush, and I laughed. "I'll not hurt you, little one," I called, racing ahead.

By the time I neared our meeting place, my neck and hands were damp with sweat. I slowed my pace to a brisk walk, mopping my neck with a rough cloth from my pocket. It reminded me that the rose stone was still there, and I paused to take it in my hand and hold it up to the glowing day moon.

"I thank thee, Goddess, for the use of thy power."

When I lowered my hands, the stone winked at me, ever cheerful and appealing. I lifted the top of my dress and dropped the stone down into the hollow between my breasts. Its warm glow worked its magick there, emanating from the middle of my body like a ray of sunshine breaking through clouds.

"Rose?"

It was him. He appeared directly before me, slipping from the trees as though he had materialized out of thin air.

I laughed heartily. "My love! How is it that you seem to appear out of nowhere?"

My boy chuckled happily, his eyes crinkling at the corners. "I did a see-me-not spell, Rose. You are familiar with these?"

I nodded. It is a simple spell one does when wanting to mask oneself from another's eyes. I had never seen it done quite so convincingly. "Diarmuid," I said, loving the sound of his name.

"So, you've discovered me." He moved closer, chuckling and reaching out to me. I gave him my hand and was startled by a beautiful spark of magick. He led me down the path, toward my special altar. "I suppose you've also learned that I'm a not-to-be-trusted Leapvaughn."

"A Leapvaughn, aye, though I find you trustworthy." I lifted my chin to study his face. "You may be full of tricks, swinging from trees and juggling vegetables in the marketplace. But I find you to be honest."

"I believe you are wise beyond your years, Rose."

Under the cover of trees he pulled me into his arms, my body pressing against his. I had never known a man or boy in this way, feeling his legs and chest and hands upon me, enveloping me, inciting tiny wildfires beneath my skin.

Who could have imagined the power of love?

I had felt drawn to the Goddess on many occasions, but never had I felt this incredible desire to press into another person, to combine our two bodies in the simplest of unions.

He lowered his head, his soft lips meeting mine. I sucked in my breath and fell deep into his kiss, a sweet, languorous kiss. Then another, and another, and soon we were touching each other and performing a dance of kisses, soft, then severe, light, then dark and torturous. I wrapped my arms around his neck, gave myself over to him, and we tumbled onto a bed of moss, still kissing.

I don't know how long we danced that way—a chorus of moans and breathless sighs. When we fell apart and lay side by side, staring up at the Goddess's sky, our words seemed to shimmer like leaves in the summer breeze. I learned that he lived in Lillipool, a Leapvaughn village several miles down the road. His father was a sheepherder, a job that Diarmuid hated. He preferred trade, which his father occasionally let him handle. He had been in Kirkloch trading sheep at auction the very day we met. He learned that my father had died when I was young, that I lived with my mother, who was the high priestess of our coven.

"I don't care that you're a Wodebayne," he said. "I wouldn't care if you were Ruanwande or Burnhyde or the daughter of a bestial dragon. I love you, Rose. As you are."

I dipped my hand into the opening of his shirt, pressing against his warm chest. "My friends cannot believe I have fallen into the arms of a Leapvaughn. Yet here I am, body and soul."

"We are *mùirn beatha dàns*," he whispered.

I nodded silently. Yes . . . my love knew it, too.

Two days—we'd had barely time to know each other. Yet I was utterly certain that he spoke the truth. We were soul mates. "So mote it be," I said.

"Aye, the Goddess has certainly brought us together." His fingers stroked the hair at the tender nape of my neck. "Who could imagine that She would bring me a tiny Wodebayne girl, with hair as black as a Samhain sky?"

" 'Tis an extraordinary match, to be sure. But the Goddess must have a purpose." I stared at the sky, watching as two fast-moving clouds raced into each other's path, melding into one. "Do you think we are to be the example to all clans? To prove that if the two of us, members of rival clans among many rivals, can come together in peace, so can all the clans?"

Diarmuid sat up and pulled my shoulders from the ground. "We are to be the champions of love. Our union will settle clan differences. End the age-old wars." He smiled proudly. "Could it be that the Goddess has chosen us for this noble task?"

"We will be the example of harmony under the Goddess's great blue sky." I leaned forward, brushing my cheek against his. "A noble task, yet hardly a task at all."

"Mmm . . ." His lips met mine for another deep kiss.

I melted against him, knowing it was true. We had been chosen. Ours would be an extraordinary love. The charm glowing at my breast was just the beginning of it all, thanks to the Goddess. I knew that we needed to pay homage to Her.

When the kiss ended, I arose and prepared a circle, sweeping it clean with my broom. Without wasting words, Diarmuid joined the cleansing ritual, working with me so naturally I felt as if we'd been raised in the same coven. He picked up two handfuls of dirt and spread them around the circle, moving so beautifully I nearly lost my way in the cleansing ritual.

Diarmuid turned to the east and stretched out his arms. "Ye Watchtowers of the East, I summon you, stir and call you, to witness this rite and watch over this circle." He waved his hand through the air, drawing something. A star? No, a pentagram.

I watched in wonder as he moved to the south quarter of the circle and beckoned the Watchtowers there. This was a practice I had never witnessed, and I wondered at the many things I might learn from him.

When he had called to the Watchtowers of the West and North, we ended up together in the center of the circle, facing the altar.

I lifted my hands to the moon. "The circle is cast, and we are between the worlds. We are far from the bonds of time, in a place where night and day, birth and death, joy and sorrow meet as one."

The forest seemed suddenly silent, our circle a haven of peace apart from the wars of the nearby clans and dreary villagers.

"O mighty Goddess, I have come this day to honor Your presence and to give thanksgiving for bringing Diarmuid to me. We who once were two will become one, Goddess, as we dedicate ourselves to You." I went to the altar and removed a pouch from my pocket. It was filled with dried sage, good for protection and wisdom. I poured the sage onto the altar, crushed it fine with a smooth stone, and pushed the tiny flakes onto the palm of my hand.

"We offer sage," I said, returning to Diarmuid's side. "Sage for protection against those who would harm us." I sprinkled the flaked herb over Diarmuid's head, then over my own. "Sage for the wisdom to fulfill the Goddess's will." I held my hand to his face, and he tipped back his head. I sprinkled sage onto his tongue, then poured the remainder into my own mouth. "Sage for protection and wisdom," I said, feeling a mist come over me.

"But you are wise already," Diarmuid said, taking my hands. He began to turn us in a circle. We moved slowly, but the earth seemed to race under our feet. "We have been chosen. The Goddess looks upon us with favor. How is it that She knows you so well?"

"I, Rose, am the Goddess incarnate," I answered. I was

beyond thinking. Where had those words come from? Had I heard my mother chant them in an Esbat rite of long ago, or had the Goddess lifted my tongue like a winged bird at my back?

My whole world was spinning, my head dizzy with the whirring motion. Hands joined with Diarmuid, I lifted my face to the sky. It opened up upon me, sending a crushing blade of lightning to my chest.

The jolt lifted me off my feet. Suddenly my stomach was sour, my knees turning to mush beneath me. The ground seemed to rush up, sucking my body onto it.

The next thing I knew, my cheek was pressed to the earth, my knees curled beneath me like those of a child suckling its mother. My eyes were closed, but the whirring noise had stopped. The only sound was Diarmuid's voice calling my name.

"Rose? Are you all right?"

His hands were upon me, rubbing my shoulders, stroking my cheek.

"Aye." I sighed and sat up in his arms. "What happened? I've never been struck like that before."

"I don't know." Diarmuid pulled me closer into the cradle of his chest. "Are you sure you're not hurt?"

"Just . . . feeling in a haze." I brushed a lock of dark hair out of my eyes. I was stunned at the Goddess's sudden attack. Had I displeased Her? "I'm so confused. Why did that happen to me?"

"I've seen something like that, but only once. Our coven was gathered in a circle for Esbat rites, and the Goddess struck one of the witches down, very much like that. The coveners saw it as the hand of the Goddess reaching down, pointing to Her chosen one, her priestess. Soon after, the woman was anointed high priestess of our coven."

"High priestess . . ." I rubbed my eyes, still queasy from a churning inside me. "But I'm not in a coven looking for a leader."

"Ah, but the Goddess has chosen you," Diarmuid insisted. "I know that deep down inside me, Rose. You are destined for greatness. Have you not thought of inheriting your mother's role as high priestess?"

"Aye, but not for many years. Ma is not ready to relinquish her role, and she still sees me as a babe in the ways of the Goddess. She's always checking my Book of Spells and trying to pry into my rituals. Truly, she has no confidence in me."

"Well, on that she's mistaken." Diarmuid slid a hand around my waist, nearly knocking the air from me. "I'm sure you're destined to lead your own coven—or something even greater. You are special, Rose. Not just in my eyes, but in the eyes of the Goddess."

"I have to get home," I said, trying to rise. I coughed, and Diarmuid knelt beside me, then lifted me to my feet.

"Can you walk?" he asked. "For I can readily carry you there, such a wisp of a thing."

I tried a few steps. "I can make it. But I hate to go."

"I'll help you to the path," he said, lifting me into his arms.

I held fast to his shoulders, allowing myself a few moments of rest and protection in his arms. I had asked for protection, and the Goddess had answered already.

Diarmuid. He would be my pillar.

My soul mate.

5

The Witch's Jar: A Spell of Protection

As darkness fell, the whirring pain within me began to settle, though the memory of it still frightened me. As Ma and I ate our stew thickened with the potatoes from Diarmuid, I noticed that she was still in a dour mood. I kept myself steady, not wanting to draw her ire upon me.

After I had cleaned the supper dishes, Ma brought out a clay jar to prepare for the spell of protection. "I don't believe you've ever done a witch's jar before, have you?"

I shook my head. "No, but I've collected many sharp objects. Just as you said." I opened the thick pouch and shook its contents onto the table with a tinny clatter.

"Fill the jar with everything you've found," Ma told me. "And as I remember, there are a few herbs that need to be added. Let me see." She took her Book of Shadows from its hiding place under the eaves of the cottage roof and set it on the table. "This is why I expect you to chronicle everything in your Book of Shadows, Rose. The mind does not always record as well as parchment and quill."

Another criticism. I dropped nails into the jar, wondering what I would have to do to please my mother in the ways of the Goddess.

My mother leafed through her book, her teeth pressed over her lower lip, until she found the right page. "Aye, we need sage and ivy," she said. "And a touch of bay should warn us of any further act of evil coming upon the MacGreavys." She ran her finger down the page, nodding. "And marjoram. Do we have that in our collection, Rose?"

"I think so." I got up from the table to check the pouches hanging from the rafters. "Aye, Ma, here it is." As I placed the pouch on the table, she caught my hand in hers.

Her touch sent a spark through me. Surprise, perhaps. Although I already knew I felt guilty for hiding so much from her.

"Something's changed, like shifting winds." She glanced up at me, her dark eyes locking on me. "Why do I have the feeling you're not telling me something, Rose? Are you all right?"

I nodded, trying to look away from her.

Ma rose to her feet, facing me. "What happened to you today? Did something go wrong in your ritual?"

I nodded again, too frightened of the painful experience to keep it pent up inside me. "I was . . . I was thanking the Goddess when She struck me down from the sky." I clasped my hands to my chest. "The force hit me here, knocking me to the ground. 'Twas like a lightning bolt on a sunny day and . . . oh, Ma, 'twas painful."

She folded me into her arms. "Child, child. Were you harmed?"

I closed my eyes and pressed my head to her blouse, relieved to have the truth out. "At first I could barely breathe, but I'm better now. Still frightened, though. Why would the Goddess strike me down?"

"'Tis hard to say." Ma stroked my hair, then moved me to a chair. "Have you done anything that might offend Her? Think hard, Rose, and be honest. What kind of spells have you been working on of late?"

I rubbed my forehead, wondering how to get through my web of lies without tripping over it. Surely my love spell for Diarmuid had not offended the Goddess so greatly? "Well, there was drawing down the moon. I did that with Kyra."

"'Tis not a spell, though."

"But we did work magick," I insisted. "We had a charm that needed to be charged."

"What sort of charm?"

As soon as she asked the question, I knew trouble was brewing for me. "It was a moonstone for Kyra," I said simply.

"And the purpose of the charm?"

"To bring her the love of Falkner Radburn."

"Oh, by the Goddess . . ." Ma banged her fist on the table, making the witch's jar jump a bit. "How many times have I told you not to meddle with a person's free will? You can make a charm or a poppet to attract love, but it's wrong to ensnare the love of a specific person. To meddle with a person's life, to control his destiny . . . that's dark magick." She banged her fist again. "It's wrong, Rose!"

My insides turned stone cold at her anger. Couldn't she see I was just helping a very desperate friend?

"Why is it that all my instructions to you fly through the air and fall to the soil?" my mother asked. "You are not listening,

Rose, and today is just one example of how the power of the Goddess can harm if you don't practice witchcraft in the ways of the elders. Do you want to hurt people, Rose?"

"No, Ma," I said quietly. That much was true.

"Then why do you insist on meddling with a person's will? 'Tis not right, Rose. When you go out to gather plants, do you strike down a plant without apology? Do you slash through stems at will, taking more than you need, harming nature?"

"No." I dug my fingers into my hair, dropping my chin against my chest. I hated being chastised this way. I thought of Diarmuid's comment that he had seen a woman struck down the same way because she was destined to be the high priestess of the coven. Why could my ma not even entertain the thought that there was a positive reason? Could it be that she knew I had been chosen by the Goddess for greatness, and she was jealous of my connection to Her? My face burned at the thought.

"So why would you strike out at a person that way, tampering with his destiny?"

There was no answer—at least, none that would suit her—so I kept quiet.

"You must go back to your earlier lessons," Ma said sternly. "Starting tomorrow, you will look over your Book of Shadows from the beginning. You will spend less time afield with your friends and more time studying from my Book of Shadows, too. And you will stop making up your own spells until I can be sure you're fulfilling the Goddess's will. Do you understand?"

"I understand," I said. I pressed my teeth into my lower lip, wondering if she would realize that I had not promised her anything.

It was all so unfair. I had tried to gain my mother's support by telling her about the painful strike from the sky, and in turn she merely wanted to cripple me. If Síle the high priestess had her way, I'd be locked in the cottage, drying herbs and inscribing spells.

How could I stop making spells when I knew the Goddess was calling me to Her? How dare my mother try to interfere with the Goddess's destiny for me?

Ma did not understand about my powers. And from her tart reaction on that front, I knew that it would be a catastrophe to tell her about Diarmuid.

For now he would be a secret, and until my mother learned to see me as more than her incapable daughter, he would remain a secret.

Down the dark road, Miller MacGreavy led the way. He was followed by his wife, who walked beside my mother, their voices lowered so as not to wake anyone in the cottages we passed. I walked behind them, feeling dull and tired. The night's Esbat rites had hardly moved me. They had only emphasized how Síle and her coven were following a weary, timeworn road while I was on the verge of opening an exciting new doorway to the Goddess.

The breeze rustled the trees so ripe with bud; their clattering branches reminded me of the bell rung at Esbat.

Three times.

"An ye harm none, do what thou wilt," Síle chanted.

"An ye harm none, do what thou wilt," we all repeated.

"Thus runs the Witch's Rede," Síle went on. "Remember it well. Whatever you desire; whatever you would ask of the Goddess, be assured that it will harm no one—not even yourself. And remember that as you give, so it shall return threefold."

I trudged along, trying to clear my mother's voice from my head. I had heard her words in the circle so many times, I could recite them by heart.

"I am She who watches over thee," said High Priestess Síle. "Mother of you all. Know that I rejoice that you do not forget me, paying me homage at the full of the moon. Know that I weave the skein of life for each and every one of you. . . ."

"Enough, enough, enough!" I grumbled through gritted teeth. I had heard my mother's words so many times, they had become meaningless for me.

As we neared the mill, I wondered if Ma's spell of protection would work. At least this was something that interested me, as I'd never worked one before. Miller MacGreavy unlatched the big door to the mill, and the four of us filed inside. During the Esbat rites, Ma and the MacGreavys had summoned the Goddess to protect them and the mill, so I imagined that this would entail more spell casting than the ritual had.

Soon Ma had candles lit, and Mrs. MacGreavy set her tools on the table, which we assembled around. Normally I would have helped with preparations, but since Ma had made it clear I was being punished, I held back. Ma had already placed herbs in the witch's jar, which now sat at the center of the table, but I knew there was something more to be added before we sealed it.

Closing her eyes, Ma held up her hands, opened to the Goddess. "With this witch's jar we will cast a spell of protection over this mill and this miller's family," she said. Looking down at the table, she moved the jar toward Mrs. MacGreavy.

"'Twill need a drop of blood from you. Take your bolline and give your finger the slightest prick."

The miller's wife pressed the sharp end of her bolline against her fingertip. A crimson drop began to form, and she squeezed it into the jar.

Then my mother passed the jar over to the miller. "Spit in it," she said. He did so. Then Ma began to seal the top of the jar, using hot candle wax. As she worked, she chanted:

> *"Protect this mill, protect these folk,*
> *Guard them from illness and harm.*
> *Send back the darkness to those who sent it.*
> *Cast a light of goodness around,*
> *Let love and protection abound."*

Glancing up from the sealed jar, my mother told the MacGreavys to join hands. "You must remain here in the mill while Rose and I circle it with the jar. Three times." She pulled on her cloak and went to the door. "We'll be back when the spell is finished."

Silently I followed my mother. I was allowed to hold the jar as we traced a wide circle around the mill. On the side where the brook ran deep and fast, there was a crossing bridge. But as we reached the shallows on the other side of the mill, it was clear there was no way across.

"No way across but in," Ma said, gathering up her skirts. "Pull up your gown, Rose. We'll be walking through the Goddess's waters tonight." She stuck out her foot, eyeing her sandal. "Too bad it's not a cobbler we're casting a spell for. We'll be in need of new footwear after this."

I laughed, taken aback at Ma's impetuous humor. This was

a side of her I rarely saw. I hitched up my skirts and stepped into the brook. Cold water swirled around my legs and mud seeped into my shoes, but I tramped on beside Ma, the witch's jar tucked into the crook of my arm.

We circled the mill three times, then ducked inside with sodden shoes and wet legs. The cold didn't bother me. It was sort of refreshing on a warm night, and I counted this spell as something of value, certainly worth including in my Book of Shadows.

Inside the mill, the MacGreavys waited in the flickering candlelight.

"The spell is done," Ma said. "We need to bury the jar, but there's no safe place around here. Rose and I will hide it in the woods where no one will find it."

The miller went over to my mother, clasping her hands. "Thank you, Síle."

She nodded. "And now I think I need a rag to wipe down my shoes. Seems that Rose and I had to go for a late-night dip in the brook." She pushed off her shoe, and it flopped onto the floor like a dead fish.

"Oh, my!" Mrs. MacGreavy laughed, rushing off to find some cloths.

The miller brought out chairs and wine for all of us, and he and his wife talked in the quiet, dark room while Ma and I dried our feet. I took a sip of wine—sweet and heady. Just like Diarmuid's kisses. Of course, nearly everything made me think of Diarmuid. It was an effort to concentrate on what was before me instead of the lovely picture floating in my mind of him. And at the moment, the conversation was so gloomy, with the miller complaining of slow business, that I preferred to dream of my love.

"At least it was our slow season," Mrs. MacGreavy was saying.

"Aye, but if we don't get that broken gear fixed soon, we'll have no business at all," Miller MacGreavy said. "It's all a result of the curse upon us, probably from those vile Burnhydes." He turned to Ma. "And I thank you for wiping it away. Our luck will change now, though I can't say that I see better days ahead for the Seven Clans. It's an age-old battle we're fighting, and it's getting worse instead of better, with curses and sheep thieves and vendors picking on innocent young girls at market." His eyes burned with conviction as he glanced at me, and I bit my lower lip, wondering if everyone in the Highlands had heard of my escapades at the market. If the story was floating around, soon the real details—of the boy who had saved me—would wend their way to my mother. More trouble for me.

"Ian . . ." The miller's wife tried to soothe him, but he forged on.

"I say it's high time we Wodebaynes stopped taking the prejudice against us," he insisted. "Time to use magick to fight back."

Closing her eyes, my mother shook her head gently. "No, Ian, that's not the answer."

"Well, then, how are we going to stop it, Síle?" the miller asked. "You know the stories—though there are so many, I've lost count. A Leapvaughn tricking a Wodebayne farmer out of his land. A Ruanwande casting a spell that makes a Wodebayne girl go mad. Even your own husband, Gowan, was prey to the prejudice, Síle."

"My father?" I dropped the rag on the floor. So long had I craved to hear stories of my father, Gowan MacEwan, but every time I asked, my request was headed off by a severe look from my mother. "Tell me," I begged, turning to the man.

"'Tis not much of a story, Rose," the miller said, touching his beard. "But one day, when your father was on the road traveling to a nearby village, he came across a Wyndonkylle man on a horse. The horseman rode past without incident but then returned to harass your father. He accused your father of looking upon him with evil in his eyes. Then, when he learned that your father was a Wodebayne, he reared up his horse and trampled your father under its hooves."

I winced. "That's a terrible tale. But Da survived it."

Ma nodded. "Aye, but he walked with a limp ever after."

As Mr. MacGreavy went on lamenting the clan differences, I thought of my father. He had died when I was young, so I remembered little of him. I'd heard a few dark rumors—tales that he had been interested in dark magick—though no one spoke of him to me directly. And my mother refused to fill in any of the missing details. Why was she so reluctant to speak of him?

After the conversation and wine ran out, we said our good-byes and headed home. Ma and I were across the river and down the road a bit when she realized we had forgotten the witch's jar.

"Make haste and fetch it," she told me. "I shall wait here."

Lifting my skirts, I ran back along the road. But as I approached the mill, I saw a solitary candle burning upon the threshold. I slowed my pace as my feet silently crept over the cooling earth. There was magick here—I felt the boundaries of a witch's circle, and I was forced to stop at its perimeters. I used my magesight to study the details. Was that a pentagram drawn in the dirt by the door? But it was upside down! 'Twas not part of the spell Ma had cast. . . .

As I stood in the shadows, a figure loomed in the open

doorway—Miller MacGreavy. He did not sense my presence as he leaned out and poured a dark liquid over the pentagram, all the while uttering words I did not understand. I gasped, realizing that the liquid Ian MacGreavy was using was blood.

The very tone of the scene made me shudder. 'Twas as if a cold wind had swept up the river, turning everything in its path to ice.

Dark magick. I gasped.

Miller MacGreavy twitched in fear, darting a look toward me. "Rose?" he asked suspiciously. "What are you doing here?"

"The witch's jar," I croaked in fear. "We . . . we left it behind."

He scowled at me, then ducked back inside. A moment later he reappeared with the jar, stepping around the pentagram and drawing a door in his circle to step out toward me.

His eyes glittered in the candlelight as he handed me the jar. "Begone with you, Rose MacEwan," he said angrily. "And not a word to anyone of what you witnessed here tonight."

"Aye, sir," I said breathlessly. Although I feared his magick, I knew it was not cast against me. Still, his warning frightened me. Best to keep it to myself. After all, it appeared he wasn't harming an innocent.

Yet even as I tucked away my memory of Miller MacGreavy, I decided not to let the matter of my father rest. On the way home from the mill that night I waited until my heartbeat slowed to a more relaxed pace, then launched into the subject. "I was glad to hear the story of Da," I said, walking slowly under the orange moonlight. "We set a place for him every year at the Samhain table, yet you never tell me stories about him. You never speak of him, Ma. Why is that?"

My mother took a deep breath, searching for the answer. "It always pained me to speak of him. The way his life was snuffed out . . . the way it ended. It was a terrible thing, Rose." She linked her arm through mine. "I supposed I thought that if we didn't talk about it, you might be spared the pain that I felt."

I shook my head. "When I think of him, there's no pain, really. Just curiosity."

"What do you remember of him?"

Thinking of Da, I smiled. "His largeness. He was a bear of a man, was he not?"

"Quite large," Ma agreed.

"I remember riding on his shoulders—big, broad shoulders. And his hands. They were so huge, my little hand disappeared inside his. I remember his deep, ringing laugh. And a trip to the coast. Did he take me to the seacoast?"

My mother nodded.

"I've heard the rumors of him," I said. "That he subscribed to dark magic. Is that true, Ma?"

"No," she said gently. "I'll never believe that. He was a good man; he loved his family, his child, his clan. He was simply misunderstood."

Like me, I thought. Ma didn't understand my powers or my adventurous spirit. She couldn't accept that her path to the Goddess was not the only way.

"I wish you'd had a chance to know him well," my mother said.

We walked for a few moments, then I asked, "What of his death? Did he not die in his sleep?"

"He did."

"Then what of all the rumors? That he was cursed—or poisoned by a rival clan?"

"That is the most difficult part," my mother admitted. "His

death was suspicious. Sudden and unexplainable. Some say a rival clan cursed him in retaliation; I don't know."

"Retaliation for what?"

Ma shook her head and her mouth grew tight. "I cannot speak of matters that I know nothing of." When she turned to me, tears glimmered in her eyes. "And I tell you truly, Rose, I do not know the truth of his death."

She fell silent, but that silence haunted me as we walked on. Aye, Ma might not have understood Da's death, but certainly she knew more of the details than I. As usual, she wasn't giving me enough pieces to patch the thing together in my mind.

I thought of Ian MacGreavy, of the way his body had loomed over the bloody pentagram. Had my father dabbled with *taibhs*, too? I cast my eyes to the distant moon, wondering. . . .

The next day, after hiding the witch's jar in a deserted thicket, I met Diarmuid at our secret place in the woods. On this day we wasted no time with small talk or teasing. He pulled me into his arms and placed his lips on mine. The kiss stole my breath away, and we tumbled onto the green moss and lay there, kissing and holding and stroking each other until the sun ventured below the treetops.

He told me that the magick in his own Esbat circle had paled in comparison to what we had done together.

"Aye," I told him, "I felt the same way last night." I went over to my small, makeshift altar and smoothed my hands over the surface of the boulder. Looking around, I realized that this was the perfect place for a circle—our circle.

I grabbed my broom and with measured steps walked farther than I had before. I would make the circle wider, this time including the moss bed we liked to frolic upon. Was not our love dedicated to the Goddess—a result of her blessings?

Diarmuid went to the four corners of the new, bigger circle, where he summoned the Watchtowers once again, drawing a pentagram in the air each time. Watching Diarmuid, I felt my world swelling with newfound knowledge and love. The rose stone between my breasts set my heart aglow, reminding me of my good fortune at having found a true love who was also a blood witch.

The day after that we met again, same time, same place. And the day after that and the day after that. My spring afternoons were lush affairs of lips trailing on skin and countless whispered dreams under the cool cover of spring leaves. Each day we maintained our altar, always thanking the Goddess for bringing us together, for bringing us so much pleasure.

"Our destiny is not clear to me yet," I once told Diarmuid. "But I know there's a reason we've been brought together."

He dipped his face into the bodice of my gown, nuzzling there seductively. "'Tis not enough that we were brought together to love?"

"Love is a gift, indeed," I said, slipping my hands into the top of his shirt to find his gold pentagram. "But I'm talking about a greater purpose. Bringing the Seven Clans together, perhaps."

He moved up to kiss my neck. "Our love is truly beyond all others." He stopped kissing me to look me in the eye. "I've known people who say they are *mùirn beatha dàns*. They truly believe they are soul mates for life. But I can't imagine that they would understand the way I feel about you."

He smoothed his hand over my bodice, cupping one breast gently. "I love you, Rose."

I gasped, feeling myself melt at his fingertips. I had never known a man before, and Diarmuid swore I was his first love, yet he seemed to know so much of a woman's body—the places to stroke, to brush, or to touch ever so lightly. Now he was down at my feet, his hands gliding up under my skirts. His fingers whispered over my knees to my thighs until I was unable to still the trembling inside me.

"We'll be together forever," he whispered.

"We'll have no secrets," I vowed.

"I shall be your first and only love," he said, moving his hand up between my legs. "And you shall be mine."

"So mote it be," I whispered, offering our love to the Goddess.

There, in our secret circle in the woods, we met every afternoon. One day as Diarmuid and I lay together on the moss, I realized that we had been together for nearly a full cycle of the moon. The May celebration of Beltane was but a few weeks away, and Diarmuid and I had met just before the full moon of April.

I thought of the two charmed gemstones that had been the seeds of love: the rose stone and Kyra's moonstone. Two charms with very different powers.

Oh, Kyra and Falkner were still together and very much in love. But not like Diarmuid and me. Just that morning I had seen Kyra at Sunday mass, and she had been full of giggles and squeals for her boy. Like a child. She knew that I met Diarmuid each day, and she couldn't believe I'd allowed him a kiss, let alone other pleasures.

"But what do you do with Falkner?" I asked.

"I bring him biscuits and shortbread every time Ma and I bake," she said. "And he stops by the cottage if he has to deliver a newly shod horse nearby. Which isn't often. So sometimes Ma allows me to accompany her to market in Kirkloch and we stop in at the blacksmith's shop."

"Oh." I didn't tell her that it all sounded tedious and lackluster to me. If it suited Kyra, that was fine. But hearing about her love for Falkner made me realize the level of maturity Diarmuid and I had reached. We were far beyond blushes and giggles. Our love had ventured into passion, promise . . .

And commitment.

"Come back to me, my love," Diarmuid said, pulling me onto my side. "You've wandered so far into the clouds, I'd dare not venture to guess your thoughts."

"Ah, but I'm here," I said, "thinking of you."

As Beltane approached and preparations began, it became more and more difficult for Diarmuid and me to steal away for our afternoon meetings. One day he was late, and I worried the time away, despairing that I would not see him at all. I was about to leave when I received a *tua labra* from Diarmuid, a silent message that only witches can send: *Wait for me, my love.* I waited, and within moments he was dashing into my arms, apologizing and explaining about the tedious chores his father had given him that day. Another day Ma seemed more suspicious than usual, and I had to concoct a preposterous lie to sneak off to his arms.

"The strain of saying good-bye to you each afternoon is wearing on me," I told him as we sat in the moss.

"Aye, and each time it's without knowing that we'll both make it back." He sucked in a deep breath. "It's getting more and more difficult for us to be together, Rose. Your ma is suspicious, and my da keeps loading me up with work."

"I know it, and I thought the Goddess would ease our burdens." He lifted his hand to my cheek, and I pressed against him longingly.

"Blast them all, we should tell them! Let them know of our love!"

His brash spirit made my heart soar. "Would you?" I said. "And would that be an act of courage or foolishness? For no one is ready to learn of us yet. They would either try to tear us apart—or banish us from our clans!"

Diarmuid's blue eyes clouded with concern. "You're right. And I will protect you, Rose. I won't have you ostracized by Leapvaughns or Wodebaynes or anyone."

"We must go forth with caution," I said. I knew the Goddess had deigned that we be together, but how could we begin to clear the way with the rest of the world?

As Diarmuid stroked my hair gently, the answer came upon me.

Make final the bond.

"The Goddess wants us to be together," I said. "Heart, spirit . . . and body." Grabbing Diarmuid's shirt, I pulled him closer. "We must seal our love with a physical union."

His eyes sparkled with wonder. "'Tis the Goddess's will?"

"Aye." I nodded, thinking of the upcoming celebration. There would be maypole ribbons fluttering in the breeze, flowers and songs and the scent of burning sage. Each covener would take a ribbon and dance around the maypole, symbolizing the union of man and woman, the joining of all together. "And Beltane will be the perfect time."

6

Night Visions

Tiny fingers.

I have short, pudgy fingers, and my da has the hands of a giant. Sometimes he holds me in his palm and lifts me in the air, allowing me to see the world the way birds and flies do. Other times, like now, I ride on his shoulders, laughing because he is reaching up to tickle me behind the knees.

We are at the seashore. The grass is so green here, and from the high cliffs you can see miles and miles of emerald field and roiling teal waters. Da hikes along the cliffside with me upon his shoulders. Occasionally the ocean rises up and smashes against the rocky cliff with a fierce temper, but we laugh at it. My da even dances closer, trying to catch the spray. Tiny droplets of water drench us, but we rejoice.

Da turns so suddenly that I am nearly wrenched out of his arms. I look to see what has alarmed him, and there it is, rising up like a dragon. The ocean is rising, higher and higher in a ferocious wave.

And then, when I look again, my da is not there. Only his

laughter remains—a hollow, mean sound as the giant wave looms over me. Its monstrous tendrils rise, its power surging overhead.

I am alone on the cliff, a wave curling over me.

I try to run, but my tiny legs are weak, like the twig legs of a marionette. There is really no escape . . . yet escape is everything.

Somehow I know there is much to be lost if I succumb to the wave. It's not only my life at stake, but also the lives and futures of all my clan, all the Wodebaynes, as well as the Braytindales and Leapvaughns and the witches of all Seven Clans.

So much at stake, but how can I escape?

How to get away from the ominous wave closing over my head?

"Rose? Rose! You must awaken."

Gasping for breath, I tried to pull myself from sleep and navigate safely to the sound of my mother's voice.

"Rose, child, you've had a night vision."

I felt her hands on my arms, shaking me gently. Opening my eyes, I realized that I was in the cottage, safe and dry. But fear held me in its grip, and I was unable to shake it.

"It's all right, child," Ma said. "Tell me what you saw."

I squeezed my eyes shut, afraid to talk about it. Afraid to open up to the woman I'd lied to so much of late. I had guarded my feelings and fears from Ma. How could I open up to her now?

She rubbed my back gently but firmly, up and down between my shoulders. A soothing warmth went through me, reminding me of all the times Ma had rubbed my back when I was sick or frightened or frustrated at not being able to master something. Whether it was the emotion of the dream or the tenderness of Ma's gesture, I wasn't sure. But suddenly I was crying.

"I was at the coast with Da," I said, spilling out the details of my dream. I told Ma everything . . . about my father leaving me and about the giant wave that had been about to slam into me. "I don't understand it. Please, Ma, please tell me the truth," I said. "Was Da an evil man? Did he ever try to hurt me?"

"Oh, no, child!" Ma insisted. "Gowan MacEwan loved you dearly. The man did everything in his power to protect us."

"Then why did he leave me behind in the dream, Ma? What does it mean?"

My mother pursed her lips thoughtfully. In the dim moonlight seeping in through the window she looked old, with lines creasing the corners of her mouth. "Perhaps he left you in the dream because he left you so early in life," she said. "Or perhaps the rumors of his death make you suspicious of him."

"Did he really die in his sleep, here in the cottage?"

"Aye." She sighed, and I felt sure she would change the subject as usual. "'Twas so sudden, his death," she murmured, as if to herself. "All the coveners suspected that someone had cast a dark spell upon him. Many said that the threefold law of magick was the reason for his death."

I thought about the threefold law—that magick returns to the sender magnified three times. In this way dark magick would hurt the sender the most. "But that would mean that he was practicing dark magick, that he had fallen away from the ways of the Goddess."

"Aye," Ma agreed, staring off into the distance, "and I'll never believe that of your father." She stood up from my bedside and beckoned me to follow. "Come. Let's cleanse the cottage for sweet dreams."

While Ma lit the candles, I swept the center of the cottage to create a small circle around our table. I was surprised to see that she had taken out our yellow candles, which were usually reserved for special occasions, but she explained that they were to help me gain true vision. "It's time you learned to have a second sight, to see past the ordinary and witness the Goddess's will."

I swallowed hard in amazement. How was it that she knew of my own plan? At that moment I wanted to sit down and tell her everything about Diarmuid, but as she started chanting over the candles, something held me back. Standing in the lemon circle of light, I watched as Ma beseeched the Goddess to bring me vision, to show me Her will for me.

Then Ma brought me to the center of the circle, and, standing behind me, she wrapped her arms around me. I felt so loved and protected there in her arms—like a child again.

"Gracious Goddess," she said, "let Your love rain down upon Rose. Show her the path she must pursue to fulfill her destiny. Walk with her through this time of darkness to come again into the light."

"So mote it be," I said.

My mother's hands went to my head. She stroked my hair back gently, then clasped her hands around my skull. "Rid her mind of frightening night visions. Let her see only Your vision, Goddess. Rid both our minds of dark thoughts. Chase evil from our home."

"So mote it be," I repeated as a warm feeling came over me. Leaning back against Ma, I remembered how she had summoned the Goddess to help me when I was little—to cool a feverish head, to guard me against eating a poisonous herb, to give me the wisdom to learn my runes. Ma and I had been at odds so much of late, but I knew that despite all of her disapproval and criticism, she did love me, her only daughter.

And in time, she would come to love Diarmuid as a son.

7

Beltane Rites, the Fifth Day of May

"Spring daisies and cornflowers," Kyra said, climbing over some flat rocks to reach another patch of wildflowers. "With the early spring we've had this year, 'twill be one of the most colorful Beltane rites ever."

As was our annual practice, Kyra and I had risen before dawn to creep into the woods on a quest for flowers. We would hang fresh flowers on the doors of our cottages and strew them about the circle in gay decoration for the night's festivities. We would also make a crown of fresh flowers to be worn by the high priestess. Today I would make an extra crown—one for myself.

"I think Beltane is my favorite celebration of the year," I said. "And this year 'twill be my most memorable." I silently thanked the lilac bush for her offering, then used my bolline to cut off a fat bunch of fragrant flowers.

"Because you are in love?" Kyra asked.

I pressed the lavender blooms to my cheek. "Because I shall become a woman in love, in every rite." When Kyra's brows lifted in curiosity, I explained, "Diarmuid and I shall have our own maypole celebration tonight. Do you see the ribbons I took from the cottage?" I reached into my pocket and pulled out streamers of red and white ribbons.

"What?" Kyra's mouth dropped open.

"Aye, red and white ribbons to signify the blood that flows from a woman when her purity is taken. For that's how Diarmuid and I will celebrate Beltane."

"This I cannot believe!" Kyra screeched. "Do you know what you're doing, Rose?"

"Aye." I twirled around in the field, letting the ribbons stream behind me. "I know quite well. I believe the Goddess has called us together for this. And Beltane is a festival of love and union, is it not?"

Kyra swallowed hard. "I don't know that the Goddess intends us to take every detail so literally."

I danced over to Kyra and tugged on her hand. "Don't be an old toad in the mire! We're seventeen years under the Goddess's sky."

"Aye, but there's been no handfasting, no joining of the two of you in the circle."

"That will come later," I insisted, pulling her into my dance.

She dropped her basket and spun around with me, our eyes meeting in laughter until we grew dizzy and dropped to the grass.

"Oh, dear Goddess, now You've convinced me," Kyra said, staring up into the clear blue sky. "Rose has lost her wits."

"I have not!" I protested. "And I'll wager that you'll be telling me the same thing soon, about you and Falkner."

"I can't imagine it, though I am so in love."

I rolled onto my side and squeezed her arm. "You must pretend that I'm with you, tonight after the circle."

"Oh, Rose, you know I am a terrible teller of tales."

"'Twill be nothing. The younger coveners always end up celebrating a bit on their own as the others dance by the light of the Beltane fires. Just tell Ma I am with you."

"Lying to the high priestess," she said. "Goddess, forgive me."

"I knew I could rely on you." I stood up and brushed grass from my hair. "We'd best go and see to the decorations."

We filled our baskets until they were brimming over with blossoms, then headed back to our cottage. Ma looked on as we made bunches to hang on the doors, leaving aside other flowers to decorate the circle. Then Ma set some sage leaves afire in a clay pot, and we blew off the flames until the burning ashes produced a pungent smoke, which we spread through the cottage.

As we set about our tasks, Kyra spoke of Falkner, how he thought her the best baker in the Highlands, how he had come to visit her just the day before. Ma did not comment until we were finished smoking the house and ready to head over and do the same to Kyra's cottage. That was when she brought out the sewing basket along with a few old snatches of cloth.

"Hearing you talk of young Falkner, I've come to think you should put your thoughts into action," Ma told Kyra. "If you truly want to bring love into your life, it's wrong to trap a particular person, as you did with the charmed moonstone."

Kyra lowered her head. "I'm sorry, ma'am. I know."

"Trapping a person with a spell is dark magick," Síle said. "It has the potential to harm someone by tinkering with their destiny and stripping away their free will. However," Ma went on, "the Goddess can help you bring love into your life, as long as you're not targeting a particular person and meddling with their destiny. You can work love magick through poppets." She placed two pieces of cloth together and began to cut. As she trimmed away the cloth, the shape of a gingerbread man began to emerge. "You must make two small dolls—one to represent you, the other to represent the boy, or man, of your dreams."

I watched carefully as Ma showed us how to make the poppets. She helped Kyra sew brown ribbon on the girl doll to make it resemble herself.

Then Ma handed Kyra the boy doll to decorate. "Make him handsome in your eyes, but don't inscribe him with a name or a rune that points to a particular person."

Kyra thanked Ma when we finished, then we raced off to decorate her cottage and our coven's meeting place in the woods. It was afternoon when our work was done. Kyra headed home to bake some of the ceremonial cakes with her ma, and I headed off to decorate my own maypole. We were just about to go our separate ways, when a tall chestnut horse came trotting up the road. It was a majestic sight, the rider sitting tall.

"It's Falkner," Kyra said, patting down her hair.

"'Tis not," I muttered, blinking into the sunlight. Kyra was right, though I had not expected this beanpole of a boy to be transformed into a knight.

"Good day!" Kyra called, waving wildly.

Falkner stopped his horse as it reached us, then swept down and landed at Kyra's feet. "Would you like a ride?" he offered Kyra and me. "I've got to return the horse. Da just fixed his shoes, but you may ride along the way."

"I'm headed off into the woods," I said, "but Kyra has been afoot all day, preparing for tonight."

"Are you tired, then?" he asked her, the fondness in his eyes unmistakable.

She nodded at him sweetly, and he boosted her up onto the horse's back. "There you go."

"Thank you." Gazing down at him, Kyra seemed like a different person. Not the gawky braided girl who used to skip over stones in the brook, but . . . a woman.

The image stayed in my head as we parted ways. On my way through the woods I stopped by the brook and sat down at the water's edge. Here the water slowed into a clear, still pool, where tiny minnows darted through the weeds and bugs skittered along the glassy surface. I reached down to cup a drink of water but stopped, startled. Staring back at me was the face of the Goddess.

No, 'twas but a reflection of a woman. Me.

I had grown in the ways of the Goddess, and I was ready to take the next step. For Beltane was not only a feast of love, it was a feast of fertility. It was a time for joining two halves to make a whole—the third entity. And although every young witch knew the spell to cast to close the door to the womb, I would not speak that spell. My lunar bleeding was but a week's past, and my body was ripe for his seed.

Tonight we would make a child.

*   *   *

Laughter rumbled through the forest as the coven's Beltane celebration wound down. Sitting on a log, Kyra's father strummed a lute and another covener piped, making merry music for revelers to enjoy. In another part of the circle I sat with the young coveners, finishing up the last of the cakes and wine.

"There you are," Falkner said to Kyra, who giggled behind her hand. "I tell you, it looks quite fine that way, unbridled and untethered." He had removed one of the braids from her hair and was now combing through it intimately with his fingers.

Kyra pressed a fat flower into his face. "You are such a silly goose," she teased.

As far as I was concerned, they were both quite silly, but perhaps I was just impatient to be off to my own Beltane celebration. And worried. What if Ma would not let me go? What if Diarmuid could not get away?

"'Tis time to leave the circle to the elders," I told the others around me. Kyra agreed, and plans were made to head off to Falkner's cottage. I crossed my fingers as we went to our parents for approval, but the festive, relaxed mood prevailed. "Just beware that you are not spotted traveling in a group," my mother advised us. "'Tis a night to revel, but we must not let the Christians get wind of our celebration."

I could hear my mother laughing with friends as we left the circle. Within minutes we were a distance away, and I was saying good-bye to Kyra.

"Be careful!" she whispered before Falkner pulled her away with the others.

I just smiled as I walked quickly through the dark night.

Diarmuid's dark figure was unmistakable. Standing naked under the maypole tree, he was silhouetted by the small fire he had lit in the north quarter of the circle. Now my eyes feasted on what my hands had explored, his rounded muscles, long limbs, smooth skin. He was a god. The red and white ribbons fluttered in the air over his head; the same wind feathered the hair from his noble forehead. The night was dark, the new moon having just passed, but Diarmuid's skin seemed to glow from across the clearing as I paused.

The space between us seemed alive with warmth. Around us the forest sang, its crickets and toads and swaying trees a symphony so clear and sweet, even a deaf man could hear its answer.

I loosened the girdle at my waist, then dropped my own gown to the ground so that I was wearing only a shift. The rustle of cloth made him turn my way, and he smiled. I ran across the clearing, and Diarmuid caught me in his arms against his warm body. We were meant to be together, to participate in this rite tonight. I noticed that he had already lit the candles, so I swept the circle while he called upon the four Watchtowers, drawing pentagrams in the air. Then we went to the maypole and each took a ribbon.

"'Tis a time for joy and a time for sharing," I said as I started to walk around the tree. "The richness of the soil accepts the seeds. For now is the time that seed should be spilled." I knew the words to most Greater Sabbats by heart, but today this particular ritual seemed so fitting! "Let us celebrate the planting of abundance," I went on. "The turning of the Wheel, the season of the Goddess. Let us say farewell to the darkness and greet the light."

"The Wheel turns," Diarmuid said. He walked behind me, wrapping his ribbon over mine.

"Without ceasing, the Wheel turns."

"And turns again," he said as our ribbons twined as inexorably as our love.

When the tree was wrapped with a lovely weave of red and white, we went to the altar, where the crown of early red roses and daisies lay. Diarmuid lifted off my shift, then picked up the crown and held it over my head.

"The Goddess has brought us through the darkness to the light," he said. He lowered the crown to my head, and I felt the heady fragrance of the roses surround me. "Now our Goddess is among us," Diarmuid whispered, his eyes sparkling. "Speak, Lady."

"I am the one who turns the Wheel," I said evenly. I felt the pulse of the Goddess within me, steady and strong, hungry and ravenous. My body was ready to take on his seed, my spirit prepared to mingle with his. "When you thirst," I said, "let my tears fall upon you as gentle rain. When you tire, pause to rest upon the earth that is my breast. Know that love is the spark of life, the fire within you. Love is the beginning and the end of all things."

I opened my arms to Diarmuid, the light of the fire dancing over my naked body. "And I am love," I whispered.

The next morning I left my bed at dawn to bathe in the spring. Most days I simply wash with a rag, but today I went to the deep part of the brook for a more thorough cleansing.

On the grassy bank I glanced around to make sure no one else was afoot. A peahen rushed through the bushes, but otherwise the woods were quiet. Quickly I slipped out of my robe and stepped into the brook. The water was cold, barely two lunar cycles away from the last winter snow, but I ventured all the way in, submerging myself to my neck, just below where my hair was knotted.

A cleansing.

And an offering.

I touched my belly, wondering at the tiny babe inside me. I had a new life to offer up to the Goddess—Diarmuid's baby. Already I knew it to be true, but my secret would grow safe within my belly for a few months. There would be enough time to work on our two clans, time to help them accept Diarmuid and me as man and wife.

Waving my arms through the water, I smiled. My whole body felt aglow with the promise of motherhood. This child would tie us together in a physical way. I knew our baby was another part of the Goddess's plan, which was slowly being revealed to us. I was eager to tell Diarmuid, but for now I would keep my secret as a delightful surprise to be enjoyed after our love was sanctioned by the clans.

Feeling cleansed and refreshed, I arose from the waters and climbed onto the muddy bank. Quickly I pulled on my robe and stepped into my sandals.

But what was that noise?

I peered out of the bushes, searching the path. There was no one in sight, though I felt a strong sense of another's presence.

Had someone been watching me?

8

Esbat Rites, Mid-July

"When the moon is full and the sky is dark,
We meet within our circle.
Now hear the singing of the lark
And dance in the circle, move in the circle.
Do what thou wilt if it harms none,
As the Goddess wills it, may it be done."

A covener sang as we stood in the coven circle, surrounding the High Priestess Síle. Falkner played a pipe, and Kyra joined in the music by beating on a small drum. I think she and Falkner had devised the ruse of practicing their music in order to spend time together—as if their parents weren't wise to their swelling emotions. Kyra had mentioned something of it, but I had been so wrapped up in attempting to see Diarmuid that I'd lost track of the details.

The music ended, and Síle called two coveners—Kyra's

parents—to come forward for the cake and wine ceremony. Side by side, Lyndon and Paige stepped before the altar, where Ma handed Paige a goblet of wine.

Paige lifted the goblet with both hands and held it between her breasts. Facing her, Lyndon took his athame and held the handle between his two palms, the blade pointing down.

Slowly he dipped his blade into the wine, saying: "In like fashion may male join female for the happiness of both."

"Let the fruits of union promote life," Paige responded. "Let all be fruitful and let prosperity spread throughout the land."

Lyndon raised his athame, and his wife held the goblet to his lips so that he could drink. When he finished, he held the goblet for her affectionately.

Watching them, I felt a stirring inside me. Could it be my child waking lazily? My belly had not begun to grow yet, but I had noticed a heaviness in my breasts. Diarmuid had noticed, too, and had teased me that I was coming into womanhood. I still had not told him, and he did not yet realize that my body was preparing to nurse a child. Glancing around the circle, my eyes fixed upon Kyra, whose face was alight tonight, probably warmed by her love for Falkner. A few times I had almost slipped and told her about my baby. I wanted her to know in the worst way but didn't think it fair for her to find out before Diarmuid.

As the wine was passed, I thought of all the couples blessed by the Goddess: Kyra and Falkner, Lyndon and Paige, Diarmuid and me. We had been together for over three months now, seeing each other nearly every day despite the obstacles. Last month we had celebrated the summer solstice by coming together in our circle, surrounded by red feathers for passion. I was more in love with him now than ever, still happy to guard our secret love, our secret child, but I had to admit, I wanted more. Watching a ceremony like tonight's, I realized that change must come. If we were to raise our child together, in a strong coven, it was time to reveal our love to our clans.

After the wine and cakes were passed around, the talk turned to spells to be cast and tales of witch hangings. One covener reported that a Wyndonkylle woman from a village to the south had been pulled from her home and charged with human sacrifice. She was still in prison—if the frightened guards had restrained themselves from burning her without trial.

"'Tis worse than you say," said Ian MacGreavy. "For that woman's coven believes that she was turned in to the authorities by two of our own! They're accusing Wodebaynes of naming her as a witch!"

"No!" everyone grumbled. "It can't be!"

"But there are no Wodebaynes residing in the south," said Falkner's mother.

"Aye, but at the time two of our own happened to be traveling south, right through the Wyndonkylles' village," the miller answered.

"Will we never have justice?" one elder railed. It was Howland Bigelow, an old woodcrafter. "Once again we're being blamed for someone else's evil! Why don't they just heap more condemnation upon our already burdened reputation?"

I felt the ire of the coveners rising as folks broke into smaller groups to tell their own tales of hateful acts against Wodebaynes. A few times in the past we had discussed bigotry in the circle, but never with this level of unrest and anger. The glitter of hatred in Ian MacGreavy's eyes harkened me back to the time I had witnessed him casting a dark spell, and I wondered if any of the other coveners had turned to black magick in private. Perhaps Aislinn, the young rebel, not much older than me, who often railed against the bigots who hated us?

I pressed a hand to my bodice, worried about the child within. I was convinced my bairn was a girl—another future high priestess. But she could not come into a world of hatred and chaos; this rancor had to subside before my child entered this life.

"'Twould be wise to calm your tempers and your fears," came a firm voice. Coveners looked to my mother, who spoke with the authority of the high priestess. "I daresay this is nothing new."

"But Síle, it's getting worse!" old man Bigelow claimed. "I've half a mind to cast a dark spell upon the Wyndonkylles to show them what real black magick is. We're taking the blame for it; we might as well do the deed!"

My mother remained quiet while people grumbled, then answered, "Howland, I know you are far too gentle a man to ever wish harm upon another."

"Oh, I can wish," he said. "I can wish the Goddess would send a mist over their fields to dampen the soil. Ruin their planting!"

"He's right!" Aislinn pushed into the center of the group. "Haven't we endured enough hatred? Isn't it time to fight back?"

People murmured in approval, nodding.

I couldn't believe how eager the folks in our coven were to engage in a war between clans. I winced, realizing how impossible it would be to see Diarmuid if we took to fighting.

"That is quite enough!" Síle said sternly.

The coveners fell silent as she demanded their attention. "We'll have no more talk of evil spells. Have you all forgotten your own initiation into the circle? Your vow to do the

Goddess's will? Have you forgotten that you committed yourself to foster love and peace under the Goddess's sky?"

Aislinn tucked a loose tress of red hair behind her ear and let out a disappointed sigh, but most of the others seemed thoughtful. They seemed to be listening to Ma's words.

"Remember the Witch's Rede?" Síle asked in a commanding voice. "Whatever you desire, whatever you ask of the Goddess, let it harm no one. And remember that as you give, so it shall return threefold."

"'Tis right thinking, Síle," Ian MacGreavy said. "This coven will never engage in dark magick, so 'tis futile to waste words upon it."

I looked at him in awe, remembering his own dark rite. What a hypocrite he was!

But Ma seemed satisfied as the coveners broke into small groups and talked of other matters. My mother had calmed the uproar, but discontent hung in the warm summer night. I worried that this could brew into a terrible storm and vowed to share my fears with Diarmuid.

The next morning as I went to meet Diarmuid, I felt a strange heaviness inside. The coven's anger was still roiling inside me, along with my breakfast. I realized that the sour feeling might be from carrying my baby. Perhaps there was a spell in Ma's Book of Shadows to alleviate it? I would have to take another look. I had been reading up on many of her spells lately—including one I wanted to try with Diarmuid. Although Ma had encouraged me to study her Book of Shadows, I didn't think she had expected me to find the entry on love magick. It claimed that couples sometimes made love in the center of the circle, offering their love force to the Goddess! Nothing like that had ever taken place in our coven circles, but I felt drawn to the idea of making love magick with Diarmuid.

I was also unsettled by the fact that I had lost my love charm. I had taken to carrying the rose stone in my pocket ever since Diarmuid and I first shed our clothes, but I had not come across it for weeks now. 'Twas not the best of days.

Diarmuid was in a far better mood. He chased me through the clearing, swiping at my skirts and wrestling me onto the grassy moss. The carefree play lifted my spirits, but after we kissed for a while, he sensed that something was wrong.

"Rose, there's no light in your eyes today. What is it, love?"

I told him about the trouble brewing between the Wyndonkylles and Wodebaynes.

"I've heard the same tale," he said. "But surely the Wodebaynes aren't involved."

"We are not, but we're being blamed, and I fear a storm brewing among the clans. A war that would destroy our chances of ever seeing each other again."

"I won't let that happen," he insisted.

"Then we must take action now." I paused, reluctant to push. "Let me ask you, Diarmuid, when you think of us, how do you picture us being together?"

"I have always wanted to marry you, Rose," he said, his eyes bright with promise. "Can't you see us two in the circle for a handfasting?"

"I'll wager I've imagined it," I said, studying his beautiful face. "Oh, Diarmuid, we should marry. And soon. Let it happen now."

"Today?" he joked. "Let me run and fetch my ma, for she won't want to miss it."

"Would that it could happen so soon."

"Aye, sooner. That it happened yesterday and we're an old married couple, with me poking around the cottage and asking you what's for dinner."

" 'Twould be a blessing. Far better than what I fear might happen."

"Stop that!" He pressed his hands over my eyes, then over my ears. "Don't listen to what the coven folk say. We are going to be married." He stood up and straightened his white shirt. "I'll go to my coven today and tell them everything. That I love you, that you're the best thing under the Goddess's blue sky, and that we're to be married."

"And if they argue that you're marrying a Wodebayne—"

"They won't. I will not give them the chance." He pulled me to my feet. "I love you, Rose. I'll make things right for us."

In that moment I knew he would. The Goddess had chosen a true hero for me.

I went up on my toes and kissed him. "And I have a spell to help us through. Have you ever heard of love magick?"

Diarmuid smiled. "No, but I think I will like it."

The spell in Ma's Book of Shadows was simple. I swept the circle and told Diarmuid to shed his clothes, lie back, and think of what we wanted to dedicate ourselves to.

When I had finished the preparations, I lay beside him, staring at the cloudy sky. "Picture us together," I whispered, "our union accepted by our clans, by all clans." I reached over and touched his shoulder. He quickly turned on his side and kissed me.

"Would we be together like this?" he asked, running a hand along my thigh.

"Aye, always."

"As close as this?" He lifted his body over mine and pressed against me.

"Aye," I whispered, focusing on our union, offering our act to the Goddess. Within the circle our bodies rose in heat and splendor, and I felt the glow of our love rising to the heavens.

"Aye, Goddess, we are here for You," I whispered as Diarmuid and I tumbled into passion.

Our love magick was strong. That night when I left our circle I heard thunder rumbling overhead. I felt sure the Goddess had received our offering. She was shaking up the heavens in preparation for Diarmuid's big announcement.

But the next day, when Diarmuid was to have met me at our secret place, he did not appear. Nor did he make it there the day after that. On the third day I sent him a *tua labra*: *Where are you? Why can you not meet your love?* But I received no response. I wondered whether he had received my message. Had something terrible happened? As each day passed, I waited for the rumble in the heavens to manifest itself on earth. Surely if I looked carefully, I would see Diarmuid tramping up the path to our cottage, his parents marching dutifully behind him, eager to work out with Síle the details of our union.

With the dawn of yet another morning I pushed open the shutter and peered out, longing for the glimpse of a Leapvaughn tartan or a flash of Diarmuid's lovely blue eyes. The path was still but for a jackrabbit searching for greens. My rescuer had not come for me . . . at least, I thought, not yet.

That afternoon Kyra and I went to the woods to gather fresh summer herbs. While Kyra was cutting clover, I went in search of clove, which was good for settling the stomach. When our pouches were full, we went to the circle Diarmuid and I had gathered in so many times. There, on the rock altar, we consecrated our herbs. As we finished, I noticed that Kyra had been unusually quiet today. I watched her sorting herb pouches in her basket, her chestnut hair braided into a twist at the top of her head.

"You know, with your hair up like that, you look like your ma," I said.

She smiled. "Falkner likes my hair free and loose, but 'tis too much to endure in this heat." Leaving her basket, she lifted my hair from my shoulders and waved it over my neck. "You'll roast under the sun with your hair down."

"I'll be fine."

"I must say I am worried about you, Rose. How many days has it been?"

I knew she was talking about how long since I'd seen Diarmuid. "Seven . . . no, eight."

"Eight days and you still believe he's coming back?"

"Of course he is. We rendered some powerful magick together, Kyra. Right here in this circle." My hair slipped out of her hands as I kicked off my shoes and walked the circle. I had come to know every tree root and dirt clod in this sacred place. I went over to the green moss that had often served as our bed and sat down. "The last time I saw him, we performed love magick. Did you hear the thunder in the sky that night? 'Twas us, devoting our love to the Goddess."

"I thought the rumbling was the sound of coming rain," Kyra said. "Rose, I really am worried about you."

"Don't despair for me," I said. "My Diarmuid will be here soon. You must help me plan the handfasting ceremony."

Kyra smiled. "I shall be so happy for you on your wedding day, Rose. That a Leapvaughn could love you so . . . 'tis truly the work of the Goddess."

I smiled back, trying not to worry. I didn't want to admit to Kyra that I had begun to wonder what had happened to Diarmuid. Where was my love? Why was he taking so long to come to my clan and my coven and announce his intentions to marry me? I knew the Goddess intended us to be together, but my patience was beginning to wear thin.

We returned to my cottage and found it empty.

"Ma said she was going into Kirkloch today," I said, pouring two mugs of cool tea. We set my share of the herbs out to dry, then went outside to sit in the shady grass, hoping to catch a breeze. Kyra told me of her first kiss with Falkner and of how they now kissed constantly, as if they'd both had their first taste of honey cakes. As I listened, I stared intently at the edge of the cottage path, willing Diarmuid to appear.

And lo, as my eyes strained in the distance, I saw the brush move, giving way to a pair of feet.

"He's coming!" I cried, scrambling to stand and adjust my skirts. As I settled myself, I saw that it wasn't Diarmuid, but a young boy. "It's not him." My voice dropped off in disappointment.

"But it is a Leapvaughn," Kyra said excitedly. "Look at the plaid of his tartan."

"Indeed." My heart swelled as the young boy smiled at us shyly.

"I've a message here for Rose MacEwan."

"That's me," I said, coming forward to meet him.

He reached into his satchel and removed a piece of pressed linen, much like the parchment we used in our Books of Shadows. Handing it to me, he bowed. "Good day to you."

My heart swelled with joy as I held the note to my breast. "I can barely breathe!"

"Read it! Read it!" Kyra gasped.

I started to read. " 'My dearest Rose, it is with heavy heart that I write to you. I will always love you, but . . .' "

The words began to stick in my throat. I could not speak, but neither could I tear my eyes away.

I have come to see that we can never be together. It was foolish of me to think we could marry, though I will ever think of you longingly in our special place of the forest. Think of me when you go there, for mine eyes will never feast on that place or on you again.

Please, Rose, do not cry for me. There will be others for you. Perhaps a stout, hearty Wodebayne lad? In the meantime, the best thing you can do is forget me.

Truly,

Diarmuid

Pain cut me like a spear through the middle of my body. I folded myself over the note, collapsing onto the ground. Sobbing in the dirt, I was barely aware of Kyra fluttering about, trying to get me inside, to fetch some water, to stroke my hair.

Diarmuid was not coming.

He would not marry me.

My life was truly coming to an end.

*   *   *

The days were a blur of swallowed tears and pain. When Ma first found me abed in the cottage, she pressed her hand to my forehead in alarm. "Are you ill?" she asked, her eyes stricken with concern.

"Quite ill," I told her. " 'Tis my digestion. Nothing tastes quite right anymore."

She quickly set about placing cool rags upon my head and wrists and making me a special potion to drink. I watched as she boiled together meadowsweet, mint, and catnip leaves and flowers. 'Twas a lesson in herbs, but a painful one. I didn't know how long I could pretend that all my pain was physical, but I couldn't begin to tell my mother the truth about Diarmuid.

My Diarmuid!

I was devastated. How could he turn away from me? I pressed my face to the pillow as a new round of tears racked my body. Ma kept asking me where it hurt, and I lied and said that the pain was in my belly. I couldn't bear to reveal that I was suffering a broken heart.

Kyra came to see me every day, bringing me flowers and fresh-baked biscuits that did sit well once swallowed. One afternoon Kyra stayed with me while Ma went out on an errand, and she encouraged me to throw on a summer shawl and venture outside the cottage for some fresh air.

The sun was hot, but there was a cooling breeze, making the heat tolerable. My body felt feeble, like a creaking old cart, but Kyra said that was from staying in bed so long. We sat under an ancient tree by the path.

"You cannot let one boy strike you down so," Kyra told me. "You'll forget about him in time."

"Never," I said, reaching to touch my belly. A tiny mound was growing there, though it was still too soon for anyone else to notice. "I cannot let Diarmuid go, for I am to have his child come Imbolc."

Kyra gasped. "A babe! 'Tis no wonder you're feeling ill."

"Aye, but Ma's teas of mint and meadowsweet have helped the illness in my body. 'Tis the pain in my heart that will not relent."

"Oh, Rose . . . poor Rose!" Kyra rubbed my back gently through the shawl. "To be with child! It must be terrible for you. I wish you had told me earlier. I'll help you be rid of it. There are herbs that—"

"I want the child," I said.

She shook her head sadly. "Not here, not now? To bear a bastard child in these parts is dangerous. You'll be ostracized by everyone—even some in our own coven!"

Kyra was right. To give birth to a child out of wedlock was a sin shunned by all in the Highlands. My life would be ruined. I folded my arms across my belly. "'Twill be fine, for the child has a father. Diarmuid will come to me before Imbolc."

"And if he doesn't?"

I bit my lips tight, refusing to answer.

"No one has to know you lost the babe! I've heard you can brew a tea—"

"'Tis enough talk of that!" I insisted. "Diarmuid will be a father to my child." I drew the shawl around me closer. "I'm sure he would be here now if he knew. . . ." As my words trailed off, I realized I had stumbled upon the solution.

This baby would bring Diarmuid to me. Once he knew of its life, he would leap over the obstacles between us.

"That's it," I said, blinking. "I must tell him." I stood up, feeling strength rise within me. "I must go to him."

Kyra stared up at me, shaking her head.

"If I go to him with news of our child, surely he will think of a way for us to be together! He will be so overcome with joy, nothing will deter him."

"But the note . . ." Kyra stood up and brushed her skirts. "He said that . . ."

I waved her off. "He knew nothing of our child when he

wrote that." I headed toward the cottage, thinking of the new possibilities. "Perhaps when his parents learn of our babe, they will soften, too. We could live with them. Or if they reject us, Diarmuid shall come live among the Wodebaynes. I know our coveners will be suspicious of him, but once they come to know him, they will accept him."

With each breath, the flush of health filled my body. I had been sick over Diarmuid, but the cure was within my grasp now. I could go to my love. And once he learned of the blessed child within my womb, he would welcome me with open arms.

The following day I set off in a horse-drawn cart toward Diarmuid's village of Lillipool. Falkner had managed to secure the cart and horse from his father's shop, and Kyra sat between us, warning of the punishment the three of us would face if our parents found out the true reason for our visit to Lillipool. She could be so mettlesome at times, though I did have her to thank for arranging for the cart. In my current condition, I was not sure I could walk all the way to Lillipool without incident.

Lillipool was considered to be a Christian village, though for some time our coven had known that the Vykrothes had a circle nearby and Leapvaughn sheepherders lived in cottages on its outskirts. There was the usual small church, which I assumed Diarmuid's clan attended to avoid persecution as witches. A mill cranked at the edge of the village. We passed by it, then came upon the village center. In Lillipool's small, dusty square, peddlers displayed their wares amid clouds of blowing dirt. No one knew why grass refused to grow on the village green here, but my mother had once told me that although Leapvaughns have a gift for sales and carpentry, they were known to be barren farmers.

Falkner guided the wagon through the lane, stopping for passing villagers who paid us little mind. He brought the cart over to a small wagon at the end of the square, its side panel painted Ye Finest Wood Crafters. "I've got to pick up a table for Da," he said. "'Twill be a short while, if you want to walk around."

He helped us down from the cart, and we dusted our skirts and stepped forward gingerly, our arms linked.

"I hope he is here," I said. "His father likes him to tend the sheep, but Diarmuid prefers to spend his time in the village and at market."

Kyra nodded, averting her eyes as a tin peddler leered at her. "'Tis an odd village," she said. "Like a desert in the Highlands."

As we walked past a tinker's wagon, a cart laden with fruits, and another with an array of bonnets, I kept searching for Diarmuid. I spotted a lad who walked with the same gait and another who seemed to share his broad smile, but I did not see my love.

When we reached the end of the row of carts, I spied a head of gingery brown hair. It was feathered back from his face, revealing startling blue eyes and a smile that warmed my heart.

Diarmuid.

"There he is!" I gasped.

Kyra squeezed my arm. "You found him."

But he was not alone. A tall, swanlike girl with pale yellow hair walked beside him.

"Who is she?" Kyra muttered.

"I don't know. Perhaps a friend."

Kyra looked back toward the cart. "I'll go see if Falkner can find out."

I barely noticed that she had left my side. My Diarmuid was within reach, so close I could run into his arms, yet something kept me there, my feet mired to the ground. Who was the girl? I watched in horror as she said something to him, making him laugh. It had all the markings of flirtation. But then he chucked her under the chin, seeming more like an older brother. An older woman came by and handed the girl a tart. She took a taste, then fed the rest to Diarmuid with her bare fingers.

Such an intimate gesture. And he took it from her hand, licking his lips. Oh, Goddess, what did it mean?

"Rose," Kyra said, softly resting her hand on my arm. "'Tis terrible . . . your worst fears confirmed! She is Diarmuid's betrothed! They were promised to each other as children, and they are to be wed upon next Samhain!"

I shook my head. "An arranged marriage?" How could it be? Why had he never told me? I pressed my hands to my hot cheeks. If Diarmuid was promised to another, we had no chance of being married.

"Oh, Rose!" Kyra squeezed my arm. "Such dire news, and you with child . . ."

It couldn't be. My hands dropped to fists at my side, and for a moment I wanted to rush over and pummel him. Diarmuid was not the hero I had thought him to be. He had lied to me.

But then, he'd faced overwhelming obstacles. Perhaps he'd been trying to protect me from this until he sorted it out? And if his parents had arranged the marriage, that meant he'd had no choice. "So he doesn't love her," I said, thinking aloud. "And of course, his parents would want him to marry within his clan. I'm sure it's part of the reason they don't want him to marry me."

"Not really," Kyra said. "The girl's name is Siobhan MacMahon, and she is not a Leapvaughn, but a Vykrothe."

"An arranged marriage to someone from another clan?"

Anger rose in my throat, hot and painful. His parents thought it acceptable for him to marry outside his clan but not to marry me? Or was it that he could not marry a Wodebayne?

"Falkner has the table loaded in the cart," Kyra said. "He's ready to leave."

"But I haven't . . ." I glanced over at Diarmuid. Siobhan still hovered about him like a bee collecting nectar from a flower. It was hardly the time to march over and tell the boy I was going to bear his child.

This meeting had not worked out the way I'd planned. Not at all.

"Rose, you're crying," Kyra said gently.

"No matter." I swiped the tears out of my eyes with the backs of my hands. I needed to see him with her. I needed to see the enemy.

I stared at the swan-necked girl who was fawning over Diarmuid. She was tall and lithe, with flaxen gold hair. Everything about her was the physical opposite of me.

Diarmuid could not love one so unlike me. How could it be, Goddess? How was it possible that he could love another at all?

"We'd better go," Kyra said.

I felt her clamp my arm and pull me away toward the cart, my eyes still on Diarmuid's betrothed. How could he even think of marrying another?

How could he?

9

On the Making and Charming of Poppets

I promised myself I would cry no more. Everyone knew too much sobbing could harm the child in a mother's womb, and I was beginning to learn that tears were futile. I needed to do something to secure my baby's happiness and health.

It was time to use my powers.

Why had I not thought of this before? I wondered as I steadfastly sewed and decorated my poppets, working a little each day and night. The course of my relationship with Diarmuid ran parallel to my magick. Had I not captivated him completely with the rose stone? And then, when I'd misplaced it, he had fallen away, never returning to our secret circle. It was so clear. I needed to enlist the Goddess's help to get him back in my arms.

I went through Ma's cupboard of stones, searching for a gem to replace the rose stone. I weighed each stone in my palm and turned it about, hoping to feel a swell or glow of power, but nothing moved me. Perhaps a charm wasn't the right thing anymore. Time for a spell.

First I dedicated a candle to him, carving runes up the side that spelled his name. Although I had to hide the candle from Ma, I burned it whenever she went out, chanting to the Goddess to rekindle the love flame in this boy. And when the flame was doused, I censed my belly with the smoke, inviting my babe to feel my love for her father.

While working candle magick, I also searched for a powerful love spell. Although Ma had instructed Kyra on the making of love dolls, I could not recall the details. Searching my mother's Book of Shadows, I came across the spell. It was called simply Poppets.

> Thou must craft two poppets to represent the two lovers.
>
> What is done to the poppets shall be done to the lovers.
>
> Cut two pieces of cloth shaped like a man, then two shaped like a woman. While cutting the cloth, bring to mind the person it represents. If the ideal lover has long, flowing hair or a comely beard, so should the poppet. Thou must heed—the lover thou seekest is thine ideal mate, not a named lord or lady.
>
> Stuff the figure with herbs governed by Venus. Such herbs: verbena, feverfew, yarrow, motherwort, rosebuds, or damiana.
>
> 'Tis strong magick! Use only for a love that will have permanence, not for a mere dalliance.

Thou must thrice perform a love ritual over the poppets during the waxing moon.

The spell was very specific and promised to be very powerful. And I would give it all the more power by making my doll look just like Diarmuid and embroidering his name upon it. My own brand of magick had worked well when charming the rose stone; I felt sure this would be even stronger.

It took me days to construct the dolls, during which Ma noticed and encouraged my work. "You are seventeen years of age, Rose. Perhaps 'tis time for you to fall in love with a gentle witch." She didn't see the name I had stitched upon it, didn't realize that I was making a Diarmuid poppet, designed to capture *his* love, and I didn't dare tell her that I was working magick she considered to be dark. When the dolls were done, I had to wait for the waxing moon to begin the spell. I felt impatient, but I knew that the spell would have its full potency only if I followed the instructions.

By the time I was ready to perform the spell for the third time, it was August and Lughnassadh preparations were upon us. During the weeks of preparing the dolls and consecrating them, I missed Diarmuid desperately. My only consolation was that we would have the rest of our lives together once we made it past this obstacle. I also noticed that the babe was growing, pushing at the swath of cloth I belted around my skirts. I had to adjust the girdle higher, which only seemed to accent the new lushness of my breasts. Perhaps this was the Goddess's purpose in waiting—to give Diarmuid a visible sign of my love for him, the child within my womb.

10

Lughnassadh

Rising before dawn on the day of Lughnassadh, the celebration to honor the Sun God, I set off to my secret circle to complete the love spell. As I had done before, I placed the poppets facedown on the stone altar and consecrated the circle. I charged the girl poppet to be me, then picked up the boy, with feathery brown hair made of spun wool. Sprinkling it with salted water and censing it, I chanted: "This poppet is Diarmuid, my *mùirn beatha dàn* in every way. As Diarmuid lives, so lives this poppet. Aught that I do to it, I do to him."

I kissed the Diarmuid poppet, then put him back beside the other on the altar. Kneeling before them, I moved the two poppets closer to each other, touching, turning, pressing face-to-face. As I moved them, I pictured myself reaching out to Diarmuid, meeting him, touching him, kissing and holding him so close in my arms, I could taste the salt on his skin.

When the poppets were face-to-face, I wrapped my red ribbon around them. "Now may the Goddess bind these two together, as I do bind them here," I said. Around and around I circled them with ribbon, then tied it tightly so they would never, ever break apart. "Now they are forever one. May each truly become a part of the other. Separated, they shall seem incomplete. So mote it be!"

I rested my athame over the bound puppets, asking the Goddess to lend Her power to this and all spells I cast. Then I wrapped the poppets in a clean white cloth. I would stow them in the rafters of the cottage so that no animal or human could meddle with my magick.

After my task was done, I lifted my head to the bright midday sky. The heat was blistering hot today, casting a white glow across the land. Aye, 'twas the right day to honor the Sun God. I would go to Lillipool, but not until the sun had passed. 'Twas best not to make such a journey in the heat. Besides, of late my babe had drained me of strength. I no longer needed special herbs to calm my dizziness, but it seemed the babe wanted me to sleep the day away! I needed rest and a sip of cool tea.

By late afternoon, when the air had cooled and Ma was off preparing for the Lughnassadh celebration, I knew 'twas time to go. As I walked, I chanted bits and pieces of the love spell. "Now may the Goddess bind these two together, as I do bind them here. . . . Separated they would seem incomplete. . . ." The spell sustained me, and in no time the old mill of Lillipool loomed before me.

Today I was not so lucky as to find him in the dusty marketplace. I knew his coven would also be preparing to celebrate the sun festival, but what were his assigned tasks? To mull the wine—or consecrate the circle? I wouldn't dare go near another coven's circle, not that I would be able to find it.

Help me, Goddess, I prayed. Point me in the direction of my love.

I circled the dismal marketplace, hoping for an answer. Diarmuid did not appear, but as I paced, I came across a red feather. It sat in the middle of the lane, alone and abandoned, and the sight of it reminded me of the red feathers twined with ivy that I had used for our celebration of midsummer night. I had twined ivy around the feathers—red for sexuality—and festooned them around our circle.

Now this feather pointed down a lane. Was it pointing me toward my love?

I believed it to be so. Making haste, I followed the lane, which led past the church and quaint cottages to the countryside. My eyes followed the dark green patches of grass to a small hollow where a figure lay sleeping in the shade.

Diarmuid.

He was probably supposed to be tending sheep, though this summer heat would drive any lad to napping. I ventured off the road and crossed to him, my shoes whispering in the crisp grass. Although I did not call out to him, he stirred with my approach, rubbing his eyes. He turned toward me, saw me, then bolted upright.

"What vision is this?" he gasped. "Has the Goddess herself descended, or am I but asleep and dreaming of love?"

My heart melted. He was still the same Diarmuid, a poet and a tease.

"I have come to reclaim you," I said firmly.

He took my hand and lifted it to his lips. "You will always have my heart, Rose."

"I want more," I said, thrilled by the spark of his lips upon my hand. "We summoned the Goddess to bless our union, and she did. She looks down upon us with favor, yet you allow another to become your betrothed?"

He stared at the ground. "'Twas not my doing, Rose."

"Do you not remember your last words to me? That we were to be married forthwith?"

"I do," he said sheepishly. "But 'tis not so simple a matter."

"Aye, there are complications, but I have come to help you through them."

His blue eyes sparkled with regret. "I'm afraid you can't help, Rose. No one can help me. I have learned that a man cannot cross his elders or defy his clan. I need the approval of my coven, and they have vowed not to give it."

"Aye, I face the same challenges," I said, thinking of my ma and the coveners who wanted to rail against rival clans. "But this is no surprise, Diarmuid. We talked of it often. 'Twill not be easy, but you must remain steadfast and strong, lower your head and charge, like the ram in yonder field."

"Would that I were a ram, destined to chew grass and laze in the sun." He reached for his throat and nervously squeezed the pentagram concealed by his shirt. "Instead, I am a marriageable lad, a property of my parents dangled like a carrot before a horse."

"Tell me you don't love her," I said.

"She has her fair attractions," he said, cutting me.

My knees nearly buckled beneath me. Was this my love, the one who had pledged his love in the Goddess's circle?

He had promised to love me and only me. He was supposed to see only my charms.

Did he kiss her the way he had kissed me? Did he touch her and . . . oh, excruciating torture! I could not think of such things now. Think of the spell, I told myself. Your reason for being here—your baby.

"But mostly, it is the ease with which my life will progress if I take her hand."

His words gave me some relief. I realized it was time to tell him. "Yet I offer not a life of ease, but a sign of our bond." Boldly I took his hand and placed it on my belly. "There is a child within, Diarmuid. Do you feel it stirring?"

He gasped, stepping closer to me. There was power in his touch, magnified all the more by the glow of the child growing inside me.

"The Goddess has given us a babe, a sign of our union. 'Twill be the child that unites the Wodebaynes and the Leapvaughns. Perhaps our child will unite all clans. Oh, Diarmuid, this is how the Goddess intended it. Could you deny such a powerful destiny?"

"I could not," he gasped. "I will not." His face softened as he stroked my belly. "A man does not abandon his child, no matter what the obstacles."

My spirits lifted. He understood. He knew that our baby was a sign from the Goddess.

"We must marry now—today!" he said, pulling me into his arms for a kiss. Then he pulled away and dropped to his knees to kiss my belly. "My child. Goddess be praised!" He kissed the baby over and over again.

I smiled. "How would you marry? In a church? Or do you

think one of our covens would add a highly unusual hand-fasting to the Lughnassadh rites?"

"We'll do it any way we can," he insisted. "Mayhap your village is best, away from Siobhan and my family. We'll go to the Presbyterian reverend first—tonight. Surely he will help us."

My heart lifted. Diarmuid was coming home with me. We would be together—married!

"After that we'll arrange a handfasting," he went on. "No one dare deny us once we're together. I must first run home for a few belongings, then I shall meet you." He glanced up, gauging the position of the sun. "Let us meet at our circle in the woods before the sun sets."

I put my hand in his hair, loving the feel of it. "Would that we could travel together."

"Aye, but your presence would raise too much of a stir at my cottage right now. We'll meet in the woods at our circle before sunset." He stood up and kissed me again. "Oh, Rose, you are the world to me. After today we shall never be separated again."

"Never," I said, thinking of the words of the love spell. "Never."

The journey back to my own woods was cooled by afternoon breezes and dreams of lingering in Diarmuid's arms. On the way I stopped at the brook for a drink of water, then headed off to prepare the circle for our formal reunion. I swept the circle, then decided to rest on the moss for a while, as the long journeys had taken their toll on my strength. I sat there chanting from the love spell and picturing Diarmuid in my bed each morning when I arose. Where would we live? Perhaps Ma would have us once she got over her initial anger. Besides, she would want to be near the babe, to help nurse her, then to teach her the ways of the Goddess as she grew older. Listening to the sounds of the woods—to the trill of birds and the rustle of wind in the trees—I dozed off.

When I awoke, it was dark but for the sickly glow of a yellow moon.

Where was Diarmuid? I sat up suddenly, and my sacred place seemed like a strange wilderness. My life force hammered in my chest as reality hit me.

He was not here. Was he coming?

What had happened? "Oh, Goddess, keep and protect him," I whispered, sure that something dreadful had happened to him. There could be no other explanation. I had seen the determination in his eyes, I had felt his commitment. Nothing could stay him from me. Nothing but . . . something terrible and evil.

I stood up, brushing dust and seeds from my hair. I would return to Diarmuid's village. I had surely missed the coven circle, but I planned to miss many more in my life with Diarmuid. Who knew where our adventures would take us? And right now he needed me. I had to go to him.

Darkness closed in around me as I crept through the woods, following my familiar landmarks to the road. I started on my way, wending over a rise. Glancing up, I saw a girl my own age approaching.

Swanlike neck. Flaxen hair.

Siobhan MacMahon.

I was gripped by hatred for her—everything about her, from her sun-kissed hair to her long, graceful neck. But as she caught sight of me, I realized that perhaps I was being unfair. Perhaps, in Diarmuid's troubles, he had sent her to come for me. Perhaps she was the messenger of my love. I stepped toward her, eager for news.

"Hark!" I called out to her. "Have you come in search of me, Rose MacEwan?"

"Aye." She drew close, a sourness pinching her mouth. "I have come in search of Diarmuid's harlot."

I felt stung.

"I have just come from him, the poor lad," she said. "He was about to ruin his life by running off with a woman who could satisfy only his base desires. A Wodebayne! Such foolishness. I stopped him in the nick of time."

"How did you stop him?" I asked, afraid of the harm she might have done to him. "Did you hurt him?"

" 'Twas not necessary. I needed only to sate his desires to remind him of his attraction to me. He's fine. Sleeping like a babe, if you must know."

I felt my hands clenching into fists at the implications. Had she lain with him? I could not believe it to be true. He had sworn to be my first and last love and I his. "I don't believe you," I said. "I do not believe a word you are saying."

"Aye, but then, you Wodebaynes aren't bright, are you? That's what I told him. Why throw away a beautiful life with me so that you can waste away with a savage, uneducated Wodebayne?"

"Perhaps he does not want to be counted among warmongers like the Vykrothes?" I jabbed.

She cocked her head, as if weary. "He is perfectly fine with my clan. That's part of his problem. Diarmuid gets on with everyone. At least, every lass. I guess you might call it the charm of the Leapvaughns. They do like to trick us. You are not his first little mistake, you know. He has had others before you." She folded her arms contentedly. "But he always comes back to me."

A mistake? A trick? Her words darted through the air like arrows. I sized her up. If I were to battle her, I felt, I would win, and the temptation to cast her to the ground was irresistible.

"How dare you!" I seethed, reaching for her arm.

Siobhan stepped away, avoiding me. "Take heed." She smiled like a cat who has fallen but landed on her feet. "You cannot fight the forces at work here. He and I were promised by our parents long ago. 'Twas a plan to unite the Vykrothes and Leapvaughns. And although my Diarmuid has strayed with the likes of you, he always comes back to me." Her pale gray eyes were full of spite. "He loves me. You are just a passing fancy."

"So you say," I said tartly, though I felt my strength washing away in the rising tide of doubt. I stood there, trying to fight the feelings that swept through me at the implication that Diarmuid had lain with another, perhaps many others. *Oh, Goddess!* I wanted to fall to the ground and sob but wouldn't give Siobhan the satisfaction of witnessing my fully blossomed pain.

Would he betray me?

Would he lie with another?

Oh, Diarmuid . . .

"I've come here not to fight with you, but to give you a warning," Siobhan went on. "I know of your silly magick and your Wodebayne tendency to turn to the dark forces."

She reached into her pocket and took out a small object. She
held it up to the moon, then tossed it to my feet.

The rose stone! How had she come to have it?

"It is worthless now," she said. "I saw to that."

The small stone looked dim and gray in the dust of the
road. I felt too startled to pick it up or respond.

"Stay away from Diarmuid, or you will regret it for as
long as you live." With that, Siobhan turned away and
marched off toward Lillipool.

I stared after her in utter shock. Ordering me away from
my love? Crossing my magick charm! Defying the Goddess!
Malice rose within me, churning, burning. The urge to shoot
dealan-dé at her made my hands twitch. I lifted my hand . . .

But she turned back with a scowl.

I held the fire within me, held on to the desire to blast her
in the face. "You haven't seen the end of me!" I shouted. "You
will not have Diarmuid, and you will pay for foiling our plans."

Siobhan laughed. It was a cruel, cold sound that seemed
to dance on the summer breeze. She was still laughing when
she turned away and strode off. Even from behind, her long
neck and pale beauty were regal and comely. I wished she
would shape-shift into a fat swan and fly away!

There in the center of the road, I stretched my arms out
to the Goddess and lifted my face to the sky. I was so frustrated! Why did I keep losing my love at every turn? Despite
Diarmuid's weaknesses, I knew the Goddess intended us to
be together. I knew he was destined to be a father to the
child in my womb.

The moon above me was ringed with a watery halo—a
sign of disruption. As I watched, it moved like a ring of oil,

snaking in and out. A ring of madness. It made me wary. Nothing in the air tonight was reliable. It was a moon of illusions and interruptions. I half expected the ground beneath my feet to buckle and give way, dropping me deep into an earthly grave.

Oh, what was I doing, suffering hysterics here in the middle of the road, where murderers, thieves, and disapproving Christians could come along at any second? Overwhelmed, I moved off the road to hide behind some bushes, pressed my palms to my face, and began to cry. It was too much to bear—losing my love again! And it hurt all the more now that he knew of our child. He was not just turning against me: he was rejecting the tiny babe in my womb!

I was on my knees, sobbing, when I sensed another blood witch in the brush behind me. I turned and stared into the darkness, using my magesight. Aislinn, the young witch from Síle's coven, was closing in on a rabbit. She leaped into a patch of watery moonlight, trying to catch it, but the animal slipped away at the last second.

She was probably on her way home from the Lughnassadh circle, but what was she doing trying to catch a rabbit? "Aislinn?" I called through my tears. "What are you doing?" Could she be trying to capture a creature to spill its blood in a dark spell?

"Oh, just having a game with the creature," Aislinn said, closing the distance between us. Her mouth twitched a bit, making me wonder if my suspicions were correct. "What say you, Rose? Your ma said you were ill, but here, collapsed along the road?" She hurried over and helped me to my feet. "Can you walk?"

"I think so," I said, "though I have nowhere to go now that . . ." A new wave of hysteria came over me, and I choked on my words.

Aislinn patted my back. "Come now, Rose. I've never seen you in such a state. We must sit." She led me to a fallen log, where we sat amid the fireflies. "We missed you at the circle tonight, and I know your ma was worried, though she made your excuses, claiming that your sickness had arisen once again. I sense that it is not sickness that kept you away, but some other distressing matter."

As she talked, I dried my eyes with the hem of my summer skirt. When she pushed back her red hair, I noticed that she had inscribed runes of plant dye on her forehead as part of her devotion to the Sun God. I gasped. It was typical Aislinn, but Reverend Winthrop of the village would have her hanged for the pagan practice if he saw the markings. It seemed as though she were risking her life to flaunt her devotion to the Goddess. Aislinn had always been a rebel, and I found much of her behavior shocking. I was not sure that I could trust her, but she was a member of my coven, and at the moment I had so few choices.

"You have guessed right," I told her. "It seems I am caught in a terrible love triangle, and I have spent the evening grappling with a vicious Vykrothe girl who intends to steal my love away!"

Her face was awash with moonlight and interest, so I told her of my sorrows. Of my love for Diarmuid despite our clan differences. Of his intentions to run away with me. Of Siobhan's interference. I managed to exclude mention of my baby, not wanting to give Aislinn more than her share of sordid details. And it seemed that her ardor was fired by the situation alone.

"Yet another example of the other clans conspiring against us!" she railed. "Oh, you poor girl! To be the victim of their hatred."

I felt new tears slip down my cheeks at her words. At the moment I didn't care so much about the hatred among the clans, I just wanted Diarmuid back.

"I don't blame you for crying," Aislinn said. Her red hair fell over one cheek like a thick veil as she leaned toward me. "It's a heavy burden upon your shoulders now, made all the worse by the fact that your ma doesn't understand at all. She keeps telling Wodebayne folks to lie down while the other clans trample over us!"

I sniffed, surprised that Aislinn understood how difficult it was to be the daughter of a high priestess, especially one with such strong views. Although the Wodebaynes had endured bigotry throughout my life, my mother had never wavered from her position of peace among the clans. I wondered about Ma now. She would be annoyed at my disappearance. But her true fury would pour out when she learned of my love for a boy from another clan and of my pregnancy.

Pressing a hand against my belly, I realized I would have to return to Síle tonight. It was late, and it would be far too dangerous, not to mention foolhardy, for me and my babe to try to make the journey into Lillipool tonight.

Oh, how had I gotten myself into such a position?

"You cannot let this matter rest," Aislinn said, her eyes lit with determination.

"Aye, my heart will not let me." Nor will the child inside me, I thought as I slid off the log.

"You must fight back," Aislinn went on. "Síle and her coveners keep trying to tamp down the fires, but there's no quenching the blaze now. The other clans have struck the first blows, and now it's up to us to show them the strength of our magick. We have the power to punish the other clans. Why don't we use it?"

"Indeed." For once I agreed with Aislinn. I had borne so many slights as a result of hatred against the Wodebaynes. It was all too much. I could barely hold my head steady as I started to trundle home.

"I will see you home," Aislinn said, slipping an arm around my waist. "We'll talk more when you're feeling better."

Grateful for the firm hand at my waist, I tried to concentrate on making my way home. What would I say to Ma when I got there, and how would she react?

I meandered up the path to Ma's cottage cautiously, expecting her to fly out the door and have at me. But the cottage was silent and dark, and when I opened the door, I saw that Ma was not there. I stepped inside the shadowed house and slipped off my shoes, greatly relieved. Sleep could not come soon enough. Wanting nothing more than to fall into bed, I removed the girdle at my waist and slipped off my light summer gown. Standing before the washbasin, I tipped the water pitcher over it to rinse my face and hands . . .

And out hopped a frog.

I shrank back. A frog? In the cottage? As I went to light a candle from the fire, I heard a croak. And when I turned back toward the room, I saw them—frogs everywhere! Bumpy, spotted frogs dotted the floor, rode the chairs, perched on the bed.

I shrieked. They were surrounding me! How had they gotten in here?

Feeling as if I had nowhere to turn, I grabbed the broom, threw open the door, and began to coax them out. "Begone!" I said. "Back to where you belong!" I didn't want to harm the Goddess's creatures, but their presence unnerved me. I scooted them off the bed, pushed them from the chairs, swept them across the floor. The fat, slimy creatures burped in response. I swung the broom, sending them hopping. "Begone!" I cried through tears of frustration.

As I shooed out a tiny creature who seemed determined to turn back, I noticed a lantern bobbing along the path. It was Ma. Her face seemed placid, even amused as she ventured closer for a better look. She eyed the creatures now dotting the path to our cottage. "Frogs?"

"The cottage was riddled with them when I returned."

"What sort of infantile spell is this?" she asked, stepping aside as a frog skittered out the door.

A spell! Of course. 'Twas a spell from Siobhan, the wicked wench.

"I haven't seen the likes of it since I was a young girl," Ma said. "'Tis a silly little thing, usually in a child's Book of Shadows."

I stopped sweeping as a tear rolled down to my chin and fell, plopping onto a frog. Suddenly something inside me snapped, and my tears turned to laughter. The tear-struck creature hopped out the door, croaking its complaint.

Ma laughed, too, and we fell together, embracing in the midst of the ludicrous scene. Soon after, we recovered enough to shoo the remaining frogs out the door. As Ma moved about with the lantern, checking the corners of the cottage for stragglers, she spoke. "I have been worried about you. I was just out searching, knowing how unlike you it is to miss a Greater Sabbat. Are you ill?"

"'Tis terrible, Ma," I said. "Though I am not ill." I sat down at the table and told her. I told her how I had fallen in love with someone from another clan, another coven, and how I had lost my Leapvaughn love because of his arranged marriage to a Vykrothe. I told her everything—omitting only the mention of the babe, for 'twould be too much to lay upon her in one sitting.

"'Tis no wonder I've been concerned," Ma said. "I knew you were carrying a heavy load these days, though I did not know the specifics." She stood up from the table and went over to her cupboard of magickal things. "I must admit, Rose, I was quite alarmed to discover this just before I left for the Sabbat." From the cupboard she removed a white satchel. No, not a satchel—a white cloth. She lifted it to reveal the two poppets I'd made! But they were no longer bound together with red ribbon! They were separated. Ma placed them on the table between us.

"Where did you find these?" I asked.

"On the floor."

They must have dropped out of the rafters! And Ma had been the one to cut them apart. "Why did you meddle with them?" I asked. "Why did you foil the magick?"

"I was going to leave them together until I noticed the runes you'd embroidered upon them." She held up the one that said Diarmuid. "You put a boy's name on this! Truly, Rose, you know it's wrong. I've said that time and again. This is dark magick, and I'll not have it coming from my daughter, or any Wodebayne, if I can prevent it."

The sight of the unbound poppets frustrated me so, I barely heard her words. So my spell had worked until Ma had discovered the dolls and separated them. I felt fresh anger, this time at Síle. She was putting her beliefs about magick before me.

And what of Diarmuid's own love for me? Was it not strong enough to see our marriage through without help of my magick? It was all so confusing.

"Rose . . ." Ma's voice interrupted my thoughts. "You're not listening! You have no right to tamper with that boy's destiny! It may seem like 'tis the easy way out, but your intrusive spell will come back to haunt you—threefold! And I worry about you tangling with a Vykrothe girl. They are a fierce tribe, and you have a history with them that I've dared not speak of before this."

"I do?" I winced. "When did I engage a Vykrothe?"

"Do you remember your trip to the coast with your father?" she asked. When I nodded, she went on. "While you were there, the rains fell, causing terrible coastal flooding. Many of the neighboring Vykrothe homes and fields were flooded . . . ruined. And there's rumor that the floods came as a result of a spell cast by your father."

"So Da did practice dark magick?"

Ma sighed deeply. "I do not think so, but that is how the rumor goes. They say there was an angry confrontation between Gowan and a Vykrothe man in a village inn. As a result, they say, your father cast a black spell upon the village. . . . Hence the flooding."

"Did you ever ask Da about it?"

Ma looked down. "I didn't even know of the flooding at the coast until after your da was gone."

I shook my head. "'Tis quite a tale."

"Aye, that's what I believe it to be—a fanciful tale." Ma rose from the table and poured fresh water into the basin. "Now, off to bed. We'll talk more of this come the morning."

I washed off and curled onto my sleeping pallet. Sleep would come quickly, I knew, as my body and mind were worn weary. But as I drifted off, the image of Aislinn popped into my head. Her fiery red hair was aglow in the moonlight, her eyes wild. "We have the power to punish the other clans," she'd said. "Why don't we use it?"

Because power could be dangerous? But witches wielded the Goddess's power all the time. Did not the Goddess impose her own sense of justice? Besides, I had not cast the spell of frogs. And I had not stolen another's love away. Diarmuid had pledged himself to me under the Goddess; his bond with Siobhan was a business matter determined by his parents. Could I not defend myself against this vengeful girl? I was merely protecting myself and my babe. Even as my father might have defended himself from a Vykrothe all those years ago.

It was all too much to sort out this night. I yawned as Ma came close, tucking a light blanket over me. "Good night, Rose. We'll undo your spell in the morn."

Mayhap, I thought. Or mayhap I would find a way to cast a new spell upon Diarmuid. I breathed softly, feeling coddled by her love. 'Twas a lovely feeling for now, but I knew it would not sustain me.

I had reached a time when a mother's love was not enough.

I needed Diarmuid.

The next day the Sun God sent splinters of sunlight into the cottage. The light awakened me, infusing my body with refreshed strength and hope. I thought of the words from the Lughnassadh rites.

> *"Goddess, we thank thee*
> *for all that has been raised from the soil.*
> *May it grow in strength*
> *from now till harvest.*
> *We thank thee for this promise of fruits to come."*

I rubbed my belly. My baby had been but a seed at Beltane, but 'twould be a fine child to be born around the time of the Imbolc rites.

Grow in peace, little one, I thought as I rose from my bed. Your ma will take care of these difficult matters and bring your da to you.

That morning I enlisted Kyra's help in fighting the battle. I knew if I wanted to get to Diarmuid, I would first have to stave off Siobhan.

"A minor spell is necessary," I told Kyra. "Something to scare her off." After some thought I added, "Something to mar her lovely golden hair." We were sitting in my sacred circle, trying to remember anything we'd ever heard of dark spells. This was not the sort of thing you learned at the circle or looked up in your mother's Book of Shadows.

"I've heard tell of turning a person's nails black," she said. "Or perhaps you can send a lightning bolt upon her head?"

"That's a bit too much," I said. "I can't be causing her serious harm, though I must say, 'tis tempting." We meandered through the woods, talking about what we knew of herbs and spells. When we came upon a thorny plant, I went over and circled it with my bolline. "'Tis just the thing to tangle her lovely hair. Can you imagine Siobhan stuck among a bramble of thorns?" On the way back to my altar I cut a lovely purple iris to give me the wisdom to work a new spell. Working together, Kyra and I swept the circle and consecrated the thorns. Then I made up a chant:

> *"O Goddess of Light, Goddess so fair,*
> *Please bring these thorns upon her hair.*
> *Let Siobhan know my wrath,*
> *Let her nevermore cross my path!"*

"So mote it be!" Kyra said, her eyes lit with expectation.

Afterward we could barely contain our curiosity. Would our spell be a success?

"Perhaps we should go and see with our own eyes," I said. "Besides, I am due a trip to Lillipool. I must speak to Diarmuid and try to work things out."

Kyra tucked a cornflower behind her ear. "Perhaps we should pay a visit to Falkner at his father's shop? If he can get use of a horse, we'll be in Lillipool in no time."

I smiled. "Is it because you want to see the spell or because you want to see Falkner?"

A mischievous gleam danced in her eyes. "Both!"

*　　　*　　　*

At the Kirkloch blacksmith's shop we found Falkner, who talked his da into making a run to a merchant in Lillipool. Falkner had met Siobhan at market on more than one occasion. "That one thinks she's the queen of the Highlands," he said, rolling his eyes. "'Twould be quite satisfying to see her get her comeuppance."

In no time we were in the dusty Leapvaughn village, searching the marketplace for Diarmuid. It turned out that he was off tending sheep in the hills, but Falkner managed to learn the location of Siobhan's cottage. We left the horse tethered near a water trough in the village and went out to the MacMahon cottage on foot. The house was a small affair, overlooking a field of dry heather that gave way to a bog. The shutters had been thrown open from the windows, and smoke rose from the chimney.

We perched on a nearby hillside, just behind a fallen log.

"Is she home?" Kyra asked. "I don't see anyone about."

"I don't know," Falkner said, "but I cannot stay here watching a lone cottage all afternoon. Da's got work to be done. Besides, 'tis deadly dull."

"A bit of waiting would be well worth the sight of seeing Siobhan in distress," I said, watching the cottage.

Over in the bogs a few birds squawked. It was a lazy, still August afternoon. "Perhaps we could take turns napping while we wait?" I added.

Just then the wind kicked up over the heather, rattling through the weeds. It swept up from the bogs, bypassing our little hill but heading straight toward the cottage. As it churned, it blew seeds and thistle toward the house.

The door of the cottage swung open, and Siobhan flew out in a fury.

"There she is!" Kyra cried.

With her skirts gathered high Siobhan raced about the cottage, trying to shutter the windows. She pressed a shutter closed, but the strong wind sucked it back open. She reached for the shutter again, but dust and thistles and seed clods were swarming to her face, forcing her to cower. The thorny seeds blew directly upon her, hooking onto her skirts and apron. Dozens of burrs snagged in her hair, but when she reached up to tug them out, they pierced her fingertips.

"Eeow! Ow! Ooh!" she yelped, dancing about as the thorny seeds flew under the straps of her sandals.

"Ha!" I laughed with satisfaction. The three of us no longer hid behind the log but sat up for the best view of our quarry.

"Oh, Goddess, look at her!" Kyra laughed with me. "She's a sorry sight."

"From what I know of her, she quite deserves it," Falkner said. "I never thought I'd see the likes of her yelping about."

"Indeed," I said as Siobhan continued to hop around, pulling burrs from her clothes and hair. "At least this should stop her from sending more spells my way." And, I thought, perhaps it will keep her away from Diarmuid, too!

"Oh, dear," Kyra said, her hand flying to her mouth. "She sees us! She's coming this way."

I arose and stood tall, not afraid of this petty Vykrothe whore.

"It's you!" Siobhan yelped, stomping toward me. "This is your magick, is it not?"

"Aye, though I must admit, I had to practice restraint," I said. "It's far less than you deserve."

"Blast you all!" Siobhan said, raising a fist in the air. "I'll curse you and your families, too!" She was quite a sight, her blond hair matted and tangled like so many rough cuttings of dirty wool. She moved without grace, as if every turn pained her.

'Twas satisfying indeed.

"Easy!" Falkner stepped toward her and gently touched her shoulder. "Easy, now! You rail like a savage beast. Perhaps you're in need of soothing!"

"Don't touch me!" she shrieked, stepping away from him. "I'll have you know that I'm betrothed, and you must mind your hands."

Falkner lifted his hands defensively. "I apologize! I was just trying to help."

"Take your leave, all of you!" Siobhan cried as she turned back to the cottage. "Begone, you and your vicious spells."

"Likewise to any witch who would summon frogs from the pond," I called to her.

As Siobhan slammed into the cottage, I turned to my friends. "That was worth waiting for, and you'll be back to your da's shop in no time," I told Falkner.

"But wait!" he said mysteriously. He held out one hand as if he were cradling an invisible tool.

"What's this?" Kyra said. "More magick?"

He smiled. "When I touched Siobhan's shoulder, I managed to extract a valuable item—a strand of her hair." He waved his closed fingers before me, and I saw it—a thin line of gold.

I was most impressed. All this time I had thought Falkner a bit dim-witted, but perhaps he had simply been keeping his thoughts to himself. In any case, I had to admire his foresight in stealing something that could prove quite valuable—especially if I needed to cast another spell against Siobhan. "Thank you," I said, sweeping the golden hair from his hand and tucking it into a tiny pouch from my pocket.

Kyra brushed off her skirts as we headed back toward the center of Lillipool. "That was amusing indeed, though I think Siobhan is a waste of your time and power," she told me. "You need to go directly to Diarmuid. Speak to him. The true power is with him, not that silly girl."

"I do believe you are right," I said as we walked along. "And I shall go to him tonight when he has returned from the fields. The Goddess will give him the strength to defy his name and clan. I know it to be our destiny."

I could not wait for the evening.

11

Spelling a Death Drink with Dark Powers

Falkner delivered me to the path to Ma's cottage, and I waved good-bye to my friends with a firm resolution to work things out before nightfall. But as I neared the clearing, I noticed a group of coveners lingering outside our cottage. Panic ran cold within me. Something was wrong. Their expressions were somber as I ran up to them.

"What is it?" I called breathlessly. "What's happened?"

"'Tis your ma," Ian MacGreavy answered. He came to me and took my hand. "She's been hurt, Rose."

Gripped with fear, I broke loose from him and pushed past the others into the cottage. A few women from the coven were huddled around Ma's bed, stroking her hair and speaking in hushed tones. As I pressed closer, I saw Ma lying there, her eyes open but glazed. A pool of blood stained the blanket beneath her.

"Ma!" I knelt beside her, taking her hand. "What happened?"

Her face was a mask of pain, and from the look in her eyes I could see she was not completely in this world.

"She cannot speak," one of the elders told me. Mrs. Hazelton put her hand on my shoulder. "Seems that a stray hunter's arrow hit your ma. She was just leaving my cottage, having delivered a salve for my husband's breathing. She went down so fast! The huntsman never came forward, but I did hear his arrow whirring amid the tree."

"I'll wager it was an arrow from a rival clan," Aislinn said, her face pinched with anger. "A deliberate act of aggression."

"We don't know that," Mrs. Hazelton pointed out.

I stood and looked over Ma's body. The arrow was still in her back. "This must be removed," I said, wondering how deep it had penetrated.

"But the heat in her body is high," said another elder who went by the name of Norn. She was a shriveled prune of a woman, but I had always been fond of her humor and her spirit. Norn touched Ma's forehead, clucking her tongue. "'Tis dangerous to take the arrow while she is feverish."

"Then we must take care of her fever." I pushed back my hair, then went to the basin to wash my hands. If there was ever an occasion that I needed to call upon the magick I had learned, this was it. I handed the broom to Aislinn to sweep the circle, then I went to Ma's Book of Shadows for remedies. "We need something to bring down the fever, and we must help her sleep. Removing the arrow might cause her great pain—it's better if she can rest." I leafed through the book. "I know we can start with chamomile and passionflowers."

"Anise in the tea will help her sleep," Norn told me. "And rosemary will help the pain."

"Add cayenne to stay the flow of blood," Mrs. Hazelton said.

I nodded as I leafed through the book. Finally I found a remedy for fever. "We'll need boneset in the tea to lower the fever," I said, rushing over to the jars and pouches to retrieve the herbs. "Pray Goddess that she's able to drink this at all!"

Norn had already put the kettle on the fire. Working together, we steeped a strong tea for Ma. As it brewed, I went to the altar and consecrated the tea and the comfrey poultice that Norn was preparing. I don't know what I said in the heated, dreadful moment, only that I summoned the Goddess to heal Her daughter and to work through my hands, and the others chanted, "So mote it be!"

We managed to prop my mother up so that the tea could pass over her lips. Still dazed, she sipped most of the contents. After that, her eyes closed and her breathing slowed.

"'Tis working," Norn said, dousing my mother's head with a cool cloth. "The fever is lifting."

Thanking the Goddess, I set to work on the arrow. I had to cut the skin a bit with my bolline to remove the barbed head, and as I worked, Ma's blood ran out steadily. At last the arrow was out, and I dressed the wound with the poultice and covered it with a clean white cloth.

"Now . . . she must rest," Norn said, her own voice cracking with weariness. "As should we. We'll know more when she awakens."

I lifted the plate containing the bloodied dressings and the arrow that I'd removed. Glancing down at the base, I noticed that it was marked with runes.

My body went cold as I deciphered their meaning. "Vykrothes . . ." So this was no hunting accident. The arrow was part of a spell cast by Siobhan, I was sure of it. Had not Mrs. Hazelton said that a hunter had never appeared? Surely a hunter would come forward to claim his prized deer or rabbit? No, this was not a normal arrow. It had been spelled by Siobhan.

Had she intended to hit me? I couldn't be sure. But one thing I was sure of: Siobhan had gone too far. She had to be stopped.

"A Vykrothe arrow . . ." Norn gasped.

"What?" Aislinn darted over to my side to study the arrow. "Oh, Goddess, this is truly war! To have our high priestess struck down by another clan!"

"It might have been an accident," Norn pointed out. "Come along now, Aislinn. You get yourself all liverish at every turn, girl!"

"Oh, some accident!" Aislinn exclaimed. "If it were not intended for Síle, why did the huntsman not come forward and state his mistake?"

"Quiet, girl!" Mrs. Hazelton hushed her. "You're loud enough to wake the dead, and Síle must sleep."

"Sleep, she will," Aislinn said in a quieter voice. "But when she awakens, she will find a changed world. A clan at war! For we cannot sit back and let our priestess be attacked!"

"Enough!" Placing a wrinkled hand on Aislinn's shoulder, Norn led her to the door. "Let us go so Síle can rest. Rose will watch over her." She ushered Aislinn out, then turned back to me. "You performed some powerful magick today," she told me softly, her eyes gleaming. "Your ma would be proud."

I nodded, my lips twisted with pain as the women filed out the door and returned to their own cottages. I closed the door and sighed, alone but for the quiet breathing of my mother in the bed. I cleaned up the bloodied things, dumped the old water, tidied the cottage, nursed Ma's head with a cool cloth. All the while I felt embittered and frightened.

I had brought a Vykrothe arrow upon my mother.

It was time for Siobhan to have a taste of her own evil.

Listlessly I paged through Ma's Book of Spells, praying for an answer. Aislinn was right. The Vykrothes deserved a taste of their own dark magick. But where do you begin if you've not been trained in the ways of darkness?

I turned to a spell called Death Drink and paused. I had never had much interest in this ritual. It called for a covener who wanted to visit their own mortality to drink a bitter brew. The potion sometimes made them a bit ill, but it was never fatal. As far as I was concerned, this was a tedious mind journey. So what if it led to inner wisdom?

But now, in this light, I wondered if I could use the death drink as a spell upon an unwilling victim . . . Siobhan.

I would add a few poisonous ingredients and a dark spell that would send Siobhan to death's door. She would not die, though she might wish she could. As I doused Ma's forehead with a cloth, I imagined Siobhan writhing in pain. Oh, I would send her a spell to end her viciousness.

"I'll need bitter ingredients," I whispered as I combed Ma's hair back with my fingers. "Cranberries from the bogs. Toadstools. And bitter essence of appleseeds."

Ma sighed contentedly, and I realized her fever had cooled. She slept soundly while I shuffled about the cottage, assembling herbs from our collection. When I was sure she was resting comfortably, with no sign of fever, I slipped out to consecrate the brew at my sacred circle.

Along the way I found a small wren hiding in the bushes. I paused, my life force pounding in my ears. I had never hurt one of the Goddess's creatures before, but everyone knew that the blood of a living animal made for potent dark magick. Quietly I knelt beside it, taking a large pouch from my belt. In the blink of an eye I swung the open pouch over the bird, trapping it with such deftness, I felt sure the Goddess intended it.

The stars were shrouded by clouds as I reached the clearing. I had expected darkness, with the new moon this eve. I squeezed the nectar from some sweet honeysuckles, thinking that if the potion tasted a bit palatable, Siobhan might drink it all. I added Siobhan's golden hair from her very own body. And much to my surprise, I barely flinched when it was time to cut the wren's neck and add its blood to the potion. There . . . the death drink was complete.

"Oh, Goddess," I whispered, "here I do display the chalice of death. Whoever drinks this shall journey to the land of darkness and dwell there until she comes to realize the error of her ways."

I dipped my athame in the chalice, then held the blade up to the sky. "A bitter potion to end a bitter evil!" I said. I placed a cloth over the chalice as drops began to fall from the sky. Cool, cleansing raindrops. From the distant hills came the rumble of thunder—the Goddess's answer. She had heard me. "So mote it be," I whispered.

*   *   *

The sun rose on a newly cleansed earth. I sat in bed, grateful that Síle was still resting comfortably. I arose and began to wash and dress. It was getting more and more difficult to find a place for my girdle between my belly and my breasts. Soon the world would know I was expecting a child. If all went well, I would have a husband before then.

I had just finished eating my breakfast of warm gruel and apples when Norn appeared at the cottage door, bearing a basket of biscuits.

"I have come to give you a rest from nursing your ma," she said, her beady eyes shining in her wrinkled face. "Go forth. You need some fresh air and release."

"Thank you," I said, taking a cloak to cover my belly and ward off the morning dew. "I have need of some time to commune with the Goddess," I told her. I started out the door, then turned back to retrieve the pitcher containing the death drink. "Let me not forget the ceremonial wine," I said.

"It is good that you are working your own spells," Norn told me. "Your mother must be pleased. Has she told you that you're likely to be our coven's next high priestess?"

"N-no," I said, surprised at her words. "But Ma has taught me well."

Norn smiled brightly as I headed down the path, on my way to Siobhan's cottage.

The trip to Lillipool had begun to seem shorter now that I'd traveled this way so oft of late. The sun was still low on the eastern hills when I rounded the hilltop near the heather fields. The MacMahon cottage sat in the sun, a young lad of five or six playing about near the woodpile beyond the house. He had long golden hair that hung to his shoulders and a smudge on his cheek. Probably Siobhan's younger brother, I wagered as I approached him. Perfect!

He was scalping the bark from various tree branches, his own unskilled attempts at carving figurines. When I drew close, he glanced up at me curiously. "Hark!" he said. "Do you come to visit me?"

"I come with a gift for Siobhan," I said, holding up the pitcher. "But since the hour is so early, I dare not disturb the household. Do you know her?" I asked.

"Aye! I am her brother Tysen." He eyed the pitcher curiously. "But what gift have you there?"

" 'Tis a sweet nectar from her love," I said. "Siobhan is to drink this first thing upon awakening." I lowered my voice, adding, "I think perhaps he has put a love spell upon it, hoping to capture your sister's heart. Do you know Diarmuid?"

He grinned. "Aye, I know him well. He owes me a ride upon his shoulders."

"I shall remind him of that," I said. Carefully I handed the pitcher to the boy. "Do you think you can handle a task of this magnitude?"

"Aye." He smiled proudly, his pale eyes gleaming. " 'Tis an easy task."

Tysen headed toward the house, and I headed back the way I had come with a new sense of righteousness and balance. Siobhan had struck down my mother, but her evil magick was now cycling back to her.

When I returned to the cottage, Ma was sitting up and eating biscuits with Norn.

"Look who's feeling better," Norn said, all smiles as she

took the kettle of tea off the fire. "That's some powerful magick you wrought yesterday, Rose. Síle, your daughter is truly blessed by the Goddess."

"Indeed," my mother said. "I have always admired her powers. I am fortunate she was at hand yesterday when I was in dire need of them."

I thanked Norn for her help, and she insisted on leaving the biscuits behind. After she departed, Ma moved back to the bed to drink her tea.

"What a world of difference," I told her as I sat at the table. I bit into a biscuit and brushed flour from my fingers. "You look so much better."

"Thanks to you," she said. "You have come a long way in your magick, Rose."

I smiled. Perhaps Ma finally realized that I'd been working hard to learn the ways of the Goddess.

Ma sipped her tea, then let her head drop back. "But I must say, my mind traveled to some frightening places in my dreams. I saw you concocting a dark spell, inviting in evil, conjuring a potion with the intention to hurt someone. I saw your athame raised to dark thunderclouds and—did it rain last night?"

"I think it did," I said innocently. The biscuit was now wedged in my throat, and I no longer had the appetite for it. Ma's insightfulness scared me. It was difficult to fool a high priestess—especially if she was your mother!

"Such frightening visions," Ma said.

Brushing off my hands, I went to my mother's bedside. "Shall I change the dressing or wait?"

"Let it wait," Ma said, lifting the cloth to show me the wound. "It seems to be healing."

I nodded. "It does look much better. But you should sleep. You need to heal."

"I will, though I fear my sleep will be haunted by more of the same dreams."

"'Twas but a vision of your delirium," I assured her. "Now that you have no fever, your dreams will be gentle."

Síle smiled. "Advice from my daughter?"

I nodded. "Sage advice."

12

Reversing
a Spell

While Ma slept, I went down to wash at the brook, trying to think of a way to sneak off and see Diarmuid. I could not abandon Ma in her current state, not for a long period. And although I was grateful that she was healing quickly, my patience was wearing thin.

"You need your da," I said, rubbing my belly as I waded in the cool shallows.

I would have to give Ma one more day. After that, perhaps I could convince Kyra or Norn to stay with her while I went to fetch the man who would become my husband.

Feeling cleansed and refreshed, I headed back to the cottage. When I came upon the main road, I spied Kyra tramping along, a basket on her arm.

"I have sweet oat cakes for your ma," she said, "and dreadful news for you." She took my hand and pulled me off the road. "Did you cast a spell over Siobhan? Some kind of deadly potion?"

"I did." I squared my shoulders. "After what she did to my mother, I—"

"I'm not blaming you," Kyra interrupted, "but rumor has it that Siobhan's younger brother has fallen ill. The boy seems to have a sleeping sickness, his breathing slowed to frightening depths, his body racked by convulsions."

I gasped. "He drank the potion?"

Kyra nodded sadly. "The poor little thing."

I thought of Tysen, carving the bark diligently. The way he had been so proud to bear the pitcher to his sister. I'd had no idea he would drink it himself. But then, he was only a child—perhaps a mischievous one. I should have realized that when I handed him the death drink. I bit my lower lip, wondering if all of the death drink had gone to the wrong person. "And how is Siobhan?" I asked, hoping that she might have had a few sips herself.

"In a fury," Kyra answered. "Siobhan is telling everyone that the potion was spelled, an evil spell cast by you!"

I folded my arms defensively. "The cup was not marked, and no one saw me give it to Tysen." At least, I didn't think anyone saw me. "Siobhan will never be able to prove her suspicions," I said.

"Perhaps not," Kyra agreed. "Still, 'tis a sad thing to see sickness in one so young."

"Indeed." With every ounce of my might I wished that I could take back the spell—take it all back and restore Tysen's good health. Perhaps I could.

But I didn't want to involve Kyra in this, especially now that I had dabbled in dark magick. I thanked her for the cakes and headed back to the cottage, thinking of possible spells. There was a spell intended to undo the original spell—certainly worth a try. And there was an endless variety of healing spells. Surely any combination of those would cure the boy.

Back at the cottage, Ma was asleep. I checked her for fever, then sat at the table with her Book of Shadows. After much searching I found the spell of reversal:

> *On the eve of the new moon I cast a spell,*
> *And the effects I created, I must now quell.*
> *May this spell be lifted and I now gifted with . . .*

"With good health for Tysen," I whispered aloud.

The spell called for protective stones such as amethyst or smokey quartz, and I was to use one white and one black candle for balance. I bit my lips, determined to sneak out to my sacred place in the woods as soon as night fell and save Tysen. For now I could only assemble the things I would need.

Night had fallen. Ma had been to the table to eat, but now she was back in bed again, too weak to stay up for long. Still, she was healing well. I had cleaned and dressed her wound, and it was starting to close with no redness or discharge. I was grateful that she would recover.

She dozed upon her pillow now, and I was ready to slip out and reverse the spell that had befallen poor Tysen. My tools and herbs were assembled. All that I needed was a gemstone from Ma's cupboard. I opened the cabinet door and poked about, searching for a stone with the right charge. I found a malachite, a bluish stone with bands of white. Holding it thoughtfully in my hands, I realized it would be a good stone to keep near me. Malachite was known to give wisdom, pointing one in the right direction, giving guidance. I was about to slip it in my pocket when the stone broke in half! Part of it tumbled from my hand, falling to the table with a thud.

Ma bolted up in bed. "What was that?" she asked.

"This malachite," I told her, picking up the pieces from the floor. "It broke in two!"

"Oh, dear Goddess!" Ma exclaimed. She tried to rise from her bed, but I could see that the movement drained her.

"Don't get up, Ma," I said, tucking the blanket over her. "It's all right."

"But it's not! This has dire meaning. Malachite breaks in two to give you a warning of danger. Something terrible is going to happen, Rose!"

I swallowed hard, trying to hold back my own panic. *Oh, Goddess, are my dark spells coming back to me?* I couldn't bear to tell Ma the truth of my worries, to admit how deep I had fallen into spells she didn't approve of.

"Oh, then . . . it must have been predicting your accident with the arrow," I said, turning my face to the cupboard. I put the two pieces of malachite back on the shelf. "Because, actually, the stone broke last week. I simply forgot to mention it to you."

"It was already broken?"

I could feel her fear draining away.

"Well, then, let's hope you are right. Perhaps you are." She turned on her side, content to fall back asleep.

I found an amethyst in her collection, then collected the candles and herbs I had gathered. It was time to save Tysen.

Quietly I slipped out the door and started up the path.

Ahead of me light spilled down the lane. What was it from? A moment later torches floated up the path, heading this way.

I recoiled in fear. What had happened? Had Tysen died already and the Vykrothes come to punish me? I backed up to the door and nearly fell inside. Ma was already up, hobbling toward me.

"What is it, Rose?" she asked in a hoarse voice. "I sense the danger. What's happening?"

"A band of people is coming," I said, rushing to stow away the things I had collected for my spell. "I don't know who they are, but they are not Vykrothes."

"Let us see," Ma said, shuffling painfully to the door.

I followed her out to the sea of darkness bobbing with torches and ghostly faces. In the lead the village reverend stepped forward, his mouth a slash of contempt.

"What business do you have with us so late at night, Reverend Winthrop?" my mother asked politely. "Have you come to pay a call upon the sick, for that is what I am. A victim of a hunter's arrow."

"I am sorry for your hardship," Reverend Winthrop said. "But I am here on a mission from the Almighty Father. I have come to take your daughter to prison, Síle. On the morrow she will be tried as a witch."

"It cannot be!" my mother protested.

"No!" I cried. I clutched my belly, buckling to my knees. A witch! How could it be that these people knew of my love for the Goddess? I had moved stealthily, attending church on Sundays and always careful not to speak of my true life around the villagers. A coldness overcame me as I stared out at them, my tears blurring their faces.

How could it be?

"Upon whose order do you take her?" my mother demanded.

The reverend did not answer. But someone stepped forward from the crowd—Siobhan!

"Upon my word!" she shouted. "I know her to be a witch, and I will testify against her."

"No!" I pleaded. "'Tis not fair. She hates me! She wants to have revenge!"

But no one seemed to hear my cries as the men stepped forward and grabbed me by the shoulders. Brusquely they bound my wrists behind me and shoved me away from the cottage.

"No!" I cried, turning back to see Ma huddled at the doorway. "Ma! Please!"

But she merely watched me go with a stricken expression on her face. She held out a hand to me, as if I could clasp on and save myself from drowning.

But I could not. I marched off to prison, my heart hammering with fear that this was truly my death march. Because of Siobhan, I had been named as a witch. And no one, no one in the Highlands, had ever faced those charges and escaped alive.

On the morning of my trial a guard woke me and roughly ushered me into a cottage near the village center. I hoped they were bringing me to the table to break my fast, but when I saw the minister, Reverend Winthrop, along with a stout, bearded man, I reared back in fear.

"Dr. Wellington is here to examine you for the mark of the devil, Rose MacEwan," said the reverend. "Off with your gown."

The guard at the door crossed his arms, smiling at me.

I had never been ashamed of my body, having been raised among circles of unclad witches, but to go naked before such hostile eyes . . . I began to tremble. Would he realize that I was with child? If he did, 'twould prejudice the town against me.

"I cannot," I said, folding my arms across my chest protectively.

"Balderdash!" the reverend shouted. He stepped forward and tore at the collar of my gown. "Remove your clothes, and I'll remind you to make haste, for your trial is upon us."

"No!" I shrieked, trying to pull away from him. I felt like a trapped animal; there was no way out. Closing my eyes, I began to take off my gown.

I stood there naked, feeling their lust and hatred swirl around me. Something jabbed at my buttocks, and I opened my eyes to see the physician jabbing at me with a stick, as if I were chattel in a field. Keeping his distance, he touched my buttocks, my thighs, my belly, my breasts. Humiliation burned in my throat, and I closed my eyes again.

I could not tell whether he knew I was with child. At this point the mound at my belly was quite pronounced and my breasts were swollen with milk, but I wasn't sure this physician knew the realities of a woman's body. His examination seemed more motivated by lust than professional interest.

And thus I began the day of my trial, naked before three peculiar men. After that I was allowed to dress and given a bowl of gruel, which I gobbled up eagerly. It was not enough food to sustain my babe, and I wondered if there would be more at lunch.

After breakfast I was dragged out to the center of our village, where I was tied rather barbarically to a hitching post. Villagers were free to assemble around me and witness the nightmare, and most of the villagers I saw every Sunday in church were in attendance. Among the faces gathered there, I saw the members of our coven—the MacGreavys, Norn, Aislinn, and the others. Ma was there, leaning gingerly on Miller MacGreavy's cart. I spied Meara with two of the little ones in tow, and I wondered if she was their ma now. Kyra and Falkner were conspicuously absent, but I suspected that their parents had been fearful for their safety. If the village reverend started to get greedy, he might look for others who were guilty by association.

Standing in the center of the village, sweating under the late August sun and the scrutiny of so-called holy men, I felt horribly exposed. An alarming odor filled the air, something I could not identify. Was it a burning herb?

No, I thought, swallowing against the biting taste in my throat. It's the smell of fear. My fear.

Reverend Winthrop began talking to the crowd, telling of evils prevailing among us. I was trying to listen, trying to create a defense in my mind when I saw someone moving through the crowd—a lean, solid figure.

Diarmuid!

I felt my life force rising as he turned toward me. Our eyes locked, and I could feel it in the air between us. He still loved me. He had come to tell me that and to free me from these charges. He would come forward during the trial and rescue me. I closed my eyes and focused on sending him a message. Diarmuid would rescue me once again. This would all be over soon.

You've come to save me! I told him in a *tua labra*. *I knew you would come for me.*

I waited for an answer.

But all I heard was the voice of the reverend accusing me of being a witch. "Coming upon her at the brook one morning, I saw her conducting what must certainly be a pagan ritual," he said in his whiny voice.

I suddenly recalled the morning when I'd heard someone on the path. The morning after Beltane, when I'd slipped off my clothes for a thorough cleansing . . .

"I was washing," I said, looking out at the crowd for validation. "Do not most maidens bathe upon rising?"

"Without a stitch of clothing?" Reverend Winthrop asked.

A few of the Presbyterians snickered, as if he'd made a coarse joke.

"Why do you laugh, when most of you could use a thorough cleansing in the river?" Ma said, standing tall. The crowd grew silent. "Or is that odor the stench of hysteria? For I have yet to see a person so accused treated fairly in these Highlands."

The minister folded his arms, appraising my mother. "Woman, what is your claim here? This is a formal inquisition."

"I am the mother of Rose MacEwan, and I know her to be a kind and noble child," Síle said. Her hair was covered by a modest veil, her voice filled with a fortitude that belied her injury. "Whatever evil you have charged her with is false, I swear a solemn oath to that. And I charge you to release her and return her to her proper home."

It was dangerous for anyone to speak in my defense, but Ma had been willing to take that chance. In some ways, I knew I didn't deserve it. Pressing one hand against the child in my belly, I marveled at how deep a mother's love could run.

Reverend Winthrop puckered his lips, as if Síle's words had left a sour taste in his mouth. "These are the words of her mother," he announced formally. "Although I've yet to know a mother who clearly sees her child's true flaws."

I turned to Diarmuid and sent him an urgent message: *The man shows disrespect toward my mother!* I wanted to say. *Step forward and set him aright!* But now he was watching the reverend, pretending not to understand me.

"So," the minister went on, "it was no surprise when this young maiden came to me with proof that Rose MacEwan is a witch." He gestured toward Siobhan. "Tell us what you know, please."

Siobhan stepped forward, her long neck craning as she lifted her chin proudly. "She is a witch!" she said in a tinny voice. "I have witnessed her performing her craft."

Although she was hardly convincing, she smiled gleefully.

I turned to Diarmuid, wondering what he thought of his betrothed now. Had he known that she was a backstabbing hypocrite?

Diarmuid's face was pale, his blue eyes flashing with something I couldn't determine. Surprise? Perhaps he hadn't heard that Siobhan was my chief accuser.

Step forward and make her cease, I ordered him. *You have the power to stop her. . . . Don't let this drag on!*

But he didn't seem to be receiving my messages. Where was his mind today?

"What have you seen Rose MacEwan doing?" Reverend Winthrop prodded Siobhan. "Remember what you told me?"

"Aye!" Siobhan answered. "I have seen her dancing in the woods at night! Dancing with the devil!"

Her words lashed out like the crack of a whip. How could she say that? Even if she hated me, did she not realize those words would be my death sentence? I pressed my hands to my hot cheeks, too afraid to respond, too frightened to cry.

The crowd gasped and murmured.

"Quiet, please!" the reverend shouted. "Let's not waver from the point at hand. Did you or did you not see Rose MacEwan in her dance with Satan?" he asked Siobhan.

"I did!" she shouted. "And I can prove it." She pointed a finger at me, hatred gleaming in her pale gray eyes. "Rose MacEwan is with child! She is carrying the devil's spawn!"

I felt stung. How did she know I was with child? Had Diarmuid told her? It would have been a huge betrayal, something I could not believe of him. She must have found out some other way. But how?

The crowd was rumbling with speculation. Ma had collapsed onto Miller MacGreavy's cart, and I saw Norn embrace her. I tried to catch Diarmuid's eye, but he was blocked by one of the villagers, who was laughing heartily. Should I send him another *tua labra*, or was that a waste of time? *Oh, Goddess, help me!*

"Is it true, Dr. Wellington?" Reverend Winthrop asked the physician. "Is Rose MacEwan with child?"

Dr. Wellington stroked his bristly beard as if the answer lay there in the folds of his chin. "Well, aye, 'tis true."

"My child is not the devil's spawn," I cried. "She is a healthy, human child with a father who will love her!"

"Liar!" Siobhan shouted. "There is no father! Rose MacEwan has lain with the devil. That is why her belly is swollen with his evil seed!"

Reverend Winthrop made the sign of the cross, and those standing closest to me took a step back, as if my evil could spread to them.

"There is a father for my child!" I insisted. "He is among us now." I dared not name him, for fear that the crowd would turn on him, too. The answer had to come from him; Diarmuid had to be the one to stand up and lay claim to me as his future bride and mother of his child. By doing so he could turn this scandalous dilemma into something honorable in the eyes of the Christians, who at least believed in redemption.

I glanced toward him, beseeching him, but he did not move. What was he waiting for? *I need you—now! It's time for you to save me. Denounce Siobhan's lie. Claim me as your own true love and lover.*

"A father among us?" Reverend Winthrop said tartly. He glanced over his shoulders at the men in the crowd. "All right, then. Let the father of Rose MacEwan's child step forward. What human among us has lain with this woman?"

I looked at Diarmuid, begging him to act now.

But he would not meet my glance. It was as if he were cast in stone, a useless pillar of rock.

Please! I thought, beseeching him with every fiber of my being. *Please . . . they're going to kill me and our baby!*

But he did not move.

"Oh, Goddess," I mumbled under my breath. "Let it not be. He is choosing her! He is choosing her over me!"

"Just as I suspected." The reverend shook his head, eyeing me with mock sadness. "There is no father, is there?" His eyes glittered with malice.

"There is!" I insisted.

I wanted to protest, but my throat had gone dry.

Going over to a horse trough, Reverend Winthrop pushed back the sleeves of his gown, making a show of washing his hands. "I wash my hands of the matter of your redemption. I do believe you are guilty as charged."

"Aye, she is guilty!" someone cried.

"Guilty! Guilty!" The cry became a chant taken up by the villagers around me.

I felt myself collapsing against the hitching post, my hands hugging my belly. I couldn't let them hurt my babe. But how could I stop the swell of hatred that raged out of control?

"Guilty! Guilty! Guilty!"

Strong arms clamped around me. I felt myself being lifted, then dragged off through the crowd. Villagers stared at me, their eyes full of scorn or pity or curiosity. One woman snatched her children away and tucked them behind her skirts, as if I would harm them. How wrong she was. Didn't she know I would defend any child, especially my own, to the ends of time?

"Another useless Wodebayne to the gallows," I heard a Vykrothe man mutter just loud enough for me to hear. "'Tis no loss for us."

Is that what all of this had boiled down to? Hatred and prejudice? I wondered, but my thoughts were clouded with pain and confusion.

"At last she'll be getting what she deserves," said a familiar voice.

I glanced up to see Siobhan sidling up to Diarmuid, a smug expression on her face. Beside her Diarmuid stood staring at the ground.

Not man enough to defend me! I wanted to say, but the words were caught in the painful lump lodged in my throat.

I dug my heels into the ground, making the guards halt for a moment. "Mark my words, Siobhan," I told her, my voice cracking with emotion. "Your evil will come back to you threefold!"

"Begone!" she said, waggling her fingers at me like a sprite. "You'll not harm me again."

Without thought I was upon her, grabbing and scraping in an attempt to shatter her silly composure. I felt my nails dig into her skin, scratching the side of her cheek.

"Aaah!" she yelped. "The witch has attacked me again!"

The men quickly yanked me off her, but before they dragged me away, I had the satisfaction of seeing her sad little pout, along with a trickle of blood running down her graceful neck.

That is the neck that should be snapped at the gallows! I wanted to scream. She had tried to kill my mother, had she not? The urge to send *dealan-dé* her way was strong, and it took all my restraint to control myself as the men took me off to my tiny prison.

My cell was actually the springhouse behind a villager's cottage. The roof was made of leaky straw thatching, but the mud-plastered stone walls prevented my escape. Tossed onto the dirt floor there, I curled into a ball and thought of Diarmuid, my heart truly breaking. What had happened to the power of our love?

He had said that I was destined for great things—to become high priestess! And he knew the Goddess's plan for our union—that together we could unite all the clans!

But no. The path to redemption had been crossed by Siobhan, and Diarmuid had succumbed to her. He had failed me, failed us, failed our child.

Oh, Goddess, how could he be so disloyal? Disappointment overwhelmed me as I fell into a dark state, my hand resting upon the child within my belly.

13

A Spell for the
Darkest Hour

The creak of a door. A sliver of light.

Someone was entering my chamber.

"Hark!" he said, peering over the flame of the candle.

I sat up on the dirt floor. "Diarmuid?" My head was clogged from sleep, but indeed it was him, coming into the cell.

"Where are the guards?" I asked in surprise.

"They are blind to me," he said as the door creaked closed behind him. "I cast a see-me-not spell, rather successfully, I might add. And those bumblers are spelled deep asleep."

How could he joke at a time like this? I turned my face away, not willing to meet his eyes. "Have you come to gloat over my demise?" I asked.

"Of course not. I've come to extract one last promise. I was pleased by the way you held your tongue today, not mentioning my name. I trust you'll keep silent till the end."

I spun around to glare at him. "Silent!" I shouted. "Silence is the reason I am here! Why did you not answer my messages?" I stamped the ground with my foot. "Why did you not come forward to defend me and claim your child?"

He lowered his chin, his blue eyes abrasive. "How am I to know the bairn is mine?"

Furious, I took a swing at him, but he bobbed so that my fist caught only air. As I stumbled back, he caught my arms and held me in place. His eyes swept down my body to my breasts, my swollen belly. "And you thought I would claim your child?" he said with sudden disdain. "Knowing your wanton ways, you've probably bedded dozens like me."

His words infuriated me, but my fury was checked by my revelation. The man standing before me was not noble nor true nor even kind. And he had never been the sweet perfection I'd glimpsed under the Goddess's sky.

His pentagram dangled at his neck, glinting mockingly.

Suddenly I wanted to scratch out his glittering eyes and smite the grin from his pretty face. I did not love this man. How had I ever loved one who so cagily used me, took of my body and my heart, then abandoned me for dead?

"Get out!" I growled. I kicked at his legs, aiming high but just glancing off the top of his thigh.

Still, it was enough to scare him off. He released my hands as he doubled over.

Reaching out, I grabbed at his pentagram and pulled. He did not deserve to wear this! He did not deserve to pay homage to the Goddess! He made a little choking sound as it snapped off. With a feeling of righteousness I dropped the pentagram to the ground.

Diarmuid rubbed his neck. "You're rather feisty for a con-demned woman," he said. "And I should be the one throw-ing punches, what with the way you charmed me. I found the rose stone in your pocket. Powerful magick you make. 'Twas lovely while it lasted, but love soon fades to lust and needs. And my needs are well fulfilled by my own coven."

Fury burned inside me. "And Siobhan," I said. "You have lain with her because . . . because 'tis the easiest path to take."

He shrugged. "A man has certain obligations to his clan, and to marry a Wodebayne, I would have been falling short of everyone's expectations. You truly caught my eye. Even when Siobhan undid the power of your charmed stone, my desire to take you did not abate. Even now . . . I long to hold you one last time. . . ." He reached for me hungrily.

"In a pig's eye!" I shouted, pushing him away. "Begone from here, Diarmuid! For our passion was not about lust nor favor! Did you not stand in the circle with me and sum-mon the Goddess? Did we not pledge our love under her sky and promise to—"

"A witch says many things, chants many things," he said. "Often we say words we do not comprehend. 'Tis part of the—"

"I knew what I was saying!" Hatred swelled within me as all illusions of beauty and goodness melted away from him, revealing a diabolical monster. I pointed to the door. "Begone from here before I have at you, for I swear, I will tear the hair from your lovely head."

"Don't you threaten me, Rose!" Diarmuid lunged at me, backing me against the wall. "For despite your powers with the Goddess, I have the physical power to overcome you, and aye, I am stirring at the very touch of you, wench!" His eyes sparkled deviously. I felt stunned, unable to move. Was it possible that this boy—this boy I had seen as the answer to all of my prayers—would ravish me by force?

I struggled to get away, but he only tightened his grip.

"I will have you, Rose, for who will stop me? You are locked in prison, completely alone. Do you think the guards will answer your cries? The pleas of a witch sentenced to die?" He pressed his hips against me, pushing me into the cold stone wall.

I felt sickened by his touch, furious at his determination to overcome me. And I had loved him! How had I ever loved this cruel, conniving beast? Feeling it was hopeless to fight him, I collapsed against the wall. He was stronger than I. I knew I had to summon magick, but my mind was wild and scattered.

Seeing me relax, he released my hands and lifted my skirts. "Come on, Rose," he said, fingering my thighs. "I shall make it painful if you fight me."

Seizing the freedom of my hands, I grasped his face and pressed my nails in, hoping to scratch his pretty blue eyes out. "Aye, then let's make it painful!"

He gasped as my fingers penetrated his skin. His hands quickly encircled my wrists and pried me off, but not before I'd managed to scratch his cheeks. "Are you mad?"

"So they say!" I wrenched my hands free of him and backed away, rubbing my wrists. "But I'll not spend my last night on earth being defiled by the lust of a lying coward."

He pressed his fingers to his cheek and saw the crimson smear there. "You drew blood," he said in horror. For a moment I thought he would weep with despair.

Focusing my mind, I held up my hands to ward him off.

"Next time I'll use *dealan-dé*," I told him. "And if I had an athame, I would plunge it right through your festering heart."

Holding a hand against his cheek, he sucked in his breath. "I cannot wait till the morrow." His face was hollow and angular in the candlelight, a hideous, hateful specter. "I will relish the moment of your death."

Before I could respond, he fled from the cell, leaving only a lit candle behind.

A lit candle. Fire of the Goddess.

Diarmuid had left behind the one element I needed to balance out my circle. I had earth, wind, water, air . . . and now, despite all the attempts of the guards to keep it away from me, I had fire.

My fists clenched, I stared at the flame as fury raged within me. I burned for all the Wodebaynes who had suffered injustice at the hands of rival witches. Fire raged within me for Diarmuid—not the fires of passion, but the fires of hatred and fury. I burned with vengeance for Siobhan, who had stolen my place as Diarmuid's wife and sentenced me to death, who had tried to take my mother's life, too. And above all I was afire with love and sorrow for the babe in my belly, the child who had been condemned before she'd had a chance to take her first breath.

Sweat beaded on my forehead and dripped down my neck. What was happening? Pressing my hands to my cheeks, I found that my skin was sizzling hot to the touch, feverish despite the cool night air.

A fire raged within me, a fire from the Goddess, and I realized she was summoning me to a mystickal destiny.

What? I asked. *Where shall I go? Which way to turn?* I felt pent up and trapped, unable to commune with her. I needed to see the moon.

Glancing up at the thatched roof, I realized that I could probably reach it with the help of the one chair in my prison. I pulled the chair to the highest spot and climbed up. Aye, my fingertips pressed against the thatching. I pulled at the straw, tugging it loose. I would claw and scrape until my fingers bled if it meant reaching out to the Goddess on my last night upon this earth.

As I plucked at the straw, I thought of my purpose. I could not see my way to escape from my death or to save my child. But what of my legacy . . . my destiny before the Goddess? Would I be known only as a young witch who had feuded with a Vykrothe girl?

I recalled what my mother had said about Da, about his feud with the Vykrothes. Now, so many years later, I had become entangled with the same clan. Was that part of the Goddess's plan? Perhaps my very purpose was to dismantle the Vykrothes' power once and for all. I could not actively go after Siobhan, but I could place a curse upon her from behind these prison walls. One last spell, one final wave of revenge before she had me killed.

Bit by bit, the straw tumbled down to the earth. Then I yanked on a thick piece, and a fat section of thatching fell to the floor of the stone hut, making a crumbling sound that might have been heard by the guard if he had not been still asleep and snoring thanks to Diarmuid's spell. When the dust cleared, I was gazing upon a dark patch of sky with a virgin crescent moon.

I came down from the chair and stood, arms up, in the sliver of pale moonlight. 'Twas but a dim patch, but I could feel its power lifting me to the sky. I no longer felt trapped. I was communing with the Goddess, opening myself up to my own destiny.

The air seemed to crackle with magick as I held my hands open to the Goddess. "Show me the tools and how to use them," I begged.

In the candlelight the tips of my fingernails seemed black. Examining them, I realized it was blood. Blood and skin scraped from Siobhan and Diarmuid. 'Twas a powerful beginning, to have a piece of their body to place upon my makeshift altar. I scraped the dried crust from under my nails and placed it carefully on a clean tin plate left to me by the guards.

Staring at the scraps of Diarmuid and Siobhan, I began to feel the way clearly. 'Twas the Goddess's will, this spell, and she lit my path.

"Sweep the circle," came the Goddess's voice. Or was I remembering Ma's voice from one of the coven circles? *"Sweep . . . sweep,"* it called out to me, stirring my powers.

I gathered straw from my sleeping pallet and wove it into a small broom, which I used to sweep a circle inside the springhouse. Then I lit my makeshift broom afire and swept my circle with flames. The smoke burned my throat, but I breathed it gladly, wanting to cense my hair and skin with this powerful spell. Finally I left the broom to burn in the center and turned to the candle.

Carefully, so as not to extinguish the flame, I carved runes into the single candle that Diarmuid had brought. I spelled out the Vykrothe name, then wrote the runes for death beside it. Then I added runes for Diarmuid's name, for truly he deserved the wrath of the Goddess for his betrayal of Her, his betrayal of me and my child.

As I set the candle down, I noticed Diarmuid's pentagram on the ground. I picked up the gold coin and blew off the dust. 'Twould make a fine brand upon my body. If I was to go to the gallows, I would want to have the mark of the Goddess upon me and my child.

I built up the center fire with twigs and straw of the thatching. Blowing on the flames until the embers glowed, I knew what I had to do.

A spell to put an end to treachery.

A spell to destroy Siobhan and Diarmuid. To punish their evil. Mayhap this was the Goddess's will for me—my destiny.

A spell to set the balance among the clans aright once again.

Casting Diarmuid's pentagram into the flames, I felt the fever within me rise. Gasping, I threw back my head and cast my eyes upon the crescent in the sky. The fire within me was raging, my skin dripping, my cheeks burning. I slipped off my gown and stood naked in the square of light.

"I draw the power of generations of Wodebaynes into myself, merging with her power, the pure essence of the Goddess."

Gazing down into the crusty blood, I said: "I have cast this circle to perform the act of vengeance that the Vykrothes have truly earned. I place a curse upon their feet, that they may stumble along the path of light and fall into darkness. Cursed be their wombs, that they shall fail to produce new offspring. Cursed be their warmongering hearts, that they will no longer beat steady and true. Cursed be their sight, that they shall never again see through the Goddess's veil to her true beauty."

Holding the tin of blood over the flame, I charged it with fire, saying: "As Siobhan lit a fire of hatred in this world, so shall her blood boil. Send her own malice, greed, and wickedness back to her—threefold!" I tossed the dried blood into the fire, and a sizzling sound issued forth. I imagined leagues of *taibhs*—a huge wave of them—rising up and sweeping over Siobhan's pretty flaxen head. Black droplets of pain rained down upon Diarmuid, staining his sparkling blue eyes, burning his hair, sinking into his lovely cheeks. The black spells danced over them, blocking out all light until their bodies were a dissolving mass of darkness.

"This offering is for you, Goddess," I said. "Cast your hatred upon the head of Siobhan and her Vykrothe family. Cast darkness upon Diarmuid and his cruel family. And if you have no evil to send, I summon the fallen angels, arbiters of evil! Use my powers to mete out this justice!"

The powers of darkness swirled around me. I felt buffeted by smoky darkness, mired in the pain and suffering that I was sending from my heart to the hearts of mine enemies.

Using a thick piece of straw, I fished Diarmuid's pentagram out of the fire. I thought of the way Diarmuid had drawn pentagrams in the air . . . the foolish boy. His magick was so weak!

The pentagram had turned black with heat, but I reached for it. 'Twas time to brand myself to the ways of the Goddess, despite the pain.

My fingertips singed as I picked it up, but the pain seemed cool against the fire that raged inside me. Pressing the pentagram to my belly, I charged each point of the star.

"I summon the powers of earth," I whispered hoarsely, "wind, water, fire, and spirit." Pain brought tears to my eyes, but it seemed minor in comparison to the pain that filled me. The pain of losing my baby, of losing my life and love.

My pain must not go unpunished!

Kneeling before the fire, I imagined the wave of evil surrounding Siobhan, sucking her in, slamming her, crashing over her helpless body and swallowing the other cruel Vykrothes in its wake.

"I cast this spell for my baby," I said. "For myself, and for every other Wodebayne who has ever been wronged. Goddess, sweep over the treacherous ones and let their own evil be compounded!" I felt a surge of power, a wave that drew me up, thrumming around me, buoying my body above the chaotic forces at work. I was rising up, hovering above my cell, above my own village and Ma's cottage, above the Highlands. Beneath me were the soft greens of summer fields, the crisp dark crown of woodlands, the silver blue of lochs with the cool mist of evening rising up from them.

Wondering what held me suspended, I looked down and saw a wave of pure darkness. I was riding a crescent of black, a coursing molten liquid wrought of the blood of dead Wodebaynes, of my father and his father, of Fionnula and other tormented clan members. 'Twas my blood and my child's blood, raging and thrashing over the Highlands—a river of evil crashing into the village of Lillipool.

Then, all at once, I was released.

I collapsed to the ground, weak and spent. I slipped into a dream state, feeling fires raging around me. Was my cell burning? Had I remembered to douse the burning broom?

I wasn't sure, but I could not summon the strength to lift myself from the floor. If I were destined to die now, perhaps it was better at my own hand than at the hands of the villagers. What was to come at the end of this life? I remembered Ma speaking of death being rebirth . . . the Wheel turns and we move on to a new life. Would I find my baby in that new world? I hugged my belly, feeling the child kick. "I will be there for you," I whispered tearfully. "I will be there."

I am riding upon his shoulders at the seashore. Then suddenly we are here in the town square, dancing with torches like witches around the Beltane fires. Then I am on a seaside cliff, holding a soft bundle in my arms. When I open the flap, I peer into the face of my own baby. A girl, of course. She smells of honeysuckle and clover. But we cannot stay here. The ocean is rising from a storm. And suddenly the wave is cresting, taller and taller, over our heads. I must run to save her. . . .

I lifted my head and reached forward, trying to grasp my baby. My fingers brushed the ashes of my ceremonial fire, and I remembered that I was in my cell, sleeping in my circle under a smoky gray sky.

I arose and slipped on my gown, struggling to fasten the girdle over my bulging belly. Throughout the night the shouts of villagers and the noise of people scrambling about had penetrated the numbness that gripped me. Now that daylight was flooding in through the ceiling, the smell of fire was thick in the air. How could the smoke from my spell linger so?

The door opened, and a bowl of biscuits was tossed in. "Here's your milk," the guard said, eyeing me warily as he placed the pitcher inside the door. "And don't be laying a curse upon my head, for I am just doing my job, and I have three young bairns at home."

I blinked. What was he blubbering about? But before I could ask, the door slammed shut, leaving me to my breakfast. I ate every last crumb, surprised at the calm that had overtaken me. I had resigned myself that my baby and I would be reborn together; that was the vision I would cling to in my last hours.

When the door opened for me to go to the gallows, I stepped into the smoky haze with my chin high and a small measure of courage. If Siobhan and the others were going to condemn me, I would not let them have the satisfaction of seeing that they had indeed broken my spirit.

I will see you when the Wheel turns, I told the child within me. How I will delight in the sight of your sweet face!

I followed the guards to the gallows, surprised that they did not try to bind my hands or manhandle me today. They did cast nervous glances, but somehow their eyes no longer held the utter disdain I'd seen the day before.

Arriving at the village square, I was surprised to see such a small group of witnesses assembled. I wondered at the scarcity of onlookers, especially when I had been such a spectacle the day before. And where was Ma? I couldn't believe she wouldn't come to be with me as I took my last breath. Kyra stood by the gallows, swathed in black. But Diarmuid and Siobhan were absent, as was the village reverend, who had been my chief persecutor.

I looked at the strange faces, wondering what had

happened to my enemies. Had the spell worked? Perhaps Siobhan had been stricken down, unable to attend my execution. The thought offered some satisfaction.

As I walked up to the gallows, Kyra came up to me. "If I may have a moment," she told the guards, and they stepped back. Kyra put her arms around me for a hug, and I wanted to cry, feeling as if she were the last person on earth who cared for me. I hugged her back, the sting of tears in my eyes.

"You shouldn't be doing this," I told her, my voice cracking with emotion. "They'll persecute you just for knowing me."

"I have lied to them, Rose, and they remember me not," she whispered in my ear. "As I stand here, the guards think I'm a preacher's daughter from a village to the north, come to speak the word of the Christian God to a condemned prisoner."

I sobbed, afraid to let her go.

"Don't look down," she whispered, "but I'm pressing a charm into your hands for protection. Amber. I charged it myself." She winced, adding, "I hope it works."

"Thank you," I whispered, pleased that Kyra was working her own magick at last. "You are the only one who's come to say good-bye."

"Many did not survive the night." She frowned. "It seems there was a terrible fire in Lillipool last night. That is why smoke hangs in the air."

"A fire?" I tried to tamp down my curiosity. What had my spell done?

Kyra nodded. "Nobody was present to see the flames, only the ruin left in its wake. It appears that it swept through the village, then leaped to neighboring cottages in the countryside. I . . . I'm afraid Diarmuid was lost in it."

I blinked, feeling no sense of loss. 'Twas a marvel how drastically my feelings for him had changed, yet Diarmuid was the reason I was here. I rubbed my eyes, wondering if the fire had been the result of my spell. "What of Siobhan?" I asked.

"She died, as did her whole family and Reverend Winthrop, who was celebrating with them. The Highlands have never seen such an act of destruction; 'tis no doubt the fury of the Goddess." Kyra narrowed her eyes, studying me curiously. "So you do not know anything of this?"

"Is that what people think?"

"Some say you cast a spell in your fury over being condemned to die." She nodded toward the guards. "That's why they are so afraid of you today."

I turned toward the guards. One of them caught my eye and turned away quickly, as if he could avoid a curse by keeping his back turned. And with Reverend Winthrop gone . . . who would see to it that my sentence was carried out? These cowering guards?

The winds of fate had shifted, and I could feel the power of the Goddess swirling around me.

I was not going to die. I knew that now.

"So my spell worked," I said, loud enough for everyone in the square to hear. 'Twas a strange thrill to speak of witch matters before the Christian villagers. Heads snapped toward me in fear, and I smiled. "Yes, the fire was my doing. I used all my powers to punish the evil. They not only persecuted me, they acted on their hatred of my clan every day. They've been persecuting Wodebaynes for years!"

The few people assembled in the square began to disperse

in fear. One lady hitched up her skirts and quickly ran off. Two men meandered toward the church as if they were taking an afternoon stroll.

I swung toward the guards, wondering if I would need to shoot *dealan-dé* to scare them off.

"Don't curse us!" one of them said, covering his face with his hands. "We mean you no harm!"

"I thought you were about to hang me?" I asked.

The heavyset guard shook his head. "We'll not lay a finger on you, as long as you promise not to practice your sorcery on us."

"All right, then . . ." I cast them a fierce look. "Begone, before I turn you into toads or peahens."

They hurried off, not even looking back. I crossed my arms over my belly, aware of the tingling power inside me. My spell had worked. I knew I should feel jubilant—elated! Instead, I felt only a compulsion to leave the scene of my trial.

"By the Goddess, I cannot believe I am walking away from my own execution," I said as Kyra and I strode through the town. I was beyond feeling relief as I walked stiffly down the lane.

"So you really did cast a spell?" she asked wonderingly.

"Indeed, and by the grace of the Goddess, she fulfilled it."

"Many say it wasn't the Goddess," she said quietly. "Some say it was dark magick. A huge *taibhs*."

I sighed. "Let their tongues wag. The spell I cast was just a return of all the evil Siobhan had sent my way, threefold."

Kyra nodded, but I could tell she wasn't convinced. Let her be, I thought. She had always been näive. Someday she would understand.

*   *   *

As I walked home, I was surprised at the respect paid me by passersby. A man with a cart offered me a ride, and two passing ladies actually bowed before me. I knew they had heard of the fires, which had quickly turned me into a local legend, it seemed. I had always known of my powers, but for once it was nice to have others acknowledge my gifts.

When I reached the cottage, I found Síle sitting at the table, staring off at nothingness.

"Are you all right, Ma?"

She looked up at me, startled, as though she were seeing a ghost. Slowly she shook her head, pointing a finger at me. "My fury and disappointment know no bounds. Have you any idea what you have unleashed?"

" 'Twas a spell," I said simply. "A spell against my persecutors—those who would have taken the life of my baby!"

"No evil action deserves the black magick you conjured. I have never seen anything like it—never! You have caused a split in our coven, some arguing that you created the spell in your own defense. But they are wrong." My ma tried to sniff back tears. "You have created a horrible evil, Rose. Your spell ushers in the advent of a very dark time. A terrible reign of darkness! I have seen it!" Her voice broke in a sob, and she rested her head in her hands, shaking.

I folded my arms, unable to comfort her. "You make it sound as if I were a selfish child. I did not create the spell just for myself. I was acting for all Wodebaynes. This is the type of vengeance our clan needs."

Ma shook her head. "No, Rose. There is nothing anyone could have done to warrant this horrible violence. You didn't only hurt Siobhan—you destroyed her entire family! Her entire coven! And all of the villagers of Lillipool—Vykrothes,

Leapvaughns, and Christians alike. You burned little children and women expecting bairns, like yourself."

"I didn't . . . I didn't mean for *that* to happen, but—"

"Oh, dear Goddess!" Síle wailed. "How could my daughter, my own flesh and blood, be capable of such evil?"

I sat down on my bed in disbelief. She didn't understand, and I didn't have the strength to enlighten her. I did not enjoy seeing her in pain like this, though I truly thought she was being overly dramatic.

"It must be Gowan's blood," she muttered. "Your actions make it clear. The evil must have started with him, dabbling in dark magick like a foolish child who knows no better. The man always did want to take the easy road. He must have planted the seed of evil, and now you've nurtured it." She took a deep breath and collapsed into sobs once again.

" 'Tis not so," I said, touching her shoulder. "In time you will understand—"

"I will not!" Ma winced, pulling away from me. "Time will not heal this wound, Rose, and you may not remain under this roof for even a single night." She steeled herself, fixing me with a scowl. "You are not my daughter anymore. I do not care where you go, but I never want to see you again."

Beneath my overriding numbness, I felt the last vestige of hope crushed within me. My mother was abandoning me. My baby and I would have no one in the world, no safe harbor. Only each another.

My mouth felt dry as I moved about the cottage, gathering up my meager belongings. How would it feel never to return here? To have no one to watch over me, to console me over night visions? No one to see that I got enough to eat or had a place to sleep? No one to teach me new spells? No one to help me care for the coming child? Fear tightened my chest at the prospect of walking out the door . . . fear and dread. My mother was the last vestige of my old life, and I longed to cling to her.

But I had no choice. Ma would not have me. She watched me pack like a hawk waiting to pounce.

When I had everything in a satchel, I turned to her. "I'll say good-bye," I told her, "but surely we will meet again?"

She turned her head away and staved me off with one hand. "I cannot bear to lay eyes upon you," she said. "Just begone!"

Swallowing the lump that had formed in my throat, I stepped out the door and ventured into the woods. I had nowhere to go but my sacred circle, and even that seemed tainted by the hands of Diarmuid. Still, I swept the circle and raised my hands to the Goddess.

"I have a need that must be met," I said. "I beg You, Goddess, that I obtain a home, a place to live for me and my babe to come." I stood there under the hazy sky, wondering where I would go. "Goddess, I know You do not intend for me and my child to starve."

I thought of my mother, cursing her weakness. "She has never understood my powers, Goddess." I had always believed that someday I would inherit Ma's stature as high priestess of our coven . . . but now it was not to be. "Perhaps it is envy," I said aloud.

But there was no one to answer. Letting my hands drop to my sides, I realized that this circle had truly lost its magic for me. I packed my tools in my satchel, then set fire to my broom. I swept the wide circle with the flaming broom, wiping it all away. The Goddess would no longer visit this part of the woods. The magick was now gone from the stone altar, the green moss, and the tree that had once served as a Beltane maypole.

Once the circle was broken, I took my satchel and walked down the road. I decided to walk to Lillipool to witness the harvest of my spell. I walked as if in a daze until I reached a section of the woods that was now charred black and nearly empty, as if the trees and cottage there had simply melted into the earth.

I paused, pinching my nose against the smoking ash. What had stood here? I could not remember. I pressed closer, realizing that the striated rows of ash were charred skeletons. Three skeletons pressed against a door. Had they been unable to escape in time? I pressed my hands to my mouth, horrified at the thought. To imagine a sudden fire, the choking smoke, the need to get out before the flames swept over you . . .

Closing my eyes, I swallowed hard, trying to ignore the sting in my throat. 'Twas destruction at the hands of the Goddess, I told myself, and she smites evil. These villagers may have been nothing to me, but surely they were evil?

I didn't feel ready to see more, yet I felt compelled to walk on, past yet another and another scene of the fire, now merely a blackened square upon the earth. When I reached the river, I had a vague sense that the mill had once stood here, with cottages all around. But now I stood amid a smoky landscape of embers, an endless horizon of ash and blackened earth.

"So mote it be," I said aloud to ward off any doubts I had over the devastation surrounding me.

Down the lane of ashes I saw the charred skeletons of three children lined up, as if prepared for burial rites. I thought of the children I'd seen playing in the dusty square when I'd come to Lillipool to see Diarmuid. A pang of regret tightened in my breast, but again I told myself 'twas the Goddess's will. Were not these children being groomed in the bigoted ways of their clans?

I moved toward the center of what was once Lillipool. The charred skin of a man's hand reached out from a fallen window ledge, though there was no body to be seen. Stepping around it, I shuddered and rubbed my belly. "'Tis a gruesome sight," I said aloud. "But surely he was an evildoer."

Even the dusty village square had been transformed to thick, dark ash. Ashes of bones and buildings, embers of my enemies' dreams and hatred.

So much hatred.

Yet I could feel neither jubilation over the success of my spell nor sorrow for the lives lost upon this doomed patch of the Highlands. The Goddess had pushed me beyond feeling, beyond tears.

Walk. Breathe. Rest. My strength was focused on the simplest matters right now, the need to survive and care for my baby. *See here the fruits of your spell,* the Goddess was telling me. *Witness and learn, for the destruction wrought here is the result of your summons.*

Near the river sat a row of buildings that had not completely burned, but only collapsed into ash. Mayhap the people in them had used the water of the river to fend off the fire? I stepped near one sagging doorway and peered inside. The bodies here were not completely charred, and perhaps they were worse for their rotting stench, their distinguishable features. Was that the tinker? And the children . . .

I turned away, wanting only to see the corpses of those most deserving.

I walked into a tangle of smoking embers that I thought to be Diarmuid's cottage. Kicking at a gray ashen stump, I thought of the hungry look in Diarmuid's eyes the night before. His denial of our love, his retreat from the Goddess's plan. Goddess, please grant me that my child will not have those eyes, those lustful, glittery eyes. . . .

The ash below my shoe crunched apart, lowering me into a burning ember. I stomped out the heat, then noticed two skeletons, their charred limbs entwined.

Could it be Diarmuid and . . . and Siobhan?

Was this the spot where they had died?

I climbed over the ashes to study the skeletons. A gold ring was still wrapped around one of the charred finger bones—Diarmuid's ring. I pressed my lips together, feeling a sting as I understood that the burned girl was Siobhan.

'Twould be the last time she hurt me.

I reached down and snapped the ring off Diarmuid's charred finger bone. I would save it for my child. "I won't tell your daughter the truth about you," I told him, then thought better of it. How many years had I tried to pry the truth about Da from Ma? "Or mayhap I'll tell her everything . . . every sordid detail of your weak and cowardly character."

I laughed, realizing that Diarmuid no longer had any power in this life. Lifting my gown, I gazed upon the marking that I had branded on my belly. The pentagram was there, inverted. I blinked in awe. I had branded it so that I could look down and see it—but that meant the star shape was actually upside down upon my belly. An inverted pentagram was a legendary symbol for the harnessing of evil, though I'd never before used it.

I pressed Diarmuid's ring against my own inverted marking. Somehow it brought me a dark pleasure, and I was glad to feel something even if it was a bitter end.

"'Tis your heritage," I told my child. "The inverted pentagram, the dark spell, the dark wave, the origin of our redemption. This will be the spell I pass on to you to protect you and yours for all time."

The babe gave a hearty kick, and I lowered my gown. 'Twas time to rest, but I could not find comfort here in this landscape of charred ruin. I tucked the ring into a satchel on my belt and moved on.

Instead of heading back to my own village, I kept going east, past the burned bog and heather that had surrounded Siobhan's house. I paid no homage to the smoking remains there as I walked past, my sights set on a distant village where I might find lodging at an inn.

I came to a fork in the road and decided to continue east, to the place where the sun rose. Just beyond the fork someone called my name. I turned to find Aislinn waving at me, her red hair flying as she ran to catch up with me. Her energy seemed jarring in the silent woods, the site of so much recent destruction.

"Rose! Rose! It *was* you, wasn't it? Did you see the ruin?" Her face was lit with a predatory smile. "Your spell wiped them out, the whole lot of them! By the Goddess, we really showed them! It will be a long time before anyone else crosses a Wodebayne."

I rocked back on my heels, weary but relieved that Aislinn understood.

"You must be filled with wonder at what you've accomplished."

"I can't say that I am," I admitted, wishing that I could summon some emotion.

"Well, then I am proud on your behalf," Aislinn said. "Your dark wave of a spell has put an end to our persecution. You have altered our fate, Rose. Nevermore will we be downtrodden, nevermore the outcasts."

"My ma does not agree," I said. "She's banished me from our coven."

"Síle is a foolish woman," Aislinn said. "She has no vision, no courage. Did you know that many of us had already abandoned her coven, long before last night? Coveners were tiring of Síle's failure to take action. We've begun to have our own circle in the woods east of here, near a village called Druinden. Though sometimes we flounder. We haven't really found a high priestess with the power to summon the Goddess."

"Really?" I felt bolstered by this news. Perhaps I had not been abandoned as I'd thought. Perhaps it was Síle who was wrong. Perhaps she had been denying the ways of the Goddess, and that was why I was here traveling down this unknown road with barely a stitch to my name.

"Is that where you're headed?" Aislinn asked. "Druinden?"

"I suppose, if I can get a room at the inn there." I felt awkward revealing myself to Aislinn, yet I suspected she knew my entire story already. "I've not only been banished from the coven, but also from the cottage. And . . . you probably know, I'm with child."

"Don't even think of the inn!" she insisted, her face flushing with pride. "You must stay with my sister and me! It's my father's cottage, but he's off at sea most of the time. And you mustn't worry about the bairn. The Goddess will provide. Especially if you decide you want to be high priestess of the new coven. Of course, the others must agree, but how could they not see your power? The whole village of Druinden knows of the dark wave. I'll wager everyone from here to Londinium knows. That spell has made you the high priestess of the Highlands."

I hardly felt like royalty, shuffling down that long road upon my aching feet. At the moment all I wanted was a place to rest and a pitcher of water to wash the smell of death from me. Wash away the soot, and the grime, and the bitter memory of betrayal.

14

Samhain

" 'Tis time to leave the light and enter the darkness," I said from the center of the circle. My coveners gathered around me, listening intently as their new high priestess spoke the words of the Samhain rite. "I plunge the blade of my athame deep into the heart of my enemy," I said, lowering my athame into a goblet of wine held by Aislinn.

"Plunge the blade, let evil die," they chanted, circling around me.

I went over to the ceremonial fire and stirred it with a stick until embers flew through the darkness. "I stoke the fires of vengeance and point the wrath of the Goddess toward their evil."

"Stoke the fires, let evil die," they chanted.

I stood naked before them, the round ripeness of my body so befitting the harvest ritual. The coveners were also unclad, and I noticed that a few others had taken to branding their bellies with the inverted pentagram. Aislinn had done it first, inspired by the marking on my belly, which had healed but was now a deep brown—a permanent sign of the powerful spell I had created.

Around my neck I wore a necklace with the amber stone Kyra had charged for me along with jet black beads to signify my position as high priestess. I had not seen Kyra or my mother since the day after the dark wave. At times tales of Síle's coven trickled into our circle, and I listened with interest, despite the fact that I knew I would never see my mother again. I realized now how she had tried to undermine my strength, depriving me of the power the Goddess intended me to wield.

I touched the golden stone at my neck, wondering if Kyra knew the power of her charm. Amber was also an excellent protector of children and a spell strengthener, and I often held the charmed stone close to my breast in anticipation of the birthing rite. My child would be here before Imbolc, I knew it. I had enjoyed visions of her—a tiny bundle in my arms as I knelt before Aislinn, summoning the Goddess's power through the lighting of the candles in the crown upon my head.

"Let us reenact the great event of our year," I said, moving to the side of the circle, "the dark wave."

Aislinn led the dance, playing me as I crafted the spell in my prison cell. Other coveners played the forces of earth, wind, water, and fire. As I watched the dancers move, leaping in the air and dipping to the ground, I thought of the hours I had spent schooling my coveners in the elements of the dark wave. We planned to cast the spell over the Burnhydes to the north, for they had been stealing sheep from Wodebayne herders repeatedly. 'Twas unforgivable, the way they committed crime with abandon. "They must be stopped," Aislinn said often. "And we have the power to do it."

The dark wave.

The coveners had proven to be apt students of the grave spell. Already they had collected hair and fingernails from Burnhydes for use in the magick.

My baby shifted inside me, and I smiled. Aye, little one, you will learn the spell, too. I will pass it on to you. It is your legacy.

When the drama before me ended, I arose and held my hands up to the Goddess. "I fell into deep darkness," I said. "I greeted death. I tore the velvet darkness of everlasting light. Ablaze with glory, I was reborn. Now the old year ends."

"The new year begins!" the coveners responded. "Plunge the blade! Stoke the fires!"

I went to the center of the circle, saying: "Their evil shall burn their own funeral pyres!"

The coveners danced around me, chanting: "Plunge the blade! Stoke the fires!"

I felt the power of the Goddess swirl around us. Aye, we were nearly ready to send the dark wave, so mote it be. "Welcome, new year, farewell, strife. From fiery embers arises life."

"Plunge the blade! Stoke the fires. . . ."

Epilogue

Hunter and I still sat silently on the couch. *Plunge the blade! Stoke the fires!* The words kept running through my head, like a mantra. This girl, this young, seventeen-year-old girl. I tried to imagine going through what she went through. Would I have reacted the same way?

"Morgan?"

I realized that Hunter was looking at me with concern. His hand lay on my arm. He seemed to be waiting for me to respond. Had he asked me a question? I shook my head, trying to clear it, and then reached for my cold chamomile tea. "Yes," I said quietly. When I raised the cup to my lips, I realized that my face was wet with tears.

"Morgan, are you all right?"

I looked down at the closed book. Rose MacEwan, I thought, my ancestor. The creator of the dark wave. How was it possible? But I knew, I realized almost immediately, with a sinking feeling in the pit of my stomach. I remembered the few times I had practiced dark magick—shape-shifting with Ciaran. Weather magick with my half brother Killian. It had felt so right, pure, and natural. Hunter realized it, too, I thought—when strange things had started happening at our circles, he had believed it was me. Rose could have been me, I thought with sickening clarity. We were so alike: blood relatives. *I could have been Rose.*

Hunter had knelt on the floor before me, and he sat now with his hands on my knees, begging me to speak.

"No," I said softly, shaking my head. "I don't know what I am."

Hunter looked up at me, his eyes warm with concern. I could see pain there, pain at seeing me cry. Oh, Goddess, he loved me, without tricks or reservations. What he had done with Justine seemed so trivial now.

He sat back on the couch, reached out, and folded me into his arms. I didn't resist. "She didn't know, love. She didn't know what she was doing."

"But she still did it." I shivered involuntarily, thinking of Rose and Diarmuid—she had been so sure of their love, as sure as I had been—*was*—of Hunter's. And look where it had led. The same place my birth parents' love had led—to death, destruction, and misery.

I looked up at Hunter's face—the face that I dreamed of, the face that I believed to be there for me. Only me. I reached up and touched Hunter's cheek—my *mùirn beatha dàn*. Even his parents' love had led to hurt—abandoning their children, Hunter's father hurting himself in an attempt to re-create what they had had after his love's death.

"I know you, love. You're not like Rose. You've chosen good." Hunter whispered, stroking my hair.

I nodded, wanting to believe him. But as a daughter of such dark origins, I could only hope that he was right.

Book Twelve

SWEEP

Eclipse

All quoted materials in this work were created by the author.
Any resemblance to existing works is accidental.

Eclipse

SPEAK
Published by the Penguin Group
Penguin Group (USA) Inc., 345 Hudson Street, New York, New York 10014, U.S.A.
Penguin Group (Canada), 90 Eglinton Avenue East, Suite 700, Toronto, Ontario, Canada M4P 2Y3
(a division of Pearson Penguin Canada Inc.)
Penguin Books Ltd, 80 Strand, London WC2R 0RL, England
Penguin Ireland, 25 St Stephen's Green, Dublin 2, Ireland (a division of Penguin Books Ltd)
Penguin Group (Australia), 250 Camberwell Road, Camberwell, Victoria 3124, Australia
(a division of Pearson Australia Group Pty Ltd)
Penguin Books India Pvt Ltd, 11 Community Centre, Panchsheel Park, New Delhi - 110 017, India
Penguin Group (NZ), 67 Apollo Drive, Rosedale, Auckland 0632, New Zealand
(a division of Pearson New Zealand Ltd)
Penguin Books (South Africa) (Pty) Ltd, 24 Sturdee Avenue, Rosebank, Johannesburg 2196, South Africa

Registered Offices: Penguin Books Ltd, 80 Strand, London WC2R 0RL, England

Published by Puffin Books, a division of Penguin Young Readers Group, 2002
Published by Speak, an imprint of Penguin Group (USA) Inc., 2008
This omnibus edition published by Speak, an imprint of Penguin Group (USA) Inc., 2011

1 3 5 7 9 10 8 6 4 2

Copyright © 2002 17th Street Productions, an Alloy company, and Gabrielle Charbonnet
All rights reserved

Produced by 17th Street Productions,
an Alloy company
151 West 26th Street
New York, NY 10001

17th Street Productions and associated logos
are trademarks and/or registered trademarks of Alloy, Inc.

Speak ISBN 978-0-14-241027-1
This omnibus ISBN 978-0-14-242010-2

Printed in the United States of America

To Stephanie Lane, with gratitude

1

Morgan

><"And then the hand of God swept away the
heathen witches, and their village was leveled
and burned to the ground. This I saw with my
own eyes."

—Susanna Garvey, Cumberland, England, from
A BRIEF COLLOQUIAL HISTORY OF CUMBERLAND,
Thomas Franklinton, 1715><

"Oh, please. Will you two stop already? This is disgusting," I teased.

On Ethan Sharp's front step Bree Warren and Robbie Gurevitch tried to disentangle themselves from their lip-to-lip suction lock. Robbie gave a little cough.

"Hey, Morgan." He stood off to one side, trying to act casual—hard to do when you're flushed and breathing hard. It was still a tiny bit of a novelty to see Robbie and Bree, my best friends from childhood, in a romantic relationship. I loved it.

"Perfect timing, Sister Mary Morgan," said Bree, pushing a hand through her minky dark hair. But she grinned at me, and I smiled back. Robbie rang Ethan's doorbell.

Ethan opened the door almost immediately. Two yipping Pomeranians bounced at his feet. "Down," he said, pushing them gently with his foot as he smiled at us. "Come on in. Most everyone's here. Still waiting on a couple. Down!" he said again. "Brandy! Kahlua! Down! Okay, you're going in the bedroom."

We entered Ethan's small brick ranch house and saw Sharon Goodfine, Ethan's girlfriend, pushing furniture back against the wall. Ethan disappeared down the hall, snapping his fingers so the dogs would follow him. Robbie went to help Sharon, and Bree and I took off our jackets and threw them on an armchair with several others.

"You two look like you're getting along," I said brightly.

"Yeah," Bree admitted. "I'm still waiting for him to figure out who the real me is and then dump me."

I shook my head. "He's loved you for a long time and seen you go through a lot. He's going to be harder to shake off than that."

Bree nodded, her gaze wandering till it fixed on Robbie. I looked around, mentally taking attendance for the circle. Our regular Saturday night circles had been different lately because Hunter had been in Canada. He'd returned a few days ago and sent my emotions into an uproar with two bits of news: one, that he'd kissed another woman in Canada, which was bad enough, and two, that he'd found a book—written by one of my ancestors—that recounted the creation of the dark wave. Learning that my soul mate had been attracted to someone else *and* that I was descended from the woman who created one of the most destructive forces imaginable had left me devastated and confused. I felt a little better now, more confident in Hunter's love and in my ability to choose to do only good magick, but both of these revelations still weighed heavily on my mind.

Hunter would be here tonight. He hadn't arrived yet, because I would have felt him. My witchy short-range sensors would have told me.

Twenty minutes later everyone in our coven, Kithic, was there, except for Hunter's cousin, Sky Eventide. She was in England recovering from a failed romance, and I couldn't help glancing across the circle at the source of her pain, Raven Meltzer. As usual, Raven had dressed for attention, wearing a red satin corset from the forties, complete with cone boobs and garters, which held up fishnet stockings marred by large, gaping holes. Men's camouflage fatigues, hacked off to make shorts, completed the outfit, along with the motorcycle boots on her feet.

"Right, then, everyone," Hunter said in that English accent that made me wild. "Let's begin."

"Welcome back, Hunter," said Jenna Ruiz.

"Yeah, welcome back," said Simon Bakehouse, Jenna's boyfriend.

"It's good to be back," Hunter said, meeting my eyes. It was like being zapped by static electricity.

Hunter Niall. The love of my life. He was tall, thin, impossibly blond, and two years older than me. Besides having the English accent that I could listen to all day, he was brave, a strong blood witch, and knew more about magick and Wicca than I could imagine learning, despite my dedication to it. He had just gotten back from two weeks in Canada, where he had found his father, Daniel. And where he had met someone named Justine Courceau. Finding out that he had kissed her had been one of the hardest things I'd ever learned. I'd forgiven him—I believed that he loved me and hadn't meant to hurt me—but I didn't think I'd ever be able to forget.

Ethan's living room was carpeted, so Hunter had used sidewalk chalk to draw a perfect circle. The eleven of us stepped inside it; then Hunter closed it with a chalk line. He took four brass goblets and placed them at east, south, west, and north. One held dirt, to symbolize earth. Another held water, and a candle burned in the third: water and fire. The last cup held a cone of smoldering incense to represent air. When these were in place, he looked up and smiled at us. "Did you all enjoy Bethany Malone's circles while I was away?"

"She was pretty cool," Raven said.

"She was really nice, in a different way," Simon agreed. "There's a difference in how you make a circle and how she did."

I nodded. "That's true. And I liked all the healing stuff she taught us." An understatement. I was now taking private lessons from Bethany, focusing almost exclusively on healing. Giving my Wicca studies this focus seemed to have helped the rest of my life come into focus, too.

"Good," said Hunter. "Maybe we'll have her back as a guest circle leader sometime."

Some of us grinned, and Hunter went on. "Now, is there any circle business we need to take care of before we start? Where are we meeting next week?"

"We can have it at my house," said Thalia Cutter.

After that, there was no more Kithic business, so Hunter cast our circle, dedicated it to the Goddess, and invoked the God and the Goddess to hear us.

"Now let's raise our power," said Hunter. "And while our power is high, we can each think about the meaning of rebirth, of spring, about how we can each strive to, in a sense, re-create our lives each spring."

We joined hands—I was between Matt Adler and Sharon. This time Hunter began with a power chant, and we all added our voices to it as we felt ready. The ancient Gaelic words seemed to float above us, weaving a circle of power above our heads. Hunter's voice was strong and sure, and in another minute I began to feel the incredible lightening of my heart that told me I had connected with the Goddess. It wasn't like she spoke to me—but when I made a real connection to magick, the magick that exists everywhere, my worries dropped away. Pure, unquestioning joy filled my heart and my mind, and I felt a rush of love for everyone in my circle—even me—and everyone outside of my circle. It was this connection that made coming back to magick so necessary for me. It was question and answer, reason and instinct, need and fulfillment all at the same time.

Hands locked, we circled deasil around the room, our feet moving faster and faster as smiles lit our faces. Rebirth, I thought with wonder. Re-create my life. Begin anew. The quickening of life. These concepts seemed full of promise and hope, and I knew my exploration of them would be joyous and exciting.

"Morgan."

With zero warning my birth father, Ciaran MacEwan, was standing in front of me. My hands ripped away from Matt's and Sharon's, and my feet stumbled on the blue carpet.

I stared at him, my eyes widening with fear and shock. In a moment I realized that he was an image in front of me, not the real person. But a complete, realistic image, shimmering gently, as if with heat.

"Morgan," he said again, his Scottish accent coming through. His brownish hazel eyes, exactly like mine, examined me.

"What do you want?" I whispered. All I could see was him; my circle, the room, my friends had faded out of sight, replaced by this glowing image of my father, the man who had burned my mother to death more than sixteen years ago.

"I know you put the watch sigil on me," he said softly, and fear clenched my stomach. "But I forgive you."

The last time I had seen Ciaran, we had shape-shifted together. At the council's request, I had traced a watch sigil onto him so that council members could track Ciaran's movements and eventually take him into custody. It had been a betrayal of him, but the risk had outweighed the danger of the deeds he would commit if left free. My birth father was one of the most evil witches in existence. He had murdered scores of people, including my birth mother, Maeve Riordan, as well as the lover she had known from childhood. I had chosen to betray Ciaran. I had chosen good over evil.

"I've . . . dismantled the watch sigil," Ciaran went on, and my knees almost buckled. "It was beautifully done, Morgan. So subtle, so elegant, yet so powerful." He shook his head admiringly. "Your powers . . ."

Oh, Goddess, I thought in panic.

"Of course, I was unhappy that you chose to betray me to the council jackals," Ciaran said dryly. "My own daughter. My favored one. But I do forgive you. And it's gone now— they have no idea where I am." He gave a mischievous chuckle, making him appear younger than his early forties. "But I'm coming to see you, daughter. I have some questions for you."

His image faded quickly. Blinking, I felt like a wall I had been leaning against had suddenly been taken away. There was a split second of seeing the members of Kithic staring at me in concern; then everything went fuzzy, and I felt myself fall.

"Stay still." Hunter's reassuring voice made me quit trying to sit up. My eyes opened, then shut again—everything looked too bright.

"What happened?" I murmured.

"I was hoping you could tell me," said Hunter. He gently lifted my head and rested it on his crossed legs. "You just stopped dead in the middle of our power chant and turned as white as a sheet of paper. You said, 'What do you want?' and stared at nothing. Then you keeled over."

Just like that, it all came back with a sickening rush. "It was Ciaran," I said softly, looking up at Hunter. Above me, his green eyes narrowed.

"What happened?" he asked, almost fiercely. But I knew his anger wasn't directed at me.

I struggled to sit up, feeling my elbow aching where I must have hit it. The rest of the coven was gathered around, looking at me in concern. Then Bree knelt close to me, holding out a glass of water.

"Thanks," I said gratefully. I took it and sipped, and felt a bit stronger.

"What happened?" Bree asked also, her dark eyes worried.

"It was Ciaran MacEwan," I explained more loudly. "I just . . .

suddenly had a vision of Ciaran. And then I fainted."

That was all I wanted to say in front of everyone, and Hunter must have understood because he said, "I think perhaps we should call it a night." He put his arm around my shoulders and helped me stand up. "It would be hard to recapture the energy, anyway."

Still looking concerned, the members of Kithic started pulling on their jackets.

"Do you want me to follow you home?" Robbie asked. "Or drive you?"

I smiled at him. After Bree, Robbie had been my best friend since grade school. "No thanks," I said. "I'll be okay."

"I'll make sure she gets home," said Hunter.

We said good-bye to Ethan and Sharon, who decided to stay, and walked out into the brisk late-winter evening. I breathed in the damp night air, trying to detect the first hint of spring. The change of seasons would do a lot for me. It had been a long, hard winter.

I stood next to my beloved white whale of a car, Das Boot, and rubbed my hands on my arms. I cast my senses but picked up nothing. "Hunter, Ciaran said he's taken off the watch sigil and that he knows I put it on him."

"Bloody hell," Hunter breathed.

"Yeah. Let's go to your place." I felt nervous, as if my father would leap out at me from behind Ethan's holly bush.

Hunter agreed and followed me in his own car to his house. I would feel safer there—it was a blood witch's house, spelled, protected, and familiar. I almost ran inside.

The overheated living room felt like a haven. Automatically I cast my senses again and felt Daniel Niall,

Hunter's father, in the kitchen. I tried not to let Hunter see my disappointment. Until three weeks ago, Hunter hadn't seen his parents in eleven years. They had been in hiding from Ciaran and his coven, Amyranth. Though Hunter's mom had died before he'd been able to see her, his father was still alive, and the danger seemed to be gone. Things had gotten pretty bad for Mr. Niall in Canada, and Hunter's trip had ended with Hunter's bringing his father home to live with him. Mr. Niall was staying in Sky's room until she came back. If she ever did.

"Sit down," Hunter said. "I'll get you some tea." He headed to the kitchen, and soon I heard murmured voices.

The truth was, I couldn't help it—I didn't like Mr. Niall. I had been so excited to meet Hunter's father, whom I'd heard so much about, whom I knew meant so much to Hunter. But I'd been shocked by his appearance—he looked like a homeless person, all bones and pale skin, mussed gray hair, eyes that looked half crazy. Still, I had put on my best manners, smiling and shaking hands—and he had reacted to me as if I were a gift his cat had left on the doorstep. He wasn't mean, exactly—just standoffish and reserved. I wasn't looking forward to seeing him again.

Hunter was soon back. "Drink this," he said, holding out a small glass with an inch of dark amber liquid in it. I sniffed it. "It's sherry," he explained. "Just a tiny bit. For medicinal purposes."

I sipped it hesitantly. It didn't really ring my bells, but after it was down, I felt a bit warmer and more able to deal. Then Hunter handed me a cup of tea, and I could sense that he'd added herbs and also spelled it to be healing and soothing. It was very convenient, having a witch for a boyfriend.

"Now," said Hunter, sitting next to me on the couch, so I felt his leg warm against mine. "Tell me everything."

Feeling safer and less freaked, and becoming more and more aware of his body next to mine, I told him everything about my vision that I could remember.

"Bloody hell," Hunter said again.

The kitchen door swung open, and Daniel Niall came out, carrying a plate with a sandwich on it. He saw me on the couch and gave me a tight little nod.

"Hi, Mr. Niall," I said, trying to sound friendly.

"So what did she say?" Hunter asked his father. Mr. Niall paused at the bottom of the steps, looking pained, as if Hunter had prevented him from making a clean escape.

"She said she'd like to," Daniel said. "And her school has a break soon."

"Da was talking to my sister, Alwyn," Hunter explained. "We're trying to get her to come visit."

I knew Alwyn was now sixteen and an initiated witch. "Oh, that would be great," I said. "I'd like to meet her."

Daniel nodded again briefly and headed upstairs. I sighed, unsure if I should mention my unease to Hunter. Did Mr. Niall treat me as he did only because I was related to Ciaran? I mean, parents *always* like me. I'm a math nerd, I'm not flashy, and I don't drink or do drugs—I'm still a virgin, for God's sake! Not that I wanted to be reminded about that. But I look like I have "future librarian" stamped on my forehead. What else could Mr. Niall have against me?

"Is he settling in better?" I asked tactfully once he had gone upstairs.

Hunter shrugged ruefully. "More or less. Mostly he's been reading Rose's diary." He was referring to Rose MacEwan, the witch who was responsible for creating the dark wave: an incredibly destructive spell that can pretty much take out a whole town and everyone in it. It didn't thrill me that a blood relative had created such a thing, but she had the same last name as Ciaran, she was Woodbane—sounded like family to me. I shuddered momentarily, thinking about her. Her story had seemed so real to me—I could almost see myself reacting the same way. It frightened me to think that such unimaginable destruction ran in my blood.

Weirdly enough, Mr. Niall had found Rose's diary in Canada, at the house of that witch, Justine Courceau. We had all read it, and then Mr. Niall had taken it back. "Da hopes that he'll find clues about how to create a spell to disband a dark wave."

"I didn't know that was possible. Goddess—if we never had to worry about it, it would be incredible. I hope he can do it." I shook my head in wonder.

"Look," Hunter said, "maybe we should scry right now, see if we can get a handle on where Ciaran is. Do you feel up to it?" He gently brushed my long hair over my shoulder. I had recently lopped off about six inches, and now it hung to the middle of my back.

"Yeah," I said, frowning. "Maybe we should. I keep feeling like he's going to drop down from the ceiling, like a spider." I followed Hunter into the large circle room, next to the dining room.

The circle room at Hunter's had once been a double parlor. Now it was a long, bare rectangle, scented with herbs and candles. There was a wood-burning stove, and in front of it Hunter made a small circle on the floor, big enough for the two of us. We sat cross-legged inside it, facing each other, our knees touching. Thoughts flew through my head as Hunter took out a large, smooth piece of obsidian: his scrying stone.

Gently we each put two fingers on the stone's edges and closed our eyes. This was where you cleared your mind and concentrated, opening yourself to what the stone wants to tell you. But all I could think about was Ciaran coming back for me, how much he scared me even as I felt oddly drawn to him. And Hunter—he wanted Hunter dead. Hunter, who was a beautiful mosaic of contradictions: strong, but infinitely gentle. Kind, but also ruthless and unforgiving when confronted by those who practiced dark magick—like Cal Blaire and Selene Belltower. I had seen Hunter flushed with desire and white-faced with anger and pain. He was my love.

"Morgan?"

"Sorry," I said.

"We don't have to do this," he offered.

"No, no, I need to." I closed my eyes again and this time, determinedly shutting out all other thoughts, I sank successfully into a deep meditation. Slowly I opened my eyes to see the smooth plane of the obsidian beneath my fingers. Lightly I murmured,

"Show me now what I should see,
What was past or what will be.
The stream of time will start to slow;
Show me where I need to go."

Hunter muttered the same words after me, and then there was silence as I focused my gaze on the stone. Minutes went by, yet the stone's face remained unchanged. It was odd—scrying is always unpredictable, but I usually got a better result than this.

Consciously I let my mind sink deeper into meditation. Everything around me faded out as I concentrated on the stone. My breathing was slow and deliberate, my chest barely moving. I no longer felt my fingers on the stone, my butt on the hard floor, my knees touching Hunter's.

The stone was black, blank. Or . . . looking closer, could I detect the barest, rounded outlines of . . . what? I looked at the stone so intently, I felt like I had fallen into a well of obsidian, surrounded by cold, hard blackness. Slowly I became aware of movement within the stone—that I *was* getting a scried vision. A vision of billowing, black, choking smoke.

"The blackness *is* the vision," I murmured. "Do you see the huge cloud of smoke?"

"Not clearly. Is it from a fire?"

I shook my head. "I can't see a fire. Just billows of black, choking smoke." An image of my birth mother, who had been killed by fire, came to me, and I frowned. What did it mean? Was this an image of the future? Was this directed at me? Did it mean I would suffer the same fate as Maeve, at Ciaran's hands?

For five more minutes I stared at the smoke, willing it to clear, to dissipate, to show me what was behind it. But I saw nothing more, and finally, my eyes stinging, I shook my head and sat back.

"I don't know what that was about," I told Hunter in frustration. "I didn't get anything besides smoke."

"It was a dark wave," Hunter said quietly.

"What?" I felt my back stiffen with tension. "What do you mean? Was this a prediction of a dark wave? It seemed to be about *me*." I got to my feet, feeling upset. "Is a dark wave coming for *me*?"

"We don't know for sure—you know scrying can be unpredictable," Hunter said, trying to comfort me.

"Yeah, and you know that almost every image I've ever seen scrying has come true," I said, rubbing my arms with my hands. I felt nervous and frightened, the way I'd felt as a kid, playing with a Ouija board, when it had moved on its own.

"I'll follow you home," Hunter said, and I nodded. Another downside of Mr. Niall living with him was that Hunter and I had no privacy anymore. It was one thing to be alone in Hunter's room when Sky was around, but there was no way I felt comfortable with his father in the next room. I felt depressed as I got into my jacket. Hunter and I really needed time alone to talk, to be together, to hold each other.

"Will you be okay at home?" he asked as we walked outside.

I thought. "Yeah. My house is protected out the wazoo."

"Still, I reckon it wouldn't hurt to add another layer of spells."

At my house, though we were both exhausted, Hunter and I made the rounds and added to or increased the protective powers of the spells on my house, on Das Boot, and on my parents' cars. When we were done, I felt drained.

"Go on inside," Hunter said. "Get some sleep. These spells are strong. But don't hesitate to call me if you sense anything odd."

I smiled and leaned against the front door, exhausted, wanting to be safely inside yet reluctant to leave Hunter. He came up the steps and I went into his arms, resting my head against his chest and feeling amazed at how, once again, he had seemed to read my mind.

"It'll be okay, my love," he said against my hair. One strong hand stroked my back soothingly while the other held me closely to him.

"I'm tired of it all," I said, suddenly feeling close to tears.

"I know. We haven't had a break. Listen, tomorrow why don't we go to Practical Magick, see Alyce? That'll be nice and normal."

I smiled at his idea of nice and normal: two blood witches going to an occult bookstore.

"Sounds good," I said. Then I lifted my face to his and was at once lost in the heady pleasure of kissing him, his warm lips against mine, the cool night air surrounding us, our bodies pressed together, magick sparking. Oh, yes, I thought. Yes. More of this.

"What's wrong?" I asked the next afternoon. Ever since Hunter had picked me up, he'd seemed edgy and distracted.

He drummed his fingers on the steering wheel. "I've been trying to reach the council for news on Ciaran," he said. "But I haven't been able to get through to anyone—not Kennet, not Eoife. I talked to some underling who wouldn't tell me anything."

Eoife was a witch who had tried to convince me to go study with Wiccan scholars in the wilds of Scotland. I had said I needed to finish high school first.

Kennet Muir was Hunter's mentor in the council and had helped guide him through the hard process of becoming a Seeker. Hunter still spoke to him about council business, but their relationship had been permanently damaged when Hunter realized Kennet had known where his parents were in Canada and hadn't bothered to tell him. If Kennet had let Hunter in on their whereabouts earlier, Hunter might have seen his mother alive. I knew this idea was hard for him to accept. In fact, he was so hurt by Kennet's betrayal, he never even confronted him about it. "It'll never be the same between us regardless," he'd reasoned.

"Okay, so we don't know," I said, watching the old farm fields fly past the car window. After being winter brown for months, it was heartening to see tinges and flecks of green here and there. Spring was coming. No matter what.

"No. Not yet." Hunter sounded irritated. Then he seemed to make an effort to cheer up. Reaching out one hand, he interlaced his fingers in mine and smiled at me. "It's good to spend time with you. I missed you so much when I was in Canada."

"I missed you, too." Once again exercising my gift for understatement. Then, taking a breath, I decided to bring up a sensitive subject. "Hunter—I've been wondering about your dad. I mean, he knows I'm not in league with Ciaran, right? He knows Ciaran tried to kill me, doesn't he?"

Hunter tugged at the neck of his sweater, pretending to not understand me. "He just needs more time."

Great. I looked out the window again.

"Is it Rose?" I asked suddenly, turning back to Hunter. "Is it because I'm a descendant of the witch who created the dark wave? I mean, he was running from the dark wave for eleven years." Eleven years, while Hunter was separated from his parents, thinking they'd abandoned him and his brother and sister. My stomach plummeted as I realized yet again how many horrible things my blood relatives were responsible for.

Hunter glanced over at me, taking his eyes off the road, and in that quick glance I caught a world of reassurance. "He just needs to get to know you, Morgan. You are not your ancestors. I know that."

I sighed, watching the bare trees pass overhead. If only I could convince *myself*.

Red Kill, the town where Practical Magick was, came into view slowly, the farm fields giving way to suburban lawns, then more streets and actual neighborhoods. Hunter turned down Main Street and drove almost to its end, where the small building that housed Practical Magick stood. He parked, but I made no move to get out of the car.

"It's just, I want your father to like me," I said, feeling self-conscious. "And I don't want to come between you and your dad. I don't want you to have to choose." I looked down at my hands, which were twisting nervously in my lap. I forced them to be still on my jeans.

"Goddess," Hunter muttered, leaning over the gear shift toward me. He took my chin in his hand and looked intently into my eyes. His were the color of olivine, a clear, deep green. "I won't need to choose. Like I said, Da just needs more time. He knows how much I love you. He just needs to get used to the idea."

I sighed and nodded. Hunter touched my cheek briefly, and then we opened the doors, climbed out, and headed for the store.

"Morgan, Hunter! Good to see you." Alyce Fernbrake waved us in from the back of the store. "I haven't seen either of you in a while. Hunter, I want to hear all about Canada. I couldn't believe your news. Wait—I'll fix tea."

We threaded our way through the scented, crowded store: my home away from home. Alyce disappeared into the small back room, separated from the main room by a tattered orange curtain. Her assistant, Finn Foster, nodded at Hunter with reserve: many witches didn't trust Seekers. "'Lo, Morgan," he said. "Have you heard Alyce's news? The shop next door is moving to a bigger location. Alyce is going to move to that space and make Practical Magick almost twice as big."

My eyebrows rose. "The dry cleaners are moving? What about her debt to Stuart Afton? Can she afford to lose their rent?"

Alyce bustled back with three mugs. "Well, fortunately, my business has been getting better and better the last couple of months. The real estate market is good enough that if I move into the store next door, I can rent this space for almost as much as the dry cleaners paid. And we'll just have to keep our fingers crossed that our increased sales will make up for the rest. It's a gamble, but I think it will be worth it in the end." She smiled.

"Congratulations," Hunter said, taking his mug. "It would be fantastic if the shop were bigger."

Alyce nodded, looking pleased. "It's going to be a lot of work," she said, "and I really don't know when I'll have the time. But I think the business could support the extra room. I would love to expand what I carry." She gestured to a pile of about five paper grocery bags, each packed with old-looking books. "I buy stuff at yard sales, estate sales, things that interest me, but I don't really have the space to put them out. You should see what I have in storage. But now I want to hear about you. It's amazing that your father has come to live with you."

Hunter nodded, and the two of them drifted over to the checkout counter, where Alyce propped herself on a stool and Hunter leaned against the lighted case. I went over to the bags of old books and started poking around, sure that Alyce wouldn't mind. I decided to sort them for her and started making piles of nonoccult books and some history books. Then, in the second bag, I found some titles about Wicca, the history of the sabbats, some spell-crafting guides, some astrology charts. Hunter and Alyce were still chatting, Alyce occasionally taking a break to wait on customers. Finn was reorganizing the essential oils shelves, and everything around me smelled like cloves and vanilla and roses.

Now I was surrounded by stacks, and in the fifth bag I found some interesting older books about weatherworking and animal magick. There were a couple of old Books of Shadows, too, handwritten, filled with writing and diagrams. One looked quite old: the writing was spiky, from a fountain pen, and the pages were deep tan with age. Another book looked newer and also less interesting: fewer drawings and long periods of no writing. There was another BOS, in a green-cloth-bound diary. It looked much newer and less romantic than the others, but I flipped through it. It was written by a witch during the seventies! So cool. Most recent Books of Shadows are still in the possession of their owners. This was unusual, and I started reading it.

"Morgan, shall we?" Hunter asked a few minutes later.

I nodded. "I sorted your books," I told Alyce, gesturing to my piles.

"Oh, how nice!" she said, clasping her hands together. She's shorter than I am and rounded in an old-fashioned womanly way. She looked like a youngish grandmother from a fairy-tale book, all in gray and lavender and purple.

"This one is great," I said, holding up the one I'd been reading. "It's from the seventies. Are you going to sell these books? Maybe I could buy it."

"Oh, please." Alyce waved her hands at me. "Take it, it's yours. Consider it payment for sorting all these bags."

"Thanks," I said, smiling. "I appreciate it. Thanks a lot."

"Come back soon," she said.

In the car Hunter and I looked at each other. I felt a tiny smile cross my lips.

"I think I need to work on convincing you of my undying love," Hunter said mischievously, reading my expression. "Let's see. I could cast a spell that would write your name in the clouds. Or I could take you out for a nice meal—or we could go to my house and fool around on my bed. You know, as practice before we do the real thing."

"Is your dad at your house?" I asked. Hunter and I had both wanted to make love for what seemed like a very long time. But the last time it came up, right before he left for Canada, Hunter had decided that we should wait. It was important to both of us for it to be just right—but who knew when that would ever happen?

"No. Today's he's at Bethany's," said Hunter. "She's been doing some deep healing work with him."

My eyes lit up. "Oh, yeah, let's go to your house!"

2

Alisa

><"The barrier between the world and the netherworld is both stronger and weaker than we ken. Strong in that it never breaches by itself, come earthquakes, floods, or famine. Weak in that one witch with a spell can rend it, allowing the passage of things unnamable."
—Mariska Svenson, Bodø, Norway, 1873><

"It's okay, Alisa," said my friend Mary K. Rowlands on Monday afternoon. "You're not a guy. You can come in."

I laughed and followed her into the living room. Both of Mary K.'s parents worked, and she and her sister, Morgan, weren't allowed to have boys over when their parents weren't there. It was so funny—almost antique. But her folks are really Catholic and keep Mary K. and Morgan on pretty tight leashes.

"Let's hang in the kitchen," Mary K. called over her shoulder.

"That's where the food is," I agreed.

Everything about the Rowlandses' house looks like it got frozen in about 1985. The living room is done in hunter green plaids with maroon accents. The kitchen is dusty blue and dusty pink, with a goose theme. It's corny, but oddly comforting. Now that my evil stepmother-to-be was madly redecorating the house I shared with my dad, I really appreciated anything familiar.

I dumped my messenger bag on the wood-grained Formica table while Mary K. rustled through the fridge and the pantry. She surfaced with a couple of bottles of Frappuccino, some apples, and a big bag of peanut M&M's.

I nodded my approval. "I see you've covered all the major food groups."

She grinned. "We aim to please."

We settled down at the kitchen table with our food and our textbooks open. I had been going to Mary K.'s pretty often after school lately—I guess to avoid going home—and Mary K. was really cool. A good friend. She seemed so normal and kind of reassuring somehow, especially compared to Morgan. Morgan had done a lot to weird me out in the past. I still wasn't sure what to make of her.

"Alisa?" Mary K. said, twirling a strand of hair around one finger as she frowned at her math book. "Do you have any idea what the difference is between real and natural numbers?"

"No," I said, and took a swig of Frappuccino. "Hey, did Mark ask you out for Friday?"

"No," she said, looking disappointed. She'd been crushing on Mark Chambers for weeks now, but though he was really nice to her, he didn't seem to be picking up on her "date me" vibes. "But it's only Monday. Maybe I could ask him, if he hasn't asked me by Thursday."

"You go, Mary K. Fight the system." I smiled, encouraging

her. Then I sighed, thinking about my own romantic possibilities. "God, I wish I had a crush on someone. Or someone had a crush on me. Anything to break up the delirious joy of being around my dad and Hilary."

Mary K. made a sympathetic face. "How's the Hiliminator?"

I shrugged, my shoulders rising and falling dramatically. "Well, she's still with us," I reported dryly, and Mary K. laughed. My dad's pregnant girlfriend had recently moved into our house, and now she was already pooching out in front, before they were actually getting hitched. I couldn't believe my straitlaced, ultraconservative dad had gotten himself into this nightmare. It was like living with a couple of strangers. "But she's quit barfing, which is good. Every time I had to listen to her hurl, I got the dry heaves."

"Maybe the baby will be incredibly cute, and you'll be a great big sister, and when she grows up, you guys will be really close," Mary K. suggested. She couldn't help it: she was born to pour sunshine on other people. It was one of the things I loved about her.

"Yeah," I allowed. "Or maybe it'll be a boy, and when I'm forced to change his diaper, he'll pee right in my face."

"Oh, gross!" Mary K. shrieked, and we both started laughing. "Alisa, that is so, so gross. If he ever does that, do not tell me about it."

"Anyway," I said with a giggle, "I've been suggesting names. If it's a girl, Alisa Junior. If it's a boy, Aliso."

We were still laughing about that one when the back door opened and Morgan came in. She smiled when she saw us, and I made myself smile back. It wasn't that I didn't like Morgan. It was mostly that I thought she was kind of dangerous—even though she could be nice and thoughtful sometimes. Morgan is a witch, a real witch. Some kids around here are—they call themselves blood witches because they're born to it, like having blue eyes or bad skin. Mary K. isn't, because though they are sisters, Morgan was adopted.

Morgan and some other kids from my high school (Mary K. is a freshman, I'm a sophomore, and Morgan is a junior) even have their own coven, called Kithic. I had been to circles with Kithic and had thought they were so . . . incredible. Special. Natural, somehow. But I had quit going a while back when Morgan had started making scary things happen, like breaking things without touching them. Like that girl in *Carrie*. And I saw her make crackling blue energy on her hand once. Mary K. had even told me (in total secret) that she thought Morgan had done something magicky when their aunt's girlfriend had cracked her head open at an ice rink. Mary K. said that Paula had looked like she was really hurt, and everyone was freaking, but Morgan put her hands on her and *fixed* her. I mean, how scary is that? It wasn't anything I wanted to be around.

"Youngsters," Morgan greeted us with a snobby nod. But she was just kidding—she and Mary K. get along really well.

"You know, Morgan," Mary K. said with an innocent expression, "I'm the same age younger than *you* as you are from *Hunter*. Isn't that funny?" No one can look more wide-eyed and who-me? than Mary K.

Morgan dropped her backpack on the kitchen table with a heavy thud and gave Mary K. a poisonous look—then they both laughed. I wished I had a sister—no, not one *fifteen* years younger than me, but a real one, whom I could talk to and hang out with, who could join forces with me against my wicked stepmonster-to-be.

"Studying, are we?" Morgan asked.

"We are," said Mary K. "Trying to, at least."

Morgan reached into the fridge and grabbed a Diet Coke. She popped the top and drank, leaning against the counter. Hilary had banished sodas from our house—we were all supposed to eat more healthily than that—and I found myself watching Morgan with envy. I almost wanted to have a soda here just because I could, even though I hate Diet Coke. Morgan set down the can, wiped her mouth on her sleeve, and breathed out. She'd gotten her fix.

"You know, watching you do that makes me feel . . . *tainted* somehow," Mary K. observed, and Morgan laughed again.

"Nature's perfect food," she said, then got some hamburger out of the fridge and pulled out a big frying pan. When the fridge door shut again, a small gray cat streaked into the room and stood around mewing.

"He heard the fridge," Mary K. said.

"Hey, Dag, sweetie," Morgan said, bending down to give him a tiny bit of hamburger. The kitten mewed loudly again, then chowed down, purring hard.

"Are we having tacos?" Mary K. asked.

"Burritos." Morgan opened the package and dumped the meat into the pan.

"The Hiliminator can't stand the smell of meat lately," I said, feeling a thin new layer of irritation settle over me. "Or fried food. Or spicy food. It makes her sick. We're down to like three acceptable food items at my house: bread, rice, and crackers."

Morgan nodded as sympathetically as Mary K. had. "You

can come over here and eat real food whenever you want."

"Thanks," I said. "So you're going to ask Mark out?" I asked Mary K.

"I guess," said Mary K.

"He's cute," said Morgan. She put a cutting board on the table, elbowing her backpack out of the way. The top hadn't been fastened tight, and a couple of books and notebooks spilled out. I glanced at them as she pushed the bag aside and set a block of cheddar cheese on the board, along with a grater. "Grate," she told Mary K.

"I'm doing my homework," Mary K. pointed out.

"You're talking about cute guys. Grate."

The books in Morgan's backpack caught my eye. One was an advanced calc book; then there were two spiral notebooks with doodles on the covers, and another, green-covered book, like an old-fashioned diary, peeped out from underneath those.

"Oh, did you notice Mom's crocuses out front?" Morgan asked, rolling up her sleeves. As usual, she looked like Morgan of the Mounties, in a plaid flannel shirt, worn jeans, and clogs. Somehow it looked okay on her. If I wore that, I would look like a truck driver.

Mary K. shook her head, busily grating. "What about 'em?"

"They're dying, dead," said Morgan. She pulled her long brown hair out of the way, braided it in back of her head, and snapped an elastic on the end. "They only started blooming last week, 'cause it's been so cold. The crocuses were up and the hyacinths were starting to poke out—now they're all brown lumps."

"It hasn't frozen lately, has it?" Mary K. asked.

Morgan shook her head. "Mom's going to be bummed

when she sees it. Maybe they have some kind of disease."
She started slicing a head of lettuce, making long strips suitable for burritoing.

"Hmmm," said Mary K.

I was listening to all this with only one ear because I just couldn't stop looking at Morgan's books. Not books, really. Book. It was freaky, but I was just dying to know what that green book was. I couldn't think about anything else until I figured it out. I didn't even know I was reaching for it when I finally realized Mary K. had been saying, "Alisa? Alisa?"

"Oh, what? Sorry," I said as Morgan turned around from the stove.

"I was saying that if you liked someone, too, then maybe we could all go out, the four of us, and then it wouldn't be so weird for me and Mark," she repeated.

"Oh." The words barely even registered. All I could think was green book, green book, green book. What was *wrong* with me? I tried to shake it off. "Um, well, I don't really like anyone. And no one likes me," I admitted. "I mean, *people* like me, but no guys specifically like me."

Mary K. frowned. "Why not? You're such a cutie."

I laughed. I knew I wasn't hideous—my dad is Hispanic, and I have his dark eyes and olive skin. My mom was Anglo, so my hair is a honey-streaked brown. I'm kind of different looking, but I don't make babies scream. But so far my sophomore year at Widow's Vale High had been a total bust, guys-wise. "I don't know."

"Morgan, do you know any guys, like friends of friends, that maybe we could set something up with?" Mary K. went on, and my mind and eyes wandered again to the stupid green book. What was it? I wanted to know. I needed to know. I shook my head silently, wondering what was going on. Why was I being so weird? It was like this crazy green book was invading my mind. Was this a temporary thing, or was it going to last? Years from now, was I going to be sitting in a padded cell somewhere, babbling, "Green book, green book, green book"? It was probably just some horrible extra-credit calc or something.

"That's a cool book," I heard Morgan say, and my head snapped up to see her and Mary K. both looking at me. I jerked back my hand, realizing with embarrassment that I had been reaching for the book again. What was *with* me? "It's a Book of Shadows," Morgan explained, glancing at Mary K., who seemed to take no notice. "I just got it today at Practical Magick."

I frowned and put both my hands in my lap. Magick. So it was a witch book. Well, that oughta cure me. I'd had enough freaky encounters with witchy things—and witchy people.

"Oh, dang!" Morgan said, turning around with irritation. "I forgot the stupid flavor packet! Well, I'm not going back to the store."

As she stood, frowning, the refrigerator door swung open. A glass butter dish, complete with butter, crashed to the ground, shattering. We all stared at it.

"Was that propped on something in there?" Mary K. asked.

"It was in the butter thing on the door," Morgan said, frowning even more.

I jumped up almost without realizing it. Oh, God, not again, I thought as horror filled my veins. Morgan just could not control her powers! She was a walking hazard! I had to get away from her. I *hated* this kind of stuff. True, this was just a broken butter dish, but I'd seen far worse happen before. Who knew what would happen next? What if she made *knives* start flying around or something?

"Did you not close the door?" Mary K. persisted. Morgan sighed and tiptoed to the broom closet, taking out a broom and a dustpan. Morgan with a broom, I thought. How appropriate.

"No, I closed it." Morgan sounded fed up. "I don't know what happened."

Uh-huh. And my mom is Queen Elizabeth, I thought.

Morgan scowled down at the broken dish as if she could reconstruct it with her eyes and make it all rush backward and mend itself, like in the movies. Actually, maybe she could. I didn't know.

"I didn't—" she began, and then her head lifted. "Hunter," she said. Wiping her hands on a kitchen towel, she walked out the kitchen door, leaving hamburger sizzling on the stove, a broken butter dish (that *she* had broken) right there on the floor. A moment later we heard the front door open and shut.

"What about Hunter?" I said.

Mary K. looked a little uncomfortable as she used a paper towel to pick up the glass-encrusted butter and put it in the trash. "Hunter's here, I guess."

"Did you hear his car?" I didn't even know why I was asking. I knew the answer. It was Morgan, Morgan the witch, Morgan and her freaky powers. She'd heard Hunter coming with her superpowerful witchy ears.

Mary K. shrugged and began to sweep up glass. I stood up

and turned off the fire under the hamburger, giving the meat a quick stir. Without meaning to, I glanced at the table and was immediately drawn again to the green book. What *was* it about that book?

3

Morgan

>< "Young Michael Orris was down to the shore, fetching seaweed for the garden. He looked up and saw a black curtain falling over the land like a sunset. Being a lad of six, he were scared and hid behind a rock. When the sun came out, he ran home to find nothing but broken stones, still smoking. Years later I heard he never made his initiation. Didn't want to be anything like a witch, not ever."
—Peg Curran, Tullamore, Ireland, 1937 ><

"You don't look like a happy camper," I said, crossing my arms over my chest. I'd come out without a jacket as soon as I'd felt Hunter's presence. The thing with the butter dish had totally thrown me—we'd never figured out why the weird telekinetic stuff happened. I was afraid that it might be a sign from Ciaran, just to let me know he was watching. "I'm glad you're here—something weird just happened—"

"I just came from a meeting with the council," Hunter uncharacteristically interrupted me. "Kennet flew in yesterday, which is why I couldn't get hold of him. They called me this morning."

"What was it about? Did you find out anything about Ciaran?"

"Yes." Hunter seemed tightly coiled, like a snake, and I felt anger coming off him in heated waves. He strode past my mother's crumpled crocuses and up onto the porch. "I did." He reached out to enfold me in his arms. "Apparently Ciaran dismantled the watch sigil two weeks ago. He hasn't been seen since."

I pulled back and stared at him. "Two *weeks* ago?" I choked out. Oh, Goddess. Oh, no. My father could in fact be hiding under my front porch *right now*. I went rigid with fear. He could have been watching me for almost *two weeks* now. "Goddess," I whispered. "And the council didn't share this because . . . ?"

He shook his head, looking disgusted. "They have no good reason. They said it was on a 'need to know' basis. Why they didn't think you or I needed to know is a complete mystery. I think they're just embarrassed that he's slipped through their fingers again. Obviously they should have taken him in before now and stripped his powers. But they were hoping he would lead them to other cells of Amyranth. Now he's gone."

The image of Ciaran having his powers stripped was disturbing—I'd seen it happen before, and it was horrifying. But the image of Ciaran coming after me with full powers—maybe *being* in Widow's Vale right *now*—was much, much worse. "I can't believe it," I said, feeling anger rise in me like acid. "Who the hell do they think they are? I don't need to know my own father is free? When I'm the one who put the watch sigil on him?"

Hunter nodded grimly. "Too right. I don't know what

they're doing. The council was never intended to be able to act with impunity. They seem to have forgotten that, and that they have a responsibility and an obligation to the witches they represent. Not to mention their own fellow council members."

"I can't believe it," I said again. "Those *asses*. So we can assume that Ciaran is around here somewhere." I thought about it. "I haven't picked up on anything, except the vision."

"Nor I. But I think we can guess he's coming to at least talk to you, like he said."

"What should we do? What are you going to do?"

"We need to be incredibly vigilant and on guard," he said. "I'm going to demand that the council take some responsibility for once, take some real action. In the meantime, your house and car are about as protected as I know how."

I closed my eyes. I had liked Eoife, the council witch I knew the best, but I was outraged that they had bungled this so badly and hadn't bothered to tell me. Surely they knew that I would be in danger. What had they been *thinking*?

"The council—" Hunter began, then stopped abruptly, clearly as upset as I was. "It's like they're falling apart, with certain factions acting without the knowledge or approval of the others. When it was first formed, they had strong witches at the head. Nowadays the whole thing is being run, and badly, by a witch named Cynthia Pratt. She doesn't seem to have a handle on anything."

"Great. So now what?"

"I don't know," he admitted. "I have to think about it. But maybe we should try scrying again, see if we can pick up on anything about Ciaran at all." He glanced over my shoulder. "Can I come in?"

My parents would be home from work soon. I had to finish getting dinner together. I glanced at my watch. "I have maybe ten minutes, max," I said. "But if my mom or dad comes home early, you'll have to get yourself out of here without them seeing."

He nodded, and I opened the front door, almost hitting Alisa, who was on her way out. She shot me a startled glance and clutched her messenger bag tighter to her chest. With a jolt I remembered the broken butter dish and sighed. Given the way Alisa was eyeing me, she thought I'd done my *Blair Witch* act. It was unfortunate that these things often seemed to happen when she was around.

"Hi, Alisa," Hunter said absently, stepping aside to let her pass. "Hope you're feeling better." Alisa had been hospitalized about a month ago for some kind of flu, but she seemed fine now.

"Thanks," Alisa muttered; then she scuttled past us on the porch and went down the stairs. I watched her for a moment; then Hunter and I entered the warmth of my house.

In my room, where the only male creatures allowed were my father and Dagda, Hunter and I sat on my woven grass rug and lit a candle. We surrounded it with protective stones: agate, jade, malachite, moonstone, olivine, a pearl, black tourmaline, a chunk of rock salt, and a pale brown topaz. We linked hands, touched knees, and looked into the candle. I knew we had only minutes, so I concentrated hard and ruthlessly shut out any extraneous thoughts. Ciaran, I thought. Ciaran. Hunter's power blended with mine, and we both focused our energy on the candle.

The glow of the candle filled my eyes until it seemed that

the whole room around me was glowing. Slowly a figure began to emerge, black, from the glow. My heart quickened, and I waited for Ciaran's face to become recognizable. But when the glow faded a bit, it revealed instead a woman or a girl—her back was to me. She raised one arm and wrote sigils in the air. I didn't recognize them. I got the impression she was working magick, powerful magick, but I didn't know what kind. Who are you? I thought. Why am I seeing you? As if in answer, the girl started turning to face me. But before I saw her features, a great, rolling wave of fire swept toward her. She crumpled underneath it, and the fire swept on. I waited to see the twisted and charred body left behind, but before I could, the image winked out, as if someone had turned off a slide projector.

I sat back, disappointed and confused.

"What I saw didn't make sense," Hunter said finally, blowing out the candle.

"It didn't to me, either," I said. "I didn't see Ciaran at all—just a girl and a fire."

"What does it mean?" he asked in frustration, and then we heard a gentle tap on the door.

"Mom just pulled up," Mary K. said quietly.

Quickly I put the candle away and Hunter slipped back into his jacket. I opened my bedroom door.

"Thanks," I told my sister.

She looked at me pointedly. "I got dinner together for you. I cleaned up the broken glass. And now I've told you mom's home so your ass won't be in a sling."

"Oh, Mary K.," I said gratefully. "Thank you. I owe you one."

"You sure do," she agreed, and I followed her down the stairs.

"Be careful," I heard Hunter barely breathe in back of me, and I nodded. Then my mom was in the living room, and I went to the kitchen to finish dinner, and soon after that my dad came home. I never heard Hunter leave, but half an hour later I remembered to glance out the window, and of course his car was gone. It made me feel incredibly alone.

4

Alisa

>< "The question is, are we going to tolerate witches who are of mixed or unknown clans? Witches whose view of magick is contrary to what we know and hold to be true? Why should we? Why should a clear stream allow mud to cloud its waters? And if we choose to keep our lines pure, how do the other clans fit in? They don't."

—Clyda Rockpell, Albertswyth, Wales, 1964 ><

This is it, I thought, staring at the green book that lay before me on my bed. This is the beginning of my complete and total slide toward hell. Now I am a thief.

I had never stolen anything in my life, yet when I saw that stupid green book of Morgan's, I had been taken over by my evil twin. My *stupid* evil twin. Only the three of us were in their kitchen. If Morgan noticed the book was gone, she'd ask Mary K. Mary K. wouldn't know, and by a lightning-swift process of elimination, one name would come up: Alisa Soto. Sticky Fingers Soto. Which is why I'd pretty much avoided both of them at school today. But neither of them had acted funny when I'd seen them, so maybe Morgan hadn't missed the book yet.

The only thing I had going for me was that Dad was at work, of course, and Hilary must be at her Mama Yoga class since it was Tuesday. Yay. I had no witnesses to my crime.

It was hard—no, impossible—to explain. But when I had seen that book fall out of Morgan's backpack, it was like it was *my* book that I had lost a long time ago, and here it was. So I took it back.

Just in case Hilary popped in anytime soon, I locked my bedroom door. I felt strange—maybe some of Morgan's weirdness was rubbing off on me. I almost felt like I was dreaming—watching myself do stuff without knowing why.

I ran my fingers over the cloth cover and felt a very faint tingle. I flipped open the cover, and the first thing I saw was a handwritten name. My eyes widened—it was Sarah Curtis, which was my own mother's maiden name! "Oh my God," I whispered, not believing what I was seeing. Was this why I had been so drawn to it?

I began to read. It was a diary, a journal, that Sarah started keeping in 1968, when she was fifteen, my age. Flipping through to the back, I saw that the book ended in 1971. I leaned back against my pillows and pulled my grandmother's flowery crocheted afghan over my feet. Ever since Hilary had moved in, our thermostat had been set to "Ice Age."

From the very first page I was totally hooked, but the book only got stranger. My jaw dropped by the second page, when I saw that Sarah Curtis lived in Gloucester, Massachusetts—just like my mom. How many Curtises could there be in one Massachusetts town? Maybe a lot. Maybe Curtises had lived there so long the name was really common. But if it wasn't, what did that mean? Could I be sitting here reading *my mom's* diary? It was impossible! I had gotten this book from Morgan! Then a chill went down my spine: Morgan had said this was a witch book. My eyes opened wider, and the back of my neck tightened.

On Saturday will be the annual Blessing of the Fleet. It's funny how today people still rely on the old traditions. Mom says the fleet has been blessed every year for over a hundred years. Of course, it's the Catholics who run it and make the big show. But I know that Róiseal always does our part as well.

I stopped for a moment. Róiseal? The Blessing of the Fleet I had heard about—a lot of fishing communities have it every year, where the priest comes out and sprinkles holy water on the bows of the fishing boats to protect them through the year and give them luck.

Sam and I went down to Filbert's today and got some orange soda pop. Mom would kill us if she knew. Mom and her "whole food, natural food" stuff. She thinks artificial flavors and tastes are enough to dull your senses and abilities. I haven't noticed any difference.

Whoa, I thought. And I thought Hilary was bad, with her organic toilet paper. I mean, she thought sodas weren't good for you, but I didn't think she actually believed they would dull your senses. A glimmer of a memory went through my head, of my mom saying something to me, telling me a story about when she was a little girl. About how funny her mom had been about some stuff. But the memory was too vague to really remember—maybe I was getting mixed up. After all, my mom had died when I was three. This *was* an amazing coincidence, though. *If* it was a coincidence, a scared little voice inside me whispered.

I'm still trying to talk Mom and Dad into an out-of-state college. I figure I have another three years to work on them—who knows what could happen? They just don't want me mixing with people who aren't like us—like if I meet enough different people, I'll leave and not come back.

I frowned as I remembered Dad telling me about how Mom's parents hadn't wanted her to go away to college, either. Oh, God—what did this mean? This couldn't just be a coincidence. But how was it possible—God! As if mesmerized, I turned back to the book for answers.

The lilacs have been blooming for a couple of weeks now. Their scent is everywhere. When I go outside, the damp salt of the sea is overlain with their gorgeous, heavy perfume. Mom's bushes are covered with bees in ecstasy. Seeing the lilacs in bloom breaks me out of my Northeast winter blues every year. I know that warm weather is coming, that summer is almost here, that school will soon be out.

My throat felt like it was closing. Once I had brought home a little bunch of lilacs from the grocery store, and Dad had looked at them and turned pale. Later he told me that they'd been Mom's favorite flower, that she had carried them at their wedding, and that it still made him sad to see them. So I'd eighty-sixed the lilacs. *Oh, Mom,* I thought desperately. *What's going on?*

In the meantime, my asinine brother, Sam, is still auditioning for the world's-biggest-pain-in-the-butt award. Last week he switched all the copper plant labels in the garden around, so the chard has "carrots" written above it and the corn has "radishes." Mom almost had a fit. And twice he's taken my bike and stored it up on the widow's walk. It was a nightmare getting it down through the trapdoor, listening to him cackling in his room. But I'm getting him back—this morning I sewed the toes of all his socks together. Insert wicked laugh here.

I chuckled, feeling relief sweep through me. Thank God. This wasn't my mom. This Sarah Curtis had a brother. My mom was an only child, and Dad had said by the time he met her, she was estranged from her family and never saw them. That's so sad. It means I grew up with only one set of grandparents and cousins. None from her side. But God, what a relief to hear this woman had a brother. I had been practically shaking with dread about this witch Sarah Curtis.

Time to go. I have to practice the full moon rite that I'm supposed to do on Litha.

I turned the page.

Okay, I'm back. Mom is in the kitchen, making a

healing tea for Aunt Jess. Her tonsilitis is acting up. I can't believe I have school tomorrow. I keep looking at the calendar: three more weeks till Litha. Litha and summer. Mom and I have been crafting a fertility spell for the last two months. Basically it's to make everything in the land and sea do well and multiply. A typical Rowanwand all-purpose spell. I can't wait. At Litha all of Ròiseal will be there, and it will be the first big spell I've cast in public since my initiation last Samhain.

With a thud all my sensations of fear and nervousness came back. This *couldn't* be my mom—I knew that. But someone with my mom's name had written this book. Hands trembling, I set it down.

She had come from Gloucester, Massachusetts. Like my mom.

Like my mom, she'd loved lilacs. It was too weird, too similar.

But some things didn't fit: her brother, Sam. The fact that *this* Sarah Curtis had been a Rowanwand *witch*.

Crash! I jumped about a foot in the air. My wooden jewelry box had fallen off my dresser and was lying on its side on the floor. How the hell had *that* happened?

This was all crazy. I closed the book without marking my place and went to my jewelry box. It was one of the very few things I had that had been my mom's. I picked it up and cradled it in my arms.

That Sarah Curtis had been a witch.

My mom hadn't been a witch. I searched my patchy, foggy memories. My mom, who smelled of lilacs. Her smile, her light brown hair, her laugh, the way it felt when she held me. There had been nothing about her that said witch. I didn't remember spells or chants or circles or even candles. There were two Sarah Curtises. One of them had been a witch. One of them had been my mom. Just my mom.

I took the box over to my bed, unlatched it, and dumped everything out on my comforter. My fingers brushed through the fake jewelry, the goofy pins I collected, the charm bracelet my dad had been adding to since I was six. There were a few pieces of my mom's jewelry, too: her engagement ring, with its tiny sapphire. Some pearl earrings. Even an anklet with little bells on it.

I looked at the empty box as if it would reassure me somehow. None of this could be real. There had to be some sort of explanation. A nonwitch explanation. My mom hadn't even *had* a brother.

Open me.

I hadn't heard the words—I had felt them. I stared down at the box as if it had turned into a snake. This was too creepy. But, compelled, I turned it upside down. I shook it, but nothing more came out. I opened and closed it a couple of times, looking for another latch somewhere, a hidden hinge. Nothing. Inside I ran my fingers around the lid and down the sides. Nothing. There was a small tray insert that I had dumped out onto my bed. The bottom of the box was lined with cushioned pink satin. I pressed it with my fingers, but there were no lumps or catches anywhere. I was imagining things.

Then I saw the pale pink loop of thread sticking out from one side of the cushion. I hooked my finger into it and pulled gently, and the whole cushion came up in my hand. Beneath the cushion was the wooden bottom of the box. There was a tiny catch on one side, tarnished and almost impossible to see. I poked it with one fingernail, and nothing happened. I turned the box another way and held it in my lap and pushed at the latch again.

With a tiny *snick* the bottom of the box swung upward. And I was staring at a yellowed pile of old letters, tied with a faded green ribbon.

The ribbon was tattered and practically untied itself in my hands. The letters were written on a bunch of different kinds of paper—loose-leaf, stationery, printer paper. I picked one up and unfolded it, feeling like I was watching someone else do this. From downstairs I heard the thud of the front door closing, but I ignored it and began to read.

Dear Sarah,

I'm so glad you finally contacted me. I can't believe you've been gone six whole months. It feels like years. I miss you so much. After you left, there was nothing but bad scenes, and now no one even speaks your name. It's like you died, and it makes me so sad, all the time. I'm glad to hear you're okay. I've set up a PO box over in North Heights, and you can write me there. I know Mom and Dad would flip right now if they saw a letter from you.

I better go—I'll write again soon. Take care.

Your brother, Sam.

Tap, tap. The knock on my bedroom door made me jerk.

"Allie?" Oh, *God*. Not Hilary. Not now. How many times had I told her I hated to be called Allie? A thousand? More?

"Yeah?"

"I'm home."

I had a feeling, I thought, since you're speaking to me. "Okay," I called.

"Do you want a snack? I have some dried fruit. Or maybe some yogurt?"

"Oh, no thanks, Hilary. I'm not really hungry."

Pause. "You shouldn't go too long without eating," she said. "Your blood sugar will crash."

I felt like screaming. Why was I having this conversation? My past was unraveling before my eyes, and she was going on about my freaking blood sugar!

"It's *okay*," I said, aware that some irritation had entered my voice. "I'll deal with my blood sugar."

Silence. Then her footsteps retreating down the hall. I sighed. No doubt I would hear about that later. For some reason, neither Hilary nor Dad could understand why I might have some trouble getting used to having his pregnant, twenty-five-year-old girlfriend living with us.

I shuffled the letters randomly and picked up another one.

Dear Sarah,

I'm sorry I couldn't make the wedding. You know October is one of our busiest times. I have to tell you: You're my sister, and I love you, but I can't help feeling disappointed that you married an outsider. I know you turned your back on your magick, but can you turn your back on your *entire heritage? What if you, by some miracle, have a child with this outsider? Can you stand to not raise the child Rowanwand? I don't get it.*

A few paragraphs down it was signed *Sam*.

I felt hot and a little dizzy. The truth kept trying to break into my consciousness, but I held it back. Just one more letter.

Dear Sarah,

Blessings on your good news. Since you moved to Texas, I've been worried about you. It seems so far away. I hope you and my new niece, Alisa, will be happy there. Dad has been sick again this spring—his heart—but no one thinks it's as serious as it was two years ago. I'll keep you posted.

The letter fluttered from my fingers like an ungainly butterfly. Oh, God. Oh, God. I swallowed convulsively, pressing my hand to my mouth. I had been born in Texas. My name was Alisa. Reality crashed down on me like a breaker at the shore, and like a shell, I felt tumbled about, rolled, torn away from land.

I, Alisa Soto, was the daughter of a witch and a nonwitch. I was half witch. Half *witch*. Everything I had always thought about my mom my whole life had been a *lie*. A rough cry escaped my throat, and I quickly smothered it in a pillow. Everything I had known about *me* my whole life was a lie, too. It was *all* lies, and none of it made sense. Suddenly furious, I picked up the damn witch's box and threw it across my room as hard as I could. It smashed against one wall and shattered into dozens of sharp pieces. Just like my heart.

"Honey, are you all right?" My dad's voice sounded tentative, worried.

I'm fine, Dad. Except for the fact that you married a *witch* and now *I* have witch blood in me, just like all the people who *freak me out.*

"Can I come in?" Of course the door was locked, but it was one of those useless dinky locks where a little metal key pops it open in about a second. Dad, assuming his parental right, unlocked the door and came in.

I was curled up on my bed, under all my covers, with my grandmother's afghan bunched around my neck. I felt cold and miserable and hadn't gone down to dinner, which had been a chickpea casserole. As if I didn't feel bad enough.

My brain had been in chaos all afternoon. Dad must not have known Mom was a witch. I think she had hidden it from him—and who wouldn't—and he had never figured it out. He'd never been thrilled about my going to Kithic circles, but he hadn't acted paranoid. Surely he would have said something if he'd known my mom had been a witch.

"I brought you some soup," he said, looking for a place to put down the tray.

"Don't tell me. Tofu soup with organic vegetables who willingly gave their lives for the greater good." Spread the misery around.

He gave me a Look and set the tray at the bottom of the bed. "Campbell's chicken noodle," he said dryly. "I found some in the pantry. It's not even Healthy Request."

I sniffed warily. Real soup. Suddenly I was a little hungry. I sat up and dipped a saltine (okay, it was whole wheat) into the soup and ate it.

"What's wrong, honey?" Dad asked. "Do you feel like you're getting sick again? Like last month?"

I wish. This was so much worse. Then tears were rolling down my face and into my bowl.

"Nothing's wrong," I said convincingly. Sniff, sniff.

"Hilary says you seemed upset when she came home." Translation: you've been being a jerk again, haven't you?

I didn't know what to say. Part of me wanted to blurt out everything, show Dad the letters, confide in him. Another part of me didn't want to ruin whatever memories he had of my mom. And *another* part didn't want him to look at me, for the rest of my life, and think, "Witch," which he definitely would once he read the letters and understood about blood witches. My shoulders shook silently as I dipped another cracker and tried to eat it.

"Honey, if you can't tell me, maybe Hilary—I mean, if it's a girl thing . . ."

As if. My soggy cracker broke off in the soup and started to dissolve.

"Or me. You can tell me anything," he said awkwardly. I wished that either one of us thought that was true. "I mean, I'm just an old guy, but I know a lot."

"That's not true," I said without meaning to. "There's a lot you don't know." I started crying again, thinking about my mom, about how my whole childhood had been a lie.

"So tell me."

I just cried harder. There was no way I could possibly tell him about this. It was like I had spent fifteen years being one person and suddenly found out I was someone completely different. My whole world was dissolving. "I can't. Just leave me alone, please."

He sat for a few more minutes but didn't come up with a plan that would suddenly make everything all right, make up for our not being close, for my not having a mom, for his marrying Hilary next month. After a while I felt his weight leave my bed, and then the door closed behind him. If only I *could* talk to him, I thought miserably. If only I could talk to *someone*. Anyone who would understand.

And then I thought of Morgan.

"Morgan?" I called on Wednesday morning. I had been lurking in the parking lot, waiting for her and Mary K. to arrive. Mary K. had popped out of the car, looking cute and fresh, the way she always did. I'd waited till she'd gone off to hang with our other friends; then Morgan had wearily swung herself out of her humongous white car and I called to her. I'd seen Morgan in the morning before and wasn't sure it was smart to talk to her this early. Besides her usual non-morning-person vibe, today she looked a little haggard, like she hadn't been sleeping.

She turned her head, and I stepped forward and waved. I saw the faint surprise in her eyes—she knew I tried to avoid her sometimes. As I got closer, I saw that she was drinking a small bottle of orange juice, trying to slug it down before the bell rang. Hilary would be glad that at least Morgan was paying attention to her blood sugar.

"Hey, Alisa," Morgan said. "Mary K. went thataway." She pointed to the main building of Widow's Vale High, then glanced around us, as if to assure herself she was actually at school.

"Uh, okay. But actually I wanted to talk to *you*," I said quickly.

She slurped her drink.

"Are you okay?" I couldn't help asking.

She nodded and wiped her mouth on her jacket sleeve. "Yeah. I just . . . didn't get much sleep last night. Maybe I'm coming down with something." She gave another sideways glance, and I wondered if she was supposed to meet someone.

"Well, I have to tell you—I took your book on Monday." There. I'd gotten it out.

She gave me a blank look.

"Your green book. That you had Monday in your backpack. Well, I took it."

Morgan's brows creased: The rusty gears of her brain were slowly creaking to a start as the OJ flowed into her system. She gave a quick glance over her shoulder to her backpack—the scene of the crime—as if clues would still be there. "Oh, that green book? The Book of Shadows? You took it? Why?"

"Yes. I took it on Monday. And I read it. And I need to talk to you about it."

Suddenly she looked more alert. "Okay. Do you still have it?"

"Yeah. I want to keep it. It's . . . it's about a woman named Sarah Curtis, who lived in Gloucester, Massachusetts, in the seventies."

"Uh-huh." Go on, and feel free to start making sense, Alisa.

I gulped down some chilly air, hating what was about to come out. "Sarah Curtis, from that book, the witch, was my mother. I'm pretty sure." Like, positive.

Morgan blinked and shifted her weight. "Why do you think that?" she said finally.

"My mom's name was Sarah Curtis, and she lived in Gloucester, Massachusetts. There were things in the diary that reminded me of things about my mom and that my dad has told me about her. And then, after I had read it, I went to the jewelry box she left me and found a secret compartment underneath. I opened it, and there were letters inside from an uncle I didn't know about, and he talked about magick. In one of the letters he said congratulations about your new daughter, Alisa. In Texas. Which is where I was born." I took a deep breath. "Sarah Curtis was a Rowanwand witch."

Now I had her complete attention. Her eyebrows raised up in pointy arches, and she seemed to stare right into my brain. "But your dad isn't, is he?" I shook my head. "So you think you're half witch?"

"Yes," I said stiffly.

She shifted her weight and glanced around again. What was with her? "Half witch. You. Jeez, how do you feel about it? It's kind of a shock."

I gave a dry laugh. "Shock doesn't cover it. I'm so . . . worried. Really, really upset. I never knew any of this. I don't think my dad knew about it, either. But all of a sudden I'm something I didn't know, and I'm just . . . freaking. I don't want to be a witch."

Nodding, Morgan looked understanding. "I know what you mean. I went through that last November. All of a sudden I was someone else."

I knew that was when she'd found out she was adopted. "It's just that you—and Hunter—and the others, well, it scares me, some of the things you do. And now I find out I'm just like you—" Okay, this was not putting it well. But Morgan didn't look offended.

"And you wish you weren't, and you're worried, and you don't know what it means."

"Yes." A rush of relief washed over me—she did understand. Someone understood what I was going through.

The first bell rang then, and we both jumped as if poked with a cattle prod.

"I'll never get used to that sound," Morgan said, looking at the students filing into the buildings. "Listen, Alisa, I know how you feel. It wasn't easy for me to find out about my heritage, either. But talking to people about it can help. Why don't you come to the next Kithic circle on Saturday? Everyone misses you. And you could talk to Hunter or me afterward. We could be your support group."

I thought for a moment. "Yeah, okay. Maybe I will." I looked down at my backpack. "So I can keep the book?"

Morgan looked at me. "I think it's already yours."

5

Morgan

><"Before the dark wave could be reproduced pretty much anywhere, the most we could have pulled off would be an epidemic, like the plague. And that's so hit-or-miss."

—Doris Grafton, New York, 1972><

Why am I doing this? I asked myself. I was sitting in Das Boot in front of Hunter's house, trying to work up the courage to just walk in. Yes, I wanted to have dinner with him; yes, I wanted to hear more about Rose MacEwan's BOS; yes, I didn't mind escaping Mary K.'s "Thursday Dinner Special": spinach pie. But I also couldn't help feeling reluctant at having to see Daniel Niall again.

I cast my senses out before I got out of the car—not that being *in* the car, even with the doors locked, was really any protection at all. Not against a witch as strong as Ciaran. I felt nothing, reminded myself dryly that this was not necessarily a guarantee, then hurried up the uneven front walk to Hunter's house.

He answered the door before I knocked.

"Hey," he said, and that one word, plus the way he looked at me, dark and intense, made my knees go wobbly.

"Hi. I brought these," I said, thrusting a paper-wrapped cone of flowers at him. I was too young to buy wine but hadn't wanted to show up empty-handed, so I'd gone to the florist on Main Street and picked out a bunch of red cockscomb. They were so odd-looking, so bloodred, I couldn't resist them.

"Cheers." He looked pleased, and leaned down to kiss me. "Are you all right? Has anything out of the ordinary . . . ?"

"No." I shook my head. "So far, so good. I just can't shake the feeling. . . ."

Hunter pulled me close and patted my back. "I know."

"He could be *anywhere*."

He nodded. "I do know, sweetie. But all we can do is be on our best guard. And know that if he does try anything, we'll battle him together."

"Together," I said softly.

Hunter smiled. "Well, take off your jacket and come sit down. Everything's almost ready."

Hunter's dad came in and looked at the table set for three. Hunter went into the kitchen, and I was left awkwardly standing there with a man who distrusted me and quite justifiably hated my father.

"Hi, Mr. Niall," I said, managing a smile.

He nodded, then turned and went into the kitchen, where I heard murmured voices. My stomach knotted up, and I wished I were at home, scarfing down spinach pie.

Five minutes later we were sitting at the small table, the three of us, and I was working my way through Hunter's pot roast with enthusiasm. A plate of Hunter's really good cooking went a long way toward making me able to stand Mr. Niall.

"Oh, so much better than spinach pie," I said, pushing my fork through a potato. I smiled at Hunter. "And you can *cook*." In addition to being a fabulous kisser, a strong witch, and incredibly gorgeous.

Hunter grinned back at me. Mr. Niall didn't look up. He was starting to lose his pinched look, I saw when I glanced at him. The first time I'd met him, he looked like someone had forgotten him under a cupboard—all gray and dried up. After more than a week, he was beginning to look more alive.

"Da, why don't you tell Morgan some of what you've been thinking about with Rose's book?" Hunter suggested. "The part about the spell against a dark wave?"

Mr. Niall looked like he'd suddenly bitten a lemon.

"Oh, you don't have to," I said, feeling a defensive anger kindle inside me. I clamped down on it.

"No, I want him to," Hunter persisted.

"I'm not ready," Daniel said, looking at Hunter. "I've gotten some help from the book, but not enough to discuss it."

Hunter turned to me, and I saw a muscle in his jaw twitching. "Da has been reading Rose's BOS. In it there are sort of clues that he thinks he could use to craft a spell, something that could possibly dismantle a dark wave."

"Oh my *God*. Mr. Niall—that's incredible!" I said sincerely.

Daniel set his napkin by his plate. Without looking at me, he said tersely, "This is all premature, Gìomanach. I'm not getting enough from the book to make it work. And I don't think Ciaran's daughter should be included in our discussion."

Well, there it was, out in the open. I felt like the town tramp sitting in at a revival meeting.

Hunter became very still, and I knew enough to think, Uh-oh. His hands rested on the table on either side of his plate, but every muscle in his body was tensed, like a leopard ready to strike. I saw Mr. Niall's eyes narrow slightly.

"Da," Hunter said very quietly, and I could tell from the tone of his voice that they'd had this conversation before, "Morgan is not in league with Ciaran. Ciaran has tried to *kill* her. She herself put a watch sigil on him for the council. Now he's on his way here, or is already here, to confront her about it. They are on opposite sides. She could be in mortal danger." There was a terrible stillness in his voice. I'd heard him sound that way only a few times before, and always in intensely horrible situations. Hearing it now sent shivers down my spine. Coming had been a mistake. As I was debating whether or not I was brave enough to just get up, grab my jacket, and walk out to my car with as much dignity as possible, Mr. Niall spoke.

"Can we afford to take the chance?" His voice was mild, unantagonistic: He was backing down.

"The chance you're taking is not the one you think," Hunter said, not breaking his gaze.

Silence.

Finally Mr. Niall looked down at his plate. His long fingers tapped gently against the table. Then he said, "A dark wave is in essence a rip in what divides this world from the nether-world. The spell to cast a dark wave has several parts. Or at least, this is my working hypothesis. First, the caster would have to protect herself, or himself, with various limitations. Then he or she would have to proscribe the boundaries of the dark wave when it forms so that it doesn't cover the entire earth, for example."

Goddess. I hadn't realized that was possible.

"The actual rip, for lack of a better word, would be caused by another part of the spell, and it basically creates an artificial opening between the two worlds," Mr. Niall went on. "Then the spell calls on dark energy, spirits, entities from the netherworld to come into this world. They form the dark wave and as a cloud of negative energy destroy any-thing that is positive energy. Which describes most of the things on the face of the earth."

"Are these ghosts?" I asked.

Mr. Niall shook his head. "Not exactly. For the most part, they've never been alive and have no individual identity. They seem to have just enough consciousness to feel hunger. The more positive energy they absorb, the stronger they are the next time. The dark waves of today are infinitely stronger than the one Rose unleashed three hundred years ago. Then the last part of the spell gathers this energy in and sends it back through the rip."

I thought. "So an opposite spell would have to take into account all the parts of the original spell. And then either permanently seal the division between the two worlds or disband the dark energy."

"Yes," Mr. Niall said. He seemed to be loosening up slightly. "I think I can somehow do this—if I have enough time, and if I can decipher enough of Rose's spell. I have knowledge of the dark waves, and my wife was a Wyndenkell, a great spellcrafter. But it's starting to look as if Rose was careful not to put the information I need in writing."

It was my ancestor who started all this, I thought glumly. It runs in my family. My family. I looked up. "Could I see Rose's book again, please?"

Hunter immediately got up and left the room. Mr. Niall opened his mouth as if to object, then thought better of it. In moments Hunter was back with the centuries-old, disintegrating Book of Shadows. I opened it carefully, trying not to harm the brittle pages.

"Does either of you have an athame?" I asked. Wordlessly Hunter went and got his. "Hold it over the page," I told him. "See if anything shows up."

"I've tried this already," Mr. Niall huffed.

"Da, I think you underestimate the benefit of Morgan's unusual powers," Hunter said evenly. "Beyond that, she's a descendant of Rose. She may connect with her writing in ways that you and I can't."

Hunter slowly moved the flat of the knife blade over the page, and we all peered at it. When I had first found my mother, Maeve's, Book of Shadows, I had used this technique to illuminate some hidden writing. I had a feeling it might work again.

"I don't see anything." Hunter sighed.

I took the athame and slid the book closer to me. I let my mind sink into the page covered with tiny, spidery writing, its ink long faded to brown. Show me, I thought in a singsong. Show me your secrets. Then I slowly moved the athame over the page, just as Hunter had done. Show me, I whispered silently. Show me.

The sudden tension of both Hunter and Mr. Niall's bodies alerted me to it even before my eyes picked up on it. Below me on the page, fine, glowy blue writing was shimmering under the knife blade. I tried to read it but couldn't—the words were strange, and some of the letters I didn't recognize.

Taking a deep breath, I straightened up and put the athame on the table. "Did you recognize those words?" I asked.

Mr. Niall nodded, looking into my face for the first time all evening. "They were an older form of Gaelic." Then he picked up the athame and held it over the page. For a long minute nothing happened; then the blue writing shone again. Mr. Niall's eyes seemed to drink it up. "This is it," he said, awe and excitement in his voice. "This is the kind of information I need. These are the secret clues I've been looking for." He looked at me with grudging respect. "Thank you."

"Nicely done, Morgan," said Hunter. I smiled at him self-consciously and saw pride and admiration in his eyes.

All of a sudden I felt physically ill, as if my body had been caught in a sneak attack by a flu virus. I realized I had a headache and felt achy and tired. I needed to go home.

"It's late," I said to Hunter. "I better get going."

Mr. Niall looked at me as I turned to go. "Cheers, Morgan."

"'Bye, Mr. Niall." I looked at Hunter. "What about the writing? Will it disappear if I leave?"

Hunter shook his head. "You've revealed it, so it should be visible for at least a few hours. Long enough for Da to transcribe it." Hunter got my jacket and walked me out onto the porch. We both gave a quick glance around and felt each other cast our senses.

"Let me get my keys," he said. "I'll follow you to your house."

I shook my head. "Let's not go through this again." Hunter was always trying to protect me more than I was comfortable with.

"How about if I just sleep outside your house, then, in my car?"

I looked up at him with amusement and saw he was only half joking. "Oh, no," I protested. "No, I don't need you to do that."

"Maybe I need to do it."

"Thank you—I know you're worried about me. But I'll be okay. You stay here and help your dad decipher Rose's spell. I'll call you when I get home, okay?"

Hunter looked unsure, but I kissed him good night about eight times and got into my car. It wasn't that I felt I was invincible—it was just that when you go up against someone like Ciaran, there isn't a whole lot you can do except face it. I knew he wanted to talk to me; I also knew that he would, when he wanted to. Whether Hunter was there or not.

As I drove off, I saw Hunter standing in the street, watching me until I turned the corner.

I felt like crap by the time I pulled into my driveway. I got out of Das Boot and locked it, grimaced at its blue hood that I still hadn't gotten painted, and headed up the walk. The air didn't smell like spring, but it didn't smell like winter, either. My mom's dying crocuses surrounded me.

It wasn't really that late—a little after nine. Maybe I would take some Tylenol and watch the tube for a while before I went to bed.

"Morgan."

My hand jerked away from the front door as if electrified. Every cell in my body went on red alert: my breathing quickened, my muscles tightened, and my stomach clenched, as if ready for war.

Slowly I turned to face Ciaran MacEwan. He was handsome, I thought, or if not strictly handsome, then charismatic. He was maybe six feet tall, shorter than Hunter. His dark brown hair was streaked with gray. When I looked into his eyes, brownish hazel and tilted slightly at the corners, it was like looking into my own. The last time I had seen him, he had taken the shape of a wolf, a powerful gray wolf. When the council had suddenly arrived, he had faded into the woods, looking back at me with those eyes.

"Yes?" I said, willing myself to appear outwardly calm.

He smiled, and I could understand how my mother had fallen in love with him more than twenty years ago. "You knew I was coming," he said in his lilting Scottish accent, softer, more beguiling than Hunter's crisp English one.

"Yes. What do you want?" I crossed my arms over my chest, trying not to show that inside, my mind was racing, wondering if I should send a witch message to Hunter, if I should try to do some sort of spell myself, if I could somehow just disappear in a puff of smoke....

"I told you, Morgan. I want to talk to you. I wanted to tell you I forgive you for the watch sigil. I wanted to try once again to convince you to join me, to take your rightful place as the heir to my power."

"I can't join you, Ciaran," I said flatly.

"But you can," he said, stepping closer. "Of course you can. You can do anything you want. Your life can be whatever you decide you want it to be. You're powerful, Morgan—you have great, untapped potential. Only I can really show you how to use it. Only I can really understand you—because we're so much alike."

I've never been good at holding my temper, and more than once my mouth has gotten me into trouble. I continued that tradition now, refusing to admit to a fear close to terror. "Except one of us is an innocent high school student and the other of us is the leader of a bunch of murdering, evil witches."

For just a moment I saw a flash of anger in his eyes, and I quit breathing, both dreading what he would do to me and wishing it were already over. My knees began to tremble, and I prayed that they wouldn't give way.

"Morgan," he said, and underlying his smooth voice was a fine edge of anger. "You're being very provincial. Unsophisticated. Close-minded."

"I know what it means." He wouldn't even need to hear the quaver in my voice—he was able to pick up on the fact that my nerves were stretched unbearably taut.

"Then how can you bear to lower yourself to that level? How can you be so judgmental? Are you so all-seeing, all-knowing that you can decide what's right and wrong for me, for others? Do you have such a perfect understanding of the world that you assume the authority to pass judgment? Morgan, magick is neither good nor evil. It just is. Power is neither good nor evil. It just is. Don't limit yourself this way. You're only seventeen: You have a whole life of making magick—beautiful, powerful magick—ahead of you. Why close all the doors now?"

"I may not be all-knowing, but I know what's right for me. I've figured out that it's wrong to wipe out whole villages, whole covens in one blow," I said, trying to keep my voice down so no one inside could hear me. "There's no way you can justify that."

Ciaran took a deep breath and clenched his fists several times. "You are my daughter; my blood is in your veins. I'm your family. I'm your father—your *real* father. Join with me and you'll have a family at last."

The quick pang of pain inside didn't distract me. "I have a family."

"They're not witches, Morgan," he said painstakingly, as if I were an idiot. "They can neither understand you nor respect your power—as I can. It's true, I'm selfish. I want the pleasure of teaching you what I know, of seeing you bloom like a rose, your extraordinary powers coming to fruition. I want to experience that with you. My other children . . . are not as promising."

I thought of my half brother Killian, the only one of Ciaran's other children I had met. I had liked Killian—he'd been fun, funny, irreverent, irresponsible. But not good material as an heir to an empire of power. Not as good as I would be.

"And you . . . you are the daughter of my *mùirn beatha dàn*," he said softly. His soul mate, my mother.

"Who you killed," I said just as softly, without anger. "You can ask me from now until I die, but I won't ever join you. I can't. In the circle of magick, I'm in the light. My power comes from the light, not the dark. I don't want the power of the dark. I will never want the power of the dark." I really hoped that was true.

"You will change your mind, you know," he said, but I detected a faint note of doubt in his voice.

"No. I can't. I don't want to."

"Morgan—please. Don't make me do this."

"Do what?" I asked, a thread of alarm lacing through me.

He sighed and looked down. "I was so hoping you'd change your mind," he said, almost to himself. "I'm sorry to hear that you won't. A power like yours—it must be allied with mine, or it presents too much of a risk."

"What the hell do you mean by that?"

He looked up at me again. "There's still time to change your mind," he said. "Time to save yourself, your family, your friends. If you make the right decision."

"You tell me what you're talking about," I demanded, my throat almost closed with fear. I thought of what he could to me, to the people I loved inside this house. To Hunter. "*Save myself, my family?* Don't you dare do *anything.* You asked your question. I answered. Now get away from me." I was almost shaking with rage and terror, remembering all too well the nightmare of New York, when he had tried to make me relinquish my power, my very soul to him. I remembered, too, the terrifying, heady sweetness of being a wolf alongside him, a ruthless, beautiful predator with indescribable strength. Oh, Goddess.

"I'll leave," Ciaran said, sounding sad. "I won't ask you again. It's a pity it all has to end this way."

"End *what* way?" I practically shrieked, almost hysterical.

"You've chosen your fate, daughter," he said, turning to leave. "It isn't what I wanted, but you leave me no choice. But know that by your decision you have sacrificed not only yourself, but everyone and everything you love." He gave a rueful, bitter smile. "Good-bye, Morgan. You were a shining star."

I felt ready to jump out of my skin and tried to choke out something, *something* to make him explain, make him tell me what he was going to do. Then I remembered: I knew his true name! The name of his very essence, the name by which I could control him absolutely. The name that was a color, a song, a rune all at once. Just as the name sprang to my trembling lips, Ciaran faded into the night. I blinked and peered into the darkness but saw nothing: no shadow, no footprints on the dead grass, no mark in the cold dew that was just starting to form.

Abruptly my knees finally gave way and I sat down, hard, on the cold cement steps. My breath felt cold and caught in my throat. My hands were shaking—I felt stupid with panic, with dread. As soon as I could get to my feet, I went inside, smiled, and said good night to my family. Then I went upstairs and called Hunter. And told him that Ciaran had gotten in touch with me.

The next morning Hunter was waiting for me outside my house when Mary K. and I came out to go to school.

"Hi, Hunter!" my sister said, looking surprised but pleased to see him at this hour.

"Hullo, Mary K.," he said. "Mind if I tag along this morning?"

Bewildered, my sister shrugged and got into the backseat of Das Boot. He and I exchanged meaningful glances.

For the rest of the day, Hunter hung out in my car outside school. Last night I had been inside my spelled house. Today, at school, I didn't have much protection. Whenever I passed a window, I looked out to see him. Even though he and I both knew this was like erecting a tissue-paper house in front of a gale-force wind, still, it made both of us feel better to be close.

At lunch he joined me and the members of Kithic in the cafeteria. After we'd talked last night, we'd agreed not to say anything to the rest of our coven until we knew more about what was going on.

"Hi, Hunter," said Bree, taking the seat next to him. "What are you doing here?"

"Just missed my girl, I guess," Hunter said, accepting half the sandwich I offered him. He immediately changed the subject. "So you're all coming to the next circle, right? At Thalia's?"

I saw Bree's beautiful, coffee-colored eyes narrow a fraction and thought it lucky that Thalia didn't go to our school. She had made it no secret that she found Robbie attractive. Privately I thought a bit of competition might be good for Bree.

Raven Meltzer clomped over in her motorcycle boots and sat down at the end of the table. She looked uncharacteristically sedate today, in a torn black sweatshirt, men's suit trousers, and less than half an inch of makeup. She nodded at the rest of the table, then surveyed her bought lunch without enthusiasm.

I looked around at my coven, my friends, remembering Ciaran's words from last night: He had said that with my decision, I had sacrificed them. At the start of the school year I had really known only Bree and Robbie. Now all of them—Jenna, Raven, Ethan, Sharon, and Matt—felt like an extended family. Despite how different we were, despite what other groups we belonged to, we were a coven. We had made magick together. And now, because of me, they might all be in serious danger. I took in a couple of shuddering breaths and opened my carton of chocolate milk. Hunter and I would somehow fix this situation. I had to believe that.

After school I joined Hunter at Das Boot. We gave Mary K. a ride home and picked up his car, and then we both drove to his house. Once there, he called upstairs to his dad. Mr. Niall soon came down and greeted me with what seemed like a fraction more warmth than usual. I felt slightly encouraged as the three of us sat around the worn wooden table in the kitchen.

"Last night Ciaran asked you to join him," Hunter said, jumping right in. I tried to ignore Mr. Niall's visible flinch.

"Yes," I said. "He's asked before. I've always said no. I said no again last night. But this felt more final. He said he was sorry to hear it—but that I could still save myself, my friends, and my family—if I made the right decision."

"He said specifically your friends, your family?" Hunter asked.

"Yes."

Hunter and Mr. Niall met eyes across the table. Mr. Niall stretched his hands out on the table and looked at them. Finally he said, "Yes, I think that sounds like a dark wave."

My mouth dropped open—somehow, despite his implications, I hadn't let myself believe Ciaran could have meant that. "So you really think Ciaran would send a dark wave *here*, to Widow's Vale? For me?"

"That's what it sounds like," said Mr. Niall, and Hunter nodded slowly. "Though it would likely be targeted to attack only the coven members and their families, and not the whole town."

"I agree with Da," said Hunter. "From what you told me last night, it sounds like Ciaran thinks your power is just too strong not to be allied with his. And I would guess he also wants revenge since you won't join him. Not to mention the added bonus of taking a Seeker out at the same time."

As much as I had tried to deny the real threat behind Ciaran's words, as soon as Hunter said "dark wave," I knew he was right. Still, it felt like a fresh, crushing blow, and I took small, shallow breaths, trying to keep calm.

"I think he's been planning it for a while," Mr. Niall went on. "I've been feeling the effects this past week. There's a feeling of deadness, of decay in the air. An oppression. At first I thought it was my mind playing tricks on me. But now I'm certain my instincts are right—there's a dark wave coming."

In a flash I remembered Mom's crocuses dying in a row beside the front walk. I thought of how the lawn hadn't begun to green up, though it was time. I thought of how awful I'd been feeling physically. "What can we do? How can we stop it?" I asked, trying not to sound completely terrified. Inside me, my mind was screaming, *There's no way to stop it, there's never been a way.*

"I contacted the council," Hunter answered me. "They were no help at all, as usual. They're looking for Ciaran, and now that they know he's here, they'll surround Widow's Vale."

"For me it means I'll devote all my time and energy to crafting a spell that could combat a dark wave," said Hunter's father. "I've been able to decipher a lot of the hidden writing in Rose's book. I've started to sketch out the basic form of the spell, its shape. I wish I had more time, but I'll work as fast as I can."

The weight of this hung over my head like an iron safe. This was happening because of *me. I* had caused this to happen. Ciaran was my biological father—and because of that, everything I held dear would be destroyed. "What if I left town?" I suggested wildly. "If I left town, Ciaran would come after just me and leave everyone else alone."

"No!" Hunter and his father cried at the same time.

Taken back by their vehemence, I started to explain, but Mr. Niall cut me off.

"No," he said. "That doesn't work. I know that all too well. It won't really solve anything. It wouldn't guarantee the town's safety, and you'd be as good as dead. No, we have to face this thing head-on."

"What about the rest of Kithic?" I asked. "Shouldn't they know? Could they help somehow? All of us together?"

Looking uncomfortable, Hunter said, "I don't think we should tell Kithic."

"What? Why not? They're in danger!"

Hunter stood and put the kettle to boil on the stove. When he turned back, his face looked pained. "It's just . . . this is blood witch business. We're not supposed to involve nonwitches in our affairs. Not only that, but there's truly nothing they can do. They might have strong wills, but they have very little power. And if we tell them, they probably wouldn't believe us, anyway. But if they did, then everyone would panic, which wouldn't help anything."

"So we just have to pretend we don't know everyone might die," I said, holding my head in my hands, my elbows on the table.

"Yes," Hunter said quietly, and once again I was reminded of the fact that he was a council Seeker and that he'd had to make hard decisions, tough calls, as part of his job. But I was new to it, and this hurt me. It was going to be literally painful not to tell my own family, or Bree, Robbie. . . . I swallowed hard.

"There's something else," Mr. Niall said. "I haven't mentioned this to you yet," he told Hunter. "With this type of spell, actually, as with most spells, the person who casts it will have to be a blood witch and will also have to be physically very close to where the dark wave would originate. My guess is that Ciaran would use the local power sink to help amplify the wave's power."

I nodded slowly. "That makes sense." At the edge of town is an old Methodist cemetery where several magickal "leys" cross. That made that area a power sink: any magick made there was stronger. Any inherent blood witch powers were also stronger there.

"The problem, of course," Mr. Niall went on, "is that to be

close enough to cast the spell, a witch is in effect sacrificing herself or himself because it will most likely cause death."

"Even if the spell works and the wave is averted?" I asked.

Hunter's dad nodded. The sudden whistle of the kettle distracted us, and Hunter mechanically made three mugs of tea. I gazed numbly at the steam rising from mine, then flicked my fingers over it widdershins and thought, Cool the fire. I took a sip. It was perfect.

"Well, that's a problem," Hunter said.

"No, it isn't," said Mr. Niall. "I'll cast the spell."

Hunter stared at him. "But you just said it would probably kill the caster!"

His father seemed calm: his mind had been made up for a while. "Yes. There are only so many blood witches around Widow's Vale. I'm the logical choice—I'm crafting the spell, so I'll know it best—and I would once again be with my *mùirn beatha dàn.*"

Hunter had told me the loss of his mother, just a few months ago, had almost destroyed his father.

"I just got you back!" Hunter said, pushing away from the table. "You can't possibly do this! There has to be some other witch who would be a better choice."

Mr. Niall smiled wryly. "Like a witch with terminal cancer? All right, we can look for one." He shook his head. "Look, lad, it's got to be me. You know it as well as I do."

"I'm stronger," Hunter said, wearing the determined look that I knew so well. "I should cast it. I'm sure I could survive. You could teach me the spell."

Mr. Niall shook his head.

"Dammit, I won't let you!" Hunter's loud voice filled the small kitchen. If he'd yelled at me like that, I would have been appalled, but his father seemed unmoved.

"It's not your decision, lad," he said. Calmly he picked up his mug of tea and drank.

"How long do we have?" I whispered, running my hands over the worn surface of the tabletop. "Is it tomorrow, or next week, or . . ."

Mr. Niall put down his mug. "It's impossible to say for certain." He looked at Hunter. "I would say, given the level of decay in the air and what I've read about the effects of an oncoming wave . . . perhaps a week. Perhaps a little less."

"Oh, *Goddess*!" I put my head down on the table and felt tears welling up behind my eyes. "A week! You're saying we might have one week left on this planet, a week before our families all die? All because of *me*? All because of my father?"

Mr. Niall surveyed me with an odd, grave expression. "I'm afraid so, lass." He stood. "I'm going back to work." Without a good-bye he left the room, and I heard him go upstairs.

"I just got him back," Hunter said, sounding near tears. I looked up from the table and realized, all at once, that no matter what happened to my family, Hunter was certainly going to lose his father. I stood up and wrapped my arms around him, pulling him close. So many times he had comforted me, and now I was glad to have the chance to give some back to him.

"I know," I said softly.

"He's got years left. Years to teach me. For me to get to know him again."

"I know." I held his head against my chest. His body was tight with tension.

"Bloody hell. This can't get any worse."

"It can always get worse," I said, and we both knew it was true.

6

Alisa

"Can I get you anything? I'm running to the store." Hilary's voice interrupted my reading, and I glanced up as the door to my room opened. There she was, in black leggings and a red tunic, her artificially streaked hair held back by a red Alice band.

"No. I'm okay," I said, raising my voice so she could hear me over my CD player.

"Ginger ale? That's what I like when I'm sick."

"No thanks."

I won the stare-down contest, and when Hilary finally broke, I went back to my reading. A minute later I heard the front door close with a little more force than necessary. I had elected to take a mental health day—going to school, having PE, eating lunch with people, paying attention in class—it all seemed ridiculous compared to finding out I was half witch. Thus my "illness" that Hilary was trying to treat. But she was gone now, and I had peace and quiet.

I pulled Sarah Curtis's Book of Shadows from under my bed and then got the small pile of letters. Since Tuesday, I had read all of them. It was like trying to absorb the news that a huge meteor was hurtling toward Earth—on some level, I just couldn't comprehend it. I mean, until a month or two ago I hadn't even known that real blood witches existed, and I kind of hadn't even believed it until I had seen Morgan Rowlands and Hunter Niall do things that couldn't be explained any other way. And now, surprise! I was half of something weird myself. Not only that, but my mom had pretty much felt the same way about being a witch— it had scared her, too, and before she met my dad, she had actually stripped herself of her powers. Which would explain why he didn't know she was a witch.

I had a lot to take in—my mother being a witch, her stripping herself of her powers, which I didn't even know you could do, and also about her family. Dad had always said that Mom had a falling-out with her family before he met her. He'd never known any of them. From the Book of Shadows and Sam Curtis's letters, it was starting to look more like they had disinherited her when she stripped her- self of her powers. So unless they had all been wiped out by a freak accident after my mother left Gloucester, there might actually still be some relatives living there. I guessed it was *possible* they were all dead—GLOUCESTER FAMILY DECI-MATED BY ROGUE TORNADO—but that seemed kind of unlikely.

Mom had been a Rowanwand. I knew from what Hunter had said in circles that Rowanwands in general had a reputation for being the "good guy" witches. They were dedicated to knowledge, they helped other witches, they had all sworn to do no evil, to not take part in clan wars. That didn't fit me at all. Dedicated to knowledge? I hated school. Sworn to do no evil? It seemed like every ten minutes, I was harshing out on someone. So I didn't feel very Rowanwandish. Which was a good thing, in my opinion.

Maybe being a witch was like a recessive gene, and you had to have copies from both parents in order for it to kick in. That would be cool. I breathed out, already feeling relieved. Since Dad was normal, maybe I only *carried* the witch gene, but it wouldn't be expressed. I frowned, thinking back to last semester's biology class. Pea plants and fruit flies popped into my mind, but what about recessive witch genes? Or was it even a gene? But what else could it be?

I groaned and leaned back against my pillows. Now I really did have a headache. I went to the bathroom and took some Tylenol and was just climbing back into bed when I heard the front door shut again downstairs. Feeling my nerves literally fraying, I pushed the letters and book under my covers and picked up *The Crucible,* which we were studying in sophomore English, ironically enough.

I was just making a mental note to pick up the CliffsNotes for it when, lo and behold, Hilary popped her head around my door because I had *forgotten to lock it.* She was carrying a tray that had a sprout-filled sandwich on it and some teen magazines that had articles like "Are You Over Your Ex? Take This Quiz and Find Out!"

For those of us who are too dumb to figure it out ourselves.

"Alisa? I thought you might be hungry. When I was sick, my mom always brought me lunch and some fun magazines."

"Oh. Thanks," I said unenthusiastically. At the risk of stating the obvious, you're not my mom. "I think I really just want to be left alone, though."

Her face fell, and I immediately felt a pang of guilt.

"I know I'm not your mom," she said, obvious hurt in her voice. "But would it be so hard for us to be friends? In a little while we're going to be related. I mean, like it or not, Alisa, your dad and I are getting married, and this baby I'm having is your half brother or half sister."

She set the tray down on my bed, and at that moment my CD player popped loudly. I smelled an electric burning smell and jumped up to unplug it. It was practically brand new! Why did everything keep self-destructing around me? Hilary gave me a long-suffering look, then swirled out of the room, slamming the door behind her.

I looked down at the plug in my hand, beginning to feel like a walking destructive force: just a few days ago, the butter dish at Mary K.'s, then my jewelry box, now the CD player. . . .

Oh my God. My breath froze in my throat. I stood stock-still, petrified by a sudden thought. I had just read about this kind of stuff in my mom's journal. When she'd been younger, she'd caused weird telekinetic things to happen—things fell off shelves, radios quit working, car horns wouldn't stop honking. Watches never worked on her—or on me, either. The batteries died instantly.

I breathed very shallowly. The horrible, unavoidable realization coming over me felt like a wave of icy water. I went through all the weird things that had happened around me for the last couple of months. Things breaking. Things falling off shelves. Things that had stopped working. I had been so sure that stuff had been caused by Morgan, with her scary powers.

The lightbulbs popping at our circle. The bookcase falling at the library. And sometimes they had happened without Morgan being there. Like on Tuesday—the jewelry box. I felt like I had been blind and now could suddenly see everything.

Crash! Pop!

I spun around to see my little collection of crystal animals fall off their shelf, one by one, and shatter on the floor. *Stop!* I thought desperately, and a small unicorn teetered on the edge of the shelf but didn't fall.

Oh God, oh God, oh God. Numbly I stared down at the shattered animals, then up at the rest of the collection. The shelf looked rock solid. Unless a tiny, unnoticeable earthquake had just shaken Widow's Vale, I had some awful truths to face.

It had been *me.* I had caused that to happen. I had caused the CD player to self-destruct. I had caused my jewelry box to leap off my dresser. Why hadn't that struck me as more odd? I mean, how good was I at lying to myself? All this time I had blamed Morgan and avoided her for being freaky and hated the things that I thought her powers did.

But it had been *me,* with my mom's witch gene, all along. Just like my mom, I was a walking telekinetic nightmare. God, my mother had been a full blood witch, and she couldn't even control her own powers. What was going to happen to *me?*

*   *   *

Thalia Cutter lived on Montpelier Avenue. Dad gave me a ride over on Saturday night. I hadn't mentioned that it was a circle, and he hadn't asked. It had taken me all day to psych myself into going. But in the end I accepted that this was probably the only place I could find help or information.

"Thanks, Dad," I said, opening my door.

"Call me when you need me to come get you," he said.

"Okay. Or maybe I can get a ride."

"Alisa—" He leaned out toward me, but stopped as if he'd changed his mind. "Have a good time."

"Thanks." I left him and headed up the walk to the front porch, where I rang the bell.

"Alisa! Come on in," said Jenna, who opened the door.

"Hi." I've always liked Jenna—she's really nice.

Other people greeted me: Ethan Sharp, who had been one of the biggest potheads in school; Simon Bakehouse and Raven Meltzer, who had both been in the original Kithic with me. Raven cracks me up. I was dumping my jacket on a sofa when I felt a prickling at the base of my neck. Turning around, I saw that Hunter Niall and Morgan were coming in together.

It was a fact: Hunter was *hot,* even though he was four years older than me, a witch, and went out with Morgan. Despite all those drawbacks, he tended to cause a lot of head turning when he walked into a room. And even though right then he looked like he was hungover and simultaneously fighting a virus, I felt a little quiver when he saw me and immediately came to talk to me.

"Hey, Hunter," I said.

"Hi," he said, bending down to talk to me. I'm not a shrimp, but he's over six feet tall. "Morgan told me about what you just found out." He stopped and gave a grin that would have melted Alaska. He's usually kind of serious, so when he does smile, everyone's knees go weak. Or at least I'm assuming I'm not the only one. "I would say congratulations, but I understand you don't feel that way."

My cheeks burned, and I looked away. "No."

He immediately sobered and leaned closer so only I could hear. "I know it must have been a shock. And I understand how you've been feeling about magick and witches. I'd like to talk to you about it, try to help if I can."

I nodded. "Thanks." I stood very still, waiting for a picture to fall off the wall, the door to fly open, or a window to crack. Nothing happened, and I held my breath, determined to stay very, very calm this evening.

Hunter went back to Morgan's side, and I saw that she looked pretty bad, too. They must have been passing germs back and forth. Yuck.

"We can get started," said Hunter. "I think everyone's here. Is there any coven business first? I think Simon has volunteered to host next Saturday, right? Good. Okay, now. Tonight I'd like to talk a bit about magick."

Hunter knelt and drew a large circle on Thalia's living room floor. He always started by drawing a circle, but this time he added another circle around it and then one more circle around that. Then he took a small cloth bag of stones and placed different-colored stones around the outside circle. Standing, he gestured us into the little "door" he had left, and once we were all in the smallest circle, he closed the circles with chalk, stones, and also some runes that he traced in the air. I wondered what was going on.

"Now, magick," he said, rubbing the chalk off his hands.

He looked pale and tired. "Magick is basically energy, life force, chi, whatever you want to call it. The same magick that makes a flower bloom, produces fruit on a tree, brings a baby into the world is the exact same magick that can light fires spontaneously, move objects, and work invisibly within the universal construct in order to effect change—such as casting a protective spell, a fertility spell, or a healing spell. Now, can I have each of your impressions about magick?"

He nodded to Sharon Goodfine.

She frowned thoughtfully, her shiny dark hair brushing her shoulders. "To me, magick is potential—the possibility of doing something."

"That's a nice thought," said Hunter. "Thalia?"

"It's just cool," she said, shrugging. "It's different, out of the ordinary."

Ethan said, "It's like a different kind of control, a different way of getting a handle on things."

"It's being connected with the life force," said Jenna.

"It's beautiful," Bree said.

Next was Morgan. "It's . . . another dimension to life, an added meaning to regular life. It's a power and a responsibility."

Hunter nodded again. "Robbie?"

"It's mysterious," said Robbie.

"Alisa, how about you?" Hunter asked.

"It's scary," I said abruptly, thinking of my own experiences with it. As soon as I said that, all my feelings came rushing out. "It's uncontrollable. It's dangerous. It's awful, like having some genetic error. You never know when it's going to wreck your life."

My fists were clenching, and my mouth felt tight. I realized

I was surrounded by silence and looked up to see eleven pairs of eyes watching me. Nine pairs were surprised. Hunter was calm, accepting. Morgan looked understanding.

"Oh. Did I say that out loud?" I said, feeling embarrassed.

"It's all right," Hunter said. "Magick strikes everyone differently. I understand how you feel." He turned to the others. "Now, since we have stones of protection, I won't call on earth, air, fire, or water. But I do cast this circle in the name of the Goddess and the God and ask them to join us and bless our power tonight. Join hands."

I took hold of Simon's hand and Raven's, feeling an impending sense of doom. If I was in this circle and it got all magicky, what would happen? What would I destroy?

Slowly we began to walk deasil, clockwise. Hunter started a chanting kind of song. It was incredibly pretty and easy to follow, and soon all of us were joining in. It was kind of like aural Prozac, because soon I began to feel calmer and more cheerful than I had in days. I felt like everyone here was my friend, that I was safe, that we were singing the most beautiful song, that I was filled with a light that made all my troubles seem bearable.

I was processing these feelings, and suddenly I realized that this was magick, too. This was a positive, gentle kind of magick. As the chant rose and grew, I felt better and better. It was like I was trying to worry about it being magick but just couldn't. I knew it was weird, but it all felt okay. When we threw our hands apart and raised our arms to the sky, I was smiling widely, feeling loose and open instead of tight and upset.

Our circle broke apart then, and people were hugging

and patting one another's backs. Morgan came over to me and took my hand. She put her own palm on top of mine and held it there for a moment. She looked at her hand, and I felt a gentle heat. I took my hand away, and there was a rose-colored rune imprinted on my skin.

I grabbed her hand and looked at her palm. Nothing was there. I rubbed at my hand and realized that the rune was *raised*, it was my *skin*, raised up, like a scar. I stared at it, and Morgan gave a little smile. "That's Wynn," she said. "Happiness. Peace." She caught my expression and added, "It'll go away in a little while. It's just something to take away from here."

She went back to join Hunter, and I looked at my hand again. This was visible magick, right here on me. Peace, happiness. Did she just mean the rune or the actual feelings, too?

7
Morgan

><"The first time I saw one was in Scotland. I didn't take part, of course—I wasn't strong enough yet. But I watched from a distance as it rolled across the countryside, purging the land of everything unclean. I almost wept with the glory of it."

—Molly Shears, Ireland, 1996><

On Sunday, I went to church with my family, despite feeling definitely ill. Afterward we went to the Widow's Diner, where I could manage to choke down only a few bites of my BLT.

At home I tossed down some sinus/allergy stuff, then changed, grabbed my keys, and yelled that I was going to Hunter's. When Sky had gone to France and then England, my parents had known that left Hunter with the house to himself. For a while they had given me squirrel eyes whenever I went there and again when I got back. Now that his father lived there, they were less suspicious. Of course, they hadn't met Mr. Niall and had no clue as to how different he was from their vision of a father.

Fatherly or not, his presence was enough to make me feel weird about being alone with Hunter anywhere in his house. I sighed and got into Das Boot. Outside it was horrible—after a few misleading days of decent springlike weather, we had taken a big step backward, and it was in the mid-thirties, overcast, and smelling like snow. Before I reached Hunter's, tiny, icy raindrops starting pinging against my windshield.

"Hullo, my love," said Hunter as I approached the front door. He gave me a critical glance, then said, "How about some hot tea?"

"Do you have any cider?" I asked. "With spices in it? Or lemon?"

He nodded and I went in, glad to see the fireplace in the living room had been lit. I dropped my coat and stood before the fire, holding out my hands. The dancing flames were soothing. On his way to the kitchen, Hunter stopped in back of me, wrapped his arms around my chest, and held me close. I leaned back and let my eyes drift shut, feeling his warmth, the strength in his arms. One of his hands came up to stroke my hair, melting the few bits of ice crystal that lingered there. He leaned down and kissed my neck. I tilted my head to give him better access. Slowly he put careful kisses up my neck and across my jaw. I turned to face him and smiled wryly—he looked as bad as I felt. It seemed kind of pathetic, how bad we were both feeling, yet we still had such a strong desire to be in each other's embrace. His lips were very soft on mine, moving gently, afraid to make either of us feel worse.

When I heard Mr. Niall's footsteps on the stairs, Hunter

and I untangled and headed toward the kitchen. Moments later Mr. Niall joined us, and Hunter started mulling cider on the stove. I sat glumly at the table, my pounding head resting in my hands.

"Why do we all feel so bad?" I asked. Mr. Niall looked pale and drawn.

"It's the effect of an oncoming dark wave," Hunter's father said with little energy. "It isn't even in force yet, but the spells to call it have been started and the place and people targeted. It isn't going to be long now. A matter of days."

"Oh, Goddess," I muttered, a fresh alarm racing through my veins.

"We'll feel sicker and sicker as the dark wave draws closer, and we'll grow irritable. Which is unfortunate, because we'll need to work with one another now more than ever."

Hunter sighed. "You talked to Alyce this morning?" he asked his father, and Mr. Niall nodded.

"She and the other members of Starlocket have been holding power circles, aiming their energy at Widow's Vale and at Kithic in particular. They're hoping to help in any way they can, but there's been so little documented evidence about anyone even trying to resist a dark wave." He ran his long-fingered, bony hand over his face.

"Have you had any progress?" I asked.

He let out a breath heavily, and his shoulders sagged. "I've been working day and night. In some ways I'm making progress. I'm crafting the form of the spell, its order, its words. But it would be much stronger if I could give it more specificity. If only I had more time."

I looked up and caught Hunter's eye. I knew we were

feeling the same desperation, the same frustration: If only we could help Mr. Niall or speed him along. But we were helpless; we just had to hope that his father was up to the task.

"What do you mean by specificity?" I asked as Hunter put a mug of cider in front of me, and I inhaled. The spices of ginger and cinnamon rose up to meet me. I drank, feeling its warmth soothing my stomach.

"The spell is basic," Mr. Niall said, sounding frustrated. "It's designed to cover a certain area, at a certain time, in a certain way. It's designed to combat a dark wave, to dismantle it. But it would be so much more powerful if I could use something particular against its creator."

"What would that do?" I needed a cold cloth for my forehead.

"Spells are just as personal as the way someone looks, like their fingerprints," Hunter explained. "If you're trying to dismantle or repel another witch's spell, your own spell greatly increases in power if you can imbue it with something in particular that identifies the spellcrafter you're working against. That's why in spells, you so often need a strand of hair or an item of clothing of the person who's the focus of the spell. It gives the spell a specific target."

"Like using an arrow instead of a club," said Mr. Niall.

I sat for a few moments, thinking. I had no strand of Ciaran's hair, none of his clothes. My head felt fragile, made of china that had been broken and poorly mended. It was a struggle to put two thoughts together.

Wait—I rubbed at my eyes, catching the elusive thought. I had . . . I had something of Ciaran's. I didn't even think of it as his anymore—it was completely mine now. But it had once been his. He had handled it. I drained my mug and stood up, feeling my muscles ache naggingly.

"I'll be back," I said, and left before either Hunter or Mr. Niall could open his mouth.

It was still raining sullenly as I climbed behind the wheel of my car. Inside, the vinyl seats were freezing, and I immediately cranked the heater. I pulled away from Hunter's curb and headed toward the road that would take me out of town.

Widow's Vale was surrounded by what had once been prosperous farmland and was now only a few small family holdings, bordered on all sides by abandoned fields, overgrown orchards, and woods of tall, second-growth trees.

There was a place along here, a patch of woods completely unmarked by any physical sign but still a place I recognized at once, as if there were a large arrow spray-painted on a line of tree trunks. There it was. I pulled well over onto the road's shoulder, feeling the slipperiness of the ice-crusted gravel at the road's edge. Reluctantly I climbed out of my car, leaving its cozy warmth for the inhospitable sting of icy rain.

I pulled my collar up as far as I could and headed straight across a rough-cut field of withered grass stalks. At the first break in the woods I paused for a moment, then headed straight between two beech trees. This place was mine alone. I could feel the presence of no other human, witch or nonwitch. I felt safe here, safer than in town.

In the woods there was no path, no marked trail, but I slogged steadily forward, unerringly headed for the place that bore my spell and contained my secret. It was a good ten-minute walk—my clogs slid on the wet, decaying leaves, and tiny branches, still unbudded, whipped across my face and caught at my hair.

Then, in a small clearing, I lifted my face to the patch of bare, leaden sky. It was here, it was still here, and though animals had crisscrossed this place with any number of trails, no human had been here since my last time. Pausing, I closed my eyes and cast my senses out strongly, taking my time, going slowly, feeling the startled heartbeat of small animals, wet birds, and, farther out, the still, wary eye of an occasional deer. At last I was quite sure I was still alone, and I walked out into the clearing and knelt on the sodden forest litter.

I'd brought no shovel with me, but Das Boot had a jack and a crowbar, and it was the crowbar I used, chucking it into the cold ground and twisting it. It didn't take long. I felt layer upon layer of my amateurish spells of protection, the best I had been able to do at the time. Then, feeling close, I used my fingers to claw at the freezing earth. Another two inches and my fingers scrabbled at wet cloth. I cleared the dirt away around it and soon lifted up a silken bundle. I didn't untie the knot that held the scarf's contents in place. I didn't need to. Instead, I kicked the dirt back in place and lightly scattered some leaves and pine needles and twigs over the area until it again looked untouched. Picking up my crowbar, holding my cold, damp bundle, I headed back to my car.

"Where did you go?" Hunter asked when I returned. "Where have you been? I was worried sick! Don't go anywhere like that without telling me, all right?"

"I'm sorry." I was still chilled, my fingernails dirt-packed and broken. It seemed too hard to explain when my errand had taken so much effort. Instead, I walked into Hunter's circle room, where Mr. Niall was kneeling on the floor, his eyes closed, surrounded by papers and books and candles. He felt me come in and looked up.

I knelt beside him, the knees of my jeans soaked. "Here," I said, pulling the silk-wrapped package from my coat pocket. My fingers were cold and stiff as I picked at the knot, but I finally pulled it loose and the cloth fell open. I reached in to pick up the only thing of Ciaran's I had: a beautiful gold pocket watch, engraved with his initials and my mother's. Not only that—it had my mother's, Maeve's, image spelled into it. To be able to see my mother's face was a gift. To me, it was a concrete reminder of the relationship my blood parents had once had—the only thing that was part of both of them. My mother was dead—the spell against Ciaran couldn't rebound on her. But Ciaran's vibrations ran all through it.

When Mr. Niall reached for it, I surprised myself by pulling my hand back. Embarrassed, I pushed the watch forward again. He could use it more than I. Maybe it was better not to have any reminders of a love that had ended so tragically—even though that same love had resulted in my birth. It suddenly struck me that my parents' relationship was the epitome of magick itself: darkness and light. A great, great love and a great, great hatred. Passion, both good and bad. A powerful joining followed by an irrevocable tearing apart. The rose and the thorn.

"This was Ciaran's," I explained, offering it to Mr. Niall. I forced my hand to stay open while he took it.

"When did you get it back?" Hunter asked, surprised.

"The last time Ciaran was here," I explained, feeling very tired.

"And you kept it?" Hunter knew as well as I how dangerous it could be to have something of someone who wants to control you.

"Yes. It was my mother's." I was aware I sounded defensive—I had kept this a secret, even from Hunter. "I buried it outside of town. I was going to leave it there until it had been purified, all its dark energy gone. Years."

Mr. Niall was examining the watch, turning it over in his hands. "I can use this," he said, as if talking to himself. He looked up. "But are you sure? It will be completely destroyed, you know."

I nodded, looking at the watch. "I know. It's okay. I don't need it anymore." Still, even as I said the words, something in me knew I'd feel its loss. I shivered from leftover chill.

When I looked up, Mr. Niall was watching me. "This will help," he said. "Thank you." His eyes looked at me as if he were seeing me for the first time. I got the impression I had just moved up several notches in his estimation.

"Okay, well, I'll get out of your way," I said, standing up. In the kitchen I washed my hands, soaping them over and over, holding them under the warm water as if I were washing off more than dirt. Then I went into the living room and sank down on the floor in front of the fireplace. Hunter sat down next to me, and soon I was warm enough to take off my coat. We scooted back until we could lean against the couch, and I rested my head against his shoulder. Gently Hunter lifted me up onto his lap so I was sitting sideways across his legs. With his arms around me, I felt incredibly safe and warm. I was so happy to be there that I didn't even care if Mr. Niall came out and found us like this.

"Thank you for making that sacrifice," Hunter murmured close to my ear. "Why didn't you tell me about it?"

I shrugged, not really knowing myself. "I knew I wasn't going to use it, not for a long time."

He nodded and kissed my ear. "I know what it must mean to you."

"Not as much as my life, your life, my family. My friends," I said, closing my eyes and snuggling closer.

"Morgan," he said, his voice low. I felt his fingers under my chin, raising my face so he could kiss me. It felt so good, so right, and it made everything else fade away: all my worries, the way I felt physically, the sadness of losing my watch. Ever since Hunter had gotten back from Canada, we hadn't had much time alone together. I'd been concerned about what I had seen—Hunter and the Canadian witch—and sometimes it made me feel insecure and out of sync with him. But right now those feelings were melting away, and once again I felt that quickening, that rush of desire that made me tremble.

We clung together, kissing, and I now knew him well enough for there to be comforting familiarity mixed in with the rush. I remembered the last night we'd been together, before he'd left for Canada. I had planned for us to make love for the first time: I'd actually started taking the Pill because I didn't know how witch birth control worked, I'd psyched myself up, shaved my legs, everything. And we had almost done it. We'd come so, so close. Then Hunter had talked me into waiting until after he got back from Canada so we wouldn't have to say good-bye afterward. Of course, we didn't know that he'd be bringing his dad back with him and that almost immediately we'd be threatened by a dark wave.

I gripped Hunter's collar in one hand and pulled him closer, kissing his mouth hard, feeling his fingers tighten around my waist. Hunter, I thought. I want to be joined with you. Are we ever going to get there? Or are we going to die before we get the chance?

8

Alisa

><"Tonight we opened a rift in the world, in time, in life. I fell to my knees in awe as the source of our power swelled above my head. I could only stare in wonder as my coven leader called upon the dark power, right in front of us. Every day I thank the Goddess I found this coven, Amyranth."

—Melissa Felton, California, 1996><

"Alisa, are you okay?"

My head snapped up to see Mary K.'s big brown eyes gazing at me with concern. We were sprawled in Mary K.'s room after school on Monday, listening to music and sort of doing homework.

"I'm okay." I shook my head. "It's just, like, everything's coming down on me at once. It's giving me a headache."

Mary K. nodded sympathetically. "Everyone has a headache lately. It must be the weather." I was so glad that we were friends. My best friend had moved away at the end of last summer, and though I still missed her, being friends with Mary K. had helped a lot.

"Like the wedding and Ms. Herbert's science fair project?" she asked.

"Yeah." Oh, and the fact that I was half witch. That, too. I hadn't told Mary K. about my realization—I knew that she still had a problem with Morgan's involvement with Wicca, and I wasn't ready to test her reaction.

"Any ideas for the science project?"

I thought. "Maybe a life-size modeling-clay version of a digestive system?"

Mary K. giggled. "Fun. I'm thinking about something with plants."

"Can you be more specific?"

Her shiny russet hair bounced as she shook her head. "I haven't worked out the details."

We both laughed, and I pulled over the box of Girl Scout cookies and had another Thin Mint.

"Any wedding news?"

My eyes closed in painful memory. "Right now the flower-girl dress of choice is emerald green, which will basically make me look like I died of jaundice, and it has a big wide bow across the ass. Like, look at my humongous big butt, everyone! In case you missed it!"

"I still can't get over the fact that you're the *flower girl*," Mary K. laughed, falling back on her bed, and it was hard for me to remain sour.

"My backup plan is to break my leg the morning of the ceremony," I told her. "So I'll be bringing you a baseball bat soon, just in case."

I turned my attention back to my algebra problems. Art class I was good at. But all these little numbers jumping around the page just left me cold. "What did you get for the equation for number seven?" I asked, tapping my pencil against my teeth.

"A big blank. Maybe we should get Morgan."

"I'll get her," I said casually, getting to my feet. There was the slightest surprise in Mary K.'s eyes that I would voluntarily talk to the witch queen. "Where is she?"

"In her room, I think."

Mary K. and Morgan's rooms were connected by the bathroom they shared. The door to Morgan's room was ajar, and I tapped on it.

"Morgan?"

"Mpfh?" I heard in response, and I pushed open the door. Morgan was lying on her bed, a wet washcloth draped over her forehead. Her long hair spilled over the side of her bed. She looked awful.

As I approached the bed, she mumbled, "Alisa? What's up?" She hadn't opened her eyes, and I got a little nervous shiver from this evidence of her witch skills.

"How do you do that?" I asked quietly. "You can just feel someone's vibes or something? Or like my aura?"

At this Morgan did open her eyes and bunched her pillow under her head so she could see me. "I gave you a ride after school, so I knew you were here. I heard someone open the door and walk into my room. I knew it wasn't *me*. Mary K. sort of flounces through and makes more noise. That left you."

"Oh," I said, my cheeks flushing.

"Sometimes a cigar is just a cigar," she said.

I had no idea what that meant. "Anyway, Mary K. and I are

stuck on an algebra problem. Could you come help us? If you're up to it, I mean." She looked really sick. "Do you have the flu or something? Why were you in school?"

Morgan shook her head and sat up very slowly, like an old lady. "No. I'm okay."

"Hunter's sick, too. Why didn't you just stay home?"

"I'm okay," she said, obviously lying. "How do *you* feel?"

"Uh, I have a little headache. Mary K. thinks it's the weather."

Our eyes met just then, and I swear Morgan looked like she wanted to say something, was about to say something.

"What?" I asked.

Standing up, Morgan pulled down her sweatshirt and flipped her hair over her shoulder. "Nothing," she said, heading toward the door. "What's this problem you need help with?"

There was more here than she was telling me. I knew it. Without thinking, I reached out to grab her sleeve, and at that exact instant there was a *thud* and a sound like glass hitting something. I looked around wildly, wondering what I had destroyed this time, feeling cursed.

"That was Dagda," Morgan explained, a tinge of amusement in her voice.

Sure enough, I now saw her small gray cat getting to his feet on the floor by Morgan's bed. He looked sleepy and irritated.

"Sometimes he rolls off the bed when he's asleep," Morgan said.

Frustrated, I pulled back my hand and curled and uncurled my fingers. There was something happening here, something I didn't know about. Something Morgan wasn't telling me. I remembered the other day, when Morgan had run out of the kitchen to talk to Hunter, how upset she had seemed. But her face was now closed, like a shade being pulled down, and I knew she wouldn't tell me. We went into Mary K.'s room, back to algebra and away from magick.

That night I was slumped on my bed, taking a magazine quiz to find out if I was a flirting master or a flirting disaster. By question five, things were looking bad for me. I tossed the magazine aside, my mind going back to Morgan. For some reason I had a terrible feeling—I couldn't even describe it. But I was somehow convinced that something weird or bad was happening, and that Morgan and Hunter knew about it, and that they were keeping it to themselves. But what could it be? They both looked physically ill. Morgan had seemed so close to saying something, something hard. And last week there had been a day when Hunter had sat outside school literally all day. I didn't think it was just because he couldn't stand to be away from her.

Sitting up, I decided to confront Morgan again. I would somehow make her tell me what was going on, what was wrong with her and Hunter. The flaws in this plan were immediately obvious: (1) I had already asked Morgan, and she'd made it clear that she wasn't going to tell me. (2) Mary K. would wonder why I needed to talk to Morgan. And if it *was* some weird witch thing, I didn't want to drag her into it.

So how could I find out?

Hunter.

No. I knew him, but we weren't good friends. I was kind

of impressed by and wary of him at the same time. What would he think if I asked him to tell me their secret? Would he get mad at me?

Hunter was out. But . . . there really wasn't anyone else. I went through the members of Kithic in my mind. No one else had seemed nervous or ill. Just Morgan and Hunter. The blood witches. I shook my head. My brain kept coming back to this again and again, the way it had about my mother's green book. This felt the same.

I had to talk to Hunter.

I didn't have his phone number, but I knew where he lived. Now, did I have the nerve to ask him? I had no choice. I ran downstairs: Girl of Action. In the living room I encountered Hilary, watching a dvd of *Sex and the City*. Too late I remembered that Dad had gone to a union meeting at the post office, where he worked. Damn, damn, damn. I met Hilary's inquiring look. I had to go ahead and ask her.

"Um, I forgot my algebra book at school," I said, giving an Oscar-caliber performance. Not. "My friend has the same book and says I can borrow his. Do you think you could give me a ride to his house?"

Hilary actually looked touched to be asked, and I felt a little pang of guilt over the way I usually treated her. The fact that I would now owe her was not lost on me. Once again I wished the state of New York would lower the freaking driving age to, say, fifteen. Then I wouldn't have to ask anyone for favors.

"Sure," Hilary said easily. She clicked off the TV and stood up, stretching. She gave me a smile and almost looked pretty for a split second. "Let me go to the bathroom real quick.

Since I've been pregnant, I have to pee every five minutes."

She turned and left the room then, so she didn't see the horrified expression on my face. Oh, gross! Why did I have to know *that*?

Not being a complete idiot, I held my tongue, and a few minutes later I was directing her to Hunter's house. When Hilary parked behind Hunter's car, I said, "I'm having trouble with this one section. Is it okay if I stay for a minute so he can explain it to me?"

"Take your time," Hilary said. She clicked on the radio and closed her eyes, leaning back against the headrest.

"Thanks," I said, and hopped out of the car. Up on the porch I rang the doorbell, and after a moment it was answered by an older man I didn't know. Oh, this had to be Hunter's dad—I'd heard he'd come back from Canada to live with him. He didn't look much like Hunter—almost too old to be his real dad.

"You're a witch," he said after a moment, startling me.

"Uh—" I was caught off guard. No one had ever sensed this before. Including me.

"I get a strange reading off of you," he said, squinting at me. He had a slightly different accent from Hunter, too.

"Da," came Hunter's voice, and then I saw him push in next to his father. "Oh, hullo, Alisa. Are you all right? Did you come here alone?" He looked out past me to the dark yard.

"My stepmother-to-be drove me," I said, feeling an attack of shyness and regret sweeping over me. "I really need to talk to you."

"Sure. Come on in." Hunter turned to his father. "Da, this is Alisa Soto. She's a high school student, part of Kithic."

I noticed that Hunter looked as bad as Morgan had this afternoon. It was as if all the witches I knew had, like, witch pneumonia or something.

Mr. Niall looked at Hunter. "What's going on? Who is she? Why does she feel strange?"

"Calm down, Da," Hunter said. "She might feel different to you because she's only half witch."

I felt like a microbe, the way his dad looked at me.

"But she has power—I can feel it. How is that possible?" he asked.

Hunter shrugged. "Here she stands. So what can I do for you, Alisa?"

Unfortunately, I hadn't planned what to say. So what came out was, "Hunter, what's going on? Why do you and Morgan look like death? Why won't she tell me what's happening?"

"I'm off," Mr. Niall muttered abruptly, and left the room. Strange dad behavior.

I turned back to Hunter, aware that Hilary was waiting outside. "Hunter, what's the deal?" I asked again.

He looked uncomfortable, then ran one hand through his short blond hair, giving himself bed head. "How do you feel?" he asked.

I stared at him. Why did everyone keep asking me that? "I have a headache! *What is going on?*"

"Alisa, there's a dark wave coming to Widow's Vale," he said gently. "Do you know what that is?"

A what? "No."

"It's—a wave, a force, of destruction," Hunter said. "It's dark magick, a spell that a witch or a group of witches casts. They aim it at a particular village or coven, and basically it wipes everything out."

This was too much to take in. I wasn't following. "What are you *talking* about?"

"It's a bad spell," Hunter said simply. "Very uncommon. In the Wiccan world it's rare to come upon someone who practices dark magick. But dark witches can cast a spell when they want to kill other witches, destroy a whole coven, even level a whole village."

I stared at him. "What . . . what . . ." What he was saying sounded like the plot of a Bruce Willis movie—not something that could happen in Widow's Vale. But at the same time, I felt in my bones that he was telling the truth. I didn't understand it, but I did suddenly believe that something bad was coming. Something very bad. "Is this why you and Morgan are sick?"

Hunter nodded. "I would guess your headache is caused by it, too, but since you're half and half, it's not wrecking you as much." He went on to explain what he and Morgan had figured out and also what his father was trying to do, how he was trying to come up with a spell to disperse a dark wave. And he told me that the witch who cast this spell would probably die and that his father was going to be the one who cast it. I felt shocked. Hunter looked really grim, and I couldn't imagine what he was feeling.

"I guess you guys are pretty sure about all this," I said faintly.

He nodded. "It's a situation that's been developing for a while."

"Are you sure your dad—"

"Yes. I'd like for someone else to do it, obviously. But any blood witch is likely to die, and he won't let that happen to someone else."

"And a nonwitch can't cast it?"

"No. They have to be able to summon power. But if they're strong enough to summon power, then they're strong enough to be decimated by the dark wave." He looked frustrated. I felt so sorry for him. If only there was some alternative—a way for a witch to cast the spell yet not be susceptible to the powers of the dark wave. Like if a person were . . .

I frowned as an awful, horrifying thought seeped into my brain. Immediately I shut it down.

"I have to go," I said quickly. "My stepmonster-to-be is waiting for me."

Hunter nodded and opened the door for me.

"The rest of Kithic doesn't know about this," he reminded me. "They wouldn't be able to help, and there's no use in terrifying them."

"Okay." I looked back at him, framed in his doorway. Then I turned and ran down the stairs, to where Hilary was waiting in the car. I was actually really happy to see her.

I had always thought people exaggerated when they talked about sleepless nights. But that night I had one. Every time I felt myself drifting off, I thought, *Great, great, I'm going to sleep.* And of course as soon as I thought that, I was wide awake again. I heard my dad come home after I had gone to bed. I heard Hilary ask him if he wanted something to eat. I remembered how, before Hilary came, I used to leave him something for his dinner when he had late meetings. For twelve years it had been me and him and a succession of housekeepers. By the time I was ten, I'd been able to make dinner by myself, do laundry, and plan a week's worth of meals. I'd thought I was doing pretty damn well, but now I'd been replaced.

After they went to bed, the house was still but not quiet. I listened to the heat cycle on and off, the wind outside pressing against the windows, the creak of the wooden floorboards. Don't think about it, I told myself. Don't think about it. Just go to sleep. But again and again my mind teased the idea out of me: I was half witch. I might be able to call on the power, enough to cast the spell against the dark wave. And I was half not witch. So I might very well be able to survive the dark wave itself.

Don't think about it. Just go to sleep.

I thought about Hunter's weird dad, about his dying right in front of Hunter.

I thought about my mother, whose powers had scared her so much that she had stripped herself of them so that she couldn't cast any kind of spell, good or bad. Had that been the right thing to do? Would I want to do that?

I couldn't control my powers. Sometimes I broke things and made freaky stuff happen. I'd only just found out about being half witch—I didn't even know how I felt about it yet. It scared me; it pissed me off. Then I remembered some of the things I'd seen Morgan do. Now that I knew that *I* was the one who in fact had been causing the scary stuff to happen, I tried to separate out what had been Morgan. She had turned a ball of blue witch fire into flowers, real flowers, raining down on us. Mary K. thought she had saved their aunt's girlfriend from dying after she'd fallen and hit her head. She had come to visit me in the hospital when I had been sick. And I'd gotten better, right away. Those were good things, right?

I hadn't asked to be half witch. I didn't want to be. But since I was, I needed to decide what to do with myself. Was I going to strip myself of my powers, like my mom, and just keep being a regular human, not tuned in to the magick that existed all around me? Or was I going to try to be a Morgan, learning all I could, deciding what to do with it, maybe deciding to be a healer? Or was I going to be a total weenie and pretend none of this was happening?

Hunter was about to lose his dad, to watch him die. He didn't have the luxury of pretending none of this was happening.

My brain wound in circles all night, and when I realized that my room was growing lighter with the early dawn, I still didn't have any answers.

"Alisa." Hunter looked surprised to see me on his front porch, and frankly, I felt surprised to be there again. I'd taken a bus most of the way, then walked the rest, the cold wind whipping through my ski jacket. The school day had been endless, and after my sleepless night it had been especially painful to do laps around the gym.

"Come on in," he said. "It's nasty out there."

Inside, my hands twisted together nervously. "I could do it," I said fast, getting the words out before I lost my nerve.

Hunter looked at me blankly. "Do what?"

"I could cast the dark wave spell." I licked my lips. "I'm half and half. Witch enough to cast the spell. Unwitch enough to survive it. I'm your best hope."

I had never seen Hunter speechless—usually he seemed

unflappable. Behind him, I saw Mr. Niall come out from the circle room. He saw Hunter and me standing there and came over. Hunter still hadn't said anything. I repeated my offer, talking to Mr. Niall this time.

"You'll die if you cast the dark wave spell. I probably won't. I don't know how strong I am, but I can shatter small appliances from twenty feet," I said, trying for some lame humor. "All of you guys are sick—you look terrible and you can hardly move. All I have is a headache. You need me."

"Nonsense," said Mr. Niall gruffly. "It's out of the question."

"There's no way, Alisa," Hunter said finally. "You're completely untrained, uninitiated. There's no way of knowing if you could do it or not. There's no way we could risk it."

"You can't risk *not* using me," I said. "What if your dad is overcome by the dark wave before he finishes the spell? What happens then? Do you guys even *have* a backup plan?"

From the quick glances they exchanged, I figured they didn't.

"But Alisa," said Hunter, "you've never even cast a spell. This is incredibly difficult and complicated magick. There's no way you could ever learn it in time. Plus, we just don't know how strong you are."

"I'm no Morgan, I know that," I said. "I'm not a prodigy. But I know I have *some* powers, from all the weird telekinetic stuff that's happened. I mean, I know I'm the one who's been causing all the weird poltergeisty stuff. I have *some* kind of power. I know the spell would be complicated. But what other choice do you have?"

"I can choose not to send an uninitiated half witch to her death," said Mr. Niall.

"Okay." I met his eyes. "Can you choose to send the rest

of Kithic to their deaths because you couldn't see other options?"

Hunter and his father exchanged glances again. "Excuse us," Hunter said abruptly, and, taking his father by the arm, he led him into the next room. They were gone almost ten minutes. It felt like ten hours. When they came back, they both looked wary but as if an agreement had been reached.

"My father is going to do some basic testing of your powers," Hunter told me. "Based on that, we think it might not be the worst idea for you to at least study parts of the spell. We're not completely convinced that you could take part in this, but it won't hurt anything to have you know some of it. As you said, the fact that you're only half witch works in your favor here."

I nodded. Now that they had agreed, a whole new set of fears crossed my mind. But I wasn't able to back out now. My mother had been afraid of her powers and in the end had destroyed them. I wasn't there—not yet. I needed more information; I needed to explore their possibilities first. If I did have real powers and I could somehow learn to harness them, use them for good—well, that would be better than not having any powers at all.

9

Morgan

><"There can be great power in darkness. There can be great ecstasy in power."
>—Selene Belltower, New York, 1999><

Wednesday. Today sucked. I feel like I have the flu, but nothing I take makes any difference. I've tried every kind of sinus medicine I could find—nothing touches how I feel. Mom has noticed how yucky I look, even for me, and keeps feeling my forehead. But I have no fever. Just this horrible, ill feeling that seems to be eating at me from inside out. I'm so tired of feeling this way—I keep bursting into tears. Our situation is so dire that I can't even fully wrap my head around it. I'm trying to go to school, to eat dinner with my family, to go on as normal, and all the time I'm trying not to think about the fact that I and everyone I love might be dead in a week.

In terms of my studies, I worked on some of the correspondences that Bethany assigned. I'm studying the different structures of crystals and how their individual molecular patterns can aid or deter their powers when used in actual spells. I like this kind of stuff. It's sciency. I'm just finding it hard to think.

On Thursday, I opened my Book of Shadows to write the day's entry. I'd been trying to write a little every day, at least a few sentences about what I was doing, Wicca-wise, what I was focusing on. I realized my brain just wasn't functioning. I needed a Diet Coke. Downstairs, I heard the TV on in the family room. I got my soda from the fridge and poked my head in on my way back upstairs. Dad was working on the computer, Mary K. was on the floor, an open textbook in front of her, and Mom was on the couch, going over new real estate listings while she watched TV. My whole family might be dead in a week; this house might no longer exist; these three people who had been the only family I'd known, who had taken care of me and gotten mad at me and loved me—they might be killed. Because of Ciaran. Because of me. Through no fault of their own. Their only crime being to have adopted and loved me.

Feeling wretched, guilty, and sick, I went upstairs. I wanted to cry but knew that would only make me feel worse. It wasn't just my family. It was Hunter, the person I loved as much as my family. The person I felt so close to, so in love with, whom I wanted so desperately. The thought of him dead, lifeless and charred on the ground, made me feel like I was going to throw up.

And if by some miracle Mr. Niall managed to avert the dark wave, then what? He would still be dead. We would all be alive, but I would have indirectly caused the death of my boyfriend's father. Would Hunter ever be able to forgive me for that? Knowing him, probably. But would I ever be able to forgive myself?

I sat down at my desk, my head in my hands. My birth father was going to take Hunter's father away, just as Hunter had found him again. What could I do? A series of crazy thoughts went through my head. Could I shape-shift into a wolf and kill Ciaran? I didn't think so—I didn't know how to shape-shift by myself. The last time Ciaran had told me what to say and do. Plus, I never wanted to shape-shift again—it had been too scary. Plus, I didn't think I could really kill anyone, even Ciaran. Could I somehow warn Kithic and their families so they would leave the area? Again, I didn't think so. It would be virtually impossible to convince anyone, and it would only delay the dark wave, not dismantle it. I wondered if I could put a binding spell on Mr. Niall so he couldn't do the spell. Well, if he didn't do the spell, we would all die. On the other hand, since we would all be dead, Hunter wouldn't have to face his father's death.

Then it came to me—an idea that had been fluttering around my mind. I had been ignoring it, but it would be ignored no longer. I could confront Ciaran again. I could tell him that I would join him. A cold feeling settled over me like a mantle. No—it would be lying, and he would see through it. But maybe . . . maybe I could confront him again and then somehow use his true name against him? Maybe I could bind him, shut him down so he couldn't do the final part of the dark wave spell? Ciaran was impossibly strong, but I knew that I had an unusual strength myself. For the most part, I was untrained and uneducated, but I had always been able to call on the power when I needed to. And I had Ciaran's true name. I had discovered it in the middle of our shape-shifting spell. A witch's true name is made of song and color and rune and symbol, all at once. Everything has a true name—rock and tree and wind and bird. Animal, flower, star, river. Witch. To know something's true name is to have ultimate power over it—it can deny you nothing.

And I knew Ciaran's. Of course, he knew I knew it and would be on his guard. But it was a risk I felt I should take.

Looking up, my glance fell on my open textbook. I had a plan.

I waited until I sensed that everyone in the house was asleep. I could feel Mary K. in her room, sleeping deeply and innocently. My dad was sleeping more lightly, but I knew that soon he would go deeper and start snoring. Mom slept as she always did, or at least always had since I'd started notic-ing—with the efficient, light sleep of a mom who manages to get her rest while at the same time being poised for action in case she hears the unmistakable sound of a child crying or throwing up. Mary K. and I were in high school, but Mom would probably sleep that way until we left for college.

I crept out of bed and shut myself in my walk-in closet. In there I drew a small circle on the floor with chalk. I closed myself into the circle, then sat cross-legged and meditated. This circle would increase my powers and give me an added layer of protection. I had no idea where Ciaran was, but I had a feeling he was still nearby. I summoned as much power as I could and sent a concentrated message: *Father—I need you. Power sink.*

I felt a pang of guilt over calling him Father—especially when my real father was sleeping across the hall. I found Ciaran extremely compelling and charismatic, and the idea that he was a blood relation still confused me. For him, I was the child most like him, the one he wanted most to teach. Yet we both despised aspects of each other, and we had never really trusted each other.

I dismantled the circle, feeling sick and tired and close to tears. What was I doing? This had seemed like a good idea an hour ago, but now the whole concept frightened me. I didn't know which outcome would scare me more: that he wouldn't answer my message or that he would. I crawled back into bed, every muscle aching, and lay there in a tense half sleep for I don't know how long. Then it came to me, Ciaran's voice in my mind: *One hour.*

An hour can fly by (when I'm with Hunter) or crawl by (when I'm at school). After I got Ciaran's message, each second seemed to take an entire minute to tick past. After lying stiffly in bed for twenty minutes as if I had rigor mortis, I couldn't stand it any longer. I pulled on some jeans and a hoodie sweatshirt, whisked my hair into a long braid, and, holding my shoes, crept downstairs.

Outside, I buttoned up my coat and pulled on a knit watch cap. Everything felt tight, surreal as I crunched over the spring frost to Das Boot. I felt like I had infrared vision: I could see every tiny movement of every twig on every tree. The moonlight as it filtered through the tree branches was pale and fragile. I opened the car door, put it in neutral, then took off the parking brake. My Valiant began to roll heavily backward toward the street, and soon we bumped almost silently over the curb. I cut the wheel sharply to the left. When I was facing forward, I eased up on the brake again and let myself roll slowly downhill about thirty yards. Then I started the engine, flipped on the headlights and the heater, and headed for the power sink.

When I was younger, I was afraid of the dark. At seventeen, I was more afraid of things like becoming irreversibly evil or having my soul taken from me by force. The dark didn't seem that bad.

Since I had first started realizing I had witch powers, my magesight had developed, and now I could see quite easily with no light. I parked my car on the road's shoulder and left it unlocked. Every detail stood out as my boots crunched over frost-rimed pine needles, decaying leaves, and waterlogged twigs. I was more than twenty minutes early. Casting my senses out, I felt only sleeping animals and birds and the occasional owl or bat. No witch, no Ciaran.

The power sink was in the middle of the graveyard, and to me it felt like every age-worn headstone had something or someone hiding behind it. Ruthlessly I clamped down on my fear, relying on my senses instead of my emotions. I was cold, whipped by a wet, icy wind, but more than that, I was chilled through with fear. No, the dark didn't bother me, but the worst things that had happened in my life had all happened in the last four months, and they had mostly been caused by the man I was waiting to meet. My birth father.

I paced back and forth, and slowly I became aware of

tendrils of power beneath me in the earth, tingling energy lines of the power leys that had been there since the beginning of time. They were beneath my feet; they had fed this place for centuries. Their power was in the trees, in the dirt, in the stones, in everything around me.

"Morgan."

I spun around, my heart stopping cold. Ciaran had appeared with no warning: my senses hadn't picked up on even a ripple in the energy around me.

"I was surprised to get your call," he said in that lilting Scottish accent. His hazel eyes seemed to glow at me in the darkness. Slowly I felt the heavy thudding of my heart start up again. "I hope you called me here to make me happy—to tell me that we're going to be the most remarkable witches the world has ever seen."

I felt so many things, looking at him. Anger, regret, fear, confusion, and even, I was ashamed to admit it—love? Almost admiration? He was so powerful, so focused. He had no uncertainty in his life: his path was clear. I envied that.

I didn't have an exact plan—first I needed to know for sure what his plans were.

"I've been feeling awful," I told him. "Is it from the dark wave?"

"Aye, daughter," he said, sounding regretful. "If you know far enough in advance, you can protect yourself from the illness. But if you don't . . ." Which explained why he looked bright eyed and bushy tailed, but I felt like I was going to throw up or collapse. "I can do a lot to help your symptoms," he went on. "And then the next time you'll be protected before it starts."

"I'm not joining you," I said, drawing cold air into my lungs.

"Then why did you call me here?" There was a chill underlying his tone that was far worse than that of the night air.

"My way isn't your way," I said. "It isn't a path I can choose. Why can't you just let me be? I'm a nobody. Kithic is nothing. You don't need to destroy us. We can't do anything to hurt you."

"Kithic is nothing," he agreed, his voice like smoke rising off water. He stepped closer to me, so close I could almost touch him. "An amateurish circle of mediocre kids. But you, my dear—you are not nothing. You possess the power to devastate anything in your path—or to create unimaginable beauty."

"No, I don't," I objected. "Why do you think that? I'm not even initiated—"

"You just don't understand, do you?" he said sharply. "You don't understand who you are, *what* you are. You're the last witch of Belwicket. You're my daughter. You're the *sgiùrs dàn*."

"The what?" I felt hysteria rising in me like nausea.

"The fated scourge. The destroyer."

"The *what?*" I repeated in a squeak.

"The signs say that it's you, Morgan," he explained. "The destroyer comes every several generations to change the course of her clan. This time it's you who will change the course of the Woodbanes—just as your great ancestor Rose did centuries ago. So you see, you have more power than you realize. And I simply can't let that power be in opposition to my own. It would be ... foolish of me to go against fate."

"You're insane," I breathed.

He grinned then, his teeth shining whitely in the night. "No, Morgan. Ambitious, yes. Insane, no. It's all true. Just ask the Seeker. At any rate, you won't be around long enough for it to really matter. Either you join me now or you die."

I stared at him, seeing a reflection of my face in his more masculine features. "You wouldn't really kill me." Please don't do this, I begged silently. Please.

A look of pain crossed his face. "I don't want to. But I will." He sounded regretful. "I must. If I have to choose your life or mine, I'll choose mine."

Hearing him confirm this broke my heart. I felt a sadness in my chest like a dull weight. Any of the confused affection I had for him, any lingering hopes I had of someday, somehow having an actual relationship with the man who had fathered me dissipated. A real father would never hurt his own daughter—as a real soul mate wouldn't have killed his lover. Ciaran was failing on all counts.

With no warning I was overtaken by a wave of rage, at his arrogance, his selfishness, his shortsightedness. He would rather kill me than know me! He would rather wipe out an entire coven than achieve his ends in other ways! He was a bully and a coward, hiding behind a dark wave that had killed countless innocent people. He was going to kill me because I—a teenager, an unschooled witch—scared him. I didn't think before I moved. Suddenly I felt like I was on a playground and being picked on. I flung out my fist, catching him squarely on the shoulder. Taken by surprise, as I was, Ciaran caught my wrist in his hand, and then I was twisted down to the ground, crying out. This wasn't magick—this was just a man who was stronger than me. But then he muttered something and I felt a horrible stillness coming over me, a remote coldness that I had felt once before, when Cal had put a binding spell on me.

Dammit! My mind raced ahead in panic as I knelt, so numb

I couldn't feel the dampness of the ground seeping through my jeans. What had I been thinking? I knew Ciaran's true name! But instead of using it, I had lashed out like a stupid kid!

He released my hand and stepped back, looking angry and concerned. "What is this about, Morgan?" he said, sounding, ironically, quite fatherly. I couldn't form words—it was like being under anesthesia, those scary minutes before you go totally out. My brain felt wrapped in damp cotton, synapses firing slowly and erratically. I couldn't move; I no longer felt like I had a body. Besides sheer panic, I was now filled with anger. Could I be any stupider? Magick is all about clarity of thought. Clarity of thought dictates clarity of action. Not thinking, lashing out blindly, not having a firm plan and sticking to it, meant not only trouble—for me, now, it meant death.

I'm not one of those heroine-type people who think best under pressure. Mostly, under pressure, I just want to cry. I wanted to cry now. I was choked with frustration, with fury, with fear. Instead, I knelt on the cold ground, my father standing before me, holding my life in his hands like an egg.

"Morgan." He sounded surprised, disappointed. "What are you thinking? Are you really going up against *me*? I'm much stronger than you are."

My mouth moved, but I couldn't form words. *Then why are you so scared of me?* I thought, sending him the message.

I wondered if I could just *think* his true name—if that would be enough to control him. I was reluctant to try. If he even knew it was in my mind, I'd be toast. I had already made one terrible, possibly fatal mistake. Anything I did from now on would have to be a sure step.

Foggily, my eyes went to Ciaran's face. He was talking to

me in a low tone, and I struggled to understand what he was saying. "Would it be so terrible to join me? Am I such a monster? I'm your father. I could teach you things that would make you cry at their beauty, their perfection. Do you really want to throw this opportunity away?"

My eyes were focused on him as he spoke. Think, think, I told myself dreamily. Think or he'll win. A binding spell was one of the odder spells one could be under. There were different levels of it—from simply being unable to harm another being to being virtually comatose. The way I felt now was like being wrapped in many layers of tissue: hard to get out of, yet made of thin, tearable layers. I also knew that keeping me in this spell required Ciaran's concentration. One could work a binding spell from a distance, but he hadn't had time for that. This was a quick one, hastily put together and requiring his continued effort.

If I broke his concentration, if he for one millisecond dropped his guard, I might be able to do something. Like whimper pathetically and then fall over. Or break free. And then I was sure I could use his true name. It was just so hard to *think*. I could barely move my eyes—that was all. What were my options? I didn't think I could send a witch message to anyone not right next to me while I was bound. I couldn't form the sounds of Maeve's power chant. What could I do? What was I capable of? Starting fires was something I was good at—but everything around me seemed damp. Could I set wet leaves on fire?

Ciaran was talking, pacing back and forth, earnestly trying to convince me why black equaled white. My eyes followed him, but he didn't look at me much: he was sure I couldn't break free.

Fire. Heat. Heat plus dampness . . . made steam. Steam could be powerful. Most heavy machinery used to be run on steam. Radiators.

Then it came to me. With great effort, I slowly slid my gaze past Ciaran to the trunk of a pine tree. Heat, I thought. Heat and water. Heat. Fire. I imagined sparks, tiny flames flickering into being, fire warming bark, running beneath it. Ciaran didn't notice the very faint ribbon of steam coming from the tree behind him. His soliloquy continued, as if he thought that if he talked long enough, I would finally be convinced.

Heat, building beneath the pine bark. Pressure building. Cells expanding. Tiny fissures splitting wood fibers. The water in every cell evaporating, turning to steam. I lost myself in it, imagining that I could see the bark swelling, feel the fibers splitting, feel the pressure building.

Crack!

With the force of a small explosion, chunks of pine bark flew outward, hitting Ciaran, almost hitting me. He whirled, his hand outstretched, ready to deflect an attack, but it took him several seconds to see where the sound had come from. Seconds in which his concentration was weakened. In those precious seconds I made a tremendous effort and managed to work my right arm. Summoning every bit of power in me, I raised my voice to say his true name. He whirled as the notes began, my voice sounding dull and leaden under the binding spell. My right hand clumsily sketched runes in the air, and with a last breath I managed to complete it—his true name, a color and song and rune all at once.

He hissed something at me, but I held up my hand and deflected it.

Teeth gritted, I said, "Take off the binding spell."

The look of fury and horror on his face was frightening, even though I knew I had power over him.

"Take it off!"

His arm raised against his will, and words fell from his lips. In moments I could take deep breaths, and when the spell dissolved, I fell to my hands and knees.

"Morgan, don't make this kind of mistake," Ciaran said softly. But he wasn't in control anymore.

"Be quiet," I panted, slowly standing up, rubbing feeling back into my arms and legs. The cold of the night air made me shake: I had been motionless for too long.

I looked at him, my biological father, an extremely power-ful witch whom I had both reluctantly admired and truly feared. He had put a binding spell on me! He had planned to kill me, kill my friends, my family. I let my contempt show in my face as I looked at him.

"Ciaran of Amyranth," I said, my lungs still feeling stiff, my tongue thick, "I have power over you. I have your true name, and you are bidden to do my will." I was trying to remember the exact phrasing from various witch texts. His eyes flashed, but he stood quietly before me. "You will never hurt me again," I said strongly. I wasn't sure exactly how a true name worked—but I felt that pretty much anything I said went. "Do you understand?"

His lips were pressed tightly together.

"Say it," I said, feeling unreal, giving him orders.

"I will never hurt you again." It looked like the words were costing him.

With quick, efficient motions I put a binding spell on him, just to be safe. He stood in the darkness like a handsome mannequin, but fire was burning in his eyes and his gaze never left me. "I have your true name," I said again for good measure. "You have no power."

I backed away from him, feeling exhausted. My watch said 2:26 A.M. Pressing one hand against my temple, keeping my eyes open, I sent out a witch message as strongly as I knew how. *Hunter. Power sink. Now. Bring your dad. I need you.*

10

Alisa

><"The secret of a successful dark wave is in creating its limitations. Be clear in your intent, unemotional. Act because of a calm, logical decision—not out of anger or revenge."
—Ciaran MacEwan, Scotland, 2000><

"No, no—it's *nal nithrac*, not *nal bithdarc*," Mr. Niall said, not bothering to hide his irritation.

I gritted my teeth. "Isn't there a *nal bithdarc* in there somewhere?"

"There's a *bith dearc*," Hunter reminded me. "But not till a bit later."

I let out a breath and sank down onto the wooden floor in front of the fireplace. It was way freaking late, I was exhausted, I had a headache, and I was kind of hungry. "Is there any cake left?" I asked.

Hunter had made a killer pound cake yesterday, and we'd all been wolfing it down in between their teaching me this wretched horrible spiteful spell. Without a word Hunter went into the kitchen and came back with a slab of cake on a plate. I picked it up with my fingers and took a bite.

Mr. Niall sat on the floor next to me and held his hands out to the fire. He looked like death warmed over, gray skinned and hollow eyed. Starting last Tuesday night, he'd been working with me on the spell to fight the dark wave. Dad and Hilary thought I was working on my science project with Mary K. I had told Dad I'd be home late, and he agreed. Another sign of Hilary's turning my dad crazy: a year ago he'd never have let me stay out past his bedtime.

I looked at my watch: past midnight. And I had to go to school tomorrow. Thank God tomorrow was Friday. I could sleepwalk through classes, then go home and crash. Then come here and not have to worry about getting up the next morning.

"I'm sorry," I said, trying not to spray crumbs. "This is all new to me."

"I know," said Mr. Niall, rubbing the back of his head. "And this is a hard one. Most witches start with spells to keep flies away, things like that."

"Keep flies away," I mused. "I could probably handle something like that."

Hunter gave a dry laugh, then headed back to the kitchen when the teakettle began whistling.

He came back with three mugs. It was hot and sweet, laced with honey and lemon. I waited till Mr. Niall had drunk his, then tiredly got to my feet. "Okay. Can we start right at the beginning of the second part, where we do the sigils?"

"Lass—" Mr. Niall hesitated. "You've been trying, but—"

"But what? But I keep messing up? It's late, I'm tired, this is my first dark wave spell," I said testily. "I know I need lots more practice. That's why I'm here." My jaw jutted out, and I realized that I had some pride invested here. I *wanted* to be able to do this. Not to look good in front of Hunter and his dad, but because I was my mother's daughter. She'd come from a whole line of witches, yet she'd been so freaked out by her powers that she'd stripped herself of them. That seemed kind of cowardly to me. My powers scared me, too, but it seemed so wrong to give up like that. I felt like, I'm me, *I'm* in control of me. My powers were not in control of me. Doing the spell was a crash course in learning to channel my powers. So far it hadn't been that successful: there had been several times when I'd been so upset or frustrated that I'd popped a lightbulb overhead, caused a stack of firewood to topple (I assumed that had been me), and made a framed picture drop off the wall.

Those were the kinds of things that had scared me about Morgan and her powers—the whole idea of her being out of control. But it *hadn't* been her, and I had to live with that part of me. I needed to get it together. The weird thing was, by the time the third thing had happened (I was almost screaming in frustration after doing a whole set of sigils perfectly—but backward), Hunter and his dad started to find it funny. Funny! Stuff that had made me quit Kithic and run a mile from Morgan—made me dislike her, mistrust her. Now, after spending so many hours with me in this house, they had started making a big show of throwing out their hands to catch things—vases, lamps, mugs—every time I even raised my voice. It was like that scene in *Mary Poppins* where the admiral sets off his cannon and everyone runs to their posts.

"Look at yourselves," I said, not meanly. "You guys can hardly eat, hardly sleep. The dark wave coming is draining you. I'm the picture of health next to you. This is still a good plan. Which means you still have to teach me."

Looking defeated, Mr. Niall stood up, and we both faced west with our arms out.

"Give me the words," he said.

Concentrating, I tried to let the spell come to me instead of reaching out to grab it. *"An de allaigh, ne rith la,"* I half sang. *"Bant ne tier gan, ne rith la."* And so on it went, the words of limitation that were the second part of the spell. After one more phrase Mr. Niall and I started moving together, like synchronized swimmers. My right hand came out and traced three runes, then a sigil, a rune, and two more sigils. These would focus the spell and add power. Each rune stood not only for itself, but also for a word that began with its sound. Each word had meaning and added to the spell.

I crossed my arms over my chest, palms down, each hand on a shoulder. Standing tall, I continued, *"Sgothrain, tal nac, nal nithrac, bogread, ne rith la."*

Ten minutes later I sounded the last part of the second stage of the spell. I wanted to drop onto the floor and sleep right there for the rest of my life. But when I looked up and saw admiration on Hunter's face and a reserved approval on Mr. Niall's, I felt a rush of energy.

"Was that okay?" I asked, knowing that they would have stopped me if it wasn't.

"That was fine, Alisa," said Mr. Niall. "That was good. If we can get the other parts down as well, we'll be in good shape."

I tried not to groan out loud: there were three other parts to the spell. The whole thing took almost an hour to perform.

"I felt your power," Hunter said. "Did you feel it?"

I nodded. "Yes. It seems to be getting stronger—or maybe I'm just better at recognizing it. It's still so new to me. Is it weird for a half witch to have power?"

Hunter shrugged. "It's an exceedingly rare condition, right, Da?"

"Very rare. I don't think I've ever met another half witch, let alone one that had powers," Mr. Niall said. "I've heard stories—but usually a female witch can't conceive by an ordinary male. And when a male witch conceives with a non-witch female, their child is always relatively powerless."

Heat flushed my cheeks. I really didn't want to think about my parents conceiving anything.

"I wonder, though," said Mr. Niall. "I wonder if your having powers, or this level of powers, has anything to do with your mother stripping herself of hers. Stripping yourself of powers is rather like getting plastic surgery: on the outside, you appear different, but your genes are the same. *Your* nose looks different, but you have the ability to pass on your old nose to your offspring. The fact that your mother stripped herself of her powers didn't in any way mean she was no longer a blood witch, with the capability of passing her strength, her family's strength, on to her offspring." He frowned at me. "But you do have a high level of power, even assuming that you inherited your genetic due from your mother. Most half witches are relatively weak because they get power from only one side of the family. But you . . ."

"I break things," I supplied.

Mr. Niall chuckled—a rare occurrence. "Well, there's that, lass. No, I was getting at the fact that you seem to have as much power as a full blood witch. I wonder if it's possible that because your mother stripped herself, her powers were somehow concentrated in you."

Hunter looked curious. "You mean Alisa has not only her own powers as a half witch, but her mother's powers as a full witch."

Mr. Niall looked at me and nodded slowly. "Yes," he said. "It's something I've never seen before, but I suppose that's what I mean."

"You don't have brothers or sisters, right, Alisa?" Hunter asked.

I shook my head. "Except for the half sibling that's due in six months. But it wouldn't have any witch at all."

"It would have been interesting if you had, to see what their powers would be like," he said.

"Yeah. I'm a walking science experiment," I said tartly. "I mean, do you think I could ever learn to control my power, all the telekinetic stuff?"

Hunter's father nodded. "Yes—I can't think of any reason why you wouldn't be able to. It would be a skill to learn, like any other skill. It would take practice, commitment, and time, but I feel sure it could be done."

"Okay," I said with a sigh. "I guess I'll start on that as soon as this dark wave thing is over."

Hunter and Mr. Niall met glances over my head, and in a

flash I got what they were thinking: that if we couldn't some-how combat the dark wave, I wouldn't ever have to worry about my telekinetic stuff again. Because I would be dead.

Hunter stretched again, then frowned slightly and went still. I listened for any unusual sounds but didn't hear any-thing or see anything out of place.

"What, lad?" asked Mr. Niall, and Hunter held up a finger for silence.

"It's Morgan," he said then, getting to his feet.

"What, outside?" I asked, thinking he had sensed her coming up.

"No. At the power sink. She wants me to come there." He looked at his father. "She said to bring you."

Without discussion they walked into the front room and pulled on their coats.

Halfway out the door Hunter asked, "Do you want me to give you a ride home?"

I looked around the room at Mr. Niall's spell books, Rose's Book of Shadows, and my scrawled notes on endless messy pieces of paper. I needed more practice. "No thanks—I'll wait here, if that's okay. I'll go over the third part of the spell again."

Hunter considered it for a moment, then nodded. "Right, then. But stay close to a phone, and if anything weird hap-pens, call 911."

"Okay." Anything weird? 911? What was going on?

Then they were gone, and I was alone. It was almost two-thirty in the morning. I put another thin log on the fire in the circle room and began to work through the forms again.

11

Morgan

><"During the flu epidemic, a coven leader from Dover wanted to use a dark wave on her city. If Dover were leveled, it would reduce the chances of the disease spreading. Sound reasoning, but of course the council couldn't approve it."

—Frederica Pelsworthy,
NOTABLE DECISIONS OF THE TWENTIETH
CENTURY, Adam Press, 2000><

After ten minutes of holding Ciaran in a binding spell, I began to feel that I should have let him sit down first. Because I felt a little *guilty* that one of the most evil witches in the last two centuries, a man responsible for hundreds if not thousands of deaths, a man who had, in fact, killed my *mother,* was possibly getting uncomfortable having to stand still in one place for so long! I'm so pathetic, I just can't stand myself sometimes.

I was leaning against a headstone, occasionally walking around to keep warm, when Hunter and his father arrived. I had never been so glad to see another person in my life. I felt them get out of Hunter's car; then Hunter led his father through the woods to the Methodist cemetery. I hurried forward to meet them.

"Thanks for coming," I said, wrapping my arms around Hunter's waist and leaning my head against his chest for a second. I kept part of my concentration on Ciaran but knew he couldn't budge that binding spell. I'd always been good at them. "Things got a little crazy."

"What's going on?" Hunter held me by my shoulders and looked down into my face with concern.

"Over here." I waved my hand limply toward Ciaran, and Hunter took a few steps before he spotted him. Then he froze, his hands already coming up for ward-evil spells. "He's under a binding spell," I said quickly.

"Goddess," Mr. Niall breathed hoarsely, having spotted Ciaran.

Hunter turned and looked at me like I had suddenly revealed elf wings on my back.

I shook my head, unsure of how to begin. "I just couldn't stand the fact that all this was happening because of me. If I weren't here, Amyranth would have left Kithic alone. I felt like it was all my fault. I decided to contact Ciaran, to try to reason with him."

I glanced at Ciaran and almost shivered at the look in his eyes. He seemed less recognizable, his eyes glittering darkly, with none of the mild affection or warmth that they usually held.

"So you called him to meet you here?" Hunter asked, disbelief in his voice. "And he came?"

"Uh-huh. And he said that if I didn't join him that he

would have to take out our coven. Because I was too dangerous to live if I wasn't on his side. Because I was the—the, um, *sgiùrs dàn?* Something like that. Then he put a binding spell on me—"

"Hold it," Hunter interrupted. "Wait a second. He said you were the *sgiùrs dàn?*" He looked at Ciaran questioningly, but the older man's face didn't change.

"Yes. Then he put a binding spell on me, and I thought I was going to die, right here, tonight. But I distracted him for a second, and broke his concentration, and managed to put a binding spell on *him.*" I rubbed my hand across my forehead, feeling old and sick and tired.

"How did you distract him?" Hunter asked.

I glanced at Mr. Niall—I thought he'd been way too quiet. In the night's darkness he almost glowed with a white rage. He was standing stiffly, hands clenched into fists. He looked like he might attack Ciaran at any moment.

"I created a pocket of steam, under that tree's bark," I explained, pointing. "It made the bark pop off hard, and it distracted Ciaran just enough for me to be able to use my hand and to speak."

"What did you say that got you out of the binding spell?" asked Mr. Niall, his voice hard.

"I said . . . his true name." The last three words tiptoed out of my mouth. I had never told anyone that I knew Ciaran's true name, and part of me didn't like telling anyone now.

Hunter's eyes got so big, I could see white all around the green irises. His jaw went slack, and then he cocked his head to one side. "Morgan. You said *what?*"

"I said his true name," I repeated. "Then I made him take off the binding spell."

Both Hunter and Mr. Niall looked from me to Ciaran: they had suddenly found themselves in a situation that defied all reason. Ciaran's eyes now seemed as black as the night, and considering that all he could do was blink, he managed to put a lot of scary expression into it.

"And I put a binding spell on him," I finished. "Then I called you. I don't know what to do now."

Just then, with a hoarse cry, Mr. Niall launched himself at Ciaran. Using his shoulder, he butted Ciaran hard in the stomach, then followed him down to the ground and pulled back his fist. I was already on my way to them when Hunter's father landed a hard blow to the side of Ciaran's head. Hunter beat me there and tried to pull his father off, but finally it took both of us to drag Mr. Niall away.

"Da, stop it," Hunter panted, pinning his father down with one knee. "This isn't the time or the place. Get ahold of yourself."

"I'm going to kill him," Mr. Niall spat, and I got angry.

"No, you're not!" I snapped. "I understand how you feel, but you don't decide what happens to him. That's the council's job."

"No, not the council." Hunter shook his head. "They've bungled things twice with him already. No—it's up to us. We have to strip him of his powers."

Ciaran lay on the ground like a mummy where he had fallen. He hadn't displayed much response when Mr. Niall had attacked him, but now, at Hunter's words, real fear entered his eyes. I had seen a witch stripped of his powers once, and I'd hoped never to see it again. The idea of seeing it happen to Ciaran was stomach turning. Yet I knew, realistically, that there was no other real option. If we let Ciaran go, he would be exactly the same. He would continue to create the dark wave, killing anything that got in his way. He would always be a threat to me, no matter what kind of promise I could get out of him. Once more I met his gaze and saw the disappointment there, the rage, the regret. I looked away.

"Yeah, you're right," I said roughly, trying not to cry. "I guess you need five witches."

"We have three here," said Hunter. If he was surprised by my acquiescence, he didn't show it.

"I can't do it," I said immediately. "Get someone else."

Hunter took his knee off his dad's chest and warily let him up. Mr. Niall slowly got to his feet and stalked off to lean against a weatherworn headstone. Hunter stood quite still for a couple of minutes, and I knew he was sending witch messages. Without looking at Ciaran's face, I went over and pulled him into a sitting position, awkwardly propping him up. There was a lot I wanted or needed to say to him, but I didn't trust myself to speak. In my heart, I knew we were doing the best thing. After he was sitting up, I sank onto a cement bench nearby and concentrated on the binding spell.

Then we had to wait. Hunter came to sit next to me. I felt like I had been out here about three years and wanted to go home, curl up in my comforter, and cry until dawn.

"Morgan," Hunter said, his voice pitched for me alone. "You never told me that you knew Ciaran's true name."

It was a statement, not a question, but I knew what he wanted.

"I learned it the night we shape-shifted," I said. "It was part of his spell. I don't know why I never told anyone. It just felt . . . wrong to tell."

"Or maybe you didn't want Ciaran to be that vulnerable to anyone else. Because whatever else he is, he helped make you."

I frowned, not wanting to acknowledge this fact at the moment.

"All this time you knew his true name," Hunter continued, rubbing his chin with one hand. "You could have done anything you wanted with it. You could have killed him, controlled him, turned him in to the council or to me. You could have bound him and done a *tàth meànma brach* so that you would have all his knowledge, all his skill."

I shook my head. "No—I couldn't have. I couldn't have killed him, and somehow I just kept hoping that he would . . . be different. And I don't want his knowledge or his skill. I don't want to have anything to do with it."

Hunter nodded. He was sitting close but not touching me, and I wondered how upset he was that I hadn't told him.

It wasn't long before we heard two cars driving up, and moments later we were joined by Alyce Fernbrake, Bethany Malone, and a woman I didn't recognize.

"Where's Finn?" Hunter asked.

"He couldn't come," Alyce said, and the way she said it made me think he just hadn't wanted to come. I didn't blame him. "This is Silver Hennessy."

Awkward introductions were made—we all knew why we were here: he was sitting ten feet away from us. I started to feel queasy and had to sit down again.

"More than five witches can take part," Hunter said to me. "Five is the minimum number."

"I can't," I said, and he didn't press me.

Having to do this particular rite out in the woods, with

no advance warning, wasn't ideal. Usually the witch in charge chooses a suitable time and place, where the phase of the moon helps lessen the discomfort or the place feels more protected. Ciaran, because of his very nature, couldn't be held for any length of time. It would be here and now.

Hunter had brought his athame, and now he drew a pentacle on the ground, about eight feet across. The litter of leaves obscured the ground, but he muttered some words and raised his athame high. Then he traced it on the ground, and it left a fine, faintly glowing azure line.

I couldn't bring myself to look at Ciaran, to see the increasing rage and panic on his face. Instead, I huddled on my cement bench, my head on my knees. I knew that using his true name had been the right thing to do. I also knew that I would feel badly about doing it for a long, long time. Bethany Malone and Alyce both came and sat next to me, and I felt the warmth of them on each side of me. Bethany put her arm around my shoulders, and Alyce patted my cold knee. I leaned my head against Alyce, grateful she was here. I didn't know Silver Hennessy, but I completely trusted Bethany and Alyce and knew that Ciaran was lucky they were performing the rite.

Mr. Niall stood close to Hunter, as if watching to make sure he was setting the rite up correctly. Occasionally they murmured to each other. Mr. Niall refused to look at Ciaran or me, but I felt that he was trying to release some of his own fury and pain. He would need a clear head to participate in this.

Soon Alyce left me and went to sit by Ciaran with Silver. Alyce was just about the gentlest, least judgmental person I had ever known, but the look she gave Ciaran was reserved and sad. I knew that Ciaran must be feeling incredibly sore and stiff by now, but of course I couldn't lessen the binding spell. And this was nothing compared to how he would feel an hour from now. Not that he didn't deserve it. Every once in a while I felt a rough growl in my mind, as if a trapped animal were trying to break free. It was Ciaran, trying to claw his way through the binding spell.

Sitting there, remembering the last time I had seen this rite, I realized we needed to make some arrangement about Ciaran, for afterward. I left Bethany, went over to Hunter, and waited until he paused and met my eyes.

"I think I should call Killian to come get him," I said very quietly. "None of us is going to want to take care of him afterward."

For long moments Hunter looked at me, then he nodded. "That's good thinking, Morgan. Can you send the message?"

I nodded and went back to sit next to Bethany on my bench, where I concentrated and sent a witch message to my half brother Killian MacEwan, the only one of my half siblings I had met. Despite being extremely different, we had forged a somewhat caring relationship. After tonight, I assumed, that would be over.

When Killian answered me, he was in Poughkeepsie, an hour and a half away. I asked him to come to Widow's Vale at once and told him it was important, but didn't tell him why. He said he would, and I hoped he meant it.

At last Hunter stood. "All right, I think we can begin."

Bethany squeezed my shoulder, stroked my hair briefly, then joined Hunter, Alyce, and Silver as they lifted Ciaran and carried him into the middle of the pentacle. Mr. Niall stayed away—I wondered if he didn't trust himself to get close to Ciaran without attacking him. The four witches bent Ciaran's unresisting body so he was kneeling on the ground with his arms by his sides. Then Hunter ran his hands over Ciaran, taking off anything metal, taking off his shoes, loosening his collar, his cuffs. He was quick and efficient, but not rough. I saw a tiny muscle jerking in Ciaran's cheek. With no warning a sudden, searing pain ripped into my mind. I cried out and pressed my hand to the side of my head. I heard Hunter shout and felt a flash fire of panic in the air around me. In an instant I realized it was Ciaran, trying to break free. Without looking I flung out my hand, singing out Ciaran's true name. The pain in my head dulled, and when I raised my eyes, I saw Ciaran sprawled motionless on his side on the cold ground. He had almost made it. He had almost broken free.

Hunter looked over at me questioningly.

I nodded. "I have him," I said shakily, rubbing the dull ache in my skull.

"Right. One more time," Hunter said, and again he and the women propped Ciaran into a kneeling position. I knew that if I hadn't managed to stop Ciaran so quickly, we'd all be dead now.

Then Hunter stood at the top of the pentacle, and the other four arranged themselves around the points. With closed eyes and bowed heads, each witch concentrated on relaxing, on letting go of emotion, on releasing any anger they might have. After several minutes Hunter raised his head, and I saw that he was a Seeker and no longer just someone I loved.

"East, south, west, and north," he began, "we call on your guardians to help us in this sad rite. Goddess and God, we invoke your names, your spirits, your powers here tonight so that we may act fairly, with justice and compassion. Here, under the full moon of this, the first and last month of the year, we have gathered to take from Ciaran MacEwan his magick and his powers, as punishment for crimes committed against human and witch, woman and man and child. Alyce of Starlocket, are you in agreement?"

"Yes," Alyce said faintly.

"Bethany of Starlocket, are you in agreement?"

"Yes." Her voice was more strong.

"Silver of Starlocket, are you in agreement?"

"Yes."

"Daniel of Turloch-eigh, are you in agreement?"

"Aye." His voice was like a rasp.

"No more shall he wake a witch," Hunter said.

Silver, Alyce, Bethany, and Mr. Niall all repeated, "No more shall he wake a witch."

"No more shall he know the beauty and terror of your power," Hunter said, and they repeated it. I heard it echoing in my mind as I rocked myself back and forth on the cold cement.

"No more shall he do harm to any living thing."

"No more shall he be one of us."

"Ciaran MacEwan, we have met, and in the name of witches everywhere, we have passed judgment on you. You have called on the dark wave, you are responsible for untold deaths, you have participated in other rites of darkness that are abhorrent to those who follow the Goddess. Tonight you will have your powers stripped from you. Do you understand?"

There was no response from Ciaran, but the muffled claw-ing sensation in my head increased. I raised my voice from where I was. "He's trying to break the binding spell," I said.

"Strengthen it," Hunter said gently, and I closed my eyes and did as he said.

When Hunter had stripped David Redstone of his pow-ers, Sky had used a drumbeat to guide our energy. Tonight the five witches began chanting, first one and then another, and kept time with rhythmic stamping of their feet on the ground. Hunter's voice was deeper and rougher than the women's; Mr. Niall's sounded thinner and weaker. Everyone looked sad. Their voices blended and wove together, but instead of the beautiful, exhilarating power chants I was used to, this one seemed harsh, mournful, more cacophonous. I felt the increasing energy in the air around me; goose bumps broke out on my arms, and my hair felt full of static. I could feel that every animal and bird had left the area. I didn't blame them.

When I looked down, I saw that the star, the pentagram, had begun to glow with a whiter light—their energy. I knew what was coming next, and my stomach clenched. I drew my knees up again and held them tightly against myself and felt that I would bear the scars of this night forever. As would Ciaran.

The chanting ended abruptly, and Hunter bent to touch his athame to the white lines of energy. The knife glowed briefly, and when Hunter raised it, it seemed to draw up a pale, whitish blue film, like smoke or cotton candy. Slowly Hunter walked around the pentacle, drawing this light around Ciaran, as if he were at the bottom of a slow, beautiful tornado. When the light reached the top of Ciaran's head, Hunter gave me a sharp look.

"Take off the binding spell."

Praying he knew what he was doing, I released my father. In a split second he sprang up, roaring like a tortured animal, and just as quickly he seemed to hit the barrier of light and drop like a dead thing to the ground, where he lay on his side. He could move now, and his hands clutched at his clothes, at his hair. His bare feet moved convulsively, and he drew in on himself like a snail, trying to avoid any contact with the light. His eyes were closed, his mouth working soundlessly.

A sob erupted from deep within me, then another and another. No longer having to concentrate on holding the spell, my emotions poured out, and I was so shaken and upset that I wasn't even embarrassed. Through my tears I saw glistening traces on Alyce's face, on Bethany's. Silver looked deeply saddened. Mr. Niall looked calm, focused. Hunter looked grim, purposeful, not angry or hateful. Still chanting quietly by himself, he spiraled the energy around Ciaran, slowly and completely. When at last he lifted the athame away, it swirled around Ciaran unaided.

Then the images began, the images that defined who Ciaran had been, who he had become. Watching through my tears, still shaking with sobs, I saw a boy, handsome and happy, running across a green Scottish field with a kite. It was diving groundward, and with a flick of his hand, young Ciaran sent it back up to the clouds. I saw fourteen-year-old Ciaran being initiated, wearing a dark, almost black robe sprinkled with silver threads. He looked very solemn, and I felt that in his eyes there was already a glimmer of the witch he would become. Ciaran aged in the visions, and we saw teenage Ciaran courting girls, working on spells, having arguments with a man I thought must have been his father—my grandfather. Then to my shock, I saw a teenage Ciaran with a young Selene Belltower, just for an instant. I blinked, and there was Ciaran, being wed to Grania, her belly already round with their first child, Kyle. My breath stopped, sobs caught in my throat, as I saw Ciaran with the woman I recognized as Maeve Riordan, my birth mother. Maeve and Ciaran were wrapped tightly together, clinging to each other as if to be separated would equal death. Then Maeve was crying, turning away from him, and Ciaran was staring after her, his hands clenched. I saw Ciaran darkly silhouetted against the bright background of a burning barn. On and on it went, these images being born from the energy and floating upward to disappear into nothingness. On the ground, Ciaran lay jerking as if he were having a seizure, and I could make out a thin keening coming from him.

The images turned darker then, and I flinched as I saw Ciaran performing blood sacrifices, then using spells against other witches who cowered before him in pain. I felt ill as I saw him calling the dark wave, saw the exultation in his face, how he felt the glory of that power as before him whole villages were decimated, the people fleeing pointlessly. It grew to be too much, and I closed my eyes, resting my head on my knees.

When I looked up next, I saw myself and Ciaran hugging, I saw us turning into wolves, and even from over where I was,

I felt Alyce's and Silver's surprise. And then we were at tonight, when I had used his true name and he had been bound. When the last image had floated away and no more were coming, I knew that we had seen his life unraveling before us, seen the destruction of everything that had made him who and what he was.

My blood father lay unmoving on the cold March ground. Hunter drew his athame, and slowly the swirling energy surrounded it and seemed to be absorbed by it. When the last of the energy had gone, Hunter sheathed the knife and went to stand over Ciaran.

"Ciaran MacEwan, witch of the Woodbanes, is now ended," Hunter said. "The Goddess teaches us that every ending is also a beginning. May there be a rebirth from this death."

With those words, the rite was over.

When David had been stripped, Hunter had brought him healing tea, and Alyce had held him as he cried. I knew no one would do that for Ciaran. I wanted to go sit next to him, but my guilt was too great. Then Alyce, softly rounded, dressed in her trademark lavender and gray, knelt down on the ground near where Ciaran lay crumpled.

Hunter came and sat next to me on the cement bench, carefully not touching me. He seemed much older than nineteen and looked like he'd been battling a long illness.

Bethany stooped, touched Ciaran's temple once, then came to me and did the same thing. I felt her caring, her concern, and then she left through the woods. Silver Hennessey came to clasp Hunter's hand, then she, too, left, after a sympathetic glance at me.

Mr. Niall strode over to us. "I'm off, lad," he said in his odd, rough voice. "Good work."

I gazed stonily at the ground.

"Morgan," he said, surprising me. "It was a hard thing. But you did right." I didn't look up as he walked away.

Alyce stayed by Ciaran, and Hunter stayed by me. We were all silent. It was past four o'clock in the morning, and I felt that I would never sleep or eat or laugh again.

We sat in the darkness like that for another hour until we heard Killian crashing through the woods, and then he emerged through the cedars and pines.

"Hey, sis," he said cheerfully, and it was clear he'd been drinking. Great—he'd driven here from Poughkeepsie. He ignored Hunter, which wasn't unusual.

"Killian," I whispered. I had no idea what to say—words didn't cover this situation. I motioned over to where Ciaran lay on the ground.

If I had seen my real father, Sean Rowlands, lying on the ground in the woods in the middle of the night, I would have run over immediately. But Killian wasn't me, and Ciaran wasn't anything like my real father, so instead Killian just gaped at him.

"What's happened, then?" he asked.

"Amyranth has been casting dark wave spells," I said tonelessly. "Ciaran wanted me to join him and Amyranth. I said no. So he decided to bring the dark wave on Kithic. I met him here tonight, and then a group of five witches stripped him of his powers."

Killian's eyes widened almost comically. He couldn't even think of what to ask or say, just kept looking from me to Hunter to Ciaran in astonishment.

"No," he finally said, all traces of alcohol gone from his voice. "He has no powers? Are you sure?"

"We're sure," Hunter said, not sounding proud about it.

"You stripped Da of his powers. Ciaran MacEwan."

I understood why he was having a hard time with it. Ciaran seemed invincible—unless you knew his true name.

"Can you please take him to a safe place until he's better?" I asked.

Killian still seemed unsure whether or not this was reality. "Aye," he said hesitantly. "Aye. I know a place."

"I'll help you get him to your car," said Hunter. "Watch him closely. He'll be very weak for a while, but when he's able to move, he might . . . hurt himself."

"Aye," said Killian, slowly absorbing the meaning of Hunter's words. He gave me a quick backward glance, then walked over to the father he had feared and respected. Alyce edged back to give him room. Killian put a hand on Ciaran's shoulder and flinched when he saw Ciaran's face. I looked away. Then Hunter and Killian walked away through the woods, supporting Ciaran between them.

Alyce got up slowly and came to sit by me. "It was a hard thing, my dear," she said.

"It hurts," I said inadequately.

"It needs to hurt, Morgan," she said gently, rubbing my back. "If you had done this without it hurting, you would be a monster."

Like Ciaran, I thought. Hunter came back, alone. Alyce kissed my cheek and left, going back through the woods the way she had come. With only Hunter as my witness, I let go and began to cry. He sat down next to me and put his arms around me, hard and familiar. I leaned against him and sobbed until I thought I would make myself sick. And still there was pain inside.

"Morgan, Morgan," Hunter barely murmured. "I love you. I love you. It will be all right."

I had no idea how he could say that.

12

Alisa

><"It's a thin line between light and dark, between pain and pleasure, between heat and cold, between love and hate, between life and death, between this world and the next."

—Folk saying><

By five o'clock in the morning, I was totally ready to freak. Where the hell had Hunter and his father gone? Why weren't they back? It was going to be dawn soon, and I was supposed to be home! Any minute now, Hilary would be getting up for her sunrise yoga. Eventually she would notice I wasn't at home.

I was stalking around their house, too worried and upset to be tired, though my body felt like I'd been up for days. Should I call a taxi? Wait—this was Widow's Vale. There was no taxi service at five in the morning. I would have to wake someone up to come get me. This sucked!

I was trying to decide if I should just start walking when I heard heavy footsteps on the front porch. I almost flew to the door, just in time to see Hunter and Mr. Niall came in. They looked like someone had taken all the blood out of them while they were out.

"Are you okay?" I blurted. "What's wrong? Where were you?"

Hunter nodded, then patted his father on the back as Mr. Niall passed us, then headed slowly upstairs, his tread lifeless. "I'm sorry, Alisa," Hunter said. "I had no idea it would take so long. Do you need to get home?"

"Yes—but what's happened? Are you okay?"

"I'm all right. Morgan's waiting outside—she'll give you a ride."

"Morgan?"

He nodded, rubbing his hands over his face, pressing gently on his eyes. "Yes. Tonight Morgan met Ciaran MacEwan—we told you about him—out at the power sink. You know, that old Methodist cemetery at the edge of town. Things got strange, and then Morgan ended up putting a binding spell on him. She called me and my da, and we went out there, and we got some other witches, and we stripped Ciaran of his powers."

I stared at him. "You just stripped Ciaran of his powers? Just now?"

"Yes. It was very hard—Ciaran was incredibly powerful, and he resisted strongly. It was especially hard on Morgan."

I could hardly take it all in. "What does this mean about the dark wave?"

Hunter gave a wry smile, and I could tell all he wanted to do was drop onto his bed and sleep for a year. "I would guess there won't be a dark wave now," he said. "Looks like you're off the hook—you won't have to torture yourself with this spell anymore."

It took a moment for the words to sink in. "I can't believe it's all over," I said, getting into my coat. I had been working so hard—we all had. And it had been for nothing. I mean, I was glad there wouldn't be a dark wave coming, but at the same time, in a way I had been almost looking forward to seeing how well I did. Call me self-centered.

My adrenaline started to ebb, and suddenly I could hardly lift my feet enough to walk to the door. I looked back at Hunter, drawn and pale in the harsh overhead light of the living room. "Was it very bad?"

He nodded and looked down at the scarred wooden floor. "It was very bad."

"I'll talk to you soon," I said softly. "Take care of yourself." I gently closed the door behind me and walked across the front porch and out to the street, where Morgan was waiting in her big old car. Hunter and his father had looked awful. I wished there was something I could do for them. Maybe later today I would try to bring them something. What would be good in this situation? Chicken soup?

The door was unlocked and the engine still running when I got in. I looked over at Morgan. "Hi," I said quietly. "It sounds like you guys had a really hard time."

She inclined her head a tiny bit, then put the car into gear and pulled away from the curb. I sneaked another glance at her. Morgan usually looked pretty natural, not too spiffed up, but tonight she looked terrible. Like she had literally been through hell.

"I'm sorry, Morgan," I said. "I'm sorry tonight was so hard, and I'm sorry for how I've acted toward you the past couple of months. I wish . . . I wish I could help you somehow."

She looked over at me, a pale slash from a streetlight bisecting her face. The edges of her mouth curved in a tiny acknowledgment, and then we turned the corner onto my street. She stopped a few houses away and looked at me expectantly, like she was waiting for me to get out. "Um, should I get out here?" I asked, grabbing my purse.

Morgan nodded. "So your dad doesn't hear the car."

"Ohhh." Very wise, I thought. "You're good at this," I said in admiration, and she let out a little laugh that sounded like broken glass.

I opened the door as quietly as I could and stepped out onto the silent street. When I turned back to whisper thanks, I saw that Morgan's face was shiny with tear tracks. "I'm sorry," I whispered. It was all I could think to say. She gave a small nod and put the car back into drive. Very slowly, she turned around and headed back toward her house.

The morning air was still and heavy as I walked over to my house. It was that last moment of quiet before the early risers get up; I felt like I could breathe in the peaceful sleep of my family and my neighbors and the whole town. After silently making my way to my room, I kicked off my shoes and looked for just a minute out the window. The rim of the horizon was just barely highlighted with pink: the dawn of a new day.

I woke up later that same morning, not even caring how late I was for school. When I went downstairs Hilary looked up in surprise from the yoga mat she had spread on the living room floor. She glanced at the mantel clock, then looked thoughtful.

"It's Friday, isn't it?" she said. "Aren't you supposed to be in school?"

"Yeah," I said wearily, collapsing on the couch.

"Are you sick again, or did you and your friend stay up too late talking on the phone?"

"I'm sick again."

She uncoiled herself and came to look at me. She wasn't wearing makeup, and somehow she looked both younger and older than twenty-five. I wondered what it was that made my dad so crazy about her. Reaching out, she pressed her hand against my forehead.

"Hm. Well, I guess I should call the school."

"Thanks," I said, not having expected her cooperation. It had never occurred to me that my twenty-five-year-old stepmother-to-be would actually have the authority to do stuff like this.

"Why don't you go back upstairs and get into bed? Do you need anything?"

"No thanks." I hauled myself up and headed to my room as I heard her dialing the school's number.

When I woke up again later, I heard light footsteps in the hall. Hilary tapped on my door and opened it. "Are you awake?"

"Uh-huh." The open eyes are always a good clue.

"It's past lunch. Are you hungry?"

I thought. "Uh-huh."

"Come on downstairs and I'll fix you some nice sardines

on crackers," she said, and I stared at her in horror before I noticed she had an evil grin on her face.

I couldn't help smiling back. "Good one."

In the kitchen I fixed myself a PB&J, poured some juice, and sat down.

Hilary sat down across from me. I sighed but tried to hide it behind the sandwich. As much as I didn't want to admit it, she was going to be part of my life. And so was my half sibling. So I should probably make an effort to get along better. I should also ask my doctor for a prescription for Prozac. That could help.

"How's school going?" she asked, destroying all my good intentions.

I looked at her matter-of-factly. "It's high school. It sucks." I waited for her to tell me about how it had been the most wonderful four years of her life, how she was captain of the pep squad—

"Yeah. Mine sucked, too," she said, and my mouth dropped open. "I hated it. I thought it was so stupid and pointless. I mean, I liked a couple of classes, when I had good teachers. And I liked seeing my friends. But you couldn't pay me to go back. It didn't seem to have anything to do with real life."

She was warming to her topic. I stared at this new Hilary in fascination, chewing my sandwich.

"You know what real life is?" she went on. "Knowing how to make change from a dollar. Knowing that virtually everything is alphabetized. That's real life."

"What about mortgages, life insurance, lawn care?" I asked.

"You pick that stuff up as you go along. They don't teach

that in school, anyway. Now, college was different, I have to say. College was cool. You could control what you wanted to study and when. You could decide to go to class or not, and no one would hassle you. I looooved college. I took tons of lit and art courses, and fun stuff like women's studies and comparative religion."

"What did you graduate with?"

"A basic liberal arts degree, a bachelor's. Nothing useful for a job or anything." She laughed. "It would have been better if I had studied to be an accountant." She put her arms over her head and stretched. "Which is why I'm doing medical transcription from home. It requires knowing how to listen, read, and type. And I can set my own hours, and the money isn't bad, and I'll be able to do it after the baby's born."

"Is that what you're doing on the computer all the time?" I had thought she was writing a romance novel or having an Internet relationship or something.

"Yeah. Which reminds me. I need to get back to it. Right after *Life and Love*. Want to watch?"

"Okay." I felt compelled to follow this new, body-snatched Hilary. I wondered what they had done with the real Hilary and decided it didn't matter. We sat on the couch in the family room together and she filled me in on her favorite soap.

I watched it mindlessly, enjoying having an hour from my life gone, an hour in which I didn't have to think about magick and witches and breaking things and dark waves. I looked around the house, at Hilary, thought about my dad coming home. His face always lit up when he saw Hilary and me. That was cool. Thank God they weren't going to get wiped out by magick anytime soon.

13

Morgan

><"The thing about magick is: sometimes it looks like one thing, but it turns out to be something quite different."

—Saffy Reese, New York, 2001><

I slept all day but awoke at five in the afternoon, feeling just as crappy as when I'd gone to sleep. I heard Mary K. coming through the bathroom door and sat up to see her.

"Are you all right?" she asked, looking concerned. "Have you been in bed all day?"

I nodded. "I think I'll get up and take a shower now."

"Is this the flu or what? Alisa was out sick today, too."

"I guess it's just some bug that's going around," I said lamely. I didn't know what Alisa had told my sister, if anything, and didn't want to blow it for her.

"Well, come downstairs if you want dinner. It's little steaks and baked potatoes. And Aunt Eileen and Paula are coming."

I nodded, then pushed my way into the bathroom and shut both doors. I felt heavy and unrested, the knowledge of what I had done the night before weighing me down. My family was having one of my favorite meals, and I always loved seeing my aunt and her girlfriend. But right now the thought of food made my stomach roil, and I didn't feel up to talking to anyone. Maybe I would just go back to bed after my shower.

I made the water as hot as I could stand it and let it rain down on my neck and shoulders. Quietly I started to cry, leaning against the shower wall, my eyes closed against the splashing water. Oh, Goddess, I thought. Goddess. Get me through this. What did I do?

I saved my family, my friends, my coven.

At the expense of my father.

I had seen Ciaran after the rite. He looked dead. And I knew him well enough to know that living without magick would surely drive him insane. I had heard that a witch living without magick was like a person living a half existence, in a world where colors were grayed, scents were dulled, taste was almost nonexistent. Where your hands felt covered by plastic gloves, so when you touched things, you couldn't feel their texture, their vibrations.

That was what I had done to my father last night.

He killed your mother. He's killed hundreds of people, witches and humans. Woman, man, and child. Just like Hunter said.

I doubted that Ciaran would be alive for long. As far as I knew, there was no rite to give him his magick back—

it had been ripped from him forever. And without magick, I doubted Ciaran would feel that life was worth living.

Now he was virtually harmless, and the dark wave wasn't going to come. Not this time. I hoped I would start feeling better soon, either physically or emotionally. I would take either one. My mind was bleeding with pain and guilt and relief, and my body felt like I had fallen on rocks, again and again and again.

After my shower, I got back into bed.

It wasn't long before Mom came upstairs. She sat carefully on the side of my bed and felt my forehead. "You don't feel hot, but you certainly look sick."

"Thanks."

"Does your stomach hurt?"

"No." Just my psyche.

"Okay. How about I fix you a little tray and bring it up?"

I nodded, trying not to cry. Mom was still in her work clothes, and she looked tired. I was almost an adult, seventeen years old, yet all I wanted right now was for my mom to take care of me, to keep me safe. I never wanted to get out of this bed or leave this house again.

After Mom left, Aunt Eileen and Paula came in. Paula had completely recovered from her nasty ice-skating accident and was back at work.

"Big test today?" Aunt Eileen inquired with a smile.

"O ye of little faith."

Paula came over and felt my nose. "You're fine."

"Ha-ha." She's a vet.

"You look like death warmed over, honey," said my favorite aunt. "You need anything? Can we bring you something?"

I shook my head, and then Mom was back with my tray. I

looked at the food. It was all cut up into little pieces, and I started to cry.

"Morgan, can you talk on the phone?" Mary K. asked an hour later. "It's Hunter."

I nodded, and she brought the cordless phone in and gave it to me.

"Hello, my love," he said, and my heart hurt. "How are you doing?"

"Not great. How are you?"

"Bloody awful. Did you get any sleep today?"

"I slept, but it didn't help."

There were a few moments of silence, and I knew what was coming.

"Morgan—I wish you had told me you knew his true name. I thought we trusted each other."

Unexpectedly I felt a little spark of irritation. "If you're pissed, say you're pissed. Don't try to make me feel guilty about my decisions."

"I'm not trying to make you feel guilty," he said more strongly. "I just thought we had total trust and honesty between us."

"The way I trusted you when you were in Canada?"

Long silence. "I guess we have a ways to go."

"I guess we do." I felt upset at what that implied, for both of us.

"Well, I want to work to get there," he said, surprising me. "I want us to grow closer, to earn each other's trust, to be able to count on each other more than we count on other people. I *do* want us to have total trust and honesty between us. That's how I want us to be."

You are perfection, I thought, calming right down. "I'd like that, too."

For a moment I just basked in the glow of having Hunter. "It was just—he's my father. I was probably the only person in the whole world who knew his true name, except him. And he knew I had it. I felt I had to keep it close to myself, in case I ever needed it, for me or for you. Not for the council."

"He knew that you had his true name?"

"He must have. I used it the night we . . . shape-shifted, to stop him. That's why he disappeared, when what he really wanted to do was kill you or me or both."

"Yet he met you at the power sink."

"I guess he trusted me or was sure he was stronger than me." I gave a brittle laugh. "He *was* stronger than me. Many times stronger than me. But he shouldn't have trusted me." Hot tears slipped from my eyes and rolled down my cheeks.

"Morgan, you know you did the right thing—not only for you, me, and the others he would have hurt, but also for Ciaran. For every evil he did, three times that was coming back to him. You've prevented him from making that any worse."

"That's one way of looking at it," I said. "I don't know. Nothing is ever black or white. Decisions are never crystal clear."

"No. What you did last night was not one hundred percent good, but certainly not one hundred percent bad. But on the whole it was much more good than bad. On the whole, you honored the Goddess much more than you dishonored her. And that's sometimes as much as we can hope for."

"I wish I could see you," I said, feeling his soothing words taking away some of my jagged edges. "But I'm a wreck, and I'm sure Mom wouldn't let me out after I've been in bed all day."

"You just rest up," Hunter said. "We can get together tomorrow. I'd like to get away from here, if possible—my da's driving me mad. He's going mental because I don't want to have anything to do with the council anymore."

"What? What do you mean?"

"I don't trust them anymore. I can't put my faith in them. I can't do as they ask simply because they ask. I can't turn to them for protection. Not only are they no use to me, they've actually been dangerous for me. And for you. And for Da, though he doesn't see it that way."

"Can you quit being a Seeker? Is that allowed?"

Hunter gave a short laugh. "It doesn't happen frequently, that's certain. I haven't talked to anyone officially about it yet—Da's still trying to talk me out of it. But in my heart I know this is what I want to do."

I was stunned. Hunter's dissatisfaction with the council had been building for a while, but it had never occurred to me that he would quit being a Seeker. It was what he was; it was a huge part of what defined him.

"Whoa," I said. "If you're not a Seeker, what will you do?"

"I don't know," he admitted. "I've never done anything else, and no one besides the council needs a Seeker. I'll have to think about it. But how do *you* feel about it, my quitting?"

"I think you should do whatever you feel like you need to do," I said. "You could do anything you want. I'll help you do anything you want."

"Oh, Morgan, that means so much to me," he said, sounding relieved. "You have no idea. If you'll support me, I'll take on anyone." He paused. "They're not going to want me to quit," he explained.

"I know. Let's talk about it tomorrow, in person," I said. "This could be good. This could be very exciting. I want to look toward the future instead of dreading everything in the present."

"I'm with you there," Hunter said. "Now I guess I'll go try to avoid Da. Goddess, fathers can be a pain in the arse."

"Yes, they can," I said with dry irony.

"See you tomorrow, my love."

"Tomorrow."

"Morgan, maybe you would feel better if you ate an actual breakfast," said Mary K., sitting across from me at the kitchen table.

I looked up, bleary-eyed. It was starting to seem that maybe I really did have the flu. I still felt awful, with bone-deep aches, a pounding headache, and lingering nausea. I had staggered down to the kitchen, grabbed a regular Coke for its medicinal properties, and now felt a tiny bit better.

"It's settling my stomach."

"There's some oatmeal left. It's got raisins in it." Mary K. took a healthy bite of her banana and gave me a perky, bright-eyed look. That was how she was. She wasn't even trying to be this way. This morning, even though she hadn't taken a shower yet, she looked fresh and clean, with perfect skin and shiny hair. I hadn't taken a shower, either, and I could scare small children.

"No, thank you. Where are Mom and Dad?"

"Dad's downstairs, rebuilding his motherboard. Mom had

to show some houses. And I am going to Jaycee's, as soon as you give me a ride." She gave me a simpering smile and batted her eyelashes at me, and I couldn't help laughing.

"Okay. Let me get a grip."

An hour later I dropped her at Jaycee's house, then swung around and headed for Hunter's. The shower had helped, and then I had taken three Tylenol. Now I'd had a second Coke and a piece of toast here in the car, and I hoped that something I'd done would start to help soon.

It was better, though, walking up to Hunter's front door without feeling like I had to be looking over my shoulder. I had no idea whether Amyranth would take up Ciaran's cause, but I had the feeling that this had been a purely personal thing. I might not matter to them at all.

The front door opened. "Hi," said Hunter.

I blinked when I saw him. "Do you still feel bad? You look awful."

He rubbed his hand over his unshaven jaw. Unlike the hair on his head, which was the color of sunlight, his beard was dark, and so was his chest hair. Which I was going to stop thinking about immediately.

He shrugged and I went past him, automatically heading for the fireplace in the living room. I dropped my coat and sank onto the couch, stretching my feet toward the flames. The house smelled pleasantly smoky, clean. Fire has great purifying qualities.

"I think I feel better than I did yesterday," he said, sitting next to me so our legs touched. "Maybe it just takes a while. I've never been around a dark wave before, so I don't know."

I leaned my head against his shoulder and shivered at the warmth I found there. "Maybe you haven't drunk enough tea," I said with a straight face.

"Quite the wit, aren't you?" He put his arms around me and we snuggled, taking comfort from being close.

"Where's your dad?" Please be out of the house. Please be gone all day.

"Getting groceries. There's nothing to eat because we've been kind of busy the last few days."

I pushed against Hunter's shoulder so he would fall sideways. "Perfect."

"Good idea," he said, sliding down and pulling me with him. Then we were lying on the couch, face-to-face, pressed together, and my entire back was toasting nicely from the fire.

Simultaneously we both made happy sounds, then laughed at ourselves. I didn't feel like making out, sadly enough, and neither did he, and instead we just held each other close, snuggling hard, feeling some of our aches disappear with the heat from each other's body. Goddess, if I could just lie like this forever. Hunter's hand stroked my back absently; our eyes were closed, and I had my arms around his waist, not even caring that one was getting smushed.

"Thursday was so awful," I murmured against his chest. "I don't think I'll ever get over it. No matter how much good I was doing, I still know I betrayed my father. And despite how bad he was, there was something in him that I felt I knew, something good, from long ago. That was the part of him I liked."

"I understand." Hunter's warm breath stirred my hair. "The only thing that will make you feel better is time. Give yourself time. I promise there will be a day when it doesn't hurt so much."

I felt tears behind my eyelids but didn't let them out. I was tired of crying, of being in pain. I wanted to lie here and feel safe and loved and warm.

"Mmm," I hummed, moving closer to him. "This feels so great. I needed this."

It wasn't long until we felt Hunter's father come home, and we sat up as if we had been discussing the weather the whole time. I'm sure Mr. Niall was fooled.

Hunter helped him carry the groceries into the kitchen. When I saw Mr. Niall's face, I thought he looked even older and grayer than usual, which was saying something. However, when he saw me, he actually nodded and said, "Hullo, Morgan. Hope you're feeling better." So he had softened up to me. Maybe I should write an article for a teen magazine about how to win over your boyfriend's parents. But I guess most girls wouldn't have my same setup.

"What's in here, Da?" Hunter said, his arms full. "This weighs a ton."

"I thought you were supposed to be so *strong*," said Mr. Niall snidely, and my eyebrows went up.

"I am strong; I just don't know why they sell lead weights at the grocery store, that's all."

Their bickering continued as they went into the kitchen, and it was still going on when they came out. I frowned, thinking. Then I glanced at the potted winter cactus by the window. It had been blooming last week. Now it was dead. My heart sank, and a cold feeling came over me. Oh, no. Oh, no. I stood up and went over to them, looking closely at their faces.

"What, Morgan?" Hunter asked.

"I—we all feel horrible. You guys are arguing. That plant is dead." I was too upset to make sense, but it took them only a moment to get it.

"Oh, Goddess," Hunter breathed.

"Of course." Mr. Niall shook his head. "I knew something was wrong—I just couldn't see what. But you're right. I know you are."

Hunter muttered a word that I was never allowed to use. "Too right," he said. "The dark wave is still coming. Either Ciaran cast it before he came to see you, or Amyranth is continuing his work without him."

"Call Alisa," said Mr. Niall grimly.

14
Alisa

><"I see one day when all witches everywhere are united in one common doctrine, one common cause. I see Woodbanes everywhere safe from prejudice. I see our detractors, our persecutors, our enemies, a threat no longer. I see one great clan, not seven, with all the members of that clan Woodbane brothers and sisters. This is my vision, the one I am working toward."

—X, an Amyranth leader, London, 2002><

It seemed that every time I looked out a window, it was darker outside, more ominous. Mr. Niall had turned on the radio in the kitchen, and every once in a while we heard faint weather reports about a bad early-spring storm coming, how unusual it was. They joked about how it was March, still roaring in like a lion, ha-ha. It had all seemed so unreal. How could the world be going on as usual when I knew that mine might end at any minute?

Concentrate, I told myself. Concentrate. Okay, third form: spell specifics. This was difficult—not as hard as the second part, but harder than the first or fourth. Facing east, I began to step in the carefully designed pattern that would help define and clarify this spell. Next to me, as if we were in pairs skating, Mr. Niall started the same motions.

"Words," Hunter muttered. He and Morgan were sitting on the floor, their backs against the wall. It had been almost six hours ago that Hunter had called me and told me the dark wave was still coming. Since then I had been struggling to understand: What? Coming? Now? It was hard to get my head around the dark wave again, and there almost wasn't time, with all the practice we were doing. It was like a strange, nightmare day, like I would wake up any minute safe in my bed. But deep in my witch bones I knew that wouldn't happen.

Morgan had her head on her knees, as if she were too miserable to move. Hunter looked like he'd been run over by a truck. Mr. Niall had a washcloth, and he kept patting his forehead with it. He looked gray and clammy and had to sit down every few minutes.

"Oh, right," I said. I rubbed my aching temples with my hands and wished I had something to drink. "*Nogac haill, bets carrein, hest farrill, mai nal nithrac, boc maigeer.*" I said the ancient words, whose meanings I knew only very sketchily, as I stepped again in the pattern I'd been taught. My hands drew patterns of sigils and runes in the air as I described exactly what we needed this spell to do, how and when and why. The third part usually took about seventeen minutes if I did it properly.

"No—arms up," Mr. Niall croaked.

His interruption broke my concentration; my foot faltered,

and all at once I fell out of sync, with no idea of where I was supposed to be in the spell. I stared at my arms, which were not up, and then a wave of tiredness and nausea swept over me.

"You're doing great, Alisa," said Hunter as I stood there dejectedly, rubbing my forehead. His voice sounded stiff and leaden, as if even talking made him feel worse. "It's just an incredibly difficult spell. It would take *me* a solid month to learn it."

"Yeah, but you would understand what the hell you were doing and saying and why. I'm just memorizing it like a parrot."

"A talented parrot," Morgan said, trying to smile.

Mr. Niall slowly lowered himself to the wooden floor and curled up there with a moan. He looked like someone had taken all his stuffing out and returned the pelt. Of the four of us, he seemed the worst off. I glanced at Hunter and met his eyes: We both knew there was no way Daniel could even pretend to cast this spell himself. I'd been here three hours, and in that short time I'd watched as the three full blood witches visibly deteriorated. Even I was starting to feel pretty bad—my headache made it hard to concentrate, and my knees felt shaky.

"I'll go make tea," said Morgan, and she carefully uncurled herself and went into the kitchen.

Hunter got up to stand next to me. "It's going to be up to you," he said, so his father couldn't hear, and I nodded, wishing I were in Florida and this were all their problem.

"I know," I whispered back. "But I'm not ready, Hunter— you know it. What if when the time comes, I can't do it? I mean, I'm trying hard, but—" My voice wobbled and broke, and I wiped a hand across my stinging eyes. I refused to cry and look like a baby in front of him.

Morgan came back with a tray of mugs. She knelt on the floor by Mr. Niall, sloshing the tea a bit. "Here," she told him. "Drink this."

He pushed himself up with effort and stretched a bony hand toward the mug. "Ta, lass."

Hunter and I sat on the floor. I was incredibly thirsty and sucked down some of the hot, sweet tea. Morgan had put extra sugar and lemon in it, and it tasted great.

"The wave is coming," Hunter said baldly, and I saw Morgan flinch. "Alisa has done an amazing job of learning the spell as much as she can, but she's not quite ready. No one could be."

"I'll do it," said Mr. Niall.

"There's no way you could do it, Da," Hunter said. "You know it and I know it. The wave has already made you so weak, I'll have to practically carry you to the car, anyway."

"You couldn't carry—" Mr. Niall began, showing a spark of life.

"Please." Morgan held up her hand. "Could we not waste time? What are we going to *do*?"

"I think I might have an idea," Hunter said slowly.

"This is going to feel terrible," Hunter warned me. My hair was whipping around in the wind, as was Morgan's. She quickly stuffed hers down the back of her coat, and I did the same. Here in the old Methodist cemetery the air felt weird, like it had an actual weight that was pressing down on us— humid but cold. We were standing before the power sink, listening as Hunter explained his big idea. Mr. Niall's head was bowed, and he was bent over on himself.

"What do you call it again?" I asked.

Hunter smiled wanly. "A *tàth meànma*."

I frowned, still confused. "And why can't I just connect—or whatever—with Mr. Niall?"

Hunter cast a glance at his father, who appeared to be in too much pain to be paying much attention. "Because my da isn't strong enough," he said quietly. "He doesn't have enough power right now to connect with you and still stay a safe distance from the dark wave. Morgan has enough power for both of them, essentially, and she'll be able to hold you two together." He looked at me. "Make sense?"

I nodded. "And, um . . . why will it hurt?" Not that it mattered.

Morgan smiled weakly. "Before you do a *tàth meànma* like this, it's best to do purification rituals, fast, drink herbal tea, and so on," she explained. "For a little *tàth meànma*, it doesn't matter so much. For one like this, it would have been better. It's going to feel bad for me, too." She made a pained expression.

"Great." I smiled wanly. "And where will you be?"

"The field across the road, on the other side of the woods. I'll be close enough to keep contact, but I hope not close enough to get hit."

A sudden sob rose in my throat and I pressed my lips together hard. Sure, we were going to try Hunter's big idea, but in the end it was up to me, and I'm not hero material by any stretch of the imagination. I had worked as hard as I knew how, I would try my best, but my best just might not be good enough. The truth was, if I didn't come through, we had all gathered out here to die. I wouldn't have to be a flower girl for Hilary after all.

"Okay," I said, trying to sound somewhat less terrified than I was.

"And Daniel will be farther away than that, on the other side of Morgan," Hunter explained. "He can keep in touch with Morgan, and Morgan will keep in touch with you, and we'll do this thing. Right?"

"Right," I said, not meaning it. This was Hunter's idea: I would still perform the spell, but my mind would be linked with Morgan's. Her mind would be linked with Mr. Niall's, and he would feed her lines if necessary that she could pass on to me. Hunter was going to stay here at the power sink with me, watching my movements and coaching me. He knew what to look for, even if he couldn't do it himself.

A chill wind smacked my face at that moment. I looked up, and on the far horizon was a hovering cloud of what looked like fine ash. It was roiling, boiling, rolling toward Widow's Vale, like an impossibly large swarm of insects.

Hunter glanced up at the sky, then at his dad, who seemed to be crumpling. "Right, everyone. Let's get going. It's on its way."

Morgan, looking pale and tense, stood facing me. We put our hands on each other's shoulders. Slowly we came together, so that our foreheads touched. Morgan's was icy cold and clammy. We both had long hair, and now the angry wind twisted the strands together around our heads. I was dimly aware of Hunter and Mr. Niall leaving, and I knew Hunter would be back. Then I shut my eyes and concentrated, the way they had told me to do. Basically I was supposed to meditate and clear my mind and let Morgan do all the heavy lifting.

I stood there, the wind creeping under my coat like icicles, and wondered when this was all going to get started. Then my consciousness seemed to wink, and I felt a fine, pointed pain, as if a metal claw were clamping down on my skull. Just as I was starting to think I couldn't stand any more of this, Morgan was there, in my mind.

"Relax," her voice came to me, though I knew my ears weren't hearing it. "Let everything go. In this moment, you are safe and everything is perfect. Let everything relax. Take down your walls, and let me in."

"It hurts," I said, feeling like a sissy.

"I know," Morgan said. "I feel it, too. We have to let go of it."

I thought about taking down walls, and slowly I realized that Morgan and I were somehow joined—I could see inside her, and she could see inside me: we were one person. I felt an unexpected elation—this was beautiful, magickal, exciting. It was a glow of golden light, surrounded by a corona of finely etched pain. I thought of what the moon's shadow looked like as it moved across the sun.

Then I followed Morgan deeper into her mind. There I saw all her knowledge of magick, her feelings for Hunter, all this stuff about Ciaran—I felt Morgan deliberately leading me away from her personal thoughts.

"Focus," came her voice, gentle and strong. "I'm going to leave now, but we'll stay joined. Soon you'll feel just a bit of Mr. Niall. We'll stay with you the whole time. You will be able to do this. You have all the support you need. You're a strong, beautiful witch, and with this one act, one spell, you will set your life on an exhilarating path."

This wasn't how Morgan usually talked, but I had the feeling it was who she really was, inside. On the outside she was kind of shy and hard to get to know. Inside, she was glowing and powerful and ancient.

"Focus," came her voice.

Slowly I opened my eyes, feeling nausea trying to take over. I clamped it down and tried to forget about it. Outside, it was almost as dark as night. What little light there was looked strange, tinted with an almost greenish hue, as if right before an eclipse. Bits of last year's leaves were whipping around, swirling in tiny dust devils on top of headstones. Feeling dreamy, relaxed, and stupidly confident, I saw Hunter coming back through the woods. I felt Morgan's awareness of him through my eyes, felt her rush of love, of longing, of uncertainty. I tried not to pay attention to it.

Hunter's eyes looked huge and green, with dark hollows beneath them. His face was white and looked carved out of marble, his cheekbones angled sharply, the skin stretched tight.

"Begin," he said.

It was an incredibly weird feeling, being connected to Morgan. As long as I didn't think about it, I was okay. Whenever I remembered it again, I felt a rush of pain and nausea. Hunter handed me a large bowl of salt, and with this I traced a circle of protection on the ground. He helped by placing stones of power and protection all around that circle. Then I buried my hands in the salt and rubbed it against my skin. The rest I sprinkled around me. I had four embossed silver bowls that Hunter had given me. In one was dirt, in

another water. In one was a tiny fire that Morgan had kindled, so it wasn't affected by the wind, and in the last was
incense burning with an orange glow. I put these cups at
east, south, west, and north to represent the four elements.
Mr. Niall had given me a gold pocket watch, and I set that in
the center of my circle. Then I was ready to begin the first
part. It should take almost twenty minutes, if I did it correctly.

Just as I raised my arms, I felt a shimmering presence: Mr.
Niall. In my mind he was called Maghach, but Morgan was
just called Morgan. After a moment to get used to this new
presence, I took a deep, cleansing breath, released it, and
began.

"On this day, at this hour, I invoke the Goddess and the
God," I said, holding my arms skyward. "You who are pure in
your intent, aid me in this spell. By earth and water and fire
and air, strengthen this spell. By spring and summer and fall
and winter, strengthen this spell. By witches both past and
present, of my blood and not of my blood, strengthen this
spell. Help my heart be pure, my crafting joyous, my hands
sure and steady, and my mind open to receive your wisdom."

Here I drew runes and sigils to identify myself as the
spellworker and Mr. Niall as the spellcrafter. I identified
the place, the time of year, the phase of the moon, the hour
of the day. Then I walked deasil in a circle three times, my
arms held out.

"I make this spell to right a wrong,
I need your help to make it strong.
Today we join to heal a wound,
My voice will lift in joyous sound.

My hope is ancient, vision sure;
The goal I seek is good and pure.
I am your servant, I ask again,
Show faith in magick, ease our pain."

After this came a simple power chant, designed to raise whatever powers I had as well as to call the Goddess and the God. Whenever I had practiced this at Hunter's, I'd caused something to explode, so I wasn't sure what would happen now.

Morgan's voice came to me in my head. *Alisa, you're doing so well.*

I drew more sigils in the air and on the ground. Mr. Niall had explained these as being a kind of history, quickly describing who he was and who I was and whatever we knew about the power sink. Then I knelt back down. The first part was done.

I heard Morgan say that the first part had been perfect and to go into the second part. I stood up and took another breath, holding my arms out to my sides. I was aware of a cold, damp wind whipping my hair around, I knew that it was pitch-dark outside, but mostly I was aware within myself of the perfect, lovely form of the spell that Maghach had crafted. In my mind I could it see it all finished, done, its layers upon layers. I needed to focus and do it step by step.

The second part was the longest and hardest. Something in me started to feel anxious, as if I were running out of time. It was either Morgan or Maghach. I stepped quickly into the form of the second part, the limitations.

"This spell is to ignite on the thirtieth day of the first month of spring," I began, my voice sounding thin against the wind. "The moon is full and on the wane. The length of the spell shall not exceed five minutes after igniting. It shall be contained within these barriers."

Here I knelt and drew sigils on the ground, then runes that further identified the exact location, to within a hundred feet, of where the spell would have life. I began to feel an urgency, and I drew more quickly. Suddenly my mind went blank, and I stared down at the ground and my unmoving hand. Another sigil? Another rune? On the ground? In the air? Do I get up now? An icy bead of sweat trickled down my back as adrenaline flooded my body. *Oh no oh no oh no.*

"Tyr," came Morgan's voice, calm and sure inside my head. I almost started weeping with relief. I drew the rune Tyr on the ground with sharp movements. "Ur," she went on patiently. "Thorn. Then Yr. Then the battle sigil, in the air."

Yes, yes, I thought, following her instructions.

"Sigils for moon phase," she coached me gently.

Yes, I know now. I thought back, recognizing my place once again. I walked in the circle in the shape of a moon, then drew its identity in the air.

"The spell shall have no other purpose than that described here," I went on. "It shall affect no other being than those described here. It shall not exist or ignite ever again in perpetuity, except for the time described here. This spell is intended only for goodness, for safety, to right a wrong. My intent is pure. I work not in anger, nor hatred, nor judgment."

On and on I went. The limitations of a spell are the most important part, especially for something like this.

This part took almost thirty minutes. I moved as quickly as I could and still be precise and exact, not skipping anything.

Three more times I forgot what to do, and each time panic overwhelmed me until Morgan talked me through the next step. Her voice sounded strained but incredibly calm and reassuring. I was no longer aware of where Hunter was or what he was doing. I felt a dim outline of Maghach in my head. Sometimes I felt cold wind, or a heavy weight pressing on me, or was aware of leaves whipping around me. I stayed within my circle and worked the spell.

At the end of the second part I wanted to lie down and cry. The air itself was starting to feel bad, to affect me as if I were breathing fumes of poison. I felt exhausted and nauseated, and my head pounded. The third part was the actual form of the spell itself. The fourth part would be fast: igniting it.

"Keep going, Alisa," said Morgan, a thin line of ice underlying her calm voice. "Keep going. You can do it. You're strong. You know it. Now state the actual spell."

I wiped the sweat off my forehead and turned to the east. "With this spell I create an opening, a *bith dearc*, between this world and the netherworld," I began, my voice sounding shaky. "I create an unnatural tear between life and death, between light and dark, between salvation and revenge." And on it went, sometimes in English, sometimes in modern Gaelic, which I had done a decent job of memorizing, and some in ancient Gaelic, which Morgan and Maghach had to coach me through, practically word by word. I walked within my circle, creating patterns, layers of patterns, layers of description, layers of intent. I drew sigils in the air and on the ground. I drew sigils on myself and around myself. Suddenly I froze, looking at the billowing, oily black cloud roaring our way. It looked sickening, tinged with green, and it was getting so close. I felt like the breath was knocked out of me. Oh my God, this was real, and it was here, and I was really going to die. We were all really going to die.

Morgan started talking to me, but I couldn't move. The closer it got, the sicker I felt, and the more Morgan's voice sounded strained and weak. I barely felt Maghach at all anymore.

It's over, I thought. I won't finish in time. I looked around wildly for Hunter and saw him hunched over next to a tombstone. When he looked up at me, he looked like he had aged thirty years.

I had so much more to go, and the black cloud of destruction was almost upon us. Morgan's voice in my head urged me on, and like a robot I started working through the last section of the third part, going as fast as I could. I was shaking all over: I thought I would throw up at any second, and basically I felt like I was standing there waiting to die.

The first blast of death, of darkness, was barely twenty yards away.

My hands trembling, I sketched an inverted pentagram in the air before me. I had finished the third part of the spell.

"Ignite it!" Hunter yelled, his voice sounding strangled.

"Ignite it!" Morgan screamed in my head.

Again I felt frozen with terror, shaky and stupid and ill. The dark wave was almost upon us, and I was mesmerized by it. In its boiling, choking clouds I could see faint outlines of faces, pinched and withered and hungry, eager. My body went cold. Each one of those people had once been someone like me—someone facing this terrible cloud. It was horrifying. The most horrible thing I had ever seen or even imagined.

"Ignite it! Alisa!" Morgan screamed.

Mindless with fear, I mechanically whispered the words that would set the spell into motion, that would let it spark into life, for good or for bad. Shaking so much I could hardly stand, I held out my arms and choked out, *"Nal nithrac, cair na rith la, cair nith la!"*

I felt a huge surge of energy inside me—it seemed to start in the ground, then it shot through me and out from my fingers and the top of my head. It was warmth and light and energy and happiness all at once: my magickal power. Then the faces were *here,* and the air and the earth ripped open in front of me, as if the whole world as I knew it, reality, were just a painting that someone had slashed. The gold pocket watch I had placed on the ground exploded, and the blast knocked me off my feet. I flew backward and my head cracked against a marble tombstone. Sparks exploded in my throbbing head, and I cried out. Ten feet away, I saw the dark wave suddenly rushing down into the rip, the *bith dearc* I had made. The ghost faces in it looked surprised, then horrified, then enraged. But they had no power over the spell I had cast. The whole wave disappeared into the rip while I stared. Then my vision went fuzzy, and everything became blessedly quiet and safe, black and still.

"Oh, God," I moaned, trying to feel the back of my head. "Oh, God, this hurts."

"Stay still for a moment," said Morgan's voice.

I blinked up at her. She was sitting next to me, and she seemed to be smashing some greenish moss together in her hands. "My head hurts," I said, like a little kid, and then I remembered everything. "Oh, God!" I cried, trying to sit up, only to be struck down by pain. "Morgan, what happened? What happened?"

When her eyes met mine, I realized that she was no longer inside my mind, but separate and herself. In her eyes I saw so much more than I had ever seen before. It was like a wise, learned woman was inside Morgan's body, and that woman's eyes were telling me things I could only barely begin to understand.

"Morgan?"

"Hold on," she said, then gently lifted my head and pressed her gunk against where it hurt.

"Ow!"

"You'll feel better soon," she said.

A shadow fell across me, and I looked up to see Hunter. He crouched down next to me, and Morgan nodded as if to tell him I would be all right.

"You did it," Hunter said, his voice sounding raspy. "Alisa, you did it. You performed the spell. It worked. You saved us."

Unexpectedly this made me start crying, which made my head hurt more. Morgan, whom I'd always thought of as a little cold, took my hand and patted it, her own eyes shining with tears.

"Morgan did it," I said, trying to stop crying. " I almost forgot everything. She told me what to do."

"Hunter's father told me what to say to you," she said. "It was him. I was just a messenger." She looked wrung out and tired, and there were bits of dried grass and leaves in her hair.

Very slowly I sat up and found that the horrible throbbing in my head had lessened. "Where is Mr. Niall?" I asked. "I don't feel him anymore."

"Right there." Hunter pointed. About fifteen feet away, Hunter's father was kneeling on the ground. "He's closing the *bith dearc* forever," Hunter explained. "Only this one, of course. There will always be more, and other dark waves, too. But as far as we know, this is the first and only time anyone's ever defeated one. Now we can teach others how to do it. By this time next year maybe we'll have put a stop to Amyranth for good."

Morgan fished in her coat and found a purple scarf, which she tied over my head. "When you get home, leave that stuff on for another two hours. Then wash your hair," she instructed me. "Then take some Tylenol and pass out. You've earned it."

I looked around. "I can't believe it," I said. "It worked. We're still alive. Everyone's still alive." More tears coursed down my cheeks, and I rubbed them away with my sleeve.

Morgan leaned against Hunter, and he put his arm around her.

"I used my powers," I said in wonder.

"You sure did." A hint of a smile crossed Morgan's face.

We looked at each other for a long moment, and I realized that Morgan and I understood each other. We had bonded. We were witches.

15

Morgan

><"The Nal Nithrac spell is lengthy and difficult, but not impossible for one witch to perform. While the basic spell can be utilized against any dark wave, care must be taken to make it accurate as to the place, time, and people involved. As was shown in Widow's Vale, it is of great value to have some item that carries the vibrations of the wave creator, but it is not always necessary."

—Daniel Niall of Turloch-eigh><

"I can't believe it's over," said Hunter.

I nodded, smiling weakly. "I just want life to get back to normal—whatever normal is," I said. I stretched my feet toward the fire in Hunter's living room. It had taken us a while to make it back to our cars and figure out if we could drive or not, but now we were resting and drinking hot mulled cider.

"All of you performed magnificently," said Hunter's father.

"We made a great team," said Hunter. Alisa looked pleased. Which reminded me. I got up and checked the back of her head. She'd stopped bleeding an hour ago, and she said it didn't hurt that much anymore. I had given her some arnica montana to take every six hours for two days, and I knew she'd heal pretty quickly.

"I can't wait for other witches to hear about this," I said. "For so long no one's had any defense against a dark wave. Now they do. It's like you discovered penicillin, Mr. Niall."

"Please call me Daniel," he said, "or Maghach."

Thank the Goddess, I thought. He was finally accepting me. Besides, my tongue kept tripping over "Mr. Niall," and we'd already been through a *tàth meànma* together.

"I'm hopeful that the spell will work in other places, when needed," Daniel said. "As long as the specifications and limitations are adjusted accordingly. But yes, this is wonderful news for the whole witch community."

"I still can't believe what it felt like, when I felt the power flow through me," Alisa said. "It was . . . really . . . "

"Indescribable," I said, and she nodded.

"In a good way," she added.

"Good," said Hunter. "Now we have to start teaching you things. But first, I'm starved—I haven't eaten in a week, it seems like."

"I'm hungry, too," said Daniel.

"Pizza would be good," Alisa suggested.

"Yeah, we could—" I stopped and gasped, then looked at the mantel clock. "Oh, no, I am way late!" I said, scrambling to my feet. I still felt like I was recovering from the flu, but I knew I was getting better, and that made it okay. "Mom is going to kill me—this is the second time this week."

When I looked up, three pairs of eyes were watching me with amusement. "What?" I said.

"You just saved all of Kithic," Alisa said, snickering.

"And you're worried about being late for dinner," said Hunter.

"Do you want me to call your parents?" Daniel offered. "I could explain why you were unavoidably delayed."

We all broke into laughter, and I shook my head.

"I really should get home," I said. "But I'll see you guys soon."

I got into my coat, and Hunter walked me out to the front porch.

"Can you make it home okay?" he asked, putting his arms around me, holding me tight.

"Yeah." I snuggled closer. "We really stopped it. We stopped the dark wave."

"Yes, we did." His hand stroked my hair, which I knew still had grass in it.

I looked up at him. "Now we have to look toward the future. Like figuring out what you want to do if you leave the council. And if we're ever going to have time *alone together*," I said meaningfully, and he grinned.

"Yes, we must talk about that soon."

We kissed good-bye, and I walked out to Das Boot. The dark wave was no more. Ciaran was no longer a threat to me or anyone else, and someday I hoped to come to terms with how that had happened. Hunter and I were thinking about our future—together.

When I pulled into my driveway and walked slowly up the path, I felt unnaturally light and free. The humidity and weight were gone from the air. I almost felt like skipping.

Then my gaze fell to the ground beneath me. I knelt

down to get a closer look, and when I saw them, I let out a gleeful little laugh.

My mother's crocuses, bright purple and yellow, had miraculously sprung back to life.